I0551930

Along Came Jones

VICTORIA BERNADINE

This book is a work of fiction. References to real people, events, establishments, organizations, websites, or locales are intended only to provide a sense of authenticity, are used fictitiously; and do not imply endorsement or relationship of any kind between this book and the referenced people, places or things. If any person or organization feels their intellectual property rights have been infringed due to such use in this book, please contact Love of Words Publishing (loveofwords@shaw.ca) for resolution. All other characters and all incidents and dialogue are drawn from the author's imagination and are not to be construed as real.

ALONG CAME JONES. Copyright © 2017 by Victoria Bernadine. All rights reserved. No part of this book may be used or reproduced in any manner whatsoever without written permission except in the case of brief quotations embodied in critical articles and reviews, or used within transformative fanworks. Transformative fanworks (e.g., fanfiction, fanart, fanvids, podfic) are permitted and encouraged so long as the transformative fanwork is provided free of charge and includes appropriate disclaimers related to ownership of copyright. **Permission to create transformative fanworks in no way implies an assignment of copyright or a waiver of moral rights.**

Cover Design by Nelly Murariu at PixBeeDesign.com.

For information, contact Love of Words Publishing, loveofwords@shaw.ca .

ISBN 978-0-9918102-3-9

m/d/y/#
12-01-17-0001

DEDICATION

To Saskatchewan and everyone in it.
I love you and I miss you.

.

"Marry me."

Olivia laughs.

"What?" she teases with a fond, slightly mocking smile. "Are you 'proposing' because you think it's what people are supposed to do on New Year's Eve?"

Ferrin smirks his lopsided, endearing smirk as he lowers himself to one knee and proffers the small, square velvet box he dug out of the pocket of his tuxedo.

The beautiful brunette laughs again. "Oh, Ferrin, get up—you're being ridiculous! And the joke really isn't all that funny."

Olivia glances at the crowd of beaming friends and family surrounding them and Ferrin watches as realization slowly dawns on her face. Her gaze snaps back to his as realization morphs into horror, and Ferrin feels a corresponding sick, sinking feeling grow in his stomach as her expression changes. His own smile slips away and his face freezes into an expressionless mask. Their spectators' hissed in-drawn breaths and sudden, uncomfortable silence barely register given his complete and utter focus on Olivia.

He knows what she's going to say before she says it, but like with any impending disaster, he can't seem to look away.

"Oh, my God," she whispers. "Oh, *shit*!" She bites her lip, then says in a rush, "I love you, Ferrin, I really, truly do...but I can't marry you." Her voice breaks; her eyes fill with tears.

The silence that follows seems to grow and envelop them in a stifling cocoon built from his humiliation and suddenly terrified heart. Ferrin hears, as if through cotton wool, subdued voices and the shuffling of feet as their family and friends gather their things and leave the apartment. In some distant corner of his mind, he's mildly surprised they're all leaving so quietly...or maybe he just can't hear them across the yawning divide that's opened between him and Olivia.

As the door closes, she whispers, "Get up. Your knee must hurt."

Does it? He can't tell over the crushing pressure in his chest, his stomach, his head, but he struggles to his feet anyway, like she asks, *because* she asks, aching and sore and suddenly ancient. He straightens and becomes, as always, self-consciously aware of how *big* he is in comparison to her, and how his bulk looming over her always makes her edgy. He automatically slouches his shoulders, trying to minimize his size, trying to make her comfortable.

"Say something," she begs, and her voice breaks.

His voice is cracked, hollow, distant, as he says, "Is this it?"

'It', he thinks with despair. Such a tiny word with such a huge meaning.

She hesitates, then nods, not quite looking at him.

"This can't come as that much of a surprise. Not if you're honest with yourself."

Ferrin can't seem to make his brain work. He shakes his head, trying to force something—anything—loose so his world—his *life*—will start to make sense again.

"I—I—no. Yes. *Why?*" he asks, and winces at just how lost he sounds.

Olivia sighs and says, very gently, "I want other things in life than you do, Ferrin. My career means everything to me and I want to make it to the top of Macon-Jones Enterprises, or as high as I can get without being a blood relative."

Finally, finally, anger flares inside him.

"And I'm holding you back?   In my own family's company?"

Olivia hesitates.

Ferrin's eyes widen.   "You really believe it," he breathes. "When have I ever stood in your way, Olivia?"

This time her sigh is long-suffering. "You've never stood in my way, no, but you've never actively helped me, either."

"I didn't think you wanted me to! If I recall correctly, you told me so in no uncertain terms when we moved in together.   That's only a couple of years ago!   What's changed?"

"I didn't want you using any undue influence with Abram to get me promotions I didn't deserve," Olivia snaps, her own anger flaring. "That didn't mean I didn't want you to help me at all!"

Ferrin snorts.   "Nobody has undue influence with Abram. You should know that by now!"

"Abram isn't the point! The point is that I could have used your support when some of my projects came up for a vote before the Board. Instead, you, as always, stayed out of it and gave your vote to the first cousin who asked for it, without any regard to how the decision would impact my career or my projects! Half the time, you didn't even bother asking me how I wanted you to vote!"

"I never ask anyone about the projects or how they want to use my vote! The cousins know how I play the game and it works well for all of us. Why do you think I'm the only one any of them will talk to without a witness present?"

Olivia throws her hands up in the air as she whirls and

paces away. "There! That's exactly the problem!"

He takes a step back, blinking. "What? The fact that I'm friendly with all my cousins? That's a problem?"

"No!" She brushes a hand over her face in exasperation. She turns to him, and now he recognizes that look on her face. It's the one she has when she's getting ready to lecture him on what, exactly, he's done wrong, and what he needs to do to avoid making the same mistake again.

She says, "It's not the fact the cousins all like you that's the problem; it's the *reason* they all like you! You're such a goddamn fixer, itching to solve everyone's problems that you've become a complete pushover! I don't want to hurt you, Ferrin, but, let's face it: you're a sucker. You're gullible. And I hate to say this, but you're also a bit of a wimp. You'll do whatever anybody tells you to do, and that's proven in spades by your so-called 'business investments'! All anybody needs in order to get money out of you is a sob story and a half-assed idea!"

His mouth sags open as he rocks beneath her barrage, every word slamming into his heart and his gut and his mind.

"What the hell?" he chokes.

Olivia deflates, pity in her eyes.

"Look," she says, and now her voice is calm and firmly matter-of-fact, the way Ferrin has so often heard her speak whenever he's forced to attend a board meeting with her, "I'm going to be CEO someday of a multi-billion-dollar multinational company. *Your* family's multi-billion-dollar multinational company. It's ruthless and cutthroat, and a spouse's strengths and talents are just as important to an executive's rise as the executive's own skills and talents, especially in Macon-Jones Enterprises. You know how outright Machiavellian your family can be, and that's when they're arranging Christmas! If you think they're ruthless in their personal lives, they're ten times worse in the boardroom, trust me!"

"Yes, I know. I have met my cousins and I've even been to a board meeting a time or two. Abram seems to have done all right without a spouse to support him."

She snorts. "He's Chair and he was handed the job by your great-grandfather! He's never had to prove anything to anybody!"

His laugh is harsh and barking. "Now you're the one who's forgotten what my cousins are like!" He waves his words away. "Doesn't matter. You knew when we met that I do everything I can to avoid anything to do with the company."

"You're not supposed to avoid it by giving your vote to whichever cousin gets to you first! Besides, you're your father's only surviving child, the last of your particular branch of the family! You out of all your cousins shouldn't avoid the company at all!"

Ferrin flinches.

Olivia grimaces. "I'm sorry; that was low...but you know I'm right. You could wield enormous influence and power in the company, and not only with the family when they want something, if you'd just take an interest! If you would listen to me, let me guide you, advise you so you don't believe everything you're told, and let me stop Carson, Dyson and Jack from constantly distracting you, you could be the next Chair of the Board instead of Jack!"

"So I'm not only gullible and a wimp, I'm also so stupid I can only trust you to advise me?" he says, incredulous.

"Of course not! But you're wasting your potential— and your birthright! Your father was Abram's second-in-command, for God's sake! All you have to do is step up and follow in his footsteps!" She runs a hand through her hair and groans. "Face it, Ferrin, I'm never going to be CEO if I remain allied with you, not unless you change your approach to the business."

Ferrin rears back and stares.

"'Allied'?" he says slowly. "Is that what the last five

years have been about, Olivia? An *alliance*?"

"No! Of course not! I love you. I do! You're a wonderful man, Ferrin. But you're..." She spreads her hands and shrugs helplessly.

"Weak," he says flatly, "and obviously a little stupid. Have I got it right?"

"Ferrin..." She takes a step towards him, but he quickly retreats. She stops and stares at him, her large, brown eyes brimming with tears. For once, he's unmoved.

"I'm sorry I've been such a *disappointment* to your professional ambitions," he grates out, a bitter twist to his lips. He turns and heads for the exit.

"Where are you going?"

"I have no idea," he says, and slams the door behind him.

Lou signs the last of the papers and sits back with a rueful scowl.

"Considering I never leave the house," she grumbles, "you'd think there'd be less paperwork."

Ike chuckles as he straightens the papers and tucks them into his briefcase.

"You have a lot of investments, Lou. You need to keep track of them all."

She shrugs. "I suppose, although I thought that's what I pay you to do."

"Lou," Ike says, and leans back in Ike's Chair with an annoyed sigh.

She grimaces and waves a hand. "Whatever. You know I don't read the things when you put them in front of me, and I tune out as soon as you start talking finances and investments and whatever the hell else you're saying when your lips are moving."

"Yes, I do know. Why do you think I gave up a long time ago on trying to convince you to pay more attention?"

She shrugs, then tugs her over-sized, dirt-brown sweater more closely around herself. Her stomach churns and tightens as she buries her suddenly shaking hands in the knitted wool. She staunchly reminds herself of her New Year's Resolution to make changes in her life, beginning with her relationship with Ike and ending with her finally figuring out a way to leave the house.

"Would you like something to drink?" she asks, carefully casual, but she can't quite keep the hopeful lilt from her voice.

It's been a long time since Ike stayed past the time it takes to get her signature on a stack of papers, or to confirm she's still breathing. She misses the days when he'd linger and talk with her, giving her news of the world outside the walls of her house. Even more, she misses those all-too-few nights, when he'd whisper against her heated skin, and leave her weak with need. But those nights, like everything else, faded away and now he barely spends any time with her at all.

She doesn't really miss people, but she misses Ike, and he's the only one right in front of her.

Now he hesitates, and the thoughtful look on his face makes her stomach drop.

This won't be good, she thinks.

"I don't want anything to drink," he says slowly, "but I do want to talk to you."

Her stomach drops even further as she shifts her weight in her seat, her fingers clutching at the strands of her sweater.

"All right," she says, feeling as wary as a rabbit sensing danger.

Ike leans forward, his gorgeous golden-brown eyes never wavering from hers. He says, very carefully and precisely, "On New Year's Eve, I asked Irish to marry me, and she said yes."

The ensuing silence lengthens, deepens, as the words

drift around her like leaves, like dust.

She loves Ike, has always loved him. Even while they played cops and robbers through the dusty streets of Ledoux, or hunted for ghosts in and around the abandoned hospital on the outskirts of town, or searched for buried treasure in the rare copses of trees that dot the prairie landscape, she also secretly dreamed of playing house. He's her white knight, riding to her rescue whenever he noticed her schoolmates teasing her or when her mother got sick or when she realized she could no longer bring herself to face the world lurking outside her windows. He starred in more dreams than she can count when she was a teenager, and he's in more fantasies than she cares to admit as an adult.

Ten years ago, he helped her cope with her mother's illness by gradually taking over all the mundane tasks she had no time or energy to do: paying bills, buying groceries, talking to the neighbours. Five years later, he stood by her side, strong and tall and comforting, when she finally laid her mother—that poor, long-suffering woman—to rest. Lou had been twenty-five then, grief-stricken and suddenly unable to cope with the world outside, but Ike remained her friend even after she crept into her house and allowed its doors to seal shut behind her.

She stayed inside, and there were those few brief months when he joined her in her bed, but then his desire faded away, and when she wasn't looking, he fell in love with Irish.

She shivers.

The cold of a Saskatchewan winter doesn't even come close to the ice growing inside her.

"Lou?"

She blinks and shifts, her fingers nervously flexing against the knitted fabric of her sweater.

"Congratulations," she croaks. Her heart clenches at the genuine happiness on his face, in his eyes. She clears her throat, then asks, her voice husky, "When's the big day?"

"The beginning of March."

"That's only six weeks away!"

He laughs. "Well, there's no reason to wait, is there? Don't worry, Lou, I'm still going to manage your finances and take care of you."

"Oh. Well. That's...good." *What does it matter*, she wants to scream, *if there's no longer any hope you'll come back to me?*

Ike nods as he smacks his hands against his knees and surges to his feet.

"Maybe someday you'll meet her," he says, grinning as he picks up his briefcase.

She forces a smile, and hopes he doesn't notice her trembling lips. "Maybe. You've told me so much about her, I feel like I know her already." She winces inside at her dry tone.

Ike either doesn't notice or decides to ignore the sarcasm.

"You'd like her, you know," he says as he walks to the door. She drifts after him and watches, helpless, as he pulls on his boots and parka. "She reminds me a lot of how you used to be."

Lou opens her mouth to say *she* could be the way she used to be; she just needs to figure out how to get there, that's all. But he's already opening the door, and she closes her mouth, the words unsaid.

He pauses on the threshold, the icy air swirling round his feet and into the large, cluttered foyer. He half-turns towards her, standing in both shadow and light. Lou swallows, once again struck by how perfect he is, from the compelling beauty of his amber eyes, high cheekbones and perfectly symmetrical features, to his crown of carefully groomed dark brown hair, now ruffled by the cold winter wind. She sometimes finds it hard to believe he's ever run barefoot through mud, or hovered over her as he patiently tried to coax her to orgasm. Maybe if she'd been able to enjoy the sex more—

"I'll be back before the wedding," he says now, startling her from her thoughts. "See you later, Lou."

He flashes his charming smile, and is gone before she even finishes nodding.

She stares at the door without seeing it before she carefully straightens her sweater, vaguely aware her feet are numb even in their wool socks. She turns and walks just as carefully back to the living room. She eases down onto the couch, feeling as if even the air touching her skin is enough to break her.

She stares at nothing and takes comfort in the silence gently settling over her.

♠ ♥ ♣ ♦

The bell of his stepmother's penthouse elevator chimes, waking Ferrin from his fretful doze on the couch. He groans as he stumbles his way to the foyer as the doors slide open. His jaw drops when he recognizes the man standing inside.

"Abram."

"Ferrin," Abram replies with an austere nod, and strides past him.

Ferrin turns to watch his oldest cousin with a mixture of wariness and curiosity. It isn't often the reigning Macon-Jones patriarch makes house calls.

At 71, Abram is still a vital, handsome man, firmly at the helm of the sprawling, family-owned conglomerate known as Macon-Jones Enterprises. He'd been given the position of Chairman of the Board by his grandfather because he was the eldest son of the eldest son, but he'd held on to it because he was—and still is—a savvy entrepreneur, fearlessly decisive, and ruthlessly brilliant when it comes to maneuvering around his cousins and against his business rivals. His cousins have never quite decided if they should love him or fear him and therefore do both. Regardless, Abram built on his grandfather's success and in the last forty years he's made Macon-Jones Enterprises one of the best known companies in the world, and the Macon-Jones family one of the wealthiest and well-known in Canada.

The physical resemblance between Ferrin and Abram is strong, as it is for all members of the family, including Jack, the lone girl in three generations. They all have a tendency towards medium-brown hair—although Abram's is now mostly grey—pleasantly ordinary, albeit charming, good looks, quirkily skewed features, and, according to Olivia, the exact same shit-eating grin.

Abram's shit-eating grin is nowhere in sight as he turns to glare at Ferrin, and his eyes narrow as he takes in the younger man's bleary eyes, whiskery jaw, and unwashed appearance...and smell, if his grimace of disgust is any indication.

"Drunk?" Abram snaps.

"No."

Abram lifts a skeptical eyebrow and casts a speaking glance around the expansive living room, larger than some ballrooms, and his gaze lingers on the empty beer and liquor bottles, dirty glasses, and crumpled snack bags and pizza boxes littered around the otherwise spotless apartment.

"Hungover, yes," Ferrin clarifies.

Abram sniffs, although his glare eases and his lips twitch.

"What's up?" Ferrin asks tiredly. "Do you need my vote for something? Just so you know, I owe Carson, Dyson and Jack all of my votes for the next three years since they're the ones to blame for all," he gestures vaguely at the debris, "*this*. I think there's a schedule on a pizza box somewhere..."

"I have no doubt there'll be copies in our e-mails along with photographic evidence once the three stooges sober up."

"Musketeers."

Abram rolls his eyes and growls, "This may surprise you, but I'm here to find out what happened with Olivia."

Now it's Ferrin's turn to raise a skeptical eyebrow.

"Yes, that does surprise me," he says and gulps as Abram's hazel-eyed stare once again turns cold and hard. "She broke up with me," he adds hastily.

"So I heard. What did you do?"

"Absolutely nothing! Not that it's any of your damn business anyway."

"Olivia is the best and brightest executive in the company. She's going to be CEO someday. I don't want anything to impede her ability to do her job, or worse: make her decide to join the competition."

"Of course it's about the company," says a new voice with a refined British accent. "Like all your cousins, it's *always* about the company."

They turn and watch the sophisticated, striking woman sweep into the room and settle gracefully onto an elegant armchair. In her late sixties, she's never been exactly beautiful, but she has an undeniable presence, poise and charm that draws and holds attention.

Abram smiles a toothy, patently insincere smile. "Gillian. I wasn't expecting to see you here."

"Why ever not? This *is* my home."

"Have you been enabling your stepson in his debauchery?"

"Debauchery? Really, Abram, I hadn't realized you'd lived such a sheltered life."

Abram quirks an eyebrow, his insincere smile now a genuinely amused lopsided smirk. "I hadn't realized you'd lived such an interesting one. My cousin must have been a man of hidden depths."

Gillian laughs, a sound tinged with bitterness. "My husband had nothing to do with it. It's amazing the things you can do when you're not born a Macon-Jones."

"Ew," Ferrin mutters as he wanders to the couch and

collapses against its plush cushions with a pained sigh. He glances up and realizes he's only succeeded in focusing their attention back on him. He glances from one to the other with growing trepidation.

"What?" he finally demands.

"It's been almost a week," Abram says. "It's time to crawl out of the bottle, apologize to Olivia, and get both your lives back on track."

"Apologize? I haven't done anything wrong, except be myself." He leans forward, his elbows resting on his knees as he scrubs his hands over his face, the stubble on his cheeks rasping against his palms. "Look, she doesn't want to be with me, okay? Not the way I am, anyway."

Gillian sniffs. "After five years, she simply decides to leave you? Please."

"*You* just want me out of the apartment!"

"Well, at least I wouldn't have all these empty bottles about the place," she murmurs.

Ferrin doesn't even have the heart to growl.

"Why aren't you out there wooing that woman to within an inch of her life?" Abram demands.

"What do you know about wooing?" Gillian asks, brightly curious, and Ferrin feels a ridiculous spurt of relief at their familiar, long-standing bickering. He doesn't think he—or any of the cousins, really—could stand against both Gillian and Abram if they ever decided to call a truce and work together for a change.

He abruptly realizes Abram is ignoring Gillian, his eyes never wavering from Ferrin's face.

"Well?" Abram demands. "Why aren't you grovelling at Olivia's feet?"

"Because when a woman says no, she means no," Ferrin mutters.

Abram grunts. "Well, I'm obviously not talking about doing anything stupid, or obsessive." He pauses then adds, "Or criminal. But Olivia loves you, God knows why. She just needs some time to forgive you for whatever you did. That's all. There's no need for you to give up on her so easily."

Ferrin stares.

"Are...are you trying to be supportive?" he asks, incredulous.

Gillian turns an interested face towards Abram.

"Don't be ridiculous," Abram snaps, but he glances away from Ferrin's stunned expression and Gillian's raised eyebrow, and clears his throat. "Olivia's a valuable executive at Macon-Jones. If she's happy, she'll do better work. If you're happy, and I'm responsible, you'll vote my way all the time, rather than with whichever cousin gets to you first." He shrugs. "Well, once you've paid your debt to the stooges, of course."

"Musketeers," Ferrin and Gillian say, and he irritably waves away their correction with a sour grimace.

"Ah," Ferrin says, "I see." He smirks his own lopsided smirk, feeling an unexpected wave of affection for the man in front of him, who had once been like a brother to Ferrin's father.

Abram shrugs. "It's business."

"Of course."

"Like I said: it's always about business," Gillian murmurs with an amused lilt.

Abram turns his glare on her. "Whose side are you on?"

"My own, Abram," she says. "It's the only one I know I can trust."

Abram scowls, then points a commanding finger at Ferrin. "Mend your relationship with Olivia. If you won't do it for the company, or for the family, then do it because she makes you happy."

He turns and leaves the apartment without another word.

Ferrin closes his mouth with a snap as the elevator door slides closed and he turns towards Gillian, who's staring thoughtfully after Abram.

"I'm still drunk, aren't I?" he says.

Gillian gives him a slight smile. "If you are, then I must be drunk on the fumes from all these empty bottles."

She stands.

"I'll never admit this while he's within earshot, but I agree with Abram. Olivia loves you; you love her. She makes you happy, and despite this temporary glitch in your relationship, I think you make her happy. Apologize, do whatever you need to do to get her to forgive you. I think you'll be very sorry if you don't." She shrugs one elegantly clad shoulder and strolls towards the hallway. "Besides, you're the only Macon-Jones who doesn't put the business first. That should make you the best catch in the family. Or at least the rarest." She waves a hand at the general chaos in the living room. "Clear up this mess sometime today, will you?"

He tilts his head back against the couch and closes his eyes with a grimace as she disappears down the hall.

"Putting business first is the problem," he whispers.

Once the shock wears off, Lou's days pass much the same as always. She putters around the house, works out on the treadmill in the basement, reads whatever books Ike brought with him from the library or bought for her on his last trip to Regina, and leaves shopping lists and instructions each day in the small cubbyhole at the back of the house that had once been used for milk deliveries.

Lou sometimes wonders why she bothers with the daily notes, considering Ike only drops by once a week or less, but she finds the peaceful routine soothing, especially when the fact Ike is marrying another woman overwhelms her at the oddest moments. The thought will suddenly strike her, leaving her doubled over, fighting to catch her breath, and desperately trying to figure out what to do to convince Ike to change his mind, to give her—*them*—

another chance.

Of course, she knows what she needs to do.

If she could just get outside, become part of the world again, maybe Ike would change how he thinks of her, and would make him realize he loves her, not Irish, and they could go back to the way things used to be.

The thought of stepping outside makes her double over again, her vision turning black with panic.

As the days turn into weeks, and February inches towards March, that black panic constantly hovers at the edges of her mind. She doesn't know the exact day Ike is getting married, and it's been years since the outside world held any real meaning for her, but now she pays attention to the passage of days. She watches for Ike every afternoon, nervous sparks dancing across her skin as his mysterious wedding day edges closer. She kicks herself for not asking for the exact date, but she'd been too stunned, too hurt, to think of it, and he hasn't stepped foot in the house since he told her the news.

But he promised to come back before the wedding...probably to make sure she has food and her bills are paid before he and Irish leave on their honeymoon.

Honeymoon.

Her breath whooshes out and her knees go out from under her as she practically collapses onto the couch, her arms wrapped tightly around her waist as she bends over, pressing her forehead to her knees.

Honeymoon.

Somewhere romantic, like...like...like Toledo.

No, not Toledo, where the hell did that come from? Isn't there a romantic island that starts with a T in the Philippines or somewhere like that? It doesn't matter. What matters is it isn't Ledoux, and it sure as fuck isn't her house, where nothing has changed since long before her father died because her mother wanted her to know her father and his family, even though they were all gone before Lou was even born. Her mother loved her father too much, even after she started dating Willis-that-bastard.

Lou half-groans, half-laughs at the shit that goes through her head.

She forces herself to breathe slowly and steadily, gradually calming as she focuses on the business of drawing air into her lungs and letting it out again. Finally she calms and lifts her head, realizing her eyes are damp. She blinks rapidly.

No, she thinks grimly, no tears. They've never solved anything and just give her a headache.

She shakes her head and gets to her feet.

She still doesn't know what she's going to do, but she's going to think of something.

Lou's not-so-patient waiting is rewarded a couple of days later when Ike finally arrives.

She forces a smile as she lets him into the house, suppressing a surge of resentment and anger at the sight of his grin and sparkling eyes and his air of nervous energy, excitement and happiness.

She wraps her arms round her waist, her fingers seeking and finding the gaps in the knitted wool of her ubiquitous sweater. The feel of the strands against her fingers calms her and she feels her anger dissipate.

"You're looking good, Lou," Ike says, patting her shoulder. "Everything been okay in here?"

Just like that, the anger's back. She wonders what he'd say if she says no, and how the hell would he know, anyway? The resentment turns to a frisson of fear as she realizes she could have broken her leg five minutes after he'd left, and been lying here in the weeks since. Who would have noticed?

She pushes the thought away as disloyal.

"Just fine," is all she says. "How have you been?"

"Busier than hell," he groans as he settles into Ike's

Chair and puts his briefcase on the coffee table. "Who knew getting married was so damn complicated? We're racing the clock now, but hopefully we'll have everything in place in time for Saturday."

Her hidden fingers clutch at her sweater as she slowly lowers herself onto 'her' spot on the couch.

"Saturday?" she asks, keeping her voice carefully neutral.

He nods, his attention on the papers in his briefcase, his grin widening. "The Big Day, eleven o'clock at St. Vincent's, then we're off for a two-week honeymoon in gorgeous, romantic Tahiti."

Tahiti, that's the place, she thinks as Ike happily continues telling her about his plans for the coming days.

"Lou? Lou!"

She jumps, startled back to reality, and stares, her eyes wide.

"Sorry," she says, giving him an apologetic smile. "I was trying to imagine what Tahiti looks like."

He places the stack of papers in front of her. "It's beautiful, but I doubt you'd like it."

She pulls the papers towards her with a slight frown. "Why do you say that?"

He laughs, and hands her a pen.

"I know you," he says fondly, and his smile widens as she begins to sign.

On Saturday morning, Lou wanders restlessly from room to room, glancing constantly at the clocks.

She wants to go.

She wants to watch with her own eyes as Ike marries another woman. She wants to stop him, before it's too late. In just under three hours, that's exactly what it's going to be: too late.

She feels a surge of anger and residual pride.

Is she truly willing to let him go without a fight?

She pauses, then nods once, decisively, and hurries upstairs to her closet. She rifles through it, searching for a dress that might still fit and which is good enough to wear to a wedding. Good enough to wear outside, past all those so-called 'family friends' she spends her life avoiding, especially Willis-that-bastard. More importantly, she wants something good enough to go into a church and knock Ike's socks off, and Irish out of the picture.

As she pulls out dress after dress, many of which she doesn't even remember wearing let alone buying, she imagines walking in, looking stunning, because of course she will. Doesn't every woman look stunning when they finally dress up for the first time in years? She imagines Ike taking one look at her and realizing he almost made a horrible, horrifying mistake, and finally admitting Lou's the woman he's meant to be with for the rest of his life, even if she never leaves her house again.

She can see the look in his eyes as he walks up to her, as he kisses her, as he leaves with her.

What Irish and the wedding guests are doing while this is going on is vague. Perhaps they're simply standing back, watching in awe as true love prevails over all obstacles, the way it did in the movies she used to watch.

She shakes her thoughts away, still pawing through her clothes. The guests and Irish don't matter. All that really matters is giving Ike the opportunity to realize his mistake. Once he does, he'll come back to the house with her and make love to her the way he used to.

No, *better* than that, because he'll finally admit he loves her and understand they're meant to be together.

She dreams of Ike's amorous reaction to seeing her as she removes her sweater and carefully folds it before draping it over the end of her bed. She hastily sheds the rest of her clothes and pulls on an old dress she dimly recalls from her university days, those days before she returned to Ledoux to look after her mother; those days before the outside world became something terrifying. The dress is a slinky little black number that still fits, although she has to suck in her stomach to get the zipper up.

Well.

Half-way up.

She tries another, but it isn't eye-catching enough, and the zipper doesn't even close half-way.

She wishes she'd been able to go shopping.

She turns to her mother's dresses, and then, in growing desperation, to her grandmother's and finally her great-grandmother's, because if she can't be beautiful she can at least be dramatic, but finds nothing that would be impressive enough to convince Ike to leave his bride-to-be at the altar.

She turns away from the last closet with a frustrated sigh. She puts her hands on her hips and stares off into space, nervously tapping her foot.

Perhaps just the fact she left the house to watch him get married will be enough, she thinks, suddenly hopeful. It is, after all, a sign she's willing to make sacrifices, to conquer her fears for him.

With that encouraging thought, she carefully dresses in a clean skirt and blouse and pulls on her sweater with relief. It wouldn't have worked with the slinky little number and she would have felt horribly exposed without it. Since she won't just see Ike but also all the townspeople who deserted her and her mother in their time of greatest need, she needs all the confidence she can get.

She loses a few precious minutes searching for the winter boots she bought more than five years ago during her last shopping trip to the Macon-Jones store in Regina, but she finally drags them from the farthest corner of the front closet. She pulls on her parka, bulky and uncomfortably binding over her sweater, before shoving her feet into the boots. She stomps first one foot then the other, swinging her arms as she tests the fit and comfort of it all. She hasn't worn these things since her mother's funeral and it's all so uncomfortable, strange...*alien*.

It doesn't matter.

She takes a deep breath and faces her front door.

She stares, suddenly transfixed, as if she's never seen it before.

It's a beautiful thing: dark, rich in colour, thick and heavy. It cost a small fortune a hundred and fifty-odd years ago when her some-number-of-great-grandfather brought it here for the mansion he built for his wife on the desolate wind-swept treeless prairie of southern Saskatchewan. In an era when most immigrants to the area were living in sod huts or crude one-room shacks, her family was building a huge brick mansion with imported oak doors.

Her stomach begins a sick, yawning churn and she grimaces as she reaches for the latch then freezes in mid-movement as the reality of what she's doing finally sinks in.

Tremors begin to ripple through her, and the familiar dark wave of panic begins to rise. She stares helplessly at her outstretched, shaking hand as the wave crashes over her, washing away her good intentions, and all her dreams of Ike's last-minute change of heart.

Ferrin sprawls in a lush leather chair facing a very large, very expensive desk that dominates a very large, very expensive office, and meets the unblinking stare of the man sitting behind it.

Pierce Killian's relationship with the Macon-Jones family is, so he claims, purely business, although he's often devilishly amused by their antics even as he's just as often devilishly annoyed by them. He began his career as a personal financial advisor for Ferrin's father, but now, almost thirty years later, all of the cousins, including Abram, are his clients as well as Ferrin. Like Ferrin, Pierce is one of the few people the entire family trusts.

To a certain Macon-Jones' definition of 'trust', of course.

Pierce is classically handsome, just turned sixty and somewhat wistfully resigned to growing old. He's been in Canada for decades but retains traces of his Black Irish roots, including a lilting accent the ladies still find irresistible, to his great delight. His thick black hair is now liberally laced with silver, but his dark blue eyes are as bright and sharply intelligent as ever.

Those eyes are now shrewdly watching Ferrin as Pierce says with amused disbelief, "You're what?"

"Leaving town. For a while. A few weeks. Or so."

Pierce leans back and tosses his sleekly expensive pen onto the desk.

"Are you honestly trying to tell me you're running away from home?"

"That sounds so cowardly," Ferrin mutters.

"But true."

"Maybe a little bit."

"Look, I don't blame you. With your family, I'm frankly amazed you didn't make a run for it decades ago."

"God knows, I've thought about it."

"No doubt. But running away from Olivia..." Pierce shakes his head. "That's a mistake."

"We have all the same friends, Pierce. We go to the same parties and the same places around town. She's also a top executive at Macon-Jones so I hear about her all the time from Carson, Dyson and Jack. Worse: my family likes her more than me!"

"Don't take it personally; your family prefers anyone who isn't blood related."

"Well, you're definitely living proof of that. The fact remains, Olivia and I...we move in the same circles. We've been running into each other everywhere. Awkward doesn't even begin to describe the situation."

"So your solution is to run away?"

Ferrin sits back in his chair with a defeated sigh, his shoulders slumping.

"It's breaking my heart," he says, his face stark with grief.

"Then stay and fight for her."

"She doesn't want me."

Pierce considers him for another long, silent moment before he straightens, shakes his head, and says, "I know I'm going to regret this, but...what do you want me to do?"

Ferrin's gratitude is palpable. "Help me fly under the radar."

"You're not that well-known!"

Ferrin rolls his eyes. "Macon-Jones is a pretty famous name."

"With four hundred stores nation-wide, and God knows how many internationally, I should damn well hope so!"

Ferrin quirks a half-smile and says, "You know damn well there are 598 stores internationally, because Abram's throwing a big bash for the one-thousandth store when it opens in Toronto in two years. Not that that's important right now. The point is, Macon-Jones is a well-known name in Canada so I want to travel under my 'Ferrin Jones' ID in a futile attempt to stay out of the public eye."

"Just what are you planning that requires anonymity?" Pierce asks, his eyes narrowing.

Ferrin waves the older man's concerns away. "Carson, Dyson and Jack have to stay here, so I won't be calling you for bail money. This time. Some friends have invited me to visit, that's all. I may as well take them up on their offers. I don't need the media dogging my every move."

Pierce laughs. "Really, Ferrin, you're not that well-known! Your picture's been in the paper what? Three times since you were twenty? Maybe four?"

"Only because I've always managed to duck behind

Carson, Dyson or Jack when I see a camera, and you forgot to count the mug shots."

"Deliberately."

Ferrin huffs something that might be a chuckle. "Okay, if not the media, then how about my family? You know they won't give me any peace, no matter where I am or what name I use."

Pierce grimaces. "I can't argue with that. You're not planning on completely disappearing, are you? As annoying and downright dangerous as they can be, they're still your family, and you're the only relative they all like at any one time. Well. To a certain definition of 'like', of course. God knows you're useful as a go-between when the feuding gets out of hand, or when the three stooges need bail money and they're too afraid to call Abram or me or their respective parents."

"Musketeers, and I'm usually in the jail cell beside them so I'm much easier to find. It might do them some good to have to find somebody else to rescue them every once in a while."

Pierce gives him a speaking look.

"All right, yes, yes, I know," Ferrin says with a lopsided half-smile. "As tempting as it is to force my cousins to come up with Carson, Dyson and Jack's bail money—and seriously, they only make me pay it because they like watching me squirm—I'm not going to just disappear. I've already told Gillian and Abram I'll be leaving after the annual gala next week, and I'll keep in touch with everyone by phone and e-mail. You know, for a family that's always feuding, the grapevine is surprisingly alive and well, considering half the cousins aren't speaking to the other half at any one time. Anyway, we both know everyone's going to know where I am no matter what I do. Just regularly remind them—gently or otherwise—that they better not bother me if they ever want me to vote their way again once my deal with Carson, Dyson and Jack ends."

Pierce's eyes narrow. "How long are you planning on being gone?"

"As long as it takes."

"To...?"

"To be able to handle being in the same room with Olivia, knowing she doesn't want me."

Pierce's scowl softens. "You've already spoken to Abram and Gillian?"

Ferrin nods.

"Well, that's something, at least. If we have them on your side, we can control the others."

Ferrin raises a skeptical eyebrow, and Pierce waves a dismissive hand.

"Well, contain them, at any rate."

Ferrin's eyebrow rises higher, and Pierce reluctantly grins.

"I'll do my best," he says.

Ferrin nods again. "I understand. And if you're unsuccessful, don't worry; I'm not like my cousins. I don't hold a grudge."

Pierce snorts. "Oh, please! In that respect, at least, you are exactly like your cousins!"

Lou mopes around the house for the next two weeks, bitterly aware that Ike is on his honeymoon in sunny Tahiti while she wanders the rooms of her mansion like a ghost. The thought scares and intrigues her, and she spends more time than she should wondering if she actually *is* a ghost. She's almost relieved when, a couple days later, she nicks her finger making lunch and decides that ghosts are unlikely to bleed, or curse so long and loudly, or have a cut hurt that fucking much for so fucking long.

The days drag on and, to her surprise, she finds herself actually craving the sound of another human voice. The craving drives her to dig out her mother's ancient radio from the clutter of one of the bedrooms even as she admits it's odd, because it isn't like Ike is around that often anymore anyway. The radio no longer works, but finding and testing it, then debating with herself whether she should put it in the cubbyhole for Ike to get it fixed or throw it in the garbage—in the end, she puts it back in the bedroom where she found it, tucked away with the rest of the ephemera of other people's lives—takes another day, and that means another day closer to Ike's return. Just knowing he's in town will make her feel better.

But until then, she's restless, lonely, and sick of the sight of the rooms of her mansion, packed full of the belongings of those who have gone before her. She passes another day going through several trunks in the attic, where she finds pictures of people she doesn't know and never will because there's no one left to ask.

She even, in a moment of extreme desperation, maneuvers around the cluttered end table blocking the window beside the front door in order to peek out from behind her heavy, dusty curtains at her yard, only to see nothing but a swirling wall of white.

She sighs.

It's mid-March, and winter is still holding on tight.

She shivers.

Maybe staying inside all the time isn't such a bad thing after all.

She doesn't look out the window again, but over the next couple of days, even she can tell the weather warms. She imagines the snow slowly melting, turning ditches and fields into mini, semi-frozen lakes, and wistfully wonders if her fear of the outside will ever melt away, too.

Three days after the weather turns, and two days after his return from Tahiti, Ike bounds up her porch steps and knocks on the door.

Lou follows Ike into the living room, where he stands, rubbing his hands together, rather than settling into Ike's Chair as he regales her with tales of the South Seas. She wraps her sweater more snugly around herself and smiles a tentative, rather puzzled smile.

They stand in awkward silence until she finally says, "So. How was your trip?"

He glances at her with a distracted frown. "Hm? Oh. Great, although I expect honeymoons always are."

She abruptly turns away. "I'm just making toast. Come into the kitchen."

"Forget the toast," he says and her stomach lurches. "I need to talk to you."

She turns back and meets his beautiful amber eyes that are now far too serious for her peace of mind.

"Please," he says and gestures towards the couch.

She hesitates, clutching her sweater, fighting the urge to run. For a wild moment, she wonders if he would try to catch her or just talk to her through her bedroom door.

She swallows then forces herself to walk to the couch and sit.

Ike lowers himself into Ike's Chair and leans forward, resting his elbows on his knees. He clasps his hands and looks at her, his gaze intent and unwavering.

"Lou," he says, and her stomach gives another sharp twist at his too-soft, too-gentle tone, "Irish and I...we're moving."

She frowns. "There's a house for sale? In *Ledoux*?"

"Out of *town*, Lou! Out of province, actually. We're going to B.C."

Lou stares.

Ike shrugs almost helplessly but his expression is resolute. "Irish was offered a great job in Vancouver and there was no way she could say no. We're leaving on Friday."

She blinks and slowly leans back against the couch cushions.

Ike's gaze never wavers.

She opens her mouth, then closes it again, a frown wrinkling her forehead.

Ike says, "I'll call regularly, and of course you know you can call me anytime."

Lou doesn't respond, just continues staring at him.

"You'll be okay, Lou."

She slowly blinks, then clears her throat. "Friday?" she croaks.

He nods.

"You only got back from your honeymoon two days ago. How long have you known you were moving?"

He glances away.

"Was I the last one to know?"

"You and I are *friends*, Lou. Irish and I...we had to tell our families first."

"Oh. Sure. Yeah. I get it. But let's not tell 'the-person-I-do-everything-for-because-she-can't-leave-her-fucking-house' until we're almost on the road!"

He glances around the dusty, cluttered living room, then back at her.

"I know I'm your only friend in town, Lou, and I know I'm the only one you can count on in this shitty little town. We both know I was the only one who helped you and your mom in her last years. You have no idea how much I hate leaving you here all alone! I hate leaving you so vulnerable, but I have to live my own life now, with Irish. While I don't like it, and I wish there was something we could do about it, right now, I think the fact you have an incurable condition that forces you to stay inside is the best thing for you. Those assholes will just turn on you again if you reach out to them. You're safe the way you are and I'll figure something out."

She barely hears him. She bows her head and hopes he can't see how rapidly she's blinking. She clutches at her sweater and takes deep, calming breaths while Ike keeps talking.

"I'll hire somebody to shovel the walk, do the yard work, and everything else. Maybe somebody from Regina, or somebody new in town...not that it matters, really, who they are or where they're from, since you'll never want to speak to them. If they don't do their job, or they try to talk to you, let me know, and I'll find somebody else when I come back, if not before."

She abruptly straightens, her eyes boring into his. "You'll come back?" she asks, her voice choked with emotion.

"Of course! I'm still going to take care of you the way I've always done; it's just going to be mostly from a distance from now on. I'll be back every three months so we can go over your financials...or you can pretend to go over them, anyway." He leans forward, his handsome face filled with concern. "Okay, Lou?"

"Does it matter?" she asks bitterly, and is grateful her tears are gone, burned away by a hot flash of anger. She tugs her sweater more closely around herself and scowls.

Ike shakes his head and stands. She's on her feet, too, although she doesn't remember standing. Everything seems to be happening at a very great distance, which gives her a moment of hope. Maybe it won't hurt so much if it stays that way.

"I'm sorry," Ike says as he walks to the door and she trails behind him. He turns, and now she avoids meeting his disappointed eyes, "but I really think you should think about how *I* feel about all this. This isn't easy for me, you know. I've lived here almost all my life and the last of my family is here, but it's a great opportunity for Irish, and I can't stand in her way. If it were up to me..." He spreads his hands in a helpless shrug.

She jerks a nod, her fingers flexing against the strands of her sweater.

He sighs. "I'll let you know as soon as I've hired somebody, okay?"

"Fine."

He smiles sadly, and holds out his arms. "It's good to see you, Lou."

She awkwardly, and rather reluctantly, moves into his embrace and hugs him, her eyes squeezed shut. He hasn't hugged her since he stopped being her lover, and now, while she longs to hold him in her arms forever, keep him here, with her, forever, she knows he won't—*can't*—stay. She appreciates the hug but it just leaves her feeling empty. She steps away as quickly as he allows and her heart shatters with the sound of the closing door.

Ferrin jolts awake as the car he's driving plows into the water and comes to a sudden, bone-jarring halt, throwing him hard against his seatbelt.

He stares around, his eyes wild, momentarily failing to understand where he is and what's happening. The dented nose of the car is tilted down at a sharp angle and submerged almost up to the windshield, there's a vast expanse of flat, endless water in front of him that stretches to the equally flat horizon, and he wonders how the hell he managed to drive into a lake.

His mind finally sputters into motion: he's on a secondary highway in southern Saskatchewan; he's been on the road for almost twenty-four hours; it's been even longer since he's slept and, he finally realizes with a sickening swoop in his stomach, he just fell asleep at the wheel and drove off the road into a water-filled ditch beside a flooded field.

He's damn lucky he only hit the ditch, he thinks with a horrified relief that turns his knees to a liquid that's even icier than what's surrounding the car and seeping inside to freeze his feet.

If he had rolled...or if there had been another car...

He swallows down a sudden surge of bile as he unbuckles his seatbelt and swings his already-numb feet out of the bone-chilling water and props them on the passenger seat. At least he's not hurt...he thinks.

He pats himself down in sudden panic and heaves a relieved sigh when he realizes his only injury is a soon-to-be-bruise he can feel forming across his chest from the seat-belt. With light-headed giddiness, he thinks how lucky he is that this old clunker didn't have an airbag because he would have broken his nose for sure, and God knows his face is skewed enough already.

He twists around to look out the window beside him and sees the water is half-way up the car door. He grimaces. It's going to be damn cold wading through this shit to get to the highway. He also has no idea how far he is from the nearest town or farmhouse, and the likelihood of somebody giving him—six-foot-two and bulky with it, and looking like he's been sleeping in the gutter for last few weeks—a ride is slim to none. He's handsome enough when he's spruced up, but he hasn't shaved in at least three weeks and he doesn't really want to think how long it's been since he showered. He wouldn't offer a ride to him, either, if he had a choice.

He shakes his head and opens the door.

Well.

Tries, anyway.

He frowns and checks the water level again. Half-way up the door, yes, but he should still be able to open the damn thing, shouldn't he? He doesn't bother trying the passenger door since it had been crumpled in when he bought the car and didn't open anyway...although it *did* have the only window that did. It was one of the reasons he decided to take the secondary roads back to Toronto: he was hoping to avoid the cops while driving this barely road-worthy piece of shit home to the Musketeers.

He tries again then groans in exasperation as he smacks his hands against the door. He vows to never again buy a two-door car, no matter how desperate the seller looks for money, or how much Carson, Dyson and Jack will love the thing, because he's sure he'd be able to at least get a back door open if this car bloody well had one! As it is, well, he has no choice but to go out the only window he can open and hope he can figure out a way to get to the road without having to wade through the icy water surrounding the car. From the looks of things, he could be walking for a very long time before he finds help and his feet already feel like blocks of clumsy ice.

He grunts and groans as he squeezes his heavy frame through the passenger window's narrow opening. He perches on the edge of the door to catch his breath and assess his situation. The car is completely in the ditch and half-drowned in water that he sees now still has a thin sheen of ice on its surface. He definitely does not want to wade through that if he can help it.

He scowls as he considers the situation and decides that if he can get on the roof and slide onto the trunk, he might be able to jump from there to the road.

He eyes the distance from the trunk to the highway.

Maybe.

He looks around.

This piece of Saskatchewan prairie is flat and empty and water-filled, with only an occasional tree to break the monotony of the landscape. The few farms in sight have all, apparently, turned into islands, and he wonders if the roads into their yards are also under water or if it's all an optical illusion. He flexes his numb toes in his soaked sneakers and grimaces.

He's not about to get any more wet and cold than he already is if he can help it.

He eyes the distance from the trunk to the highway again.

He can make it, he staunchly tells himself, then pauses when he hears the roar of an engine. His hopes rise when he sees a truck in the distance heading in his direction. He settles back on his narrow perch and watches as the truck gets closer and swerves into the wrong lane of the otherwise empty highway and slows to a stop next to his drowned car. Ferrin squirms with a mixture of relief and embarrassment as the driver's window rolls down, revealing a grizzled, whiskery face wearing a thoughtfully amused expression.

They consider each other in silence before the stranger drawls, "Need some help there, young fella?"

Ferrin's lips twitch.

"Nah, I'm good," he says with a grunt as he squirms out the window. He balances only briefly on the edge of the door before his wet sneakers slip and he topples into the frigid water.

Ferrin sighs with relief as the warm air of the coffee shop hits the few spots of his almost-frozen skin not covered by the horse blankets he's swaddled in. Unfortunately, horse blankets are also *all* he's wearing.

Once Willis—his still-chuckling rescuer now following him inside—dragged him, coughing and choking, out of his icy bath, he'd ordered Ferrin to get out of his soaked clothes and wrap himself in the horse blankets and get in the truck so Willis could drive him into town.

Even with almost nothing of him exposed and the truck heater blasting as high as it could go for the last five minutes, Ferrin's teeth are still chattering and his hair is still plastered against his scalp although he's at least managed to wipe the worst of the mud and grime from his face. The cold is ferocious, biting past bone-deep and into the very core of him. Forcing his feet back into his ruined sneakers to walk into the coffee shop has only made things worse and he's wondering if he's ever going to be warm again.

The round-faced, pretty blonde barista behind the counter stares, her mouth sagging open, before she blurts, "Holy cow, Willis, what happened?" and rushes to meet them.

If Ferrin weren't so cold, he would have taken a moment to admire her cute face, lovely brown eyes, and curvy figure. As it is, it's all he can do not to shiver his blankets off.

The only other occupant of the coffee shop, a short, wiry, sharp-featured man, joins them, dark eyes wide and worried.

Willis says, "Found this young fella trying to climb his way out of a piece of shit car that's currently drowning in the ditch on the side of highway 35. It wasn't so much the first fall into the water that did him in, but the other two when he was trying to scramble out of the ditch."

The woman rolls her eyes. "And I'll bet you just stood there and laughed, didn't you?"

Ferrin tries to speak in Willis' defense through chattering teeth but Willis forestalls him.

"I wasn't wearing my waders," he says without a trace of deception in his voice even though he'd gone into the water without hesitation to drag Ferrin, choking and coughing, to the road. Willis, however, only had one extra set of thankfully dry clothes in his truck. "Besides, he was making good progress. Anyway, from the looks of him, I suspect he's lost everything he owns. Figured you'd be able to help him, Tessa."

Ferrin's eyes widen but he can't stop his shivering long enough to force out a protest at this assessment of his fortunes—although come to think of it, everything in his wallet is likely ruined—and Tessa's already speaking before he can get any words past his clattering teeth.

"No need to be ashamed," she says to him, brisk but with a kind smile, "we've all had our share of hard times. Let's get you clean and dry and, you know, clothed before we start to worry about the car and getting you enough money to get you on your way. Juan?"

Juan nods, already pulling on his parka. "The left-over clothes from the rummage sale?"

Tessa hurries behind the counter, grabs a key and hands it to him.

"It's our best bet," she says, "especially since Rudemacher's won't give credit, even though this is an emergency and our orphan of the storm here looks like he doesn't have two nickels to rub together. Not that Rudemacher's would have anything that'd fit you, anyway, from the looks of you. Man, I wish we had a Macon-Jones store in town! Anyway, Juan, let's hope we have some clothes left from the rummage sale that'll fit—sorry— what's your name?"

"F-F-Ferrin," he stutters out and thanks his lucky stars that none of these people seem to recognize him. To be fair, he suspects his own stepmother would be hard-pressed to recognize him at the moment, and tries to remember the last time he shaved. Or was this sober. Anyway, it would probably be a good thing if he could keep his identity under wraps, if only so he can minimize the grief his cousins will dish out over this fiasco once they hear of it...and he has absolutely no doubt they'll find out about it.

They find out about *everything*.

"Nice to meet you," the blonde woman says as she eyes him critically. "I'm Tessa. The bigger the better, Juan!" she calls.

Juan waves to let her know he heard her as the door swings shut behind him.

Willis watches him go, then turns his shrewd blue eyes back to Tessa and Ferrin. "I've got to leave Ferrin in your care, Tessa; Biggie's got a cow down. That's where I was headed when I came across this guy, hanging out in a ditch full of ice and water. Good thing I had to go through town anyway or I would have had to leave him there. Could you take pity on a Good Samaritan and give me some coffee?"

"A Good Samaritan because it was convenient," Tessa sniffs, "but I suppose I can overlook that part of it, just this once." She can't hold her stern facade and she grins and winks at Willis as she goes behind the counter to efficiently fill a carafe emblazoned with 'The Row' while saying, "Get those sneakers off, Ferrin—what an unusual name!—your feet must be ready to snap off from the cold! I'll give you a couple of towels to get them warm. When Juan gets back, we'll get you fitted out at least enough to get you over to the rectory and into a hot shower."

"I'll drop your wet clothes off on my way past, and you can throw them in the washer once you get there," Willis says, grabbing the carafe with a nod of thanks. "Nobody lives there anymore but we keep everything hooked up for when the priest comes around, which is about as often as the rest of us go to church." He grins at Ferrin's questioning albeit shivering look. "Weddings and funerals. Anyway, gotta go. Biggie will understand, but I'm not too sure about the cow. I'll check in with you later, young fella."

"B-b-but...w-w-wallet!" is all Ferrin manages to shiver out before the door closes behind Willis.

"Don't worry about it," Tessa says, handing him a couple of towels and shooing him towards a nearby table, "I'll start a tab for you. Coffee? Tea? Hot chocolate? I can whip up some hot apple cider, too, if you think that will work faster. Sorry, no rum or whiskey. I don't have any here, and of course, I'm not licensed, so I wouldn't want to face the fines, not that I object to drinking, God knows I enjoy a drink or two myself on occasion, but, you know, livelihood and all that. So, what'll it be?"

He blinks, wondering if the clicking of his teeth is what caused him to lose track of the question or if she truly talks as fast as he thinks.

She watches him with wide-eyed interest.

"C-c-coffee," he manages to force out.

She nods and bustles behind the counter, if such a cute, thirty-something woman could be said to 'bustle'.

Ferrin sits then hisses in relief and pain as he pulls off

his cold, soggy sneakers and briskly rubs his numb feet with the towels. The movement seems to trigger something, and the shivers increase with a vengeance, getting even more violent, his teeth chattering harder and faster than before.

"G-G-G-God," he manages, "you'd th-think I'd have w-w-warmed up by now!"

"Not in this weather, and even though Willis would have set the heat on high, his truck probably isn't much better than the old clunker you placed in the ditch. Oh, good, Juan's back."

The bell over the door jingles as Juan walks in and places the box he's carrying on the neighbouring table.

"All that's left," he says. "Hopefully something will fit. There aren't any shoes, so I'm gonna go to the job site and grab some extra work boots so we can at least get you to the rectory even if you're wearing nothing but blankets."

He heads out the door again as Tessa absently nods and thanks him. She places a half-full cup of coffee in front of Ferrin, who cautiously wraps his still-shaking hands around it. He hisses at how fiery the cup feels against his chilled skin but after a few moments, the heat seems to seep into his bones and for the first time since his plunge into the flooded ditch, his shivering eases and his teeth finally slow their clattering.

"What happened, anyway?" Tessa asks, holding up a flannel shirt and eyeing it critically before she shakes her head and sets the shirt aside.

"I fell asleep at the wheel," he mutters before he's seized by another wave of violent shivers.

Tessa pauses and stares, wide-eyed, then bursts into rapid-fire speech. "What were you thinking? Lucky you weren't badly hurt! Or killed! Why the hell didn't you stop for a nap? You could have slept in your car if you couldn't afford a motel room!"

Ferrin speaks as quickly as he can in between shivers. "I didn't realize I was that tired! I mean, I knew I'd have to pull over soon, because I'd been on the road for the last twenty-four hours, but I didn't feel sleepy, so I just kept going, and the next thing I knew—boom! Or, rather, splash."

He shakes his head and carefully raises the cup in his still-trembling hands and takes a cautious sip. To his relief, the heat of the coffee spreads through his body as it slides down his throat.

"Believe me," he says, his face stark, "I know just how lucky I am. I could have killed myself or worse: somebody else." He shudders, this time from the possibilities rather than the cold.

He meets her eyes and they look at each other in silence before Tessa briskly says, "Well, that didn't happen, and you're not hurt." She gasps, suddenly struck by the thought, and her words begin tumbling out even faster than before. "You're not, are you? Oh my God, I never even thought about getting you to a hospital!" She whirls and rushes behind the counter. "I'll call Delaney; she can cover the store while I take you to Regina, even if she has to bring the hellspawn with her." She keeps babbling as she scrabbles for her phone. "No doctors around here. Well, there are, but none you'd want to visit, or you really will end up dead. It's tough for the older folks, and we're trying to attract better talent, but who wants to be a doctor in a pissant little town like this in the middle of bald-ass prairie? Not that there's anything wrong with bald-ass prairie, of course, because personally, I love it, but I do wish we had a decent doctor! Not to mention a Macon-Jones store of our very own, but well, I guess we can't have everything, now can we?"

Ferrin stares, his mouth hanging open, but he abruptly sits up straight when Tessa finally finds her phone and grabs it with a triumphant cry.

"I don't need a doctor!" he blurts. Loudly.

She stops and stares.

Ferrin eases back in his chair, and shrugs, which sets

off another set of shivers. He waits until his teeth stop chattering before he says, "Sorry, but there's no point in running me all the way to Regina—although I have no idea how far away that is—because I'm not hurt. Bruised a little, but not hurt."

"How would you know?" Tessa demands, hand on her hip. "You didn't even know you were sleepy!"

Ferrin chuckles. "Fair point," he says, and grins a genuinely amused, full-on, lopsided, charming grin. "But I don't need a doctor. I swear."

Tessa scowls, giving him a hard stare. "Don't try to turn on the charm, buddy; I'm immune, and I've sworn off too-handsome, too-charming men for the foreseeable future."

He preens as much as he can while unshaven, unwashed, smeared with mud and wearing a horse blanket toga because, *damn*, the family charm and good looks still shine through. Tessa's stare immediately turns into a glare. He rearranges his features into a look of bright-eyed innocence, and is rewarded with a slow, albeit reluctant, grin from Tessa.

"All right," she says, "I'll take your word for it, but don't blame me if you wake up dead tomorrow morning from internal bleeding."

"Cross my heart, although I may still come back to haunt you, just to be contrary."

She laughs. "Fine. Let's get you in some clothes. You're violating my dress code."

He glances down at his blankets. "I don't know. I think this outfit does something for a man."

She snorts as she returns to pulling clothes out of the box. "Trust me, it does nothing for any man. I'm not sure how the ancient Greeks and Romans ever got laid."

Ferrin's mouth drops open before he begins to laugh.

VICTORIA BERNADINE

Ferrin settles into one of the narrow beds at the rectory after a hot shower and being fed to within an inch of his life by Juan and his wife, Delaney, a beautiful woman with the equally lovely cadence of the Caribbean in her voice. He's also survived being peppered with questions from them, their two children, Tessa, and Willis. He finds himself grinning up at the ceiling while he ponders the events of the day.

He deftly dodged their questions, telling them as much of the truth as he could but stopped short of revealing who he really is. They're all so firmly convinced he's a down-at-the-heels drifter needing a helping hand and endearingly determined to give him one that he almost feels guilty about hiding his true identity. He's incredibly touched by everyone's enormous generosity but decides he can't risk one of them leaking the news to the media before he can do damage control with his cousins. Besides, he'll be on his way tomorrow, and they never need to know they rescued Benjamin Ferrin Macon-Jones, one of the many heirs and owners of Macon-Jones Enterprises, and wealthy in his own right.

Not that he isn't grateful and he's already thinking of ways to thank them for their kindness to a stranger. Tessa's coffee shop, The Row, could use a good refurbishing, and Willis could definitely use a new truck. Juan and Delaney look like they're doing well, with Juan's construction company profiting from the recent economic boom in Saskatchewan and the resulting building frenzy that's come with it. Still, he's sure there's something they need. Maybe something for the kids, or the hellspawn as, well, everyone calls them when they're out of earshot, or maybe they could use a new family vehicle or...*something.* He'll figure it out and work with Pierce to get everything done once he gets back to Toronto.

In an instant, his good mood is wiped away.

Toronto means both too much and not nearly enough Olivia and he's not sure he's ready to go back to face that

44

reality. The desire to hide at the bottom of a bottle has finally eased, although he'd still been drunk when he impulsively bought that barely-road-worthy piece of shit car currently drowning in a ditch. Not that he regrets buying the thing. The kid looked so desperate, and Ferrin knew Carson, Dyson and Jack would love refurbishing it...plus his liver—not to mention the rest of him—was screaming for a break from the beating he was giving it. Buying the thing and driving it back to Toronto was the perfect excuse to leave Vancouver and he hoped he'd have enough time to recover before Gillian saw him.

Seemed like a good idea at the time.

Still seemed like a good idea even after he sobered up enough to drive.

He pulls up the blankets and rolls onto his side with a sigh. The bed is narrow but surprisingly comfortable, or it may be the multitude of sleepless nights over the last two and a half months, or maybe the events of the day are finally catching up with him.

His eyes drift closed.

Well, if nothing else, at least he met a great bunch of people and has quite a story to share once he's back in Toronto.

Even if he won't be sharing it with Olivia.

The wind is howling the next morning, snow swirling around Ferrin's feet as he walks in to The Row. He's greeted like a long-lost relative by Tessa, Juan, and Willis, and subjected to a cold, hard stare from a tall, movie-star-handsome man with light brown eyes, who's standing with them at the counter.

"*This* is the guy?" the stranger demands.

The others nod and Ferrin's eyebrow goes up as the stranger, with a skeptical twist to his lips, makes a show of looking him up and down.

"You weren't kidding when you said he looks like something the cat dragged in," he says.

"Hey, now," Ferrin says indignantly, "I've cleaned up! You should have seen me yesterday!" Well, at least he showered, he adds silently. He might even shave tomorrow.

The stranger doesn't bother to acknowledge him.

"I can't believe you guys think he's even remotely suitable!"

"You're leaving tomorrow, Ike," Tessa says breezily, but with a hint of steel in her voice. "You're kinda running out of options."

Ike heaves a long-suffering sigh.

"That woman," he growls. "Some days..."

Ferrin's eyebrow rises higher. He glances at his new-found friends, and is surprised by their expressions of polite disdain as they watch the man in front of him with varying degrees of wariness. His curiosity ramps up.

Ike scowls, then mutters, "Not ideal, but Tessa's right. I'm out of options." He glares at Ferrin. "I have a job for you."

Ferrin laughs. "Sorry, what?"

"Look," Ike says impatiently, "I'm leaving town tomorrow and Lou needs somebody to look after her. You're the only one in town who doesn't know anything about her, which is good, and you're in desperate need of a job, which is even better."

"Whoa, whoa, whoa!" Ferrin says, holding up his hands. "I'm not a nurse! Or doctor or a caregiver of any kind!"

"Not that kind of looking after! She's the town recluse." Ike pauses, considering, then shrugs. "Hermit. Nut job. Whatever. She lives in the big house on the hill."

Ferrin frowns, visualizing what little he's seen of the town. It's picturesque in a stark kind of way but 'hilly' it is not. He turns to look out the front window and something clicks.

46

"You mean that slightly higher piece of ground across the street?"

That makes everyone laugh, even Ike.

"In Ledoux, that's a hill," Ike says, and Ferrin sees the charm in the other man's grin even if it doesn't quite reach his eyes. "Lou needs somebody to run her errands, shovel her walk, mow the grass, that kind of thing. You'll never see her, or even hear her, because she doesn't like the people she knows, and she likes strangers even less. I'm the only person she's spoken to in years. She leaves notes in an old cubbyhole beside the back door. You do whatever the notes ask you to do, and in return, she'll pay you—" and he names a sum that makes both of Ferrin's eyebrows soar into his hairline.

Ike says, "Trust me, you'll earn it. There's a lot to do; it's a pretty big place. She can be pretty picky, too. She's also very directive, and, quite frankly, she can be a cantankerous old bat. When she wants something done, she wants it done right."

"How's she going to know?" Ferrin asks, honestly curious.

"She's psychic," Ike replies with withering sarcasm.

"Convenient," Ferrin murmurs as he glances at the others before turning back to Ike. "Look," he says, "I'm honored, but I'm just passing through."

"From what I hear," Ike says, his voice now as cold as the air outside, "you'd be hard pressed right now to make it a mile out of town, especially with your current home and only mode of transportation frozen in the ditch. Somebody who needs money as desperately as you shouldn't be too picky."

"Hey," Willis says sharply before Ferrin can get past his shocked amusement enough to finally set the record straight, "you can't force the young fella! Like he says, he's just passing through."

"Yeah," Tessa says, "if he doesn't want to do it, he doesn't want to do it. You'll just have to figure something else out and, honestly, you should have made arrangements when you knew Irish got that job in Vancouver instead of leaving who was going to look after Lou—your only client as far as we can tell and the only job you actually have in this town—to the last minute. You have nobody to blame but yourself, and you know it."

"Well, Tessa, I was a bit busy, what with getting married and going on my honeymoon and all."

"Whoa, whoa, whoa," Ferrin says, making calming motions with his hands, hoping to prevent Tessa from literally going for Ike's throat, "back up the bus. Let's start over, okay? Why are you going to Vancouver, Ike?"

"My wife starts a new job there in two weeks. We're leaving tomorrow because we're driving and decided to make some stops along the way."

"And who, exactly, is Lou?"

"Lou Upjohn. Her great-great-grandfather was the founding father of this town and once owned every piece of land the town sits on. He's the one who built the house on the hill."

"That's...lovely," Ferrin says drily, "but that doesn't tell me anything about Lou herself."

"You don't need to know anything about Lou herself," Ike says, equally dry. "She's a recluse, remember? You're never going to meet her and you're never going to talk to her. That's the way she likes it."

Ike gives him a hard stare to emphasize his point, which fills Ferrin with mild amusement. Ike's trying to be intimidating but compared to the Macon-Jones clan, he's about as frightening as a butterfly. It's taking everything Ferrin has not to laugh out loud at the other man's posturing.

But, to his own surprise, he's finding the unexpected offer almost...*tempting*. His curiosity is piqued and if he takes this job, it gives him a reason to avoid returning to Toronto. It's not like he has anything or anyone waiting for him. Well, his cousins, of course, and Gillian, not to mention Pierce and Ferrin's many business investments, but not Olivia, and she's really the only one who defines 'anything' or 'anyone'. He has nothing but his bone-deep yearning to see Olivia again drawing him back to Toronto, fueled with the faint hope that she misses him as much as he misses her.

But he has his pride, and besides, there's something else to consider, or rather, someone: a recluse, a real person, somebody vulnerable, who needs help in keeping the world at bay. He feels a pang of compassion for this old woman, tired of the world and about to lose the only person she trusts enough to help her.

"I'm only passing through," Ferrin says slowly, "and I have plans of my own. I can't stay forever."

"What plans?" Ike snaps. "You're living out of your car!"

"For God's sake, Ike," Willis growls.

Ike rolls his eyes at the older man then returns his attention to Ferrin and heaves an impatient sigh. "I'll be back in August," he says. "I'm still Lou's financial manager and I'll have papers for her to sign by then. If you can at least hold out that long, that would help. I'll just have to make the time to take care of it when I'm back. Maybe get somebody from Regina."

Ferrin hesitates.

"Even in Ledoux, the money you're offering isn't going to go far," Juan says suddenly. "Ferrin, if you're gonna stay a while, I can give you a part-time job on my construction crew."

Ferrin's eyes widen. "I don't know anything about construction!"

Juan shrugs. "General labourer. We always need somebody to haul shit around."

Ferrin feels a surge of panic. Helping out a little old lady he'll never see is one thing but having somebody offer him a real job is something else, especially a job he doesn't need but somebody else·might. He stares at his new-found friends as he wonders how he can gracefully get himself out of this situation.

Then he glances at Ike and is caught by the other man's cold eyes and stern expression. A chill runs down Ferrin's spine. He doesn't like Ike but more than that: he doesn't trust him, and he feels a stab of real concern for that poor old lady hiding away behind her closed door.

Besides, Ferrin thinks, trying to shake away his sudden concern for a woman he's likely never going to meet, Ike doesn't seem the type to be amused to discover he's mistaken an heir to the Macon-Jones business empire for a homeless drifter desperate for work.

Ferrin turns his attention to Tessa, Juan and Willis. They might eventually be amused, he thinks, but they might also feel he's been playing them for fools. He doesn't want to repay their kindness with suddenly blurting out his true identity and possibly embarrassing them in front of this harsh man they obviously do not like.

Still...the situation is more humorous than scandalous, and really, he's the only one who has any reason to be embarrassed for longer than five seconds. Lord knows, he's done worse with Carson, Dyson and Jack, and has all the mug shots to prove it and from several countries, too.

He turns his gaze back to Ike and cocks his head as he considers the other man.

As a Macon-Jones, Ferrin's no stranger to cold-eyed men, but unlike his cousins, there's no roguish twinkle or charm or reluctant kindness lurking behind Ike's icy facade. Ferrin doesn't want to leave some poor old woman—cantankerous old bat or not—all alone without anyone to look after her, and even with less than five minutes of exposure to Ike, Ferrin has absolutely no doubt Ike will leave her to fend for herself rather than adjust his own plans. Ferrin's heart twists with sympathy because there's a real person living behind the walls of her house, needing someone to help her, just like there had been a real person in Vancouver with nothing but a shitty car to sell to keep the wolf from the door. He can't turn his back if there's something he can do to help.

He heaves a silent sigh, hearing Olivia's voice telling him he's such a goddamn fixer that it's made him gullible and weak and maybe a little stupid. Not for the first time in the last few months, he wonders if it's true.

"All right," he says slowly, "I'll do it, at least until August. But first, I need to make a phone call."

"You're *where*?" Pierce asks, and Ferrin grins at the horror in his voice.

"Ledoux, Saskatchewan."

"Where the *hell* is *that*?"

"Well, Saskatchewan's between Manitoba and Alberta, and north of—"

"*Ferrin!*"

Ferrin chuckles. "It's a small town about an hour southeast of Regina. Twenty-six hundred people, more or less. Mostly less."

"Dear Lord!"

"Don't worry, they have computers and everything. Even a pay phone. The old-fashioned kind. It works, too, because it's what I'm using to call you."

"Yes, but do they have indoor plumbing?" Pierce asks, his Irish accent even more pronounced in his agitation.

"It's supposed to be in every house by this time next year, so I'm told."

Pierce makes a scoffing noise before he says, "How long are you planning to stay...*there*?"

The very real disgust in his voice makes Ferrin laugh.

"It's not the end of the world!"

"I'll wager you can see it from there!"

"Maybe. I'll go look and let you know."

Pierce snorts. "Perhaps I should speak to your cousins and stepmother. Start a pool as to how long you'll last in the wilds of Saskatchewan." He chuckles. "What am I saying? There's absolutely nothing 'wild' about Saskatchewan!"

"You're such a snob, Pierce."

"Of course." He pauses, then sighs. "I'll tell the cousins you're alive and well, and currently safely ensconced in *Saskatchewan*, of all the ungodly places."

"And working as a day labourer on a construction crew, and as a general handyman for the town recluse."

The ensuing silence swells with possibilities, and Ferrin bites back a laugh as he imagines the look on Pierce's face.

"Why?" Pierce finally asks, and Ferrin is reluctantly impressed by his controlled tone. Then again, the man has been working for his family for at least thirty years; nothing should surprise him anymore.

"Why not?" Ferrin says lightly. "It's got to be better than drinking my way around the country, right?"

"Well, when you put it that way...do these people have any idea who you are?"

"Obviously not, or they'd know I'm unemployable. Look, I promised to stick around until August. I'll come home after that. Of course, I can't really do much anyway until we get the car out of the ditch—once it thaws again—and I either get it fixed enough so I can drive to Toronto or have it towed to the junkyard. Or maybe I'll just ship it to Carson, Dyson and Jack. They're the reason I bought the bloody thing in the first place."

Pierce sighs in weary resignation. "What do you need?"

"A bank account, a credit card, and a phone in the name of Ferrin Jones. I guess there's not much I can do about getting a driver's license in that name, is there?"

"Not one you can show the police if you're pulled over."

"Well, that's true, but I could use one just in case someone needs to look inside my wallet, or catches a glimpse inside it. I'm just lucky Willis didn't look through it when he had the chance."

"Sounds like you're planning on making sure they never find out who you are."

"We-ell, I at least want to delay it for a while. You know, it's fun being just an ordinary Jones even if everybody's firmly convinced I'm a homeless drifter and, apparently, a handy kinda guy." He pauses, frowning. "Maybe it's because I have such broad shoulders..."

Pierce snorts. "Have you ever done any manual labour in your life?"

"Well, no, but so many people do it, how hard can it be?"

Ferrin lets himself into the rectory that evening, wearily pulls off his borrowed work boots and parka in a pained daze, then limps to the shabby couch and falls face down on it with a groan.

He's exhausted, his blisters have blisters, his shoulders and legs ache, but, he concedes through the painful haze surrounding him, he feels....*satisfied*. Even proud.

But he's very grateful he doesn't have to go to Lou's place until tomorrow.

Like Juan promised, he's grunt labour. He spent the day moving loads of tile, lumber, bricks, and doing whatever the hell else the crew told him to do, including hauling out the garbage and making coffee runs to The Row. But, he has to admit, he feels like he's accomplished something, something real. Something he can see and measure and feel.

He turns his head to the other side and groans from the pain of that small movement.

Dear *God*, can he feel it.

He stands and stretches his aching back, then frowns, surprised as the doorbell rings. He grimaces as he limps over to open it, hoping it isn't another lost soul seeking refuge. He has no problem sharing the rectory, but he's in no shape to be sociable. He can barely move without yipping with pain and all he wants is to eat, shower, and crawl into bed.

He opens the door and finds Tessa, looking adorable in a stylish parka with a faux fur toque framing her pretty, round face. She holds paper bags in her mittened hands.

"I can't stop. Juan asked me to bring you this," she says cheerfully, brown eyes sparkling as she hands him the bags.

He frowns. "What's this?"

"Don't worry, it won't bite! It's just something to eat. He said it looked like you'd barely make it here, let alone cook or venture out later to find food. He would have delivered it himself, but Delaney phoned and he had to hurry home. It sounded like the hellspawn broke something vital, or, knowing them, they've taken something apart and can't figure out how to put it back together again. Either way, Juan had already bought supper for his crew, so he asked me to deliver everything to everybody."

"Wow. That's..."

"That's Juan. He appreciates a good day's work. Anyway, gotta go. I have other meals to deliver. Enjoy!"

She lifts her hand in farewell and hurries away.

Ferrin slowly closes the door and only then realizes his feet are blocks of ice, even through the thick wool socks Juan had given him that morning.

It's frickin' mid-March, he thinks as he limps to the kitchen; how long does winter last out here?

He sets the bags on the small table in the kitchen and opens them to discover lasagna, garlic toast, Caesar salad, and a cold beer. His nose twitches, his mouth waters, and he realizes he's famished. He sits and tucks in to the savory food, and as he gobbles it down, he thinks it's the best he's ever tasted, made all the better by the ache in his muscles and the still-lingering satisfaction of an honest day's work.

He finishes eating and cleans up before making his way upstairs to fall into bed, where, for the first time in months, he goes immediately and peacefully to sleep.

♠♥♣♦

"You did *what*?" Lou screeches.

Ike heaves an irritated sigh. "You know you need somebody to do the yard work and run your errands."

"And just when did you hire this...this whoever the hell he is?"

"This morning."

"And you're only telling me *now*?" This time her screech is even louder. "It's ten o'clock at night!"

"We're leaving tomorrow, Lou; you don't think I have other shit to do?" He sighs and roughly runs a hand through his carefully styled hair. "What are you so upset about? You knew this was going to happen! Did you think if you ignored it like you do everything else that somehow things would magically stay the same?"

Lou glares, arms wrapped tight round her waist, her fingers gripping the wool of her ubiquitous brown sweater like a lifeline. She wants to snap back a sharp retort, but, she grudgingly admits, he has a point. She *has* been hoping that if she ignores everything, then nothing will change.

Yeah, she thinks bitterly, because that worked so well when it came to his wedding.

"Well," she mutters, "I would have appreciated it if I'd had some input into who would be working for me."

"Right. Like you'd let me bring a stranger into the house so you could interview him."

She scowls, her fingers flexing against her sweater. "For something like this, I might have," she says, but even she has to admit her defiance is pitiful.

The look Ike gives her is pitying and she flushes and lifts her chin.

"Right," he says. "You would have tried, and you would have promptly had a panic attack, like you always do with somebody new." His expression softens. "I would never expose you to outsiders. You know that."

Lou's fingers relax as she softens beneath his warm gaze.

"I know," she says. "I know you just want to protect me." She's silent, shifting uncomfortably on the couch then says, "So. Who is this paragon of handiness you've found for me?"

"His name's Ferrin Jones. He's a drifter; just wandered into town yesterday, I think, or maybe the day before." He shrugs. "Doesn't matter, he's stuck here since he drove his car into a ditch full of water, and now it's frozen over. It'll take a few days to tow it out and get it working again...*if* they can get it working again. It's apparently been his home, too. Anyway, he's promised to stick around until I come back in August."

She fidgets for another moment then says, "What if he doesn't?"

Ike gives her a rueful smile as he leaves Ike's Chair to join her on the couch. Her heart gives an aching lurch as he puts an arm around her shoulders and gives her a comforting squeeze. "Then I'll find somebody else. Don't worry about it, okay? Leave everything to me. You won't need to go outside. You won't need to talk to anybody. Just ignore him, keep your doors and windows securely locked and blocked, and I'll be back before you know it. You'll see. It'll be just like I still live here." He tightens his arm around her. "Just remember: I'll take care of you, and you don't need to deal with gossiping neighbours or this stranger."

"I thought the gossip would have died down by now," she mutters.

Ike shrugs. "It's a small town. Besides, your house is pretty hard to ignore, and you're the last member of the Upjohn family. They wonder what you do in here all day and why you never leave the house, and that leads them to wonder if there's something wrong with you, and what that might be."

"There *is* something wrong with me."

"Well, yes, but I doubt you're going to murder all your neighbours in their sleep."

"Of course not," she snaps, "I can't leave the house."

"*You* know that, and *I* know that..."

She smacks him in the chest with the back of her hand and reluctantly smiles before she sobers, and says, "I'm going to miss you, Ike. I mean, I'm *really* going to miss you."

He pulls her into a warm hug. "I'm only a phone call away, and I'll be back in August," he murmurs against her hair, and she closes her eyes and presses her cheek against his warm, firmly-muscled chest, remembering how it felt when his body had moved against hers. She listens to his heartbeat and feels hot tears prickling beneath her eyelids. She wonders if he ever thinks about those days; ever misses them the way she does.

She doesn't have the courage to ask and instead simply mutters, "Okay."

He releases her, stands, and glances at his watch. "I have to go. Irish is finishing up the last of the packing and she won't be too pleased if I leave her to do it all on her own."

Lou forces a smile. "Okay," she says again. "What time do you leave in the morning?"

"Seven."

"How long is the drive?"

"About twenty hours, if we don't stop at all. But we're going to spend the night in Calgary and then Kelowna, make it a bit of a second honeymoon road trip." His sudden grin is wide and bright. "I know we just got back from Tahiti, but we're newlyweds; what can I say? We're going to enjoy it while we can because we're going to be hellishly busy once we get to Vancouver on Sunday."

Lou forces herself to nod and smile. It must seem sincere because his expression doesn't change.

"Sounds like fun," she manages.

"Says the woman who's never seen the mountains!" he laughs, and heads for the door.

She grits her teeth and pretends to chuckle as she follows, emptiness gnawing at her core.

"Don't let it bother you, though," Ike says as he pulls on his parka and boots, "you're really not missing much, staying inside. I envy you sometimes." He straightens and smiles at her, a broad, toothy, fond smile. He puts his hands firmly on her shoulders, and looks deep into her eyes. It's all she can do to stop herself from throwing herself against him and begging him not to go.

"Everything's going to be fine," he says, seemingly oblivious to the emotions roiling inside her. "I'm going to protect you the way I've always done our whole lives. You won't even notice anything's changed."

"If you say so," she mutters.

He pulls her into another tight hug. "You'll be okay. You'll be safe, too, if you remember not to talk to strangers, even this one I just hired, and ignore anybody who comes to the door. Not that anyone will, but just in case." He drops a light kiss on her cheek. "I'll call once we're settled, and I'll see you in August."

"Sure."

He pats her shoulder and with that, he slips through the door and is gone.

Lou is curled up on the couch, unmoving, wrapped in her comforting sweater as she stares fixedly at the clock on the wall.

It's ticking down to the time Ike and Irish are leaving town.

If there's one thing she knows about Ike, she thinks

distantly, it's that he's punctual to a fault.

The second hand sweeps its way around the clock face and she watches it, hoping against hope that Ike will knock on her door and tell her he's changed his mind; that he's realized he can't leave her.

Seven o'clock comes and goes, and still she sits, watching as the minute hand inches its way to fifteen minutes past the hour, then thirty.

There's no knock on her door. No Ike, telling her he loves her.

As the clock's hands sweep towards eight o'clock, her shoulders slump ever lower. She leans her head back and closes her eyes, tears burning beneath her lids.

He's gone. He's really gone, and now she's left to face the town—life—on her own.

Well...except for...whatshisname, the stranger with the strange name Ike told her about last night, but that's just it: he's a stranger, not even somebody she might have known, back in the days when she left the house, those days when she still thought the people of this town were friends and loved her mother, those days before those same people deserted them both.

She puts her hands over her face and struggles to blinks away the tears burning her eyes.

Whatshisname isn't Ike, and she's alone.

The next few days drift by, and Lou discovers Ike was right: if she doesn't think about things too deeply, it really does seem as if nothing has changed. It's been years, after all, since he's spent more than an hour or two with her; even longer since he dropped by every day. She can almost convince herself he's still in town and if she looks out the window at just the right time, she'll see him taking the notes out of the milkman's drop box.

On the fourth day, she finds herself sipping coffee at

her kitchen table as she dreamily imagines Ike walking down Main Street, on his way to buy the groceries she asked for the night before. She sees him, dark hair gleaming in the sun and ruffling in the breeze, amber eyes smiling as he strides up her walk. She looks towards the back door and tilts her head, warm anticipation curling in her stomach as she hears his step on the porch and waits for the chime of her doorbell.

She freezes, a creeping sense of horror crawling across her scalp and down her spine.

She slowly lowers her cup, the click of ceramic against the table loud in the silence that surrounds her. It's a silence she usually finds comforting, but now, suddenly, intensely, terrifies her.

For the first time in years—or possibly ever—she sees, with stunning clarity, her future stretching out before her. Not just the looming decades of isolation and silence, of an existence spent solely within the confines of her house, but also the very real possibility of losing touch with the reality of herself and everything that lives outside her walls.

She realizes she's shivering, and she hunches over, fingers clutching in almost feverish desperation at her sweater. She moans softly, feeling the black edges of a full-blown panic attack inching closer. She closes her eyes, her jaw clenched, and concentrates on breathing carefully and consciously as the panic sweeps over her.

When the panic finally eases, she rests her head on the table and closes her eyes.

She can't go on this way. Even if Ike learned long ago there's no cure for her, there has to be *something* she can do to make things better, to *be* better. People go outside all the time, for God's sake, how hard could it be? Hell, *she* used to go outside all the time!

She pushes away from the table and goes to the window. She inches open the heavy drapes, thick with dust, that shroud her and her home from prying eyes, and peeks out.

The day is bright, the sun sparkling off the snow that is once again thick on the ground, even with April just around the corner. There's a softness to the light, however, that whispers spring has finally arrived, even if it's only for today.

It looks inviting out there. The icicles forming on the eaves of the back porch remind her of when she was a kid, and how, on days like today, her mother would break off two icicles and they'd eat them like lollipops as they strolled down the hill to Main Street to buy real lollipops from Mr. Neil's corner store.

She smiles at the memory and presses a hand over her heart.

There are days when her mother's absence is a dark ache in her soul.

She stares at the icicles, and wonders if she'll ever be able to do that again. Will she ever be able to go outside and break off an icicle like that one right there and nibble on it, remembering those moments with her mother while she wanders down Main Street and into whatever store still sells lollipops?

Her breathing speeds up and her vision starts to narrow at the very thought. She carefully puts the curtain back into place with trembling hands.

Maybe someday...but not today.

Ferrin glances up from reading the news on the brand new phone Pierce arranged for him, and smiles as Tessa refills his cup.

"So, how's it been going with the town eccentric?" she asks with a grin.

He shrugs. "I haven't seen her, but her handwriting is very elegant."

Tessa laughs.

"Sit down, if you have a minute," Ferrin says.

She casts a speaking look around the otherwise empty room and says, "I think my hordes of adoring fans can wait a minute or two. Just let me put this back and grab a coffee."

She returns with a steaming cup and slides into the seat across from him.

He leans across the table, his expression serious and intent.

"Tell me about her," he urges quietly. "Lou," he adds at Tessa's confused face.

Tessa leans across the table.

"Why are we whispering?" she whispers.

Ferrin shrugs, and lowers his voice to an even softer rumble. "In case she's a spy as well as psychic."

Tessa considers it. "Maybe." She laughs and leans back. "What do you want to know?"

"Who is this woman? I mean, I've been here for a month now, and I've wandered all over town—"

"Didn't take long, did it?"

"It's charming," Ferrin says automatically, "and very friendly."

Tessa snorts. "Especially the women, right?"

"Well, I—I didn't really notice," he says, flushing.

"Uh-huh. Anyway, you've wandered all over town...?"

"Lou's house is a true mansion. The only one in town. I mean, two and a half storeys of red brick with a front porch that would give a southern plantation a run for its money even with all the railings missing? It tends to stand out, even if it wasn't on that pimple you call a hill. So, what? Is she the cantankerous aging matriarch of the town's first family, who's alienated all of her kids and the town, and now she's mouldering away in her mansion while her family constantly battles over the inheritance while waiting for her to die?"

Tessa stares. "Wow. That's pretty good. I'd totally watch that!" She frowns. "Although, come to think of it, it sounds too much like those potboiler miniseries from the '70s and '80s—oh, hell, who is that guy?" She scowls, clicking her fingers. "*You* know the guy I'm talking about..."

Ferrin blinks, confused. "Richard Chamberlain?"

"No! The author!"

Ferrin frowns in thought, then shakes his head. "I don't—that's not—how did—? I thought this would be a simple conversation!"

"Why would you think that?" Tessa says innocently, her brown eyes wide. "Sorry, Ferrin, I got distracted. Anyway, Lou? No."

"Did I get *any* of it right?"

"Well, she is the last surviving member of the town's first family, although I'd love to see what would happen if you call her an aging matriarch to her face. Besides the fact that, as far as I know, she has no children, she's also apparently my age, or close to it."

Ferrin's jaw drops. "You mean she's *young*?"

Tessa grins, her pretty face glowing, and winks. "You are *such* a charmer; I'm almost sorry I'm immune to you! And have I told you lately I'm glad you ditched the beard?" Her grin fades. "As for Lou, well, I've been told she's my age. I've never seen the woman."

"So, what do people think happened? I mean, what did Ike tell people when they asked?"

"Ike doesn't tell many people anything, really, except that Lou is bad-tempered, eccentric, and has decided she hates this town and everyone in it. Did you know she even refused to let anybody visit her mother in the last year her life? Her mother's, I mean, not Lou's, obviously. She had Ike turn everyone away from the door, even Willis, who was a close friend to both her parents, probably the best friend they had, although I've also heard rumors about him and Lou's mother, but that was long after Lou's dad died." She shakes her head. "Sad, really. A bit before my time, though."

Ferrin digests this in silence, then, "So why didn't she

leave after her mother died?"

"Well, that's something you'd have to ask her. I've always assumed she has enough money to live on if she stays here, but if she moves, she'd have to get a job. If she hates people as much as Ike says she does, I'd guess it's easier to stay here and just avoid everyone else. It may be a long and lonely life, but it may be better than the alternative."

"The alternative?"

"Dealing with all those fucking people."

Ferrin shakes his head and reluctantly chuckles.

Tessa looks over her shoulder as the bells over the door jingle, and she smiles a welcome at the couple who enters. She gets to her feet and looks thoughtfully at Ferrin as she grabs her cup.

"Have you seen any sign of her at all?" she asks. "Aside from the elegantly written notes, I mean."

He shakes his head. "Not a twitch. I'd think the house is empty if it weren't for those notes and the lights I see at night."

Tessa raises an eyebrow. "You walk by at night?"

Ferrin flushes again. "She's all alone in there," he mutters. "I like to do a last check before I go to bed."

Tessa flashes him a smile. "You're a sweet man, Ferrin Jones," she says, and gives his shoulder a friendly pat before she hurries to the counter to serve her customers.

Lou successfully ignores the stranger-with-the-strange-name for almost two months. She drifts through the days much as she's always done, with the highlight of her week the fifteen-minute Sunday afternoon phone call with Ike. Which, she ruefully admits, means she talks to him more now he's in Vancouver than she did when he lived in town.

She hasn't allowed herself to again pretend he's still in

Ledoux, though. She drifted dangerously close to delusional denial, and tempting as it is sometimes to leave sanity behind, she's determined that someday, if there ever is some medical breakthrough that can control or even cure her agoraphobia, she's going to take advantage of it, and step outside her house again.

Feel the breeze on her face and the wind in her hair. Smell fresh-cut grass and rain on the horizon; stand beneath endless blue sky and bask in the sun.

Maybe even speak to somebody other than Ike.

She grimaces at the thought.

Or maybe not.

But that's all in some vaguely hoped for future; in the meantime, she finds herself adjusting to the unseen yet increasingly impossible to ignore presence of the stranger-with-the-strange-name. It's so gradual she doesn't realize how familiar he's become until the day he doesn't show up. She finds herself straining her ears for the clop of his boots on the porch, the creaks and bumps and clicks as he opens and closes the milk box, and even—if she's in the kitchen—the rustle of paper as he pulls out her latest note. She occasionally hears the low rumble of his voice as he sings or talks to himself while working close to the house. On Saturdays, she hears him opening the alcove off the kitchen that Ike built for her grocery deliveries back in the days the grocery store delivered, and listens to the crinkle of plastic and the clanks, clinks and thuds as the stranger-with-the-strange-name places her weekly order inside.

But that's Saturday, and today is Thursday, well past six in the evening, and there's been no clop on the porch. No creak. No clicks. No rustle.

She can't settle.

She wanders from room to room, most of which are packed from floor to ceiling with the clutter left behind by her ancestors, but instead of the usual comfort, she somehow feels smothered by it all.

She goes to bed early with gritted teeth and an

irrational desire to throw something.

The next day she drifts through the house and finds herself listening intently for his arrival. She finally perches precariously on the sitting room's window-seat, trying not to disturb the dusty knick-knacks piled haphazardly on the cushions. She peeks through the equally dusty drapes, wondering if the loser Ike convinced to take the job of being her dogsbody is going to show up or if he quit without bothering to tell Ike...or if Ike just hasn't bothered to tell *her*.

Not that it matters if he *has* quit, she thinks with a sneer. He *is* just a loser, after all, because only someone desperate for money would have taken the job and she seems to remember Ike saying the guy was living out of his car or something.

But he's been kind enough to deal with you, a tiny, disapproving voice inside her replies, even if only from a distance and through written notes. He's done everything she's asked and even writes back to let her know if something wasn't available or why something hasn't yet been done. She should at least know what he looks like...just in case she ever *does* leave the house someday and she sees him in the street.

She settles in to wait, and amuses herself with imagining the stranger, whose name is...ah, hell, she can't remember. All she knows is it's strange, and he probably looks just as strange. A drifter, grizzled and worn, wearing his life on his face. Short and stooped and wiry, with shabby clothes and a rodent-like nervous expression.

She frowns.

Ferret? Is that his name?

She grimaces.

It doesn't matter. It isn't like she's ever going to speak to him. He's not Ike, and *Ike's* the only one she wants around her, not some stranger. For a moment, despair almost overwhelms her and she closes her eyes against it, shrinking into her sweater.

She concentrates on her breathing, careful and conscious and calm, and finally opens her eyes, feeling steadier. She takes a final deep breath and peeks again through the drapes.

She blinks, then blinks again.

The stranger has arrived, and he's nothing like she imagined.

He's big and bulky, tall and broad. Younger, too, than she imagined, looking like he's within five years or so of her own age of thirty, although the stubble on his face might be making him look older. He has crooked, craggy features which are pleasant enough in a bland, boy-next-door kind of way. Some might even consider him handsome, she grudgingly concedes, although not the way Ike is handsome, with his symmetrical, movie-star-perfect features.

The stranger-with-the-strange-name strolls up the walk, his hands shoved deep into the pockets of his jacket. His head is bent, his gaze on his feet, shaggy medium-brown hair flopping over his forehead, which somehow makes him look boyish and vulnerable, and the expression on his face is one of deep sadness.

She jerks away from the window, letting the heavy, dust-covered curtain fall back into place.

It doesn't matter. Her curiosity is satisfied. She has no need to ever see him again.

Except she finds herself at the window again the next day. And the day after that.

Lou peers from behind her kitchen curtains and watches as whatthehellishisname—Ferret? Nobody would actually name their kid *Ferret*, would they?—cuts the lawn. He's frowning and she idly wonders why. After all, the harsh spring has finally softened into summer, and it looks like a beautifully warm day for early June. The sky is a cloudless, endless blue, and the sun looks hot and enticing. She can almost smell the freshly cut grass even through her tightly closed windows and musty curtains.

She wonders if the insects still sound the same, if the birds still sing the same songs, if the sunlight still warms the skin like a lover's hand. She hasn't been out of the house in close to five years, and each day it feels like the memories fade a little more. The thought gives her mixed emotions. She's saddened to be losing her connection with the outside world, but on the other hand it makes it easier to be trapped inside if she can't really remember what it's like to be out there.

She watches as whatthehellishisname finishes cutting the back lawn and pushes the mower towards the front of the house, likely to place it back in its storage space beneath the front porch. She feels a sudden flash of irritation that she can't remember the guy's name, especially since he's been working for her for well over two months and she's been covertly keeping an eye on him for more than two weeks now.

To make sure he's doing the chores she tells him to do in her notes.

He seems to be doing a reasonable enough job, from what she can tell. She supposes that, even though she still resents the fact he isn't Ike, she should at least remember what to call him.

Just in case.

She may need to break down and ask Ike for his name.

She shakes her head as he moves round the corner of the house and she loses sight of him. She wanders to the front foyer because it provides the best view of the front lawn—or at least it would, if she ever bothered to open the curtains, which she'd do, she tells herself virtuously, if she could maneuver past all the crappy knick-knacks that stand in her way. If she could do that, then she'd be able to really look out at her front yard and not just peek out to catch a glimpse of whatthehellishisname...to ensure he's actually doing what he's paid to do.

Of course.

For a moment, she wonders if she'd still be considered a peeping Tom if she's on the inside looking out. She bites back a smile at the thought and surveys the foyer, taking in the heavy oak door that is both barrier and protection, the two long windows on either side shrouded by heavy brocade drapes with small end tables in front of them, loaded with ornaments and other little knick-knacks and those godawful ornate vases she's always hated, but they belonged to her great-grandfather and she can't do anything about them.

She feels a sudden, intense desire to open the door and step outside so she can get away from the weight of other people's lives.

She imagines it now: the brilliant green of new grass, the crystal blue of the sky, the warmth of the day heating her skin, and she's struck with a yearning so fierce, it almost drives her to her knees: a desperate, all-consuming desire to feel the sun on her face and the wind in her hair.

She could go outside after he's gone. Walk through the grass in her bare feet. See if it's really as soft as it is in her memories.

The thought makes her hands shake, and her vision begin to compress into a tight circle.

She clenches her teeth, and growls.

This time, panic meets sudden, white-hot rage.

She's tired, she thinks as she tries to control her shaking hands, so goddamned tired of being afraid—afraid of leaving the security of her home, afraid of facing the so-called friends who had deserted them in their time of need. She's sick and tired of being powerless—*she's goddamned sick of it!*

Her frustrated scream makes her ears ring, and the crash as one of those godawful vases shatters against the door leading to the sitting room shocks her back to an awareness of her surroundings, and she stands, staring stupidly at the shards on the floor. She only vaguely remembers throwing the thing, and now there it is, in pieces on the ground, looking the way she's felt ever since Ike left. Ever since she lost her mother. Ever since she realized the people who supposedly loved them had left them alone while her mother lay dying.

Her hands are still shaking, but with anger now instead of panic. Anger at her uncharacteristic outburst, at her inability to control herself enough to leave the house, at breaking the vase, at having even more mess to clean up.

The doorbell shatters the silence and she lets out a high-pitched screech as she leaps back.

"Hey!" whatthehellishisname shouts, followed by a thunderous pounding on the heavy oak door. "Are you okay in there?"

She's frozen and wide-eyed, like a rabbit gone to ground. Her breath catches in her throat as she clutches her sweater.

He thumps on the door again, even harder this time. "*Are you okay?* Answer me, damn it, or I'll break this bloody door down and come in looking for you!"

She can't make herself move or speak. She doesn't know this person at all, and she has no idea if he'll do as he threatens or not. For a moment she has a vivid image of the door splintering open as she flits away, like some nymph of old trying to outrun a rampaging god. The thought calms her with its ridiculous melodrama, because 'flitting' is virtually impossible in her musty, over-stuffed rooms, and she'll simply look awkward rather than nymph-like, wrapped as she is in her over-sized sweater, not to mention that anyone who sweats like he does is far from god-like.

Whatthehellishisname hammers on the door for a third time, this time managing to shake even that heavy, oaken thing in its moorings, and she decides she can't take the chance he'll really do as he says. That, and the realization that she's actually considering *running away* from someone trying to help her finally stirs her into action.

Before she can think any more about it, she lunges at the door and flings it open.

Ferrin doesn't know what he expected; he only knows this young woman with the sweetly pretty, albeit scowling, heart-shaped face and black hair piled haphazardly on top of her head, trying to make herself disappear inside a voluminous, shapeless, shit-brown sweater while simultaneously leveling him with a death-glare from the most remarkable brown eyes he's ever seen, is definitely not it. He always thought eyes so dark they're almost black were something out of a Louis L'Amour novel and just a myth yet here they are, filled with stark terror while glaring out at him from a defiant face with her chin lifted high.

"It's okay—it's okay!" he says, flinging up his hands in what he hopes is a soothing gesture. She flinches, and he takes several hasty steps back, then flails for balance as he teeters on the edge of the porch.

"Shit!" he yelps as he loses his battle with gravity and tumbles backwards. He desperately twists, trying to break his fall and lands on his side and outstretched hand with a thud and a loud 'oomph' as the wind is knocked out of him.

In the endless suspended moment before the shock wears off, he realizes three things: the porch isn't quite as wide as he'd thought; she really needs to put up some railings; and this is going to hurt like a son-of-a-bitch.

He tries to suck in a breath, and realizes that, on the last point at least, he's so, *so* right.

"Are you okay?" she calls from somewhere above him.

He's too busy strangling on the air he can't quite get into his lungs to let her know he heard her.

"I guess you'll let me know when the pain stops, huh?"

A sense of humor, he thinks as he finally gasps in a short breath. Who knew?

He sucks in another breath and it's already easier. He's assuring himself the pain is beginning to ease to manageable levels when he feels gentle hands on his head and neck, cool fingers brushing the side of his face as Lou says, "Tell me if this hurts."

His eyes fly open as he jerks around. His body regrets the sudden move immediately and he groans through gritted teeth even as he finds himself nose to nose with her, staring directly into those incredible eyes.

They stare at each other in frozen silence.

"Does this mean I'm fired?" Ferrin finally croaks out.

Her lips twitch, but Ferrin can't tell if they're trying to smile or frown.

"No," she says brusquely, "but I'm not offering you extra insurance to cover clumsiness. Do you think you can get up?"

"Give me a minute."

He relaxes against the ground and closes his eyes.

"Do you need a doctor?" she asks with a hint of worry.

He frowns, considering the question as he takes inventory. He hasn't hit his head, as far as he can tell, and that's a blessing. His shoulder, wrist and arm feel like they're on fire, but—he carefully wiggles his fingers, then slowly bends his elbow and raises his arm—everything seems to be working. Half his ass is sore, as is his hip, but everything seems to do as he asks when he does a similar check on his legs. Sitting for the foreseeable future might be an adventure, though.

"No," he finally mutters, "I just need to get my breath back. Nothing's broken, just bruised."

"Well, that's good. Don't think I'm going to pay you while you're laying down on the job, though."

He opens his eyes and blinks at her. She's scowling again, but there's an amused gleam in her eyes. He finds the laughter much better than the fear, even if it is at his expense.

"I'll remember that for next time," he says, his voice a warm rumble.

He gives her a slight smirk, his eyes intent on her face, and she abruptly shifts, sitting up straight and wrapping that truly atrocious sweater more closely around herself. He dimly registers her fingers flexing restlessly against the wool.

"When's the last time you were out of the house?" he asks.

Her scowl deepens, and now her eyes are angry, which has absolutely no effect on their beauty.

"None of your business!" she snaps.

He sits up slowly, and grimaces as his body protests. He's going to be limping for the next few days, and he isn't looking forward to the ribbing he'll get from Tessa and the others.

"You're right," he says. "I'm sorry."

"Is that why you knocked on my door? Just to ask me that?" she snarls. "What? Did somebody dare you?"

His eyes widen at the venom in her voice. He carefully shakes his head, and is relieved there's no pain with the movement.

"No! No." For a moment, he can't remember how he'd gotten into this mess, then memory returns. "I heard a noise, like something breaking, and I thought I heard a scream. I wanted to make sure you were all right."

He watches with interest as the colour deepens in her cheeks as she looks away.

"I...uh...I broke a glass," she mutters. Her fingers tighten and relax, tighten and relax, against the knitted wool of her sweater.

"Oh." He silently debates whether he should say anything else. She's a recluse for a reason, after all, and obviously wants to be left alone. He tells himself she's managed to survive just fine before he arrived, and she'll manage to survive just fine after he leaves. Besides, now that he's seen her, he has absolutely no doubt she'll fire him in a second if he pisses her off. He also has absolutely no doubt that she'll never come out to confront him if he simply kept showing up and doing the yard work after she fired him.

But Tessa was right: Lou is still young, late-twenties, maybe early-thirties, from the look of her; far too young to be locked away from the world, even voluntarily. Besides, as Olivia would attest, he's a nosy bastard, always getting involved in things that have nothing to do with him while adroitly avoiding all those things that do. He winces again, this time from his memories rather than the fall off the porch.

"It sounded much bigger than a glass," he says.

She jerks to her feet.

"Sound echoes in that house. Makes things seem bigger than they are. Do you need help getting up?"

He shakes his head and heaves himself to his feet, wincing as his bruises protest.

"Do you need help cleaning up the 'glass'?" he asks.

She steps back, frantically shaking her head, and now her fingers aren't flexing against her sweater; they're desperately clutching at it.

"Okay," he says slowly. "Are you sure you're all right?"

She nods just as frantically and moves onto the first step leading to the porch. Ferrin thinks she looks for all the world like a skittish cat, back arched, fur fluffed, and ready to bolt for safety at the slightest movement.

"Okay," he says again, "then I guess I'll leave you to...do...whatever it is...you do."

Her frightened look hardens into a haughty glare and she straightens, even though she doesn't loosen her grip on her sweater.

"Do that," she snaps, and moves up another step.

"I'll see you tomorrow," he says.

Her look is skeptical as she moves up to the third step.

"In a manner of speaking," he adds.

"Of course," she says, and now she's sarcastic, coldly cynical, and Ferrin frowns as she steps up on the porch and with one final, unfathomable, dark-eyed glare, turns and hurries towards her sanctuary.

"Good night!" he calls rather plaintively as she steps across the threshold. She pauses and looks over her shoulder. Her eyes narrow into suspicious slits, but she says, "Good night," politely enough and closes the door.

Ferrin stands and stares at that blank panel of oak. He wonders if she's watching him from one of the windows that flank it, safely hidden behind the heavy curtains. He wonders if she's hoping he'll leave.

He rather hopes she's wondering if he'll stay.

He blinks at the thought, and hears Olivia's voice mocking him and telling him again that all a person needs is a sob story and he's putty in their hands. He grimaces at the memory then turns and gingerly limps down the walk to the front gate.

Lou watches him through the living room window until he's latched the gate behind him. She eases the heavy, dusty curtain back into place and takes a deep, shaky breath as she turns away.

She hadn't stopped to think when he disappeared off the porch; she simply rushed to see if he was all right. The porch isn't very high but it can still be a hard landing and there isn't much time to break a fall. She'd been too panicked at the thought he might have broken a bone to panic about being outside for the first time in years.

She quickly turns her thoughts to the man himself, worried that if she pays too much attention to the fact that she was outside, she'll end up giving herself a delayed panic attack...although she's not sure if thinking about whatthehellishisname is going to be much better.

He's even bigger up close than he looks from a

distance. He towers over her and she swears he's twice as broad as any other man she's ever known...of course, she's only really ever known Ike and Willis-that-bastard, and a guy or two during her brief time at university.

Still, she's definitely never heard anything like his voice before: low and husky, distinctive, oddly gentle, and almost seductive. Of course, he did have the wind knocked out of him, which might have changed the usual timbre of his voice, but she somehow suspects he's almost always that soft-spoken, and that he can—if the urge moves him—use that voice to great effect to get what he wants.

She shivers at the thought then looks with surprise at her hands. They're trembling, only this time they aren't shaking from panic or anger but from a strange, tingling, melting sensation curling in her stomach.

She doesn't know what this feeling is but she *does* know it feels like trouble and she doesn't like it.

She doesn't like it one bit.

Lou drifts towards the living room window the following afternoon at her usual time, although if there had been anyone around who cared enough to ask, she would have denied there *was* a 'usual time'. As she perches on the cluttered window seat, safely hidden behind the still-dusty heavy curtains, she tells herself she only wants to make sure whatthehellishisname didn't hurt himself too badly after his fall from the porch. Hell, she just wants to make sure he'll arrive! The hedges still need to be trimmed, after all, and it's almost time for her weekly grocery order.

The doorbell rings and she shrieks, jumping violently. She tumbles ignominiously from the window seat, landing on the floor with a painful thump with half the knick-knacks falling with her.

The bell peals again. She closes her gaping mouth,

pulls herself off the floor and tiptoes to the door. Her heart is pounding as she peers through one of the side windows, and it speeds up even more when she sees whatthehellishisname's broad shoulders as he stands with his back to the door with his hands shoved in the pockets of his jeans. She very deliberately tells herself she's *not* looking at the way his jeans pull tight across his ass.

A wave of relief washes over her that it's just him before she grimaces and rolls her eyes.

Who else could it possibly be, she chides. It's not like Ike's in town and no one else has darkened her door since before the last year of her mother's life.

She creeps to the door, leans her forehead against it, and closes her eyes. She bites her lip as whatthehellishisname rings the bell for a third time, then knocks.

"I know you're in there!" he bellows cheerfully, and her stomach makes sickening swoops and swirls at the sound of that distinctive voice, although she'd be hard-pressed to explain what is so fascina...*unique* about it.

"Don't make me break in to make sure you're still alive!" he calls now, even more disgustingly cheerful. "I'll do it, too; don't think I wo—oh. Hello."

His wide-eyed smile doesn't falter beneath her one-eyed glare as she peers through the sliver of an opening she's allowed herself. That makes her angrier even as heat slowly curls in her stomach at the sight of his lop-sided and, even she has to admit, charming grin.

"Why are you here?" she hisses.

"I work here, remember?"

She intensifies her glare but he only laughs as he takes a careful step back and spreads his arms with a flourish. "Just wanted to show you there's no harm done from the fall," he says as he slowly turns around to show her every angle. "I'm not even limping!"

"I wasn't worried."

His face falls. "I thought we bonded yesterday!"

Her eyes widen then narrow. "You're joking."

He grins again, and that, paired with a rueful shrug, makes the curl of heat in Lou's stomach burst into furious open flame. She slams the door shut and presses her back against it like she's barricading herself against rampaging barbarian hordes. She presses her hand against her stomach, willing it to calm the fuck down, and even more furiously willing the annoying man on her front porch, with his broad shoulders and crooked grin and strange jokes, to *just go away*.

She closes her eyes and bites her lip as grief and loneliness wash over her. She misses Ike and the way things used to be. It's an almost physical ache, and she slowly slides down the door and sits with her face pressed against her knees. She wants Ike. She *doesn't* want this *stranger* ringing her doorbell or knocking on her door or buying her groceries or cutting her lawn or *talking to her*, for fuck's sake!

She doesn't want her body to be feeling these weird things, making her dizzy and off-kilter and feeling like the ground in front of her is going to fall away at any moment. She doesn't want this sudden certainty that things are going to change even more, or again, or whatever, whether she likes it or not. She wants things to go back to the way things used to be.

She wants Ike to come back.

"I'll be there in August," Ike sighs, and Lou winces at the impatient note in his voice. "That's only six weeks. What? You can't wait that long?"

"Are you coming back to stay?"

"I'm there for a week. That should be more than enough time to finish all the paperwork I have for you. I can help clean the place up, too, if Ferrin isn't doing his job. If you're really unhappy with him, I'll fire him and find somebody else while I'm there." He sighs again, a long-suffering sound. "Somewhere. Somehow."

Lou bites her lip, unhappy that she's obviously annoyed him, but she can't stop herself from muttering, "I want *you*, and the way things used to be."

She wonders if he understands she means when they were lovers.

"Things change, Lou," he says, impatient even if he's not unkind. "I'm not coming back to Ledoux to take care of you for the rest of your life. My life's in Vancouver now, with Irish. Now, if you want to relocate..."

Lou cracks out a bitter laugh. "Only if you can move my entire house, while I'm in it." *Like a snail*, she thinks, and suddenly wants to cry.

"Then you have to learn to adapt," Ike snaps. He pauses before continuing more gently. "Look, if Ferrin's ignoring your notes, I'll fire him immediately and find somebody else, probably from Regina. Okay? But he's only going to be in Ledoux until August anyway, or so he keeps telling me, so I think you can endure him for another six weeks. It's not like you're actually talking to him!"

"It's nine weeks, actually," she mutters and half-guiltily, half-defiantly ignores his last comment.

"Whatever. Do you want me to fire him right now?"

She pauses, then, "No." She has no one else.

"Good girl. Now, there are some new investments—"

She rolls her eyes even though he can't see her. "Good Lord, don't bore me with the details! Do what you think best."

"You sure?"

"Ike," she says drily, "have I ever wanted to know the details?"

He chuckles, and spends the next few minutes telling her anyway before they say good-bye. Lou sits for a few moments, holding the phone against her heart. She scrunches her eyes closed, like a child, and pretends he's standing in front of her, close enough to touch.

But, she reminds herself as she opens her eyes, imagining Ike is physically here is a dangerous pastime. It's too easy—too seductive—to slip into some kind of fantasy world and stay there when she doesn't have anything or anyone to draw her back to reality. If she's not careful, if she allows herself to pretend too much, there will be a day in the not-too-distant future when she'll slip away and never be able to find her way back.

She sighs, and slowly hangs up the phone.

Ike is over eighteen hundred kilometres away now, and married to Irish, which means he may as well be on the moon.

Her shoulders slump.

He isn't coming back, and life will never go back to the way it used to be. She needs to accept that and move on.

Well.

To a certain definition of 'move on'. After all, she hadn't left her house in years until yesterday, when whatthehellishisname—no, Ike called him Ferrin—fell off the porch.

Well, she thinks with what she assures herself is satisfaction, at least she knows this Ferrin sure as hell won't be ringing her doorbell tomorrow.

Despite her best intentions, the next day Lou finds herself, mug of tea in hand, drifting towards the living room window around the usual time. She's barely precariously perched on the window seat when the doorbell rings and she starts, spilling tea all over herself.

She's still using the edge of her sweater to sop up the liquid from her t-shirt as she flings open the door and glowers at the bane of her existence. He just stands there, big and broad and male, smirking that shit-eating, crooked smirk she's beginning to detest.

"You're early," she snaps and immediately realizes she's made a tactical error.

His smirk turns into a wide grin, eyes sparkling. "You were waiting for me? I'm flattered!"

"N-no," she stammers, wrapping her now-damp sweater closed, both for comfort and to hide her stained shirt. She lifts her chin and says, "You work for me, and you're supposed to be here at six. I'm not paying you overtime, you know."

"I do know," he says cheerfully. "I was worried I was going to be late, so I came in through the back."

"The back?" she repeats blankly, thinking of the dense, overgrown hedge that surrounds three-quarters of the property and wonders how this beefy guy managed to push his way through it.

He nods eagerly, his still-sparkling eyes—blue? grey? it's difficult to tell—are wide and his face is far too deliberately innocent. His whole demeanor is reminiscent of an overgrown, gangly puppy, eager to please. "There's a hole in the hedge, so I use it as a shortcut from Tessa's."

She's shocked at the intensity of the disappointment that floods through her at the sound of another woman's name.

"Tessa's," she says, her voice flat.

He nods again, his eyes shrewd, and now he isn't an over-eager puppy eager to please but rather a skilled herding dog, anticipating which way the sheep are going to move next.

"Well, I suppose I should say The Row, really." At Lou's confused look, he adds, "She owns the coffee shop across the street behind your house."

"Oh," she says, and goes limp with relief, imagining a plump, middle-aged woman handing out coffee and muffins with a matronly air.

She abruptly realizes Ferrin is watching her far too closely.

"You do know there's a coffee shop across the street

from your house, right?" he says slowly.

"I do now," she mutters.

The ensuing silence is almost excruciating in its awkwardness.

"Well," she finally says, her tone brisk, "I've left your instructions in the usual place."

Ferrin nods, and now his smile is deliberately charming. "Or you could just tell me. Since we're here and talking and all."

"Do your job," she growls, and closes the door.

She's half-expecting the doorbell the next day. She's still startled, but she doesn't fall or spill anything, and she feels that's a small victory of some sort or another, although over who or what is still a little vague. When she opens the door, her sense of triumph makes her 'welcoming' scowl even more fierce.

It doesn't faze him.

"Here," he says, and holds out a piece of paper, folded in half.

She stares at it like it's a poisonous snake.

"It won't bite," he says, and there's a gentleness in his low, husky voice that makes her stomach swoop and sweat prickle the backs of her knees, and it's exciting and terrifying and annoying all at once, and her own visceral reactions only manage to annoy her even more.

"I know that," she snaps, but keeps one hand on the door and the other firmly clutching her sweater.

"It's a town map," he explains in helpful tones. "I found one from five years ago, then I asked Willis—"

Her lip automatically curls up at his name. "That bastard," she growls.

Ferrin pauses and gives her a curious look, then continues. "Well, I asked him to tell me the major changes to the town since then, and I noted them on here." He waves the paper enticingly. "I thought you might like to see what's changed since you've been inside."

"I don't care. That's why I'm inside."

Ferrin shrugs, and she's suddenly very conscious of the breadth of his shoulders and how he towers over her. It makes her feel like he's as sturdy as the oak of her front door, that nothing will get through him once he's planted himself in the way...or be able to withstand him, once he starts moving. It gives her a surprising sense of security mixed with a sudden realization of her own vulnerability, and she knows—knows beyond all doubt—that her life is about to change, whether she's ready for it or not.

"Not even a *little* curious about what else is across the street from you?" he coaxes, startling her out of her thoughts. His voice is a husky rumble, slow, warm and seductive, and she realizes she's leaning towards him, yearning for the next word. The thought unnerves her, and she snatches the paper from his hand and leans back, hoping he thinks the paper had been her goal all along.

"Fine," she says sharply, looking anywhere but directly at his face, "now get to work."

His shit-eating grin is the last thing she sees as she slams the door.

♠♥♣♦

Ferrin sits with a cold beer in his hand in the back yard of the rectory that evening and listens to the sounds of the neighbourhood. As he thinks about Lou, a smirk spreads across his face and he ruefully admits he has far more of the Macon-Jones' Machiavellian tendencies than he realized...at least when it comes to getting Lou to talk to him.

He's conflicted although he can't say he feels guilty. He wonders if this is how Abram feels when he's brokering a new deal: focused on the goal and doing whatever is necessary to get there.

Ferrin sips his beer with a thoughtful air.

Not that he's planning something nefarious or anything. He just wants to understand why such a young woman would decide to be a recluse...or if she had any real choice about it at all. There had been real fear in her eyes the day he fell off the porch and that fear is still there every time she opens the door. He doesn't understand it. He sure as hell doesn't like it, but he'll never be able to help her if he can't get her to talk to him.

He takes another sip of his beer, and lets the now-familiar sounds of the neighbourhood sink into him: kids laughing, dogs barking, an occasional car, and somebody mowing the lawn. It's peaceful, and he's going to miss this place. He's still living in the rectory both because rental spaces are at a premium and also because he'll be leaving in a couple of months. He did have to insist on paying an appropriate rent, though, and let it be known he's willing to share when necessary.

So far, it hasn't been an issue. Willis wasn't kidding when he said the priest was only in town for weddings and funerals, and no other orphans of the storm—or ditch, in his case—have washed up in town, either.

Ferrin takes another sip of beer as his thoughts once again return to the town hermit.

He's leaving in August, so that doesn't give him much time to find out what's going on with Lou and see if there's anything he can do to help her. The thought of leaving Ike solely responsible for her well-being makes his lip curl in much the same way Lou's had when he mentioned Willis. The fact Ike had been taking care of her for years before Ferrin arrived doesn't change his mind: there's something about that ferret-faced little weasel he just doesn't trust. So if he's going to help Lou, he needs to get her to trust him enough to tell him what she wants...besides to be left alone. Maybe a pet, or maybe she has an old friend in town she'd like to reach out to but doesn't know how. If she's happy all alone and locked inside her house then Ferrin will accept that, but he wants *her* to tell him and not that ferret-faced little weasel.

Well, Ferrin thinks with a smirk, if there's one thing the Macon-Joneses have in abundance, it's persuasive charm. He preens a little, because he, Benjamin Ferrin Macon-Jones, has often been called the most charming of them all. He's certainly managed to sweet-talk Carson, Dyson, and Jack—and himself, because he's usually right next to them, let's be honest—out of trouble often enough.

His smirk widens.

Lou doesn't stand a chance. He'll get her to talk to him and then he'll determine how best to help her. If she's a recluse by choice, well, he'll make sure she's looked after without having to depend solely on Ike, and he can leave her to moulder away in peace with a clear conscience, but if she isn't...

He finishes his beer with a satisfied sigh, and looks at the empty bottle in his hand.

Easy pickings, he thinks smugly. She'll let him in tomorrow for sure.

"Do you drink beer?" Ferrin asks.

He decided Lou's scowl wasn't quite as strong today when she opened the door, but now it deepens, her forehead wrinkling with confusion. It makes her look even younger and almost unbearably vulnerable, and all of his protective instincts roil inside him at once. He's almost overwhelmed with sympathy and the desire to help this prickly woman trying to level him with a death-glare while simultaneously shrinking away inside that ever-present, over-sized, shit-brown sweater she clings to like it's the only thing keeping her afloat in a stormy ocean. Everything about her reminds him of a terrified kitten hissing with false bravado at anything that moves.

"*Beer?*" she asks.

85

He smirks. "You know what beer is, right?"

"Yes!"

"So? Do you drink it?"

"I—yes. But I don't drink alone."

"Ah—which means you seldom drink at all. Good to know you're not in a drunken stupor in there."

"It wouldn't be your business if I were."

"Maybe not."

"There's no 'maybe' about it!"

"Well, anyway, here," he says, his voice a bright as the sun in the sky. He picks up the six-pack of beer he placed at his feet before he rang the bell, and shoves it into her hands. "For when you have company."

He's rewarded with her jaw dropping, and he winks as he turns. He begins to whistle as he bounds down the porch steps and around the house to get the note outlining his chores for the day.

♠♥♣♦

The door flies open as Ferrin jogs up the porch steps the following evening. He comes to a stop and looks inquisitively at a glowering Lou, standing with her sweater snugged around her, arms hugging her waist. One foot is tapping angrily, while the wool of her sweater ripples from the not-quite-rhythmic clenching and unclenching of her fingers.

He stands in expectant silence, before asking, "What?" in his best 'there's nothing to see here, officer' voice.

"What. Do you. *Want?*"

"What makes you think I want something?"

"You've come to my door every damn day this week!"

"Well, then, you should be used to it by now. Look, you even came to meet me today!"

He thinks he actually hears her teeth grinding and winces in sympathy.

"Careful doing that," he says, as helpful as always, "you

could break a tooth that way."

"Sweet Jesus," she screeches, "answer my fucking question!"

His eyes widen and his smirk morphs into a sincere grin. He doesn't know if pushing her this hard is a good thing or not, but it's definitely entertaining.

"I want to make sure you're okay," he says.

"I leave you a note every damn day!"

"That's not the same as actually seeing you. What if you're sick?"

"Then I wouldn't leave you a note, would I?"

Ferrin cocks his head and considers her thoughtfully. He sees now she's trembling, and she radiates anger and fear in almost equal measure, with an underlying expression in her eyes he can't quite define. His grin fades away. He wants to help her, not make things worse.

She's right. It's time to stop playing games.

"Are you happy?" he asks, suddenly serious. "Are you happy being all alone behind that door?"

She shifts her weight from one foot to another, those unusual, darkly beautiful eyes darting around, looking everywhere but at him as she says, "Are *you*? Out here in the world?"

"No."

That snaps her gaze back to his, and they stare at each other in uncomfortable, charged silence until Lou shifts her weight from one foot to another, adjusts her sweater, and says, "So, what? You want to see if being a recluse is a good life choice for you?"

"No. And you haven't answered my question."

"I'm happy enough."

He chuckles, but there's no real humor in it. "What does that mean?"

"Exactly what I said."

Ferrin sighs, and his shoulders slump, sadness flitting across his face.

He says, "I just want you to know you're more than a

note in the milk box. That there are people out here who care about what happens to you in there."

She fidgets, her cheeks flushed.

"You don't know me," she mutters.

"Doesn't mean I don't care. As one human being for another."

Silence descends again while Lou continues to avoid his gaze.

Finally, Ferrin sighs, and says, "I'm sorry. I'm also sorry for upsetting you; that wasn't my intent. I won't try to see you again, unless I absolutely have to."

Lou bites her lip, shifts her weight again, and nervously adjusts her sweater.

"Good," she mutters, but Ferrin thinks she sounds doubtful, or perhaps it's simply wishful thinking on his part.

The silence lengthens, deepens, and now it's his turn to fidget uncomfortably. "Listen, I'm...going to get to work, just...please don't hesitate to talk to me if you need to."

She takes a step back.

"I won't need to," she says, and quietly closes the door.

For the next week and a half, Ferrin does not once ring her doorbell, and Lou reluctantly admits he's a man of his word.

It's...*annoying*. And it's annoying that it's annoying.

She grinds her teeth as she peeks around the curtain in the kitchen window and watches him trim the hedges on the east side of the property. It's brutally hot, especially for mid-June. He's stripped off his t-shirt and is now wearing only some knee-length disreputable khaki shorts that have seen better days and a pair of sneakers without socks.

She assesses him critically.

He looks ridiculous. And his feet probably stink to

high heaven.

Besides, he's tall and broad, and bulky with it, not sleek and slender like Ike. While Ferrin isn't fat, he isn't exactly Chippendale's material, either. She feels a twinge of sadness at the memory of Ike's well-defined abs that he's always been so proud of, and the smooth feel of his skin beneath her fingers. She remembers how desperately she'd wanted to please him, to feel connected to him, something she obviously and miserably failed to do since he so quickly drifted away from her.

She watches Ferrin lower the hedge clipper to the ground and wipe sweat from his face, muscles moving easily beneath the smooth skin of his back. Disgusting, and far too soft, she thinks, as he loads the branches into the wheelbarrow and pushes it to the northeast corner of her yard where he throws the debris onto the compost pile. While his torso is flat enough, there isn't a finely sculptured ab in sight.

Disgusting, she thinks again as he returns to where he left off. Too big, too bulky, too broad, too *everything*, and he probably stinks the way the boys used to stink during gym class. Except Ike, of course, she adds with a flash of guilty loyalty.

She watches as Ferrin refills the wheelbarrow, pushes it to the compost pile and empties it again, repeating his journey back and forth until all of the branches and leaves he's cut so far have been moved. He stretches, hands in the small of his back as he arches and turns from one side to another before bending to pick up the hedge trimmers from the ground. Lou's eyebrows shoot up as the material of his khaki shorts pulls tight across his ass, and she reluctantly admits that even she can't find fault with what she sees. She feels a sudden rush of heat that has nothing to do with the weather outside. She stifles a sudden urge to whimper quietly even as a vaguely creepy, vaguely guilty feeling crawls over her because she's observing him so intently without his knowledge.

She shakes her head, and tries to convince herself she's only watching him like this because...well, he *does* work for her, and she should make sure he does a good job. It's not like she has anyone else to supervise him.

Besides, she doesn't own a television or a computer, and the radio doesn't work, so it's not like there's a whole lot of other things for her to do.

Her arguments don't convince even her, and her brief flash of guilt doesn't stop her from continuing to watch as he restarts the hedge trimmer and gets back to work.

His skin is already darkly tanned as the blazing afternoon sun beats down on his mussed-up head. He looks slick with sweat...disgustingly so, she quickly clarifies...but, then again, it *is* brutally hot...and he really *is* working very hard...and she *still* has the beer he brought...

She turns and looks at the untouched six-pack. It'd be a shame if that went to waste, she thinks, and it will, because Ike doesn't drink beer, and if she doesn't want to have to explain where it came from when he's back in August, she'll have to hide it, or drink it alone, or pour it down the sink, or...

She hesitates, her hands beginning to tremble.

Is she really thinking of asking Ferrin to come inside for a beer?

Seriously?

She feels the yawning blackness of panic opening beneath her feet. She plops onto a chair, bending over until her forehead touches her knees. She breathes deeply, trying to relax, to let the panic wash over her without letting it wash her away.

For God's sake, she thinks, it's only a beer! Anger presses up against the panic until both emotions finally, slowly ease back to manageable levels.

She straightens, breathing deeply and deliberately.

It's only a beer, and he might not accept anyway. Probably won't, not after the way she treated him.

She moves on shaky legs to put four beer in the freezer

and the other two in the fridge.

She peeks out the window and sees Ferrin's once again moving loads of branches to the compost pile. She takes a final deep breath and opens the window.

Well.

Tries to.

It doesn't budge, and she hesitates, thinking it's obviously a sign that this is a very bad idea. She shakes her head. Sign or not, before Ike dropped all of his bombshells on her, she'd been determined to do something this year to change her life. If inviting a total stranger in to share the beer he brought of his own volition didn't qualify as a change, then nothing would.

She stomps to the door and yanks it open before she can change her mind.

"Hey! You!"

Ferrin jerks around, a shocked and worried frown on what Lou grudgingly admits is a rather handsome face, if a person liked that kind of thing. His shaggy brown hair is stuck to his forehead and sticking up in tufts in the back, which looks ridiculous but also somehow endearing. His eyes widen when he sees her standing in the doorway, and as he stares, she fights another sudden urge to whimper even as she fervently wishes she could turn back the clock by thirty seconds, so she could change her mind about this.

She hesitates, fidgeting nervously, but it's too late now, and she'll look and feel even more ridiculous than she does already if she bolts back into the house without saying *anything*.

"I put some of that beer in the fridge," she says. Grudgingly. "For when you're done."

His mouth slowly sags open and his expression of stunned disbelief almost makes her laugh. He quickly recovers, his lips curving into a lopsided smile. But not a gloating one, she's glad to see. If he starts to gloat—

"Sounds great," he replies, his voice carefully neutral,

"and the name's Ferrin."

"I know," she says, and closes the door with a snap.

She staggers back to the chair and collapses. She puts a trembling hand up to her face.

She hates this shit, she thinks, and why is she doing this anyway?

She doesn't know. What she *does* know is this will never happen again.

♠♥♣♦

She isn't even surprised when the doorbell rings the next day. Startled, yes, but not surprised.

She stomps to the door and opens it with a scowl that doesn't soften at the now almost-familiar sight of Ferrin's lopsided grin. She pulls her sweater more securely around herself, her fingers working against the wool, and his face slowly falls with disappointment.

"It wasn't exactly successful yesterday," she growls. "It's not like we talked!"

"Talking isn't always necessary. Sometimes it's nice to sit and drink cold beer and..." he trails off, and shrugs.

"And just sit?" Lou scoffs. "Look, I know you're only doing this because of some sick bet or something."

Ferrin's eyes widen, and in the back of her mind, she decides they're more blue than grey.

"There's no bet," he says.

"Yeah. Sure. There's always a bet. Or somebody wants something. It's the only time anyone in this town comes to my door."

He frowns. "But...you don't *want* anyone coming to your door."

She sniffs. "That's not the point." She knows she's being illogical, but she's in the throes of a different kind of panic and is beyond caring.

"Yeah, I think that *is* the point, and besides...I mean, Lou, those signs on your front gate are pretty major clues that you want everyone to stay away from you."

"Signs?"

Ferrin's frown deepens. "Okay, you do know there are these, like, giant signs all around your property saying things like 'trespassers will be shot and buried in the garden', and 'don't think I won't do it', right?"

Her eyes widen. "What? No!"

He holds his puzzled frown for another few seconds before his crooked grin breaks through. "Okay, I made that part up, but everyone thinks that's exactly what will happen to anyone foolish enough to cross onto your property without your permission."

She shifts uncomfortably, her gaze skittering away from his.

"That's good," she mutters.

"Is it?" he asks curiously.

Her eyes narrow as she looks back at him.

"Don't," she snaps.

"Don't what?"

"Don't try to save me or change me or whatever the hell it is you think you're going to manage to do for me."

He blinks, taken aback. "I'm not trying to do anything!"

"Yeah? Well, you seem awfully anxious to get to know me."

Ferrin's expression turns serious. "You're lonely. I understand that."

Lou snorts. "Yeah, right. You understand that."

Ferrin raises an eyebrow but only says, "Yes. I do. If sitting with you and having a beer or three in silence helps alleviate that loneliness for you, too, then that's not such a high price to pay, is it?"

Her eyes narrow. "It depends on who's paying, doesn't it?"

Ferrin shrugs. "We can talk about it later," he says with a charming smile, "over an ice cold beer."

She actually growls, but says "If you don't get that last

section of hedge done, you won't deserve any beer."

"Of course," he agrees solemnly, then grins and bounds off the porch and around the house, stripping off his t-shirt as he goes.

Lou leans out the door to watch him before she catches herself. She steps back and thinks she hears him laugh just before she closes the door with a decided slam.

She'll be damned if she'll give him the satisfaction of talking about loneliness and prices, she decides as she stalks into the living room and throws herself on to the couch with a huff. She won't talk to him at all.

That'll show him.

♠♥♣♦

They sit in silence, although it seems likes she's the only one who's uncomfortable with it.

Ferrin is sprawled bonelessly on the couch across from hers, that couch that always used to be filled with visitors before her mother got sick. Sweat is still beading his forehead and dampening his grey t-shirt. She's doing her best to ignore both him and the contours of his broad chest that the clinging t-shirt reveals but is failing miserably. She ruefully admits she finally understands the appeal of wet t-shirt contests as she sneaks another glance. She's feeling guiltily perverted when he speaks, startling her.

"Do you play cards?"

She blinks. "Cards?"

"Yeah, you know: crib, rummy, poker? Euchre, baccarat, whist? Bridge, hearts, spades?"

"I know what you're talking about! I just don't know why you're asking!"

"I'm just wondering if you want to play."

She stares unblinkingly at him, searching his quirkily, crookedly handsome face that still isn't Ike's, but doesn't seem quite as strange as it had several weeks ago.

"Why?" she demands.

"Why what?"

"Why are you trying to spend time with me? I don't have access to most of my money, you know. Ike takes care of all of that and I haven't been to a bank in years. I'm not even sure if I have a bank card anymore that works! Besides, it's all wrapped up in stocks or bonds or something."

For the first time, Ferrin looks angry.

"I don't want your money!"

"Everybody wants my money," she says drily. "It's the only reason anybody ever tries to talk to me."

Ferrin raises an eyebrow. "Oh?" he says silkily. "Even Ike?"

"Ike's my friend. I trust him and you don't get to question that!"

Ferrin's eyebrow inches higher but he stays silent, his jaw set in mulish anger.

She scowls, and they drink in silence for several minutes until Ferrin drains his beer and very carefully sets the empty bottle down on the coffee table.

"That tastes really good after a day working in this heat," he says, his voice neutral, and Lou realizes he's offering an olive branch.

She hesitates, then mutters, "Where else do you work?"

"I'm a general labourer with Juan Martinez' construction company."

She frowns. "Juan Martinez?"

"Yeah." He takes in her confused expression. "Maybe he came to town after you, uh, retired from public view."

"Retired from—what is this, the nineteenth century?"

"You tell me."

She glares.

His lips twitch but he doesn't smile and there's still a glimmer of anger in his eyes.

"Okay," he says, "how about since you locked yourself up in this house and threw away the key? Or since you decided to run *to* your home instead of *away* from it? How would you like me to describe it?"

Lou scowls and shrugs. "I guess retiring from public view is as good a way as any," she concedes grudgingly, "and yes."

"Yes, what?"

"Yes, I do play cards, although I haven't for a long time." She stares at her beer bottle as she picks at the label. "I used to play with my mother, before she got too sick."

"Oh."

They sit in somber silence, then Lou drains her beer and says, "Crib okay?"

"Perfect."

♠♥♣♦

Lou walks Ferrin to the door after they finish what has, over the last week, turned into their daily crib game. She grips the thick, woolly strands of her sweater and says, "Listen. Ferrin..."

"Yeah?" he says, his gaze on his feet as he pulls on his sneakers.

She hesitates, then says, "I assume you talk to Ike fairly regularly."

He shrugs. "Not really; a couple times since he left. I think he's depending on you to tell him if I'm not doing my job."

She can't hide her relief and he frowns.

"Why?" he asks.

She takes a deep breath, then says in a rush, "I don't want him to know you're coming into the house. I don't want you to tell him you've been talking to me, or even that you've seen me. Okay?"

Ferrin raises an eyebrow. "Why?" he asks again.

She scowls down at her feet as she considers the question.

"I can't really explain it," she says slowly. "I just—I'm not comfortable."

"We're not doing anything bad," he says, puzzled, "or anything we wouldn't do in public, or in front of an audience." He tilts his head, sympathy in his eyes. "He's not going to be jealous, you know."

The heat rushes into her cheeks.

"I know," she snaps. "I don't know why you would even think—that has nothing—it's not about that! Just...humor me, okay?"

He frowns, eyes narrowed as he considers her. "Okay," he finally says.

She relaxes. "Thanks," she mutters.

She waits until Ferrin bounds down the porch steps before she closes the door and wanders into the living room. As she picks up the dirty cups—they'd decided on coffee tonight rather than beer—and carries them into the kitchen, she wonders why she's so reluctant to have Ike know about her card games with Ferrin. It's not like they talk much; they just play cards, drink beer or coffee, and then he leaves.

Maybe it's because she doesn't want Ike to worry about her. He's been her protector for so long and she knows he won't be pleased to learn she's allowed a homeless drifter who is most likely just trying to take advantage of her into her house. And for the first time in years, Ike isn't around to be her first line of defense.

Lou can't really say for sure that Ferrin *isn't* trying to take advantage of her, but for some reason, she doesn't want to have to defend herself or Ferrin from Ike's suspicions or even argue with him about it.

She frowns as she finishes washing the last of the dishes and sets them to dry.

She realizes she doesn't want Ike to take away the *possibility* that something might have changed, the *possibility* that Ferrin might actually want to spend time with her and not simply want to get to her money. She can't see any harm in letting Ferrin in to play cards and drink beer or coffee. It doesn't mean she trusts the man, but she has to admit, he's good to look at it. Of course, it's been so long since she's seen anyone other than Ike that Ferrin could be a hundred years old and she'd probably *still* find him attractive.

She snickers a little then grimaces and shakes her head. There's a little too much truth in that thought.

Still, it's not like she has a lot of cash in the house. She hasn't needed much since Ike completely took over her finances a year or two before her mother died. Anything else that might be of value is far too large to easily get out of the house, and even she doesn't know where any jewelry might be, although she doubts any of it is real. She visualizes the many rooms in the mansion, and the tightly packed boxes and trunks piled high in all of them.

Well, she thinks with a rueful grimace, if he can find anything in those rooms, of value or otherwise, he *deserves* to keep it, and it might get some of that shit cleaned out.

Anyway, Ferrin's only going to be in Ledoux until August. He'll drift away when Ike comes back.

She shivers as she wanders back to the living room and curls up on the couch, snuggling into her sweater. She leans her head back and closes her eyes, letting the comforting silence of the house settle over her.

Yes, better to keep Ferrin's visits a secret. There's no need to worry Ike with something that will be over soon enough.

As Lou shuffles the cards, Ferrin takes a good look around the living room.

It's a room that seems suspended in time and not just because of the thick layer of undisturbed dust he can see on the curtains, or the slightly thinner layer of dust coating the ornaments, furniture, boxes and bags that are crammed into every spare inch of space.

No, it's more the antique furniture that looks well used, and the curtains are a heavy brocade that block out the sunlight and deaden any sound that might come in from outside. The curtains match the furniture, and it's a bit of an explosion of patterns that could have been painful if the room were smaller or less cluttered.

Even with all the clutter, the room still feels comfortably spacious, which isn't a surprise. The house is a true mansion, after all, with soaring ceilings to prove it. He idly wonders just how rich the Upjohn family is, or was, and why they stayed in a backwater town like this once they began to sell off their land—although calling this dot on the map a backwater is giving it far too much credit. Of course, he supposes being a big fish in a little pond has its perks.

"Are you going to play or judge my housekeeping skills?" Lou snaps.

Ferrin starts and meets her cynical gaze.

"Sorry," he says, picking up the cards Lou had finished dealing while he was distracted. "I was admiring the room."

"Really."

He raises an eyebrow at her drily skeptical tones.

"Really," he says, tossing two cards into the crib, then cutting the deck. "You have a beautiful home and beautiful furniture. Is it really antique?"

"I suppose," she says, turning over the card and placing it on top of the deck. "It's all hand-made—does that count as an antique?"

"Really?" Ferrin says, looking at the furniture again with interest.

"My great-great-grandfather was a carpenter." Lou glances around the room. "He built the whole place."

"Wow!"

"The fact there weren't any trees around when he showed up makes it even more impressive, huh?"

He nods.

They play the hand and as he shuffles the cards he says, "So, how many rooms are there in this place?"

"Why?"

He stops and blinks. "Why what?"

"Why do you want to know?"

He sighs. "I'm making conversation, Lou. You know what that is, right? Chit chat about your day; share past experiences; crack a few jokes; have a few laughs—remember?"

Her scowl deepens as he speaks.

"Fine," she snaps. "There are twelve rooms in total, including six bedrooms upstairs, plus the attic and basement, both of which are large storage rooms rather than living space. Happy now?"

"Ecstatic."

He deals the cards and prays for patience. He ruefully acknowledges that maybe Olivia was right; maybe he really *is* too nice for his own good. He also makes a mental note to tell Ike he's a saint. He may not trust or like the man but he has to give the ferret-faced little weasel credit where credit is due.

But, he reminds himself as he takes in her bad-tempered pout, Lou isn't Olivia, and there's really no point in trying to charm her into telling him what's wrong.

"Why are you so bitchy today?" he says as he slaps the deck down on the table.

"*What?*"

He shrugs. "More than usual, I mean. Why are you so pissed off? I know it can't be because you're tired of my wit, charm, and handsome face."

She rolls her eyes.

"You'd be surprised," she mutters.

"Lou."

She glares, those eyes that never cease to amaze him even darker than usual, then her expression changes, softens, her mouth turns down at the corners, and he feels a stab of regret as she drops her gaze to her cards, blinking rapidly.

"Ike called today," she mutters.

"You have a phone?" he blurts, then winces. "Sorry," he mutters as she glares. A sudden thought makes him freeze. "Is he okay?"

"Oh, he's just lovely. He adores Vancouver, and is having the time of his life. He and Irish are blissfully happy, and he can't wait to give me all the news in person when he's back next month."

Ferrin frowns. "You're...sorry he's happy?"

"Yes! I mean...no." She flicks a quick glance at him. "It's complicated," she mutters.

"Not that complicated: you're in love with him."

"It's none of your damn business!"

Ferrin lifts his hands in mock surrender. "I'm not saying it's a bad thing!"

"Yeah? What do you know about anything?"

Ferrin smirks. "I know lots of things, and lots about some things." He sobers. "I know what it's like to have your heart broken," he says, and stares off into the distance, Olivia's face vivid in his memory. "It takes time," he adds softly.

"Yeah? How long did it take you to get over her? Or him?"

He gives her a sad smile. "Her. And who says I am?"

♠♥♣♦

"So, why don't you leave the house?" Ferrin asks several days later.

Lou scowls. "Why don't you mind your own damn business?"

He gives her what she now calls his Best Innocent Look. She suspects he may have even trademarked it.

"You know, you say that a lot," he says as he lays down a card, "but you can't blame a guy for being curious. I mean, are you actually world famous, and you've decided to hide out here until the paparazzi stops following you? Are you in Witness Protection, and you think your best bet is to lay low, especially in Ledoux, where strangers stick out like a sore thumb?" His eyes light up. "Or are you a fabulously wealthy, world-famous heiress, hiding out incognito from all the fortune hunters lusting after your wealth and beauty?"

She flushes but her lips twitch before she presses them into a firm, tight line, and intensifies her glare.

"I *wish* I was in Witness Protection," she growls, slapping down a card and taking her points, "because then I could call somebody to keep your annoying ass out of my house."

He meets her glare with a smirk, and leans forward.

"You don't have to open the door," he murmurs, raising a suggestive eyebrow, his voice a low, seductive rumble. She wonders if he has any idea what that voice does to her. She studies his face and sparkling eyes and realizes that of course he does, the teasing bastard.

"Play," she growls, "and you know, you could have put my beauty before my wealth."

His smirk widens into a knowing grin, his blue eyes laughing as he leans back and plays his next card.

Tessa waves as Ferrin strolls into The Row and takes a seat in his usual section of the coffee shop. It's where he often finds Juan and Willis and others in his growing circle of friends, shooting the shit about politicians, the weather and the Roughriders; cattle and crops and the Roughriders; work, the neighbours...and the Roughriders. To say it's miles away from his life of bickering cousins, multi-billion dollar corporations, privilege, and luxury in Toronto is like saying Mars is just around the corner from Earth.

Today, however, the coffee shop is empty except for

four strangers at the counter who are obviously together and getting their orders to go. Once they get their coffee, they leave, chattering happily while Tessa brings two steaming cups to Ferrin's table and sits down across from him with a relieved sigh.

"Is it too early to close for the day?" she groans, and rubs her temples.

"Headache?" Ferrin asks, wincing in sympathy.

Tessa nods with a grimace. "Not to mention a sore neck and shoulders. I was painting my living room last night. I probably should have stayed home today, and I would have if I had somebody to cover the store."

"You don't make enough to hire somebody, even for a day?"

"I do, but a day is about all I can afford. Delaney's happy to help me out when I'm in a bind, only she's not available today because she's doing something with the hellspawn at school, most likely paying their bail or assessing damages. Anyway, there aren't too many people who are willing to work just one day a week, or less, because really, Delaney is all I need most of the time. Not that I blame them, people who don't want to work just one day a week or less, I mean, that's pretty chump change. It's only going to get worse when the rent goes up on this place which it's going to because the building's been sold to some big shot company out of Toronto or something. Seriously, I do all the maintenance, and I'll bet you I still won't catch a break on the rent! Ah, what the hell, I'm used to it by now because Rudemacher never did a goddamn thing with the place. Everyone warned me he was a tightwad, but he's the biggest landowner in town now that Lou's the last of the Upjohn family and she hates this town and everyone in it and sold all of her landholdings to Rudemacher after her mother died, all of which is a long way of saying this was all I could find when I was setting up. Well, at least my ten per cent volume discount at the Macon-Jones store in Regina helps a little."

All Ferrin can do is nod, mainly because he lost her somewhere in her verbal stream of consciousness and can only hope he hasn't just agreed to robbing the Macon-Jones store later that night.

Tessa gives him a rueful grimace and drops her hands. "Anyway. Not your problem. Tell me, how's Lou? Is she looking good?"

He raises an eyebrow. "What makes you think I'd know?"

Tessa bursts into loud laughter then hisses with pain. She rubs her temples again as she says, "You've never lived in a small town, have you? You don't think everybody knows you've been going inside every night for the last month? It's being talked about like it's the Miracle on Thirty-Fourth Street!"

His mouth sags open as a flush creeps into his face. "Bullshit!" he sputters. "Not a single person has said one word to me!"

"Those who know you or Lou won't, and those who don't know you enjoy the gossip too much to want the truth." She airily waves a hand. "Don't worry; we don't care what you guys are doing in there...well. Okay, we're curious as hell, but we're not judging. Much. Most of us."

In spite of his discomfort, Ferrin can't help but laugh. "Stop, Tessa! You're just digging yourself in deeper and deeper!"

She gives him a cheeky grin, her eyes sparkling, her pretty, round face glowing. "I know. I can't help it. Anyway. How is she?"

Ferrin sighs and bows to the inevitable.

"She's fine. Prickly as hell, prone to snapping my head off over the least little thing, but...yeah. She's fine." He sips his coffee then frowns. "I'd just like to get her out of the house."

"Why?"

He blinks. "What do you mean, why?"

"Why does it matter to you? She's over the age of

twenty-one...I'm assuming?"

"Yeah."

"So? If she wants to live her life without leaving her house, that's her choice, isn't it?"

"Except..." he pauses, uncertain how to put his thoughts and feelings into words, not sure he wants to, not even to Tessa, who's become his closest friend in town. His feelings for and about Lou are still too vague to share with anyone, and he's only just begun to admit to himself that things are getting more complicated than he expected. All he knows for sure is that he *likes* Lou, omnipresent scowl, snappish ways, and all. She's grouchy and suspicious, unexpectedly funny and undeniably attractive, even with that abominable sweater he isn't entirely sure she ever takes off...and he's no closer to learning why she's a recluse than before he met her.

Tessa leans forward, startling him from his thoughts. "Except?" she prompts.

He frowns, then says, "She's young, Tessa, you were right about that. She's too young to be stuck in the house all day. She should be out exploring the world, meeting people, maybe even falling in love." He ignores the twinge he feels at the thought.

"Yeah? And if she'd been eighty? What then?"

He considers Tessa's question then says, "She'd be too old to be stuck in the house all day, and she should be out, exploring the world, meeting people, and maybe even falling in love. Hell, I'd even introduce her to my oldest cousin, who could use a little fun in his life, too." He pauses, thinking of Abram, then mutters, "Now there's an understatement if ever there was one."

Tessa shakes her head and laughs. "Well, she's already in love. At least that's the story around town."

"Oh?" he says, keeping his voice neutral. "Who is she in love with?"

"Ike, of course, who else? Apparently they were an item not long after her mom died, which is about the time she went inside her house and never came out again. Nobody's really sure how long it lasted, or else they're not saying, but it was apparently pretty intense for a few months. There were even rumors around town that they were planning to get married."

"Really? What happened?"

Tessa shrugs. "You'll have to ask Lou. Or Ike." She gives Ferrin a slightly smug, slightly bitter smile. "I do know Ike wasn't nearly as committed as everyone assumed."

Ferrin raises an eyebrow. "No? And you know this because...?"

"Let's just say I've been around, and recognize the type," Tessa says, and sips her coffee with a demure air.

"Ah," Ferrin says with a knowing lift to his eyebrow, "did you know he was with Lou when you slept with him?"

Tessa sets her cup down on the table with a thud and glares.

"I did not sleep with him! I was still with Teddy at the time—the too-handsome SOB who dragged me here—so Ike didn't stand a chance." She shrugs and preens. "Didn't stop him from trying, though."

Ferrin gives her an appreciative leer. "Can't blame the guy for that!"

She rolls her eyes. "Stop looking at me like that, it's creepy."

"Hey!"

"It's like my brother's caught me in my underwear or something." She shivers dramatically with a grimace of disgust.

Ferrin holds his injured look for another second, then laughs, "That's disturbing, but I get it."

They clink their cups together and sip their coffee in perfect understanding.

"I guess I'm not really all that surprised," he murmurs. "Ike and Lou, I mean," he adds at Tessa's raised eyebrow.

The thought of Lou with Ike, that overly-smooth bastard, makes his stomach twist because there's no way that could have ended well for her. He certainly knows his share of overly-smooth bastards—hell, he's related to most of them—but there's something about Ike. He doesn't like the man very much, and trusts him even less, and if there's one thing he's learned from his lifetime of exposure to overly-smooth bastards, it's to trust his instincts.

He sets his cup down.

"Regardless," he says, hoping his thoughts aren't showing on his face, "Lou is too young and has too much potential to pine away for a guy who's married to another woman. She should be out dancing and flirting and—I don't know...*doing things*." He shrugs.

"Do you think she'd like to work for less than a day a week?"

"Hell, a job may be just what she needs! She needs to be doing *something* other than sitting in her house all alone and acting as if everyone in town hates her!"

Tessa frowns. "Nobody hates her," she says slowly, "or at least I've never heard anybody say anything like that, and trust me: sooner or later, I hear everything."

Ferrin stares into the distance in thoughtful silence, then shakes his head. "Well, we weren't born here. Things are sometimes more complicated than they appear at first glance."

"True," she concedes, "and you're definitely a living example of that!"

He feels a sudden spurt of worry as he gives her a quizzical smile. "What does that mean?"

She waggles a warning finger as she finishes her coffee. "I mean you, Mr. Jones, have hidden depths yourself." She leans forward, her brown eyes suddenly serious as she searches his face.

He forces a smirk, and doesn't allow his gaze to waver from hers. "I'm an open book, Tessa."

"Except the pages are glued together." The bell over

the door jingles and she glances over her shoulder and smiles at the person who walks in. She pushes to her feet and, as she picks up her cup, says, "I also think you're a hidden romantic, Ferrin, and that's really rather sweet."

♠ ♥ ♣ ♦

As the days turn to weeks, Lou keeps waiting for Ferrin's visits to stop. It's only a matter of time, after all.

Lou perches in her customary spot on the now cleaned window-seat in her living room and peers out from behind the curtains. She scowls as she watches for his arrival and, not for the first time, wonders what the hell she's doing. She wanted change, yes, but she's not sure this is what she meant.

He's...*unsettling*. Too big, too loud, too *much*. Every evening he breezes in, crowding her overly-cluttered living room, filling all the empty spaces of her house with the sound of his voice and the smell of sweat and earth and sun. They play cards, drink beer or coffee, talk—or not— and then he leaves with a wink, a smirk, a joke, and an airy 'see you tomorrow', which Lou can't quite bring herself to believe until the doorbell rings again.

It's confusing. Unnerving. Frightening. And every night, she closes the door on his broad back and tells herself she's going to stop letting him in; that it's time to retreat back into the safety of isolation and silence. And yet...

Every day she opens the door and steps aside.

With a scowl.

Their crib games have evolved into an on-going tournament, with Ferrin faithfully recording their wins and losses with either a triumphant grin or a ferocious scowl complete with darkly muttered comments about defending his family honour.

She sighs as he opens the front gate and heads towards the house. It's grocery day, and he's weighed down with plastic bags. It's also raining, and she has the door open as he hurries up the steps.

"Thanks," he says, shaking water from his hair. "Hopefully nothing's ruined."

She mumbles something in response, already on her way to the kitchen with some of the bags to begin putting things away. Ferrin trails behind her, and even without looking, she knows his blue eyes are watching her far too closely.

"What's wrong?" he says.

"Nothing."

"Uh-huh. Which is why you won't look at me."

She glances at him then quickly looks away.

"Ike's back tomorrow," she says.

"Yes, I know."

This time her glance is longer, more thoughtful.

"I won't need you while he's here," she says in a rush.

He blinks. "Not even for cards?" he asks, a plaintive note in his voice.

She furiously shakes her head. "I don't want him to know we're playing cards or even that we're talking."

"I remember. Why not?"

She pauses from putting cans on a shelf to scowl at him. "Because I don't want him to know."

He raises an eyebrow. "Wouldn't he be happy to know you're making friends?"

She snorts. "Friends? We don't talk except to play cards."

"We talk about lots of things, even personal things every once in a while." He shrugs under her skeptical glare. "You tell me what you want done the next day, and you remind me not to tell Ike about us."

She slams a can down on the shelf. "There is no 'us'!"

"Well, not in any romantic sense, no, but we do have a relationship. Some people would even call it a friendship. Of a sort, anyway."

She growls as she brushes past him back to the living

room. She turns to face him, her arms wrapped around her torso, her fingers gripping the wool of her sweater and stretching it out of shape.

"Are you going to do as I ask?" she demands, one foot tapping an impatient rhythm against the floor.

Ferrin's silent so long she wonders if he's ever going to speak to her again.

He finally, slowly, says, "I have no reason to tell Ike we're playing cards, but if he asks me a direct question, I'm not going to lie to him."

"I'm not asking you to lie, just...don't tell him everything."

"And if he asks if I've talked to you?"

"I'm sure you can come up with some way to avoid giving a direct answer."

He again raises an eyebrow. "I think we really do need to start talking more. You have a rather interesting perception of my character."

She rolls her eyes. "Will you do it?"

He sighs. "Of course," he says, then mutters, "Olivia is so right about me."

Her eyes narrow. "Olivia?"

"My ex," Ferrin says, and now it's his turn to scowl. "You know, if you don't mind, I think I'll pass on the cards tonight."

That startles her, her eyes widening as she nervously adjusts her sweater. "Why?"

"Because I'm suddenly in a bad mood," he growls, walking towards the door.

He puts on his shoes and turns to face her. He must see some of her dismay in her face because his own expression softens.

"Look, I'm just..." he shakes his head. "Don't worry, okay? Right now, I just think I need a drink and loud music and maybe some dancing."

Her eyes widen even more. "On a *Monday*?"

He grins at her scandalized tones, but there's no

amusement in his eyes.

"Any day," he says.

"In *Ledoux*?"

His grin instantly morphs into a grimace. "Right. Forgot where I was for a minute. Maybe just a drink, then." He shakes his head. "I've gotta go. I'll see you next week, once Ike has left the building. Or town. Whatever."

She nods, feeling more forlorn than she wants to admit. She stands in the doorway and watches as he strides away, very aware of the cold, sinking feeling in her stomach. She fights a sudden urge to call him back and shuts the door, pressing her back against it. Her breath catches in her throat because she remembers now that he was only staying in Ledoux until Ike got back.

She gulps, terrified she's once again just watched her only contact with the outside world walk away without a backwards glance.

♠♥♣♦

"So, let me get this straight," Pierce says. "You're upset because you're going to do what this Lou person— your employer—wants you to do?"

"Yes!"

"Good Lord, why would that upset you?"

"Because it proves Olivia's point! I'll do whatever anybody wants me to do! I'm even a general labourer on a construction crew, where I *literally* do what everybody tells me to do! No wonder she didn't want to marry me!" Ferrin claps a hand to his forehead and leans his head back against the couch cushions, staring up at the rectory's living room ceiling.

Pierce snorts a laugh. "I think your current circumstances are somewhat different than what Olivia was insinuating."

"Yeah? How?"

"Because it's part of your *job!* Or jobs, in your case. We all do what we're told to do by our employers, even if it's something stupid like buying a building in the middle of Nowheresville, Saskatchewan, with little to no hope of a return on investment, simply because your employer wants to give his friend a break on the rent."

Ferrin rolls his eyes so hard he wonders if Pierce can hear it.

He must have, because Pierce chuckles, and says, "It's a different situation when it's what you're paid to do, although *why* you, personally, are working those particular jobs is another question entirely. Be that as it may, this Lou is your employer. You are being paid to take care of her and to do what she asks of you. You can simply look at this latest request as just another work task."

"It's *not* a work task; that's the whole point! I'm not playing cards with her because I'm paid to do it!"

"You know that, and I know that, but does *she* know that?"

Ferrin opens his mouth, then snaps it closed as he ponders the question. Their card games are friendly enough, and usually include some superficial conversation and beer, but they don't really talk that much.

Well.

Lou doesn't really talk that much, and Ferrin is wary about giving away the fact he's a member of the Macon-Jones family, and that gives him a tendency to err on the side of silence on occasion. Not with Tessa, apparently, but Lou's different.

In all senses of the word.

"Ferrin?" Pierce asks with a note of concern.

"I'm here."

"Usually silence implies consent. Am I correct in assuming my words have merit?"

"Lou isn't the easiest person to talk to. She's a recluse for a reason, you know."

"Yes? What reason is that?"

"I have no idea." He pauses, thinking. "So you think I should do as Lou asks? Lie to Ike if he asks me a direct question about whether I've talked to her or, hell, even seen her?"

"That's between you and your conscience, although you may want to respect the fact that Lou must have a reason for wanting to keep your card games a secret from him. Just because she hasn't shared that reason with you is no excuse to go blundering in—wait. I'm speaking to a Macon-Jones, a family that's always gone where angels fear to tread."

"Hey, now, is that any way to speak to your employer?"

"It's the only way to speak to this particular employer! However, I'm not speaking as your employee, I'm speaking as your friend. Whatever this is about, it's between Lou and Ike, and it's Lou's decision, not yours."

"I don't like the idea of lying to Ike," Ferrin says with a pout.

"Considering you're already lying to Lou and everyone else in town, I'm not sure why Ike is a problem."

"I am not lying to Lou! Or anyone else!"

"Have you told her who you are? Have you told *anyone* in that backwards little town?"

Ferrin scowls fiercely. "No."

"Will you?"

"Of course. Eventually."

"You're working there, Ferrin, and you're on your way to owning commercial real estate in whatever they laughingly call their downtown core. You certainly haven't said anything during this conversation that indicates you're anxious to return home. I can only assume you're planning on continuing this current state of affairs for some time to come."

"I'm not sure."

"You'll have to face Olivia sooner or later."

"I'm not staying here because of Olivia," Ferrin says, and realizes with surprise that it's true. He still misses her;

he knows it will be painful when he sees her again, but now it's all a dull ache rather than the fresh wound it had been when he left Toronto.

"No?" Pierce asks skeptically. "Then why are you still there? Working as a common labourer, for God's sake! Your great-grandfather must be spinning in his grave!"

Ferrin laughs, and pictures his great-grandfather's craggy, homely face with its wreath of wrinkles, crooked smirk and shrewd eyes. "Gramp is probably cheering me on, and you know it," he says.

"Well...true. While coming up with some way to fleece your cousins out of a fortune by convincing them to bet against you."

"And we wonder why the family is so messed up."

"I don't," Pierce says drily and says good-bye.

Two days later, Ferrin meets with Ike during Ferrin's lunch break and gives the ferret-faced little weasel a careful update that holds no hint that he even believes Lou is real. Ferrin wears a thunderous scowl the rest of the day as he returns to the construction site and hauls garbage and building materials, putting in longer hours than usual to work off his bad mood. He's exhausted by the time he leaves the work site, but now he's fighting the urge to go to Lou's place even though Ike, too, made it painfully and condescendingly clear he isn't needed or wanted for the rest of the week.

He wanders rather disconsolately from the rectory to his favourite bar, where he greets the bartender by name, orders a steak sandwich and a beer, then turns to contemplate the few people who are in the place with him. They're all friendly faces, most of them vaguely familiar, and he smiles and nods at them all as he sips his beer. He isn't in the mood, though, for small talk, so he decides to finish his food then chat for only a minute with everyone before hiding out in the rectory for the rest of the evening.

The thought makes him even more restless.

It won't even be eight o'clock by the time he's finished, and that's if he eats his meal more slowly than a sloth. He doesn't really feel like going to a movie, even if he hadn't already seen the only one playing at the only theatre in town. There are some disadvantages to living in such a small place, he thinks sourly, taking another swig of beer. Regina's an hour away and he suspects he'd drive there only to discover there isn't a single movie he wants to see, and that's a long way to go for a beer before driving home again.

He sighs and takes another drink.

There's a two-hour time difference with Ontario, so he could phone Gillian or one of his cousins, but even on a Wednesday, he isn't likely to find anyone at home. Unlike him, they have robust and varied social lives, although half the time they're usually too busy brokering deals and verbally sparring with each other to really appreciate whatever event they're attending. Besides, he touched base with Carson, Dyson and Jack, Gillian, and even Abram just last week, and another phone call so soon would only be taken as a sign of weakness. If he called any of the other cousins they would pounce on the opportunity to start lobbying for his vote even though it's still tied up for another two and a half years. A Macon-Jones never overlooks an opportunity to gain an advantage over another Macon-Jones.

And Olivia thinks he should enjoy that shit…and most of the time he does, but that's because he's outside of it and can afford to be amused by his cousins' relentless maneuvering. It's their family game, after all.

He thanks the bartender as she sets the plate in front of him then begins to eat his steak sandwich with a singular lack of appetite.

Maybe he should go shopping tomorrow, he thinks, feeling glum. Do a big grocery run to Regina instead of the 'the cupboards are too bare to, well, bear' kind of shopping he does in Ledoux's tiny stores. His own cooking is nothing to write home about: relatively tasty but no one will ever accuse him of being a gourmet chef. But after eating in restaurants, out of cans, and endless frozen dinners for the last eight months, he's actually almost missing the taste of his own cooking. With a sharp pang, he has a sudden, desperate craving for Olivia's gumbo that she makes from a 'secret family recipe'. He smiles wistfully as he remembers how he always teased her about it, and how they talked about going to Louisiana so he could compare her gumbo with, as he called it, 'the real thing'. For a moment, he keenly feels the hole in his life where Olivia used to be, yawning black and cold at the very core of him.

He's startled from his thoughts by a flash in the corner of his eye of bright blonde hair as someone slides onto the barstool beside him.

"Hey, Tessa," he says with surprise. "What brings you here?"

"I need a drink," she sighs, pouting. "Water leak in The Row's basement. I'm shut down while the guys fix it."

"Shit. Sorry. How long are you going to be closed?"

"Hopefully I'll be open again the day after tomorrow. My landlord's awfully anxious to get it fixed, too. The final inspection for the sale is next week and Rudemacher doesn't want any more damage than what's already there. Well, at least I have a little more time before the rent goes up. It never gets easier, you know what I mean?" She brightens. "Although I am now getting a higher discount at the Macon-Jones store in Regina! Some new, long-time-preferred-customer kind of deal. I didn't ask too many questions, I'm just going to take it and run!" She shakes her head and smiles at his slightly glazed expression. "Enough about me. What are *you* doing here?"

"I'm on holiday from Lou's for a week," he mutters,

and viciously saws at his steak sandwich.

Tessa watches him with arched eyebrows and an amused smirk. "I don't think the steak is to blame for that."

He grunts in agreement, swallows his bite of food and says, "It's Ike."

Her eyebrows arch higher. "He's not my favourite person either, but you barely know the man. Is he unhappy with your work?"

"Not as far as I know," he says with a shrug, cutting off another piece of steak.

"Then what are you worried about?"

"That she's going to relapse."

Tessa laughs. "She hasn't left the house! Staying inside isn't a relapse if she hasn't actually made any progress."

"But she has!" Ferrin says, dropping his knife and fork on his plate with a clatter. "She's used to me coming into the house now. I swear, she almost cracked a smile the other day!"

Tessa laughs again. "You really like her, don't you?"

He shrugs and nods. "Although I'm not sure why," he sighs. "She's barely spoken a word to me that's actually civil."

"Even after all this time?"

"Nothing of any substance, anyway."

Tessa snickers then laughs outright at the injured look he shoots her.

"So what are you going to do with your new-found free time?" she asks, and takes a sip of her beer.

"I have no frickin' idea," he growls. "I'm tempted to go to Lou's place and crash her little party with Ike, just for spite."

"And that will be the end of your card games."

"True. Not to mention being an incredibly dickish thing to do."

"True."

They sit in silence as Ferrin finishes his meal. He

pushes his plate away and sits back with a sigh.

"What are you doing tonight, Tessa?" he asks, draining the last of his beer.

"How about a bicycle ride?"

He raises an eyebrow. "I don't own a bike."

"I know where we can borrow one." She grins, brown eyes dancing.

"I haven't ridden a bicycle in at least twenty years!"

She laughs as she slides off her stool. "They say 'it's like riding a bicycle' for a reason, Ferrin. You'll remember how. Come on. Or are you going to mope all over town for the next week?"

He rolls his eyes as he pulls out his wallet and tucks some bills beneath his plate.

"Fine," he says, following her out while lifting a hand in farewell to the others in the bar, "but if I fall over, it's gonna be your fault."

To Ferrin's surprise, remembering how to ride a bicycle really *is* just like, well, riding a bicycle. He'd forgotten how much he enjoyed it, or maybe it's just more fun in a small town where one can pedal faster than most of the people drive. By the end of the next day, he's the proud owner of his very own bicycle with snazzy racing stripes, complete with matching helmet, which sends Juan and Delaney's hellspawn into raptures. Over the next few days, he rides it everywhere instead of driving. Since his evenings are currently free, he goes for long rides on the dirt and gravel roads that crisscross the countryside. As he pedals, soaking in the immensity of the sky and the treeless land that surrounds him, he finally allows himself to really think about Olivia without distracting himself with working in Lou's yard, or their nightly card games, or trying to coax Lou into a smile.

Instead, he pedals his bike during the prairie's long

summer evenings and remembers the night he met Olivia, when he spilled his drink on her at one of his family's charity functions. He thinks of her fire and passion, he thinks of her ambition and dedication to her job. He remembers all the good things about their time together, and allows himself to acknowledge the bad. He remembers the arguments when she'd come home filled with enthusiasm for a new project only to discover he had already given his vote as a member of the board to whichever cousin got to him first.

He remembers her embarrassment the last time she bailed him and the other Musketeers out of jail for that fight they got caught up in, in that Toronto nightclub. Ferrin isn't sure which annoyed Olivia more: the fight itself and the subsequent arrests; the cost to cover the damages; or the fact that Jack is going to be the next Chair of the Board of Macon-Jones Enterprises and she's never been one to let her cousins get into trouble without her. He smiles with true affection when he thinks of his cousins and admits he misses them even if he doesn't miss the mug shots.

He feels more at peace by the end of the week than he has at any point since Olivia refused his proposal and ended their relationship. He hopes it means he's finally learning to accept what happened and the mistakes he made, and is beginning to heal. Not that he's 'over' Olivia; not by a long shot. They'd been together for five years, and he suspects a part of him will always love her and mourn for what might have been. But as the days pass and he returns to the rectory after his bike rides, exhausted and dripping with sweat, he realizes the thought of a life without Olivia isn't quite as bewildering and overwhelming as it was before.

Ferrin finds himself deeply missing his father after his rides, perhaps because he has a much better understanding now of the agony his father went through after Ferrin's mother and brother died. Gideon had been their father's

VICTORIA BERNADINE

favourite and Ferrin had been their mother's, and their parents had been devoted to each other. Gideon's and his mother's deaths left Ferrin and his father reeling and struggling to close an emotional gap between them that hadn't truly mattered until there was no longer anyone there to bridge it for them. Ferrin's feelings from the end of his relationship with Olivia remind him too much of what he felt in the terrible aftermath of the accident and he wishes he could creep into his father's study and sit in silence while his father works, gathering comfort from the sheer confirmation that his father, at least, was still there.

The cousins and his great-grandfather had rallied around, of course. Even a Macon-Jones knows when it's time to put family first. But in so many ways, they'd been alone until his dad married Gillian four years later after a short, whirlwind courtship.

Ferrin seldom allows himself to think about that time in his life very deeply, the wounds still tender even after twenty-five years. But during his rides, feeling small in comparison to the infinite prairie horizon, Ferrin finally admits that Olivia never understood how those losses shaped him, defined him, and the cold reminder that he's the last member of his family branch hurt even more than he realized at the time. Her words shouldn't have been surprising, though, because he never could get her to understand that Macon-Jones Enterprises belonged to his brother, not him. Gideon loved the company more at twelve than Ferrin has felt in his entire thirty-five years. He's already living his brother's life. He could never—still can't—bring himself to take the business, too.

He knows it's irrational, but it's his truth.

Now here he is, feeling somehow suspended in time during these hot, dusty August days. He bicycles every evening on the quiet dirt and gravel roads, breathes in the dry, hot Saskatchewan air, and remembers his lost loved ones while pedalling beneath the endless sky, the vast expanse of land and horizon surrounding him. When he stops to rest, stretching out flat on his back in a shallow ditch to stare up at the sky until it spins around him, his power and importance in the world and the universe is, once again, painfully clear. Yet he finds that very realization curiously soothing as he allows the sky and land and horizon to seep into him. It doesn't fill the holes in his life left by the loss of Olivia and his family, but it somehow smooths edges he hadn't even realized were still jagged.

He's falling in love with the open prairies stretching to the horizon beneath the endless sky, just like he's falling in love with the life he's creating as Ferrin Jones. He's working hard, he likes all the men and women on his construction crew, he enjoys Juan and Delaney and their hellspawn, just like he enjoys Tessa and Willis and their extended circle of family, friends and acquaintances.

He's not sure if he *enjoys* Lou, but he's definitely intrigued by her. She's grouchy and rude and defensive, but those devastating eyes draw him towards her, along with a growing desire to see what she looks like without that ever-present sweater covering her to her fingertips and down past her knees. It doesn't matter how hot it is outside or in, she's wrapped in that sweater like a Christmas present. Only way less cheerful. He sometimes catch himself trying to see past the knitted wool, trying to determine if she has curves or a boyishly slender figure or if she's pleasantly plump. He wonders if her legs are long and slender or short and stout. He wonders why she always wears jeans and sweat pants, or is it simply because she doesn't own anything else.

Sometimes he worries that he's a pervert or predatory when he thinks these things; he *hopes* it's only natural to be curious about what she would look like if she wore something other than all that ugly knitted wool thing. He *is* sure, though, that behind the scowls and snarled words and defensive posture, she's a person who hasn't seen anyone other than Ike for five years, which means she's incredibly vulnerable. He has no idea what the fuck Ike was thinking to just leave her to the mercy of the first stranger who came along.

He shudders and thanks every lucky star he can think of that *he's* the stranger Ike found.

Not that he'd ever let her know he thinks she's a vulnerable, easily manipulated person. He's not an idiot, after all. He has absolutely no doubt she's perfectly capable of burying his body in her basement.

Maybe she isn't quite as defenseless as she seems.

He snickers at his thoughts as he cycles back into town, only pausing to once again eye the run-down little house with the sadly sagging for-sale sign located on the western outskirts . Tessa led him past the place on their very first bike ride and he knows the devilish barista did it deliberately. The fact it worked, and he has an appointment to view it tomorrow, is something he knows Tessa won't let him live down any time soon.

He grins as he coasts into the rectory's parking lot and dismounts.

Ike's leaving tomorrow, and as soon as Ferrin finishes work, has toured the house, and tells Pierce to buy the place, he's going to Lou's for their next game of cards. He's behind in their impromptu tournament and the sooner he gets some wins under his belt, the better. The family honour is depending on him.

Lou walks Ike to the door and tugs her sweater close as she watches him put on his sneakers. He straightens and looks at her, a bittersweet smile on his handsome face. When he opens his arms, she finds herself strangely reluctant to step into them. She tells herself to stop being silly and puts her arms around him, feeling awkward.

"I'll call you next week," he says, his cheek pressed against her hair. He heaves a sigh and she stiffens as his arms tightens around her, his hands smoothing down her back. "I'd forgotten how great it is to spend time with you," he murmurs. "I miss you, Lou."

She leans back so she can see his face and forces a smile. "I miss you, too," she says and wonders why it feels so insincere. Ike's expression doesn't change so it must sound all right to him. "Have a safe trip," she adds.

He smiles, then presses a kiss to her forehead and releases her.

"Say hi to Irish," she says as he opens the door. He glances back at her, puzzled, and she shrugs. "She's your wife. I guess it's time I got used to that, huh?"

His puzzled expression doesn't change, his amber eyes intent as he searches her face. "Yes," he finally says, "I suppose so."

Lou summons up another smile. "You'd better get going or you'll miss your plane."

He jerks into motion, nodding his head. "Right. I'll call next week." He lifts a hand in farewell as he bounds out the door and down the steps.

She watches until he's out of the gate before she closes the door and leans her forehead against it with a rush of guilty relief.

The week had not gone at all the way she imagined. She thought they would easily slip back into their old relationship, and in some ways, they had. He brought her papers to sign, which she did as quickly as possible with a familiar feeling of bored impatience. He did whatever yard work needed to be done, although there wasn't much because Ferrin is keeping things neat and tidy, and he brought her what few groceries she needed, which again wasn't much because Ferrin not only brings her usual groceries but also brings her things he thinks she might find tasty or interesting. Even with occasionally feeding Ferrin, her cupboards are overflowing. Strangely, when Ike stayed and chatted for a while each evening, telling her about Vancouver and Irish, and their hopes and plans for the future, Lou found herself wistfully wishing for the card table and the score-card. She's ahead right now in her impromptu tournament with Ferrin and she wants to keep it that way.

She slowly, gently bangs her forehead against the door and groans.

Perhaps that's what's so unsettling. All Ike's talk about Irish and careers and children and houses and vacations— all those things she's never done and likely never will do— has weighed her down. She turns and presses her back against the door, and gently continues banging her head against it.

Or maybe it's because she was worried about letting it slip that Ferrin had wormed his way into the house. She took great pains to hide all evidence of Ferrin's presence, and she'd been surprised and unnerved by just how many traces of him there were. The beer bottles, the card table and its contents, including the notebook listing their wins and losses. She found one of his jackets behind one of the couches, and she can't even remember when or how it could have ended up there in the first place.

She opens her eyes and sighs.

She'd been happy to see Ike. Ecstatic, even. She was warmed by his smile, mildly turned on by his lithe body, but everything was muted somehow, like a fading echo. Even their conversations seemed off-rhythm, but she can't pinpoint how or why. As much as it horrifies and unsettles her to admit it, she's glad he's gone.

Without telling her if Ferrin is coming back.

A cold pit opens in her stomach.

Well, she tells herself in stern tones as she straightens and adjusts her sweater, she'll find out tomorrow and there's no point worrying about it tonight.

She's only gone two steps when the doorbell shatters the silence, startling a high-pitched yip out of her as she practically spins in mid-air to stare at the oak door. Her heart is hammering, her mind racing, and the cold pit in her stomach grows larger and colder.

Ike realized he forgot to tell her Ferrin left, she thinks. He's back to tell her who's going to be doing her chores from now on.

She hesitates, arms wrapped around her torso as she reflexively clutches at the wool of her sweater.

The doorbell rings again followed by a firm knock and Ferrin's voice calling, "Open up, Lou! Or did Ike finally snap and bury your body in the basem—ah! There you are!"

She glares, feeling murderous even though her knees are trembling with relief at the sight of him looming in her doorway.

"What are you doing here?" she demands.

He grins as he brushes past her. "I've heard from extremely reliable sources that Ike has left the town limits and is safely on his way back to Vancouver, so I'm here for the next round in our crib tournament."

She closes the door and scowls, crossing her arms and tapping her foot. "He literally walked out of here two minutes ago," she says, eyes narrowed with suspicion. "Who are these 'reliable sources' and what? Were they watching my house?"

Ferrin puts his hand on his heart. "I must protect my sources," he says, "and I didn't ask how they knew."

Her eyes narrow even more. "How did you get here so fast? Were *you* watching my house?"

"You worry too much, Lou," he says, his lop-sided, charming, shit-eating grin on full display, "and you're going to give me a complex with all your questions." He rubs his hands together, almost bouncing on the balls of his feet. "Now, how about some cards? Man, I've been planning my revenge all week."

"How do you plan revenge in crib?" she asks drily, then shakes her head. "Wait a minute. You're way too excited. What's going on?"

He stares, blue eyes wide, giving her his Best Innocent

Look (trademarked), which means he's anything but.

"Nothing!" he says in an injured tone.

"Hm. Why am I not convinced?"

He shrugs, his expression becoming even more innocent. "I looked at a house today."

She frowns. "Why?"

"Because it's for sale," he says as if it's the most natural reason in the world.

Her frown deepens. "How can you afford it? And aren't you leaving?"

"I can afford it," he says sharply, "and no. Why would you think I was leaving?"

"Because that's what you told Ike when he hired you in March!"

Ferrin's expression clears. "That was then," he says with a careless flick of his hand, "this is now. I like it here. I think I'll stay a while."

She stills, her eyes growing wider, her fingers flexing very slowly against the wool of her sweater. Ferrin's eyes never waver from hers and Lou feels somehow suspended, like there are a multitude of futures holding their breaths, waiting to hear whatever she says next.

"The card table's in the drawing room," she finally mutters.

"So how long do you plan on staying?" Lou asks a few days later as she gathers up the cards and begins to shuffle. "I mean, it doesn't sound like you're planning on leaving any time soon if you're thinking about buying a house."

He shrugs. "I don't know—but the house idea fell through. Got bought out from under me from some guy in Toronto. Luckily for me, he's going to let me rent it."

"Well, I'm surprised you had enough for a down payment, even for a place here in Ledoux."

"I would have managed," he murmurs, his lips quirking

into a half-smile.

"So you're going to rent from this guy, but that most likely means a lease, and that means you plan to stay here, at least for a while longer. I mean, you have a family, don't you?"

"Yeah, and I do believe it's my deal."

She rolls her eyes as she hands him the deck. "And friends, right?" she persists.

"Of course."

"So, sooner or later, you're going to want to go home, aren't you?"

"Sure. But maybe not to stay."

"Why not?"

Ferrin laughs. "If you knew my family, you'd understand," he says as he shuffles and deals the cards. He pauses, thinking, then doubles over in helpless laughter. "Oh, my God, you'd understand!"

She scowls as she waits for him to regain control.

"Anyway," he says, catching his breath, "I don't want to talk about my family, or my friends. I'd rather talk about moving into the house, and what's been going on around town, and how things are going with Ike, and how you're doing. Oh, and I won't be able to stay too long on Saturday. I'm going to Willis' place to watch the football game."

She automatically pulls a face at the name, then shifts uncomfortably at Ferrin's raised eyebrow because of course he noticed that. "The Riders must be playing," she mutters and picks up her cards.

"Yeah," he says, faintly puzzled as he picks up his own cards. "How'd you know?"

"Willis-that-bastard—" she pulls the same, disgusted face as the name leaves her lips "—only has parties when the Riders play. I doubt that's changed in the last five years." She gives him a stern look as she cuts the deck. "Be careful, though. His football parties have a tendency to get a little out of hand."

"I'm not worried. I'm actually not much of a football fan, but he did rescue me from the ditch, so I didn't feel like I could say no."

She stops and stares, opening her eyes as wide as they will go. "You're not a football fan? In *Saskatchewan?*"

He shrugs as he picks up the top card and places it face up on the deck.

"Well," he says absently, "I mean, I suppose I cheer for the Argos, or maybe the Ti-cats—"

"Oh, my God—don't say that to anybody around here!"

He stares, eyes wide. "I already have..."

"Well, whatever you do, don't eat or drink anything anyone gives you at the party."

"What, they're going to try to kill me now?"

"Of course not, but you may lose consciousness and when you wake up, you'll be a Riders' fan." She leans forward and lowers her voice to a conspiratorial whisper, "I hear it's all bright lights, watermelons, giant gophers, and endless chanting of 'let's go Riders let's go'."

His mouth sags open as he stares at her.

Her lips twitch as she nods at the cards he's holding and says, "Are you going to play or what?"

♠♥♣♦

Lou's grip on the phone tightens as she listens to Ike chattering on about everything he and Irish have been up to lately.

She's only half-listening. She's too busy trying to determine how to best broach the subject she wants to talk about and wrestling with a disloyal sense of irritation that he doesn't seem interested in letting her get a word in edgewise. It's the first time he's called since he left Ledoux two weeks ago and he only told her they'd been busy, asked if everything was all right, and didn't even wait for an answer before he launched into telling her about their plans for a fall trip to Cancun, first class, to one of the highest of the high-end hotels.

Irish's job apparently pays extremely well, Lou thinks sourly as Ike moves on to waxing poetic about the ocean view they enjoy from their house.

She bites back a sigh, grateful he's two provinces away, because she isn't sure she could maintain a pretense of polite interest if he were in the room with her.

The thought shocks her upright and she snaps, "Ike!"

He stops in mid-word, and she can imagine the shocked look on his handsome face which would be quickly replaced with irritation and anger at her interruption.

"What?" he demands.

"I want to ask you something."

"And you couldn't wait until I was finished with what I was saying?"

Lou hides a sigh.

"No," she says, softening her tone. "I was afraid I was going to lose my nerve."

"I am not coming back to Ledoux to live," Ike says firmly.

Lou laughs, surprised. "No, that's not it. I know that's not going to happen. No, this is about...about me getting out of the house."

"Oh. *Oh.*"

She presses her lips together, wanting to sound as if it doesn't matter, but the words tumble out tinged with desperation anyway. "I know you researched it a long time ago and I know there was nothing that could be done about my panic attacks back then, but it's been years, and maybe something's changed! Maybe—"

"Lou..."

The soft, gentle pity in his voice stops her cold. Her throat clicks as she swallows, the palms of her hands sweating, her knuckles white from the death-grip she has on her sweater and the phone she's pressing tight to her ear. She waits, stomach churning, and wishes she didn't already know what he's going to say.

"I've been keeping an eye out this whole time," he says, and her eyes prickle with tears. "There's nothing, Lou. Nothing at all that can be done. Don't you think I'd tell you if there were? You know I'm looking out for you."

"I know," she whispers through a throat that's almost too tight to make a sound.

"What brought this on?"

"You."

"*Me?*"

"All your stories about Vancouver and your trips and plans for the future. I just...I just don't want to think I'm going to spend the rest of my life seeing nothing but the walls of my house and whatever is out my window."

Ike sighs, and Lou closes her eyes against the mournful sound.

"Don't give up hope, Lou," he says in the tones of someone who doesn't believe the platitudes he's spouting. "Who knows what new discoveries will be made in the future? Miracles happen every day."

Ferrin eyes a scowling, tight-lipped Lou who is refusing to look him in the eyes. Or speak, except when she plays a card. He heaves a silent sigh.

Just when he thought he was making progress...

They finish the game. She gathers the cards for the next game while he records the score and the winner in their game book and says, "So, what's bothering you?"

Her hands still and he watches her without lifting his head.

"Aren't you bored yet?" she asks gruffly, and Ferrin suspects she's trying for her usual sharp tone but can't quite reach it.

Then her question sinks in, and he sits up straight,

blinking in surprise. He wonders what's going on in that messy-haired head of hers as he searches what he can see of her lowered face. The downcast curve to her mouth is nothing unusual, but her refusal to look him straight in the eye is definitely new. He's momentarily distracted by wondering once again why such a forthright and, yes, strong woman chooses to spend her days locked away from the world.

He shakes off his thoughts, and says, "Um...no?"

"You're not sure?" and there's that trace of humor that never fails to surprise and delight him.

"I'm definitely not sure what I'm supposed to be bored by," he says, "or is it with? Whatever."

Lou lifts her head and glares, her eyes even darker than usual, and gestures helplessly, angrily. "This! Me! Crib every bloody night!"

He laughs, and her eyes narrow, as if she would love to shoot lasers at his head and out the other side, which only makes him laugh even more.

"No," he finally says with a lop-sided grin, "I'm not bored. I mean, it would be nice to maybe watch a movie or TV every now and then, but you don't have a TV or anything else that we could use to play a movie, so it's not like that's an option."

She crinkles her nose. "A *movie*? TV?"

"Yeah. You know: moving pictures with sound and colour? Sometimes there's even a plot and, on rare occasions, some pretty great acting?"

She rolls her eyes so hard Ferrin imagines he can almost hear them.

"I know what they are! I just don't know why you would want to watch them!"

He raises an eyebrow. "Is this, like, a Saskatchewan thing? Does Willis have the only TV in town or something?"

She pulls her usual disgusted expression at the mention of Willis, and says, "Of course not!"

"Oh, right—the game watch party was at Tessa's last week, so she has one, too. This week we're over at Juan and Delaney's, so they must also have one. I hope that's a sign you're the odd one out. No offense."

Lou huffs, leans back in her chair, and snugs her sweater more closely around herself.

"What's this really about?" he asks.

Her fingers clench against her sweater then relax.

She shrugs. "Nothing. I just thought you might be bored with nothing to do here except play cards and make awkward conversation."

"Huh. If I say yes, does that mean I might be able to persuade you to get a TV?"

"Ha! No," she says, and rises, grabs the cups, and heads for the kitchen.

"No?" he says, hastily following her with his best eager-puppy expression. "I'm very persuasive, you know."

"Not really." She turns to face him with her arms crossed and a scowl on her face.

"No?" he asks with a raised eyebrow, his voice pitched to a low, husky rumble as he leans against the door jamb. He doesn't miss the way her eyes widen and darken before they narrow into a glare.

"Shut up and deal," she snaps, and brushes past him on her way back to the living room.

Lou opens the door the next day and her jaw drops when she realizes Ferrin, with his now all-too-familiar shit-eating grin, is standing on the porch beside the biggest box she's ever seen.

"What the bloody…?" she sputters.

Ferrin's eyes sparkle like a little boy's on Christmas morning. "Isn't it *awesome*?"

"What the hell is it?"

"A television!"

Somehow, she's not surprised.

"It's *huge*!" she says.

He nods and Lou is once again struck by his resemblance to an over-eager puppy.

"Seventy-five inches," he says, almost giddy, "which is *frickin'* huge, but your living room's really big, so it'll be just right. Now, get out of the way while I get it inside."

"Where did you find it?" she asks, retreating in front of him as he maneuvers the box through the door and into the living room.

"The Macon-Jones store in Regina is having a sale so Juan and I went and got it. Mainly because he has a truck, and I don't. I do have to buy the beer for both of us on Saturday, though." He sets the box down with a grunt, and smirks. "It's possible he may be having a similar conversation with Delaney even as we speak, but, you know, he's pretty quick on his feet. I'm sure he'll be able to dodge whatever she throws at him. Right now, you and I need to rearrange the furniture in here."

Silence descends as they survey the cluttered room, its walls crammed with boxes, shelves, bags, and a seemingly endless variety of ornaments and other knick-knacks.

"Huh," Ferrin says thoughtfully, "does your whole house look like this?"

"Pretty much, yeah."

"Huh," he says again. "We're going to have our work cut out for us."

"Assuming I want this monstrosity here in the first place."

He pulls a DVD out of his jacket pocket and shoves it into her hands. It's a Tarzan movie and her jaw drops as she takes in the preternaturally handsome, tanned, and spectacularly shirtless actor on the cover.

"Wow," she says.

"You know, that's exactly what Tessa said, too." She jerks the DVD away as he angles it so he can take another look at it. He shrugs. "Even I have to admit he's a handsome devil, but I have no idea if the movie's any good."

"Who cares?" she says, still staring at the actor in question. She yelps in protest as Ferrin plucks the DVD from her hand.

"All right," he says firmly, "you wanna look at him? Let's figure out where to set this monster up."

She scowls, then grudgingly says, "There's a plug in over there."

He looks at the spot she indicated, and ruefully considers the stacks of boxes that hide the wall from sight. He shrugs as he rubs his hands together. "Well, I didn't expect this to be easy. Let's get cracking!"

♠♥♣♦

"This movie's awful, and this guy can't act his way out of a soggy paper bag," Ferrin mutters, sprawled on the couch beside Lou. "No wonder this thing went straight to video."

"Hm," Lou replies, her eyes glued to the screen where the actor in question is wearing a loincloth that appears to still be clinging to his body through sheer luck as he rescues Jane from her latest predicament.

Ferrin heaves a long-suffering sigh, and grabs a handful of the microwave popcorn he had the foresight to bring along.

"Next time, I'm picking a movie with a plot," he mutters, "and more clothes for the men." He hesitates as Lou spares him a speaking look. "Or maybe not."

She returns her attention to the screen, and Ferrin hides a grin behind a handful of popcorn.

♠♥♣♦

The days drift by, and summer doesn't so much fade into fall as plunges into it with both feet. Ferrin misses an occasional evening with Lou, thanks to football and the social nature of his new-found friends, but by the end of September, his presence in Lou's house is surprisingly commonplace. She seems almost comfortable with him now, even if 'welcoming' is a bit of a stretch. Yet, in spite of all the time he's spent with her, he's no closer to finding out what he wants to know: he still knows next to nothing about her personally, still doesn't know what makes her tick, or why and how she ended up living behind the closed doors of her house.

Which is why, at six in the morning, he's the first of the regulars to arrive at The Row. He gets his coffee with a thoughtful air and sits at his usual table, where he stares off into space with a pensive frown. He startles back to his surroundings when Willis slides into a seat across from him, a steaming cup of coffee in hand.

"You're here early," Willis says.

"So are you."

"Haven't been to bed yet. Out at Old Man Lankowski's place dealing with one of their sows. What's your excuse?"

"Couldn't sleep. Worrying about Lou."

Willis raises his bushy, grizzled eyebrows. "Really? Giving you trouble, is she?"

"Yes. No. Not in the way you think."

Willis grins. "And what way do I think?"

Ferrin rolls his eyes.

"Awright, I'll behave," Willis laughs. "Why are you worried about Lou?"

Ferrin leans forward, his eyes intent. "You've lived here all your life."

Willis slurps his coffee then leans back in his chair, arms crossed and resting comfortably on his slightly protruding stomach. He nods, his crystal clear blue eyes bright and shrewd.

"Boy and man, as the saying goes."

"Do you have any idea why Lou's hiding in her

house?"

"Haven't the foggiest. Why don't you ask her?"

Ferrin's shoulders slump, and he sighs. "I keep chickening out. I don't want to spook her now that she's finally getting used to me." He sips his coffee, his mouth turned down at the corners.

Willis eyes him for a moment then seems to come to a decision.

"I knew her dad," he says, his voice gruff, "everyone did. Naturally." At Ferrin's puzzled look, he shrugs. "Besides this being a pretty small town and besides the fact that he was one of the kindest, friendliest men you'd ever hope to meet, he was also a really good friend to me. To everyone he ever met, truth be told. But Lou Senior died in a car accident before Lou was born, and Marigold—her mother—was..." he hesitates, an indefinable look on his face, before finally saying, "she was in pretty rough shape for a very long time."

Ferrin wonders just how much of an understatement that is.

Willis shakes his head, as if he's shaking the past away. "I did all I could for her, and we were...*close* for almost the rest of her life." He blinks rapidly before taking another slurp of coffee and meeting Ferrin's questioning eyes. He shrugs. "We talked about getting married but she wanted to wait until Lou left for university. We'd even started planning it and Lou actually seemed happy about it. Then Marigold got sick. I tried to convince her to marry me anyway, but..." He shakes his head. "It's one of the few things in my life I truly regret. I should have fought harder."

He once again stares off into the distance, his eyes sad, before he blinks and gives Ferrin a rueful smile.

"Don't look so surprised, son. Even old fellas like me fall in love and get their hearts broken. But none of this is telling you about Lou, is it?" He lifts his cup, then lowers it again without drinking. "Lou was a perfectly normal kid.

She was quiet, a little shy, and only ever had eyes for Ike, even back then, although God knows why. Trust me, he was always a little shit. Anyway, she left Ledoux and went to university in Saskatoon for a couple of years. She seemed happy while she was there, and Marigold told me some of the stories, so I know Lou had a relatively busy social life while she was there. That ended, though, when she came back home after Marigold got sick. She looked after her mother until Marigold passed away and then, after the funeral, well...Lou walked into that house and never came out." He pauses, frowning, then half-smiles and says, "She was such a cute kid. Big dark eyes, black hair, and the sweetest smile...when you could coax one out of her, that is." He shakes his head. "The spitting image of her dad, and when it came to Lou Senior, that was some comfort, at least. Everybody still misses him around here, you know, including me, even if I did fall in love with his widow. He was just a good, *good* man, he really was, just like Marigold was a good, *good* woman. They deserved better than what life gave them. Lou deserves better, too."

Ferrin's lips quirk into a half-smile. "She warned me about your football parties."

"My football parties have always been legendary, even back then. Marigold, once she started living again, was also quite the social butterfly, and Lou—" He laughs, a broad grin on his face, "The Upjohn house was the place to be, any day of the week, even with all those rooms crammed full with stuff. At least the football parties have always been for all ages—we get our Rider fans started young! Lou probably fell asleep in every house in this town before she was ten, waiting for those parties to wind down. Lou Senior was the same way, although he fell asleep for different reasons." He chuckles, then sighs. "I've sometimes wondered how things would have turned out if he hadn't died like that."

"You mean for Lou?"

"Her mom, too. Lou shut us all out, that last year.

Wouldn't let anyone see her mom, except the doctor and Ike and nurses who never seemed to stay for long, and that must have been hard for Marigold. She had a lot of friends. But Lou wouldn't even see us when we showed up at the door, just sent Ike to do her dirty work." His voice hardens. "I have to admit, when Ike holds his ground, he holds his ground. He wouldn't budge, even in the face of numbers." He softens. "I don't really know why they decided it would be better for Marigold if her friends stayed away...maybe it *was* better for her...but it must have been a lonely time for both of them, with only Ike and the local quack for company and strangers for nurses." He pauses, his face stark with grief, and Ferrin's heart goes out to the older man.

"You know," Willis continues slowly, "Lou barely seemed to be there at the funeral. Didn't say a word to anyone other than Ike and the priest." He grimaces. "She wouldn't even look me in the eye." He shrugs. "I don't know. Maybe she felt guilty that she told Ike to keep me out of the house, come hell or high water. Or maybe she thought I betrayed her mother, that it was my decision to end things after we found out just how sick she was." He shifts restlessly and shakes his head. "Well. Can't change the past. After the funeral, Ike took Lou home, and that's the last I saw of her."

They drink their coffee in melancholy but companionable silence, listening to Tessa's efficient movements as she cleans behind the counter, the chimes when the door opens, and Tessa's cheerful chattering as she serves her early morning regulars.

"It's sad," Ferrin finally murmurs, "her being in that house all day."

"Why?"

"Because she's so young! Her whole life's ahead of her."

"You know, Ferrin, some people just don't like other people. Maybe that's all it is, have you thought of that?"

"Doesn't it worry you?"

Willis gives him a thoughtful look then says, "We see the lights on at night. We see that they go on and off at different times and in different rooms, and when we know for a fact that Ike isn't there. We sometimes see a shadow moving against the curtains, again, when we know Ike isn't there. We see the smoke rising from her chimney on the cold days, so we know her furnace is working. We check the snow for footprints in the winter, and we look behind the hedges and trees in the summer. We know if anybody's been lurking outside her house, and we also know who's been visiting, how often, and for how long."

Willis smirks a little as the heat slowly rises in Ferrin's face.

"We're a small town, Ferrin, with all the good--and all the bad--that entails. We gossip about our neighbours, and we watch what they do and who they do it with. The vast majority of us are good-hearted. We don't talk because we want to cause harm, but because we're genuinely interested in our neighbours' well-being. We want to celebrate with them in triumph, and support them through their pain. Not that we're a perfect town, of course, and we have our fair share of the malicious, those who just want to cause trouble, and enjoy doing it. You learn to recognize them for who they are, and ignore whatever they say or do. The Upjohn family means a lot to this town, and not just because they settled the place. We've been taking care of Lou all along, Ferrin, we just do it from a distance, because that's what she wants. She's not hurting anybody, and it's not for us to judge the way she lives, or why."

"That's remarkably open-minded of you," Ferrin murmurs.

"We're in Saskatchewan, not the Dark Ages, although admittedly, some days it's tough to tell the difference."

Ferrin chuckles. "If you're all looking out for Lou, why was Ike reduced to hiring a perfect stranger to look after her?"

Willis snorts. "I'd do anything for Lou, but I wouldn't piss on Ike if he were on fire."

Ferrin lifts his cup in a toast. "Now, *that* I understand."

♠♥♣♦

Lou shuffles the cards, very much aware Ferrin's watching her far more intently than usual, his normally ever-present smirk nowhere in sight. His unwavering focus makes her nervous, until finally she snaps, "Why are you looking at me like that?"

He hesitates, then says, "Why don't you go outside?"

Lou freezes, then slowly relaxes. It's not like the question is a surprise. In fact, she's rather impressed it's taken this long for him to ask again, and to ask with the expectation of a serious, truthful answer. She shrugs and as she once again starts shuffling the cards, she hears him release a pent-up breath with what sounds like relief.

"There's nothing for me out there," she says, her eyes focused on the movement of her hands. There's something soothing about the fact her skill at manipulating the deck is as unconscious as breathing.

"How do you know that? Have you ever really looked? Besides, don't you want to, I don't know...see Paris in the spring? Walk the Great Wall of China? Dip your toe into every ocean of the world? Sail the seven seas? Go treasure hunting in the desert and swing through the trees of the jungle? Get into a fight in some seedy bar in some darkly exotic, tropical city, where the men wear fedoras and the women are dangerous?"

Lou stares at him, the cards forgotten in her hands.

"And yet," she says slowly, "here *you* are, in a small town. In Saskatchewan."

"Well, this place is exotic, too...in its own way."

Her skepticism rolls off her in waves.

"Or not...although the women are definitely

dangerous."

She shakes her head. "All those things you said—those are all the things the world holds for *you*."

"Lots of people want to do those things."

"Bar fights? Really?"

"At least in theory. In reality, they're not nearly as much fun as they're cracked up to be." He pauses, considering, then adds, "Not to mention they can be pretty tough to explain in court."

She ducks her head and presses her fingers against her lips, but it's too late.

"You smiled," Ferrin breathes, a slow smile of his own spreading across his face. "You actually smiled!" He leaps from his chair and does an endearingly awkward victory dance.

"Oh, shut up," she mutters, but there's no heat in her words, and she can't quite stop the gentle upward curving of her mouth.

"Hah! Like I'm going to let you live this one down! You're busted! You do smile!"

"Be careful, or I won't answer the door anymore."

He drops back down into his chair and grins at her.

"Not even threats can tarnish my triumph! You smiled!"

She sighs and rolls her eyes.

He stills, his gaze suddenly intent.

"You should do it more often," he says softly.

Heat climbs into her cheeks, and she quickly averts her gaze back to the cards in her hands and begins to deal.

"Have you done all those things?" she asks.

"Hah! Wouldn't *you* like to know?"

She gives him an annoyed look. "Well, why do you think I asked?"

He laughs, blue eyes sparkling, and Lou grudgingly admits he's rather charming in this mood. Well, he's charming all the time; he just seems even more charming when in this mood.

"I've done some of those things," he says, blessedly oblivious to her thoughts. "I haven't swung through the jungle but I have been to the Amazon, and I've worn a fedora while beside a dangerous woman in an exotic location...unfortunately, the dangerous woman is related to me and our cousins who escaped had to bribe our way out of jail, but it was still a helluva lot of fun. Well. In retrospect, at least."

"Sounds like it," she says drily. "Is that why you're not out there right now, looking for some dangerous woman who's *not* related to you and having a wild adventure? Don't call me for bail money, though."

"But I only just added you to the list!"

"You keep a list of people you can call to get you out of jail?"

"Doesn't everyone?"

She smiles again and Ferrin beams in response.

"Seriously, Ferrin," she says. "What are you doing in here with me when you could be out romancing your way through town?"

He shifts in his chair, his grin fading. "Well...my significant other, Olivia, rejected my marriage proposal on New Year's Eve. I know it's been nine months, but it still feels like it's too soon to be finding another romantic partner in crime."

"What happened?"

He pauses then says, "She said no."

He picks up his cards and studies them with a frown.

"Yes, but why?"

The look on his face is so fleeting, Lou can't quite identify it.

"She...uh..." he pauses and lowers his head, his hair flopping over his forehead, emphasizing his boyish looks. He frowns for a long moment before finally meeting her gaze with a steady one of his own. "She's an executive at a big company in Toronto. She's on the fast track to becoming their CEO, and that takes a lot of focus, hard work, and ambition, not to mention skillful and sometimes Machiavellian interpersonal maneuvering. She said I was...well, she said a lot of things, but what it boiled down to was the fact I was too nice to be of any use to her."

Lou stares. *"Really?"*

Out of all the possibilities that had flitted through her head, this had not been one of them.

"I'm paraphrasing, but, yeah. Really. And I'm apparently not that bright, either, because I wouldn't know enough not to spill her secrets to her business rivals." He shifts uncomfortably. "You know, at company parties or whatever."

Lou slowly blinks. "Really."

"Really."

"Well. That's just...odd." She frowns. "I mean, I could understand if she'd said your lifestyles didn't match, because—well, no offense, Ferrin, but you were living out of a car when you showed up here. I mean, if you were some high-powered executive in some big company back east, I doubt that's how you would have ended up."

Ferrin makes a strangled, choking noise, then clears his throat. "Highly unlikely," he agrees gravely, "but I wasn't homeless in Toronto." He pauses, suddenly struck. "Come to think of it, though, she did own the apartment, so I guess I was homeless when we broke up. In a manner of speaking. Huh. Never thought of it that way before."

"Well," Lou says, refusing to be sidetracked, "what *did* you do in Toronto? Were you working for the same company? I mean, I assume you had a job of some kind, otherwise how did you survive? Toronto's really expensive, isn't it?" She draws in a scandalized breath, her eyes wide with mock horror. "Were you a kept man? Is your ex a much older woman?"

He makes the same choking sound he'd made earlier then says, "I don't think she'd appreciate that description, but yeah, I guess you could say I was a kept man. Technically. I suppose."

There's an indecipherable expression on his face, half amusement, half something else, and suspicion ices its way down her spine. For a heart-stopping moment she's fervently grateful she hasn't told Ike about Ferrin, because she can already hear him telling her he told her so.

"Well," she says with forced lightness, "I guess I can see why she didn't want to marry you, then. I mean, a boy toy is all well and good, but if you can't support her in her career..." she trails off with an expressive shrug.

He looks affronted. "You mean I was supposed to do more than provide spectacular sex? That was *not* in the job description!"

She can't help herself: she laughs.

Ferrin claps his hands and crows in triumph, "Oh, my God—and you laugh!"

She rolls her eyes and glares, then softens. "How long were you with her?"

"Five years."

"That's a long time."

Ferrin nods. "I guess I'm more like my dad than I thought. He couldn't bring himself to even look at another woman for years after my mom died. When he met my stepmother, he married her within a few months, but that was almost four years later, and he never truly got over losing my mom."

Lou's eyes are soft as she watches him. "I'm sorry."

He ducks his head. "Thank you."

"What happened to your mom? If you don't mind my asking."

He stills, staring off into the distance, his face stark with grief.

"We were camping," he says slowly. "She and my older brother went canoeing. We're not really sure what happened exactly, but they capsized and both of them drowned." He pauses, frowning a little. "I was supposed to go with them. It took me a long time to accept that even if I'd been there, I probably wouldn't have been able to save them, or die in their place."

Lou clears her throat and says, "How old were you?"

"Ten. My brother was twelve, and my dad's favourite. They were a lot alike. I was closer to my mother and idolized my brother. It was...rough. Afterwards."

They subside into melancholy but comfortable silence, then their eyes meet and Lou can't seem to tear her gaze away. They sit, frozen in time until she finally forces herself to blink and lowers her gaze to the card table.

"Are we going to play or what?" she croaks out.

He starts and nods. "Right."

They finish the game and begin another. The lingering sadness in Ferrin's eyes makes Lou's heart do weird things, makes her feel...*strange*. She bites her lip, and—to her surprise—realizes that she wants to reach out and touch him, to make some small gesture of comfort. She hasn't felt that urge for anyone other than Ike and her mother in more years than she cares to remember. Her unusual empathy makes her uncomfortable, but it also gives her hope that perhaps she isn't as isolated from the human race as she thinks, locked away behind the walls of her house.

Twenty minutes and one more game later, Lou walks him to the door and watches as he pulls on his shoes and jacket, the memory of the expression on his face when he'd talked about his lost family in the forefront of her mind. She wonders how hard it was for him to share that with her. It obviously still hurts him to talk about it, yet he hadn't shied away from her questions. In spite of her lingering distrust—then again, she distrusts everybody— she grudgingly admits his willingness to talk to her...*matters*. She doesn't exactly know how or why, and she doesn't want to think about it too deeply, but it matters.

"I get panic attacks," she blurts almost before she realizes she's going to speak.

He drops his shoe and straightens, blue eyes popped wide.

She swallows, not quite looking at him as she tugs her sweater close, digging her fingers deep into the wool.

She opens and closes her mouth, then, "Whenever I try to leave the house. I get...I can't breathe. My hands shake, my vision narrows, and the world caves in. You know: I *panic*."

"I get it," Ferrin says slowly, "you're agoraphobic."

Lou shrugs. "I guess. That, and I don't always like people all that much."

His mouth quirks towards a smile as he asks, "Have you ever tried to get help?"

"Ike did lots of research, when I first started having them, but, you know..." she shrugs.

"No. I *don't* know."

"There's nothing that can be done."

Ferrin frowns. "What does that mean?"

"It means there's no cure. Nothing's going to make my panic attacks go away." She shrugs again, her fingers clutching the wool of her sweater in a death grip, her eyes focused firmly on the floor. "I'm pretty much stuck in here, because every time I go outside...well. It's not pretty. And that's the way it is."

She risks a glance at him, and scowls at the look on his face.

"Don't you dare pity me!" she snaps.

Ferrin sighs. "Sympathy and empathy don't automatically translate into pity, you know. Did you pity me earlier, when I was telling you about my family and Olivia?"

Her scowl deepened. "No, but don't ask what I was feeling for her, having to put up with you for all those years."

He laughs. "Well, I can't help but feel sorry for you, if you're unhappy. Are you sure there's no cure?"

"Yes."

Ferrin opens the door and pauses, his eyes thoughtful. "Well, you never know what the future holds, Lou.

Miracles happen every day." He smiles. "See you tomorrow."

That in itself is a bit of a miracle, she thinks, and closes the door behind him.

♠♥♣♦

"Ferrin still working out?" Ike asks, sounding distracted.

"Yeah, he's still working out," Lou says, her stomach tightening. She wonders why he's asking about Ferrin. He never asks about Ferrin.

"Good, good. The yard looked in great shape when I was there."

"He's very conscientious," Lou murmurs. "Never misses a day."

"I think he's been hearing the stories about you around town," he says, still distracted. "Mind you, how could he avoid them? It's Ledoux, after all, and if there's one thing the people there love more than that stupid football team, it's gossip. I'll have to warn him not to believe everything he hears, and he damn well better not let it influence him!"

For some reason, Ike's usual protectiveness sets her teeth on edge.

"Don't worry about it," she snaps, "I'll tell him myself."

Now his laugh is incredulous. "You? What are you going to do? Write him a stiffly worded note, and expect he'll listen to it? Really?"

Lou grits her teeth, because she realizes it's now or never. "You've been gone for months, Ike," she growls. "Despite what you think, it turns out even I need somebody to talk to every once in a while."

There's a sudden, tense silence on the other end of the phone.

"You've been *talking* to him?" he demands, his voice grating across her nerves.

"Yes."

"For how long?"

"A couple months or so."

"I could have...that long? What do you talk about?"

"Card games and movies, mostly. And TV shows."

"*Seriously?*"

"Yeah. He loves movies. I mean, he *really* loves movies. He's decided I need to watch the classics, and then the popular blockbusters. He's been introducing me to his favorite current TV shows, too, because the new seasons are about to start, and he wants me to understand what we're watching."

She can almost feel Ike's stunned shock through the phone. As he makes incoherent gobbling sounds, she bites back a nervous giggle as she pictures the expression that must be on his handsome face.

"What the hell are you watching on?" he finally manages.

"The TV."

"...you...bought...a *television?*"

"Yeah. Well, Ferrin bought it and I paid him for it out of the petty cash that's accumulated over the years, which was a surprisingly large amount; who knew? It was a struggle to convince him to take it, too, let me tell you."

"For God's sake, Lou! I haven't been gone that long! How come you never got a TV while I was there?"

"You never asked me."

"You never wanted one!"

"My *mother* never wanted one! I just never thought about it! I thought you'd be happy for me, Ike."

"Oh, sure! Of course! He's a fucking homeless drifter who was living out of his car when I hired him! And you want me to be happy that *this* is the asshole you finally decide to get friendly with?"

She heaves an exasperated sigh. "I'm not sleeping with him, Ike, and I haven't handed over access to my bank accounts, if that's what you're worried about!"

"Of course I'm worried about that! I'm also worried about you! He could murder you in that house, steal all your money, and who would know?"

"Well, you should have thought of that before you hired him!"

"For fuck's *sake*, Lou!"

She pinches the bridge of her nose and sighs again. "Seriously, Ike. I thought you'd be happy for me."

"*Really?*"

"At least be happy I got a TV!"

"Oh, I'm sorry! Of course that makes me happy! Welcome to the twentieth century, Lou, you got a TV!"

"And a BluRay player. All the cords are annoying, though."

"The next thing I know, you'll be getting a computer!"

"Ferrin has suggested it."

"If Ferrin suggests you jump off a cliff, are you going to do it?"

"Don't be silly. Where would I find a cliff in Saskatchewan?"

Ike is silent, then says, "What's going on with you, Lou?"

Lou sighs. "Nothing, Ike. Don't worry about me."

"You're letting a stranger in the house, and you tell me not to worry about you? Honest to God, Lou! If Ferrin's just trying to take advantage of you, I'll never forgive myself."

Lou laughs. "Take advantage of me? What century are we in again?"

"Well, you're only in the twentieth one, so you better listen to me."

She softens at the concern in his voice. "I always listen to you, Ike. You know that."

"See that you *only* listen to me. You know I'm the only one who looks out for you, Lou. You know I'm the only one you can trust."

Lou opens her mouth, then closes it. "I know," she

mutters.

"Good. Now, listen. I'm going to dig into Ferrin's background, see who—"

"*No!*"

Ike sighs. "Lou, come on—"

"No! I do not want you digging into his background, Ike. Contrary to what you seem to believe, I'm a recluse, not stupid! I like him; he makes me laugh, even if his taste in movies is sometimes spectacularly atrocious. That means I don't want you trying to scare me off, or worse: scaring him off! You're in Vancouver, and he's the only contact I have with the outside world. I'd like to keep him, if you don't mind."

"I'm only trying to protect you," Ike says, his voice sullen.

"Then you should have stayed *here!* You should have stayed with me. You should have chosen me and not Irish!"

There's a long, uncomfortable silence until Lou sighs, and says, more gently now, "You've been my only friend for most of my life, Ike. I'll always love you and trust you above anyone else. But you decided you needed to live your own life without me. You can't be upset if I decide to live my own life without you."

"Lou—"

"For God's sake, we're only watching movies!"

"Okay! Okay, fine. There's not much I can do about it from here, anyway."

"Exactly."

"But if you start thinking anything's off with him— anything at all—you tell me! You got that?"

"Yeah, I've got it."

♠♥♣♦

"Well, I'd better get going," Ferrin says to Lou a few days later, smacking his lips in appreciation after he swallows the last of his beer. "I need to get home and shower before heading over to Tessa's for Thanksgiving dinner."

He gets to his feet, a lopsided grin on his face. She stands more slowly and follows him to the door. She tugs her sweater closed and her mouth turns down at the corners as she watches him pull on his shoes and shrug into his coat. He notices her expression and raises an eyebrow in question.

She searches for something to say and settles for, "Well, I'm sure you'll have a very good time with this—this—what's her name again?"

Ferrin frowns. "I've told you about Tessa before—many times, as a matter of fact." He stares before his mouth turns up in a knowing smirk. "Are you jealous?" he asks, his blue eyes sparkling with almost unholy glee.

"What? No!"

"You are!" He chortles even as his expression softens. "You know, I can be friends with other people, and it doesn't impact my friendship with you."

Lou fidgets. "I have nothing to offer that will keep your friendship," she mutters, her eyes on her fingers twisting nervously in the wool of her sweater.

He frowns. "I'm not sure what you mean."

"I have nothing to talk about. I don't leave the house, I don't *do* anything! I'm about as much fun as—as—as a pet rock!"

Ferrin sputters with laughter. "Millions of people wanted pet rocks, though, so you're very sought after." He puts warm hands on her shoulders and looks into her eyes. "Don't worry. Pet rocks don't play cards, or drink beer, or enjoy horrible movies if the male eye candy is hot enough."

"Oh, shut up," she mutters, but a reluctant smile tugs at her mouth.

"Trust me, you're intriguing enough, and Tessa's just a friend, not a romance."

Now it's her turn to raise an eyebrow.

"No?" she asks skeptically.

"No. Not because she isn't hot as hell. Nice. Funny. Adorably cute, although she'd probably bop me between the eyes if I ever told her that."

"She sounds perfect," Lou says wistfully .

"But there's no spark, you know. On either side."

Lou flushes and takes a small step away. His hands slide away from her shoulders.

"How would I know that?" she snaps and tries to hide her shiver. "And how would you know, anyway? About the spark on her side?"

Ferrin shrugs. "Because when she invited me over for supper, she leaned very close to me, like this..." and he leans in until his lips are hovering above her ear, "and then," he murmurs, his voice low and rumbling, vibrating against her nerve endings as his lips brush her skin with the lightest of touches, "she said, 'Ferrin, you remind me of my brother'."

It takes a moment for his words to penetrate the fog that's taken over Lou's mind. She leans away and looks up at him.

"Hurt your ego?"

"You have no idea," he grumbles. "Then again, it's a relief, because while I'm fond of Tessa, I have no romantic interest in her at all."

"Even though she's—what did you say? Hot as hell, funny and adorably cute?"

Ferrin grins as he reaches out and gently tugs on a lock of her hair that has escaped the messy bun piled on top of her head.

"Yep," he says. "Anyway, gotta go. See you tomorrow."

"See you tomorrow," she says and shuts the door behind him.

Lou starts violently and gives a small shriek when the doorbell rings shortly before five the following afternoon. Then she freezes, her heart hammering in her chest, suddenly on full alert, caught between fight and flight. It won't be Ferrin, she thinks, her mind starting to whirl. Even on his days off, he doesn't arrive this early, at least not without warning her. It can't be Ike; he's in Vancouver. God knows there's no one else, although there's a slim chance Ike's decided to make an emergency trip to Ledoux in order to convince her to get rid of Ferrin. To her surprise, that thought only annoys her.

She pulls in a deep, calming breath, tells herself she'll never know if she doesn't look, and tiptoes to the door. She cautiously peeks out one of the side windows and catches a glimpse of a blonde woman standing on her porch. Lou frowns, wondering who on earth it could be, and decides it must be a stranger in town doing some kind of survey or trying to sell something.

She grimaces. There are days she's glad she doesn't open her door to just anybody.

The doorbell rings again, follows by loud knocking, and the woman shouts, "I know you're in there! Besides the fact you never leave the house, I saw the curtain move just now!"

Lou scowls, clutching her sweater close around herself, her fingers flexing against the wool.

The doorbell peals again followed by the woman once more knocking on the door.

"I'm not going away, you know!" she calls. "I'm just as stubborn as Ferrin is, or you are, come to think of it!"

Lou's scowl deepens at the mention of Ferrin's name. Who is this woman, she thinks with growing irritation.

The doorbell rings again and Lou growls as she flings open the door and glares.

The woman starts and takes half a step back, blinking before she rallies to give her a wide, sunny smile. She's holding a square pastry box in her hands.

"Hi! I'm Tessa!"

Lou doesn't deign to respond as she tries to level the irritating woman with the most unwelcoming expression she can muster.

Tessa's friendly smile doesn't change, her brown eyes wide and guileless. "I hope you don't mind me dropping by. Ferrin said you might be interested in having a bit more human contact."

"*Ferrin* said?" Lou yelps, startled into speaking in spite of herself. "He has no right—!"

"Oh, don't blame him, I nagged at him until he told me what I wanted to hear just to shut me up! I have to say I'm relieved to see you actually exist. I was beginning to think you were a figment of the town's collective imagination, although I have to admit, Willis isn't exactly what I would call overly imaginative, but on the other hand, Juan looks like he could dream up a whole bunch of intriguing things. Delaney is one lucky woman. Anyway, I thought it might be a good idea to see you with my own eyes, especially after Ferrin was all 'Lou-this' and 'Lou-that' last night. I mean, he leaves me cold, sexually speaking, but it's still tough on a girl's ego to slave over a hot, well, phone, actually, but still, slaving away, waiting for the food to arrive, only to have your guest talk so much about another woman! Not that I'm jealous, of course, but curiosity is a horrible itch, and sometimes, you know, you just have to scratch it! Wow! That sounded way worse than I intended!"

Tessa's words tumble to a halt, and she stops and grins, her pretty face glowing.

The silence stretches on and Lou slowly becomes aware her mouth is hanging open. She gently closes it, still bewildered by the barrage of words, and wonders if this is what it feels like to be in the path of stampeding cattle. No, not cattle, she thinks, bemused, this pretty blonde woman doesn't appear to be nearly that destructive. A stampede of squirrels or gophers or something equally small and cute and utterly relentless...she gives herself a mental shake, but she still can't think of a single thing to say in response.

"Well, at least you haven't slammed the door in my face," Tessa says cheerfully. "Are you able to sit out on the porch with me? I know you don't leave the house, but the porch is part of the house, isn't it? So that should be okay, right?"

Lou shuffles her feet, clutches her sweater, and says, grudgingly, "You can come in...if you want."

Unbelievably, Tessa's grin gets brighter, almost blinding her. As Lou steps aside and lets Tessa brush past her, she wonders what the hell she's thinking to let yet another stranger into her house—a woman, no less! The last time she spoke with a woman—

She closes the door with a sudden snap as she realizes that the last woman she talked to had been her mother, and that had been at least two days before that poor woman died. The sudden pain at the memory of her mother is so sharp she needs to lean her forehead against the door for a moment to recover. She takes a deep breath and turns to find Tessa gaping as she cranes her neck to look around the foyer, her wide eyes bright and curious.

"This place is amazing!" she says.

Lou snorts. "Amazingly dirty? Crowded? Cluttered?"

Tessa shrugs. "Well, sure, it could use a good de-cluttering, not to mention a dusting, and probably a good floor scrubbing or two, but all of this stuff looks fascinating. I'll bet everything in here has an interesting story!"

"Define 'interesting'," Lou says drily before reluctantly leading the way into the living room.

Tessa laughs. "You'd be surprised. Anyway, that's not why I'm here."

"Why *are* you here?" Lou sighs, turning to face her unexpected—and unwelcome—visitor. She tugs at her sweater, tapping one impatient foot as she once again intensifies her glare.

"I thought you could use a female friend."

Lou's mouth falls open again. "What the hell did Ferrin tell you last night?"

Tessa waves away Lou's question and drops down into Ike's Chair before Lou can stop her. Lou stands frozen at this blatant violation of the sanctity of Ike's Chair—even Ferrin quickly learned it's off-limits—as Tessa places the pastry box on the coffee table with an air of satisfaction.

"It's what he didn't say that convinced me," Tessa says. "Honestly, Lou, when's the last time you shared girl talk? And how much fun could that Tarzan movie have been, watching it with a straight guy? Seriously, it's tough to admire the ass on the actor in front of you while trying not to offend the guy beside you. Believe me, I know! Which isn't to say I don't also watch a movie for plot and dialogue and characterization and all that shit, but, sometimes, you know, you just need to be vocal in your appreciation, right? Of course, I suppose that means I'm a sexist pig, or piglet, or, no, sow, that's a female pig, right? But, you know, I'm okay with that and I don't mind if my straight guy friends get together and make admiring comments about an actress in front of me, or even if it's one straight guy and he's just telling me what he's admiring on the actress in a movie so long as he's not really crude, if you know what I mean. Although, I have to admit, I don't usually talk about separate body parts...except for the ass. I do love it when a guy has a gorgeous ass."

Lou slowly, gingerly, lowers herself onto the couch feeling overwhelmed by the stream of words—possibly more words than she's heard in the last year. Possibly five. She finds herself just sitting and watching Tessa with almost morbid fascination.

"But enough about all that," Tessa says.

Lou opens her mouth then decides trying to decipher what 'all that' is referring to is just going to be a quick trip to Crazy Town and closes her mouth again without saying anything.

Tessa flips open the pastry box, and the scent of cinnamon and brown sugar wafts through the room. Lou's nose twitches. Finally something about this entire situation is making sense, she thinks as her mouth waters.

Tessa chatters on. "I brought cinnamon buns with cream cheese icing—which I hope you like! If you don't, just let me know what you do like, and I'll bring that next time. And not only desserts, either! When's the last time you ate something you didn't make yourself? Or that's not out of a can or a box or something else equally boring? Which isn't a bad thing, of course, even eating out of a can or a box, but when you cook for yourself all the time, don't you sometimes crave food that's been made by somebody else? At least I do! Seriously, when's the last time you had a pizza? Delivered from a pizza place and not made from frozen, I mean. Hey! I could come and make you supper, and we could invite Ferrin, and maybe, once you're ready and if you ever want, we could invite a few other people, like Juan and Delaney, maybe, and their hellspawn, although they—the hellspawn, I mean—will find lots of things to take apart in here!"

Lou's sure her eyes are now as glazed as the cinnamon buns.

Tessa takes in her expression, and grimaces. "Sorry. When my mouth gets going, it's hard to stop sometimes, especially when I'm nervous."

Lou's slowly blinks, then shrugs.

"It's okay," she mutters. "I'll pass on the supper party, though."

Tessa nods. "Okay. Sorry." She frowns at the cinnamon buns, then gives Lou a rather forlorn look. "Do you want one?" she asks, and gestures helplessly at the open box.

Lou's nose twitches again at the delicious scent. She can't remember the last time she had a cinnamon bun. She can't even remember the last time she'd *thought* about having a cinnamon bun. She licks her lips and swallows.

"Let me get some plates."

She's everything Ferrin said, Lou thinks as she closes the door on Tessa's cheery wave almost an hour later, except he failed to do justice to just how much she's a force of nature. Standing against her is like standing against a hurricane.

Not that Lou has ever stood against a hurricane, of course, or even a stiff breeze in the last five years, but still, she has vague memories of being outside during a prairie storm and just how difficult it can be walk against the wind or even stand still, and really—

She stops her thoughts and shakes her head. Now she's thinking the way Tessa speaks, she thinks, and drops with a sigh on to the couch.

The doorbell rings and she groans.

Ferrin.

She pads to the door and opens it to see his broad, handsome, and very confused face.

"Lou?"

"Yeah?"

He takes a cautious step inside. "Did I just see Tessa leave the house?"

"You did."

He sidles towards the living room, wary eyes never leaving hers. "What? I mean, how?"

"The usual way, I think. You know, through the door. She brought cinnamon buns, by the way. There's one left for you."

He edges further inside, pausing on the threshold to the living room where he stares wordlessly at the pastry box resting innocently on the coffee table in front of Ike's Chair, a lone cinnamon bun nestled inside.

"Ummm...thanks?"

"Don't thank me; it was her idea."

Ferrin perches on the edge of Ike's Chair and she barely registers it. Tessa, it seems, has definitely broken the mental block she's had about *that*.

"Are you okay?" he asks.

"I'm fine."

"Are you angry? I mean, this wasn't my idea, if that's what you're thinking!"

"I know. Tessa was very clear it was all her idea, although she was inspired by whatever you told her last night."

Ferrin's entire demeanor is tense as he watches her.

Lou says, "She says she'll be back in a few days to visit." She frowns in puzzlement as she lowers herself to the couch.

Ferrin leans forward. "Do you want me to tell her to stay away?" he asks, his eyes and face very serious. "As much as I pushed my way in here, I don't want you to do anything that makes you uncomfortable or unhappy."

"Too late."

Ferrin flinches.

"Oh, don't look so guilty," Lou says, waving a hand, "I could have ignored you, you know. It's not like I haven't had years of practice. It's okay. *I'm* okay. Tessa is...interesting."

Ferrin flashes her a slight smile. "That's pretty lukewarm praise."

"She's everything you said: nice, funny, adorably cute. She's also exhausting! I haven't heard that many words in that short a time in years...or ever, come to think of it..."

"I know exactly what you mean."

"...I like her."

"What's that?"

"I said, I like her! Okay? I like her!"

Ferrin grins. "You've never even admitted you like me!"

She shoots him a dark, fulminating look. "That's

159

because I don't. You want your cinnamon bun now?"

"How about once I've finish the chores?"

"You're asking me to demonstrate some remarkable self-control, then."

Ferrin stands and towers over her with an insufferably smug, purely masculine smirk on his face. "You do that every second you're around me, and don't think I don't know it!"

She rolls her eyes, heat rushing to her cheeks. "Oh, for—get to work," she growls.

Life quickly falls into a new routine although, looking back, Lou is never quite sure how or when it happens. Ferrin is there every day and Tessa drops by several times a week, and somehow, without her even realizing it, sometimes they're both there *at the same time*...and it seems *normal*.

She hasn't been in the same room with more than one other person since her mother died.

She's sometimes amused, sometimes grateful, sometimes warmed by their company, and always confused, and on the bad days, she hears Ike's voice in her head, warning her they're up to something and the only one she can trust is him. He is, after all, the only one in town who didn't desert them during her mother's long illness, and he's been caring for her and her mother in one way or another for close to ten years.

But she finds Ike's voice is slowly being drowned out by the sheer force of Tessa and Ferrin's personalities, which makes her feel guilty that she seems to be replacing him, but she's also happy she doesn't feel quite so alone anymore, which only makes her feel even more guilty...and the circular thinking goes on and on.

Not that she has much time, really, to dwell on it, or to wonder what Ike is doing, or to long for him to come back to Ledoux. While she still has her days to herself—both Tessa and Ferrin have jobs, after all—she spends her time cleaning and de-cluttering her living room and kitchen with Ferrin bringing her an endless supply of plastic bins to use for storage. She finds herself wondering what the hell is in all the boxes that are crammed in every room, attic and basement of her house, and begins to think she needs to start going through everything and maybe get rid of a few things. She's the last Upjohn, the last of the town's founding family, and she doesn't like thinking about strangers coming in after she's gone and simply throwing everything away.

Her evenings and weekends are suddenly, surprisingly full, because Ferrin or Tessa or both always has some plan for something to do when they arrive. Lou finds herself learning new card games and board games and watching television shows and movies she never would have considered watching on her own and laughing more than she thought she'd ever laugh with someone who wasn't Ike.

Ah, Ike.

She's strangely reluctant to share anything when he calls and asks, more and more often and with growing suspicion, how things are going. She gives him vague responses about Ferrin and purposefully doesn't mention Tessa. That bombshell, she decides, will be best dropped face-to-face when he's back at Christmas, and in the meantime, she wants to enjoy her new-found social life without a lot of arguments, no matter how well-meaning.

It's obvious Ike is worried, though, because he calls more often, at random times of the day. He asks more questions, and pays close attention to her responses, pouncing on anything that even remotely sounds like she's trying to be evasive. If she'd known he'd react this way, she thinks ruefully after one particularly taxing conversation, she would have expanded her pool of friends years ago. If she had, maybe Ike would be living with her now instead of Irish.

At least she's finally gotten used to Ike being married to another woman. She even feels genuinely happy for him when, during their last phone call, he talks about their plans to go to the Cayman Islands after Christmas.

She is, she admits to herself with some surprise, content.

Ferrin, to his bemusement and his family's continuing shock and suspicion, finds himself fitting comfortably into small town life. True, there are those who are suspicious and cool towards him, but it isn't like he didn't experience that same attitude in Toronto, and often from his own damn family.

It helps, of course, that in addition to his strong friendships with Tessa, and Juan, Delaney and their hellspawn, Willis has also taken him firmly under his wing. A lifelong resident and the town's vet, Willis is both well-liked and somewhat feared by everyone for miles around. His approval opens almost as many doors as Abram's, albeit on a much different scale.

Of course, it also helps that Ferrin is an affable guy in his own right, and a lifetime spent persuading tightfisted millionaires to donate money to a multitude of charitable causes, not to mention being the only diplomatic Macon-Jones in the entire history of the family, means he can find common ground with practically anybody.

His friendship with Lou—news of which had spread through town at something approaching the speed of light—also opens a surprisingly large number of doors. He's beginning to understand just how much the Upjohn name is respected in the community, and how much the people of Ledoux care about Lou and her family.

It makes Lou's self-imposed isolation all the more heartbreaking.

The one flaw in his otherwise perfectly enjoyable existence is his continued refusal to tell anyone in Ledoux his true identity. He feels vaguely guilty that everyone still treats him as the down-at-the-heels drifter he appeared to be when he arrived but that doesn't stop him from maintaining the illusion by banking in Ledoux as Ferrin Jones, going to Regina if he needs more cash than he makes working for Juan and Lou, and, of course, buying his house through one of his corporations. It was both safer than risking the real estate agent sharing his real name with the world, or at least the town, and it was also a way to give the previous owner—an elderly woman moving to Edmonton to be closer to her children—more money than she might have received otherwise.

Preserving his Jones' persona is also the reason he had Pierce use a different corporation to buy the building where The Row is located, although that one was also for investment purposes. Renovations and improvements are being planned and Tessa's rent has already been lowered, news of which rendered her silent for the first time since he met her.

The reason he maintains the deception, though, is really quite simple: he *likes* being just plain Ferrin Jones.

He *likes* the simpler, more pragmatic life he's living. It's somehow refreshing to listen to the regulars at The Row talk about cattle and crops and the Roughriders, about politicians, the weather, and the Roughriders, about children and grandchildren, neighbours and friends, illnesses and hardships and hopes and dreams and...the Roughriders.

He finds the phlegmatic practicality of the conversations and the speakers strangely soothing, and it all, somehow, some way, makes him feel grounded, makes him feel connected with the real, the tangible, and the here-and-now. It's strikingly different from the never-ending discussions of fourth-quarter earnings and corporate culture and whether this or that proposed policy will have an impact on the bottom line. He likes being two minutes—five, if he walks—from anywhere in town. His new house is on the outskirts, looking out over a neighbouring field, and he loves the endless expanse of land and horizon and sky that's just outside his door. He loves how he feels when he stands in his yard and allows the prairie landscape to press in on him. He loves how it makes him feel small and insignificant and very, very human.

When his family questions him, he doesn't know how to explain that he *likes* the life he's creating and everything about it. He likes working with his hands, and Willis' snark, Juan's confidence and Delaney's warmth, Tessa's babbling, and Lou's—well, *everything,* from her constant scowl to her dry wit to her rare moments of vulnerability and her even rarer moments of laughter and smiles, from her gorgeously dark eyes to her messy hair to that shit-brown sweater she never takes off. He even likes her far-too-pale skin and the fact she looks like a plump little shit-brown dumpling when she curls up inside that ugly fucking sweater and clings to it, her fingers kneading the wool like a particularly nervous cat trying to calm itself.

Hanging over everything, though, is the knowledge that sooner or later, no matter how much he enjoys his current life, he's going to have to tell everyone his real name, and he will eventually need to return to his role as a member of the Macon-Jones dynasty. Not that there aren't a lot of perks to being disgustingly wealthy, he thinks, and he's looking forward to being back in Toronto at the end of January. He misses his cousins and stepmother, and he always helps Gillian and the others with the final run-up to the Macon-Jones' annual charity bash in February. Gillian's also wrung a promise out of him to return to Toronto in September for the grand opening of the one-thousandth Macon-Jones store while Carson, Dyson and Jack are making noises about taking him to the Dominican in April to thank him for the car he finally got out of the ditch. He knows they're hoping to get him into another drunken stupor so he'll sign away his vote for another three years, or at least give them some new pictures they can use as blackmail.

He shakes his head with a fond chuckle. Those three will be holy terrors once Jack becomes Chair of the Board, and Carson and Dyson become Vice-Presidents of their respective divisions. The thought almost makes him want to join the company while simultaneously wanting to run as fast and as far away as possible.

The thought of Jack's eventual ascension to Abram's throne just brings it home to him, though, that he's the odd one out in his family, both by choice and by inclination. His private holdings are successful enough, investments in a variety of projects or people he believes in, and the return on his investments is sometimes huge, sometimes in the hole, and sometimes worth more than mere money, and that is the part of being a Macon-Jones that he loves and enjoys, just like he loves and enjoys all his cousins...even Abram, although he'll never admit it. But he has no desire to be a part of Macon-Jones Enterprises. That had been his brother's ambition, never his.

Which all means his uncomplicated life as Ferrin Jones won't—*can't*—last forever, and he flinches away from thinking too deeply about how Lou—how *everyone*—will react when they learn the truth. But those worries will have to wait until tomorrow, because he has other plans for tonight.

He walks up to Willis' front door, rings the doorbell and walks in to the chaos of Saskatchewan Roughrider fans getting ready to go to Regina to watch their team play in the Grey Cup. As he greeted with loud shouts of welcome, he feels like he's found himself a home.

Ferrin struggles to open eyes that seem glued shut.

He finally manages to lift his lids to allow a sliver of light inside and gazes without recognition at the blurred ceiling above him.

He lets his eyes drift closed again, a frown slowly forming on his face. He smacks his lips, wondering when and how they'd gotten so dry, who put the fuzzy socks on his teeth, and which band is using his head as a drum. He hopes it's one he likes. He shifts slightly, and teeters on the edge of the—he sluggishly scrambles for purchase before unceremoniously tumbling to the floor—couch.

"Awake, are we?"

He cracks one eye open and sees, wavering…

"*Lou?*"

"Wow, is that supposed to be my name? I didn't know you could slur a one-syllable word quite that much."

"Wherm?"

Through his blurry vision, he sees something move on her forehead. He hopes it's an eyebrow.

"Well, if you're seeing me then you're either hallucinating or at my place. Do you need me to help you get back on the couch, or do you want to sleep it off on the floor?"

"Flrm," he groans, and closes his eyes.

The next time he regains consciousness, he finds himself on his side, staring at the flowery brocade of a couch skirt, and is, if anything, even more, confused. With a low groan, he carefully rolls onto his back, and blinks at the ceiling. He slowly becomes aware that his bladder is about to explode, and debates whether he should get to his feet or crawl his way to a bathroom…which he'll find once he remembers where he is.

The horrifying realization that he isn't alone creeps over him, and he turns his head to see Lou curled up on the other couch, wrapped in that infernal brown sweater, placidly reading a book.

"Finally awake?" she asks without looking up.

"...think so," he manages.

She glances at him. "Water?"

He shoots her a grateful look as he drags himself to his feet. "God, yes."

She nods, and marks her place in her book as she stands, much more gracefully than he manages to do.

"There's a toothbrush in the medicine cabinet that's never been used," she says as she heads to the kitchen. "New toothpaste, too."

He shoots her another grateful look, and only bounces once off the boxes lining the hallway to the bathroom.

He feels significantly more human when he returns to the living room.

"Bless you, my child," he breathes when he sees the pitcher of ice water and a glass on the coffee table along with a bottle of over-the-counter painkillers.

"Only bless me if you can keep it down. Drink it slow."

He splashes some water into the glass with a shaking hand then presses it thankfully against his forehead before carefully sipping the water, which seems to be absorbed directly through the parched skin of his mouth because he can't remember swallowing any of it. Finally, when his immediate thirst is quenched, he looks at her, eyes narrowed in suspicious thought, and says, "How did I get here?"

"Tessa and Willis-that-bastard poured you on to my porch early this morning, rang the doorbell then ran before I could get the door open. Well, Willis-that-bastard ran, as much as he could run, so Tessa tells me. You managed to stagger inside all on your own, and Tessa, at least, apologized before she left, laughing so hard she could barely walk."

He frowns. "Why *here*?"

"Revenge, I think."

"Revenge? For what?"

"Well, when you arrived, you were singing a very, uh,

167

lovely rendition of...well, I couldn't really tell what song you were singing, only that you were singing very loudly, and possibly even managing to hit one or two correct notes."

He groans, and rests his aching head in his hands.

"What do you remember?" Lou asks.

"Everything...up until..." he frowns. "We won the game, right?"

"How would I know? Do I watch football?"

"Good point. Well, there was the pre-trip party at Willis', the drive to Regina on the chartered bus, the tailgate parties, the game...we did win, I'm sure of it, because I remember being in the middle of a cheering crowd somewhere, then an after-party, and..." he frowns. "That's...when it goes completely blank, rather than just a little foggy."

He glances at Lou, who, he's surprised to see, is failing miserably at maintaining her usual stern and scowling facade.

"What do you know?" he asks, suspicious.

"Tessa said to make sure you saw this," she says, and picks up a tablet from the end table beside her.

His eyes widen. "Oh, no."

"Oh, yes. Apparently, it was worth capturing the moment."

He buries his face in his hands as Lou settles beside him on the couch.

"Okay, Tessa showed me how to do this," she mutters as she finds the video and gets it to play.

Ferrin groans, and peeks at the screen through his fingers as the sounds of screaming and cheering people suddenly blasts through the calm of Lou's living room. He blinks, and leans closer.

"Is that...?"

"A watermelon. Yes." Lou slowly tilts her head to one side as the video continues to play. "Although I believe you're supposed to wear it on your *head.*"

He buries his face in his hands again as she finally gives

up the struggle and begins to laugh.

As November rolls into December, and December begins barrelling towards Christmas, Lou finds herself in an unfamiliar dilemma. Both Tessa and Ferrin are being invited to parties, and are therefore not visiting her quite as often—but that isn't her dilemma; that is, after all, only to be expected, given the time of year. Hell, the last two years before he left, Ike had taken December as a holiday from running her errands, and they stopped exchanging presents not long after their sexual relationship faded away.

No, her dilemma is suddenly having friends—and just using that word still makes her twitch—and not just friends, but friends who 'do' Christmas. The Row has been decorated to within an inch of its life, so she's been told, and Tessa has a seemingly never-ending supply of Christmas-themed sweaters, pants, skirts, boots, socks, thingamabobs and doohickies, and she adorns herself with them with both aplomb and enthusiasm. Lou suspects Tessa's ideal Christmas present would be the news the season had been extended for another month.

Ferrin, on the other hand, is a bit tougher to read, but he at least goes through the motions, and he certainly seems to enjoy the parties.

Which doesn't change the fact that for the first time in years she has to think about Christmas presents.

For two people.

One of whom Ike still knows nothing about.

Well, Ike is back in town next week; she'll break the news to him then.

And send him Christmas shopping.

Lou fidgets beneath the silent weight of Ike's cold, accusing eyes. She wraps her sweater around herself, fingers gripping the thick wool strands so tightly she knows, if she looks, her knuckles will be bleached white. Still, she holds Ike's flat, unblinking stare steadily enough.

"How long has this been going on?" he finally says, his voice dangerously soft and measured, a sign that he's only holding on to his temper with his fingernails.

Lou shrugs. "Since Thanksgiving."

"*Thanksgiving?*"

"The day after, if you really want me to be precise."

"And you're just deciding to tell me about this *now*?"

Her fingers flex. "Obviously." She winces at her own sarcasm.

His eyes never waver from hers as he leans forward, elbows on his knees, hands loosely clasped in front of him.

"What's happening to us, Lou?" he asks softly, mournfully, his voice a familiar, soothing rumble, even though his eyes remain icy. "You used to tell me everything."

Lou's overwhelmed with a sudden, intense onslaught of memories and the love she's always felt for him: trailing after him and his friends, dust puffing up around their bare feet as they ran through the fields on the edge of town. Exploring the old abandoned hospital, and the hell they caught from their parents for it. The few times they danced together at school dances and local weddings and anniversaries. Later memories, after she came back from those few short years in Saskatoon because her mother was dying, and the way he took care of them when his father refused to do so any longer. Ike stepped in to pay their bills, making sure they had groceries, and the yard was clean, all while she was so desperately focused on her mother, willing her to live while struggling to control and hide her building anger as the people she'd thought were friends abandoned them.

And later still, making love and trying to make him

happy even as she mourned her mother. His dismay and confusion when she told him she couldn't leave the house, his aching sorrow when he broke the news there was no help for her, that she'd never be able to leave the house again.

She loved him through all of it. Even his gradual drift away and his subsequent relationship with Irish couldn't dim her feelings for him.

Yes, she thinks, she used to tell him everything, but then, he'd once been everything to her.

Still is, she hastily tells herself, even if he's married to another woman and living two thousand kilometres away. Guilt floods through her.

"I'm sorry," she mutters. "I should have told you about Tessa right away."

He softens, giving her a fond smile. "Well, you've told me now, about both of them. Don't worry, I'll take care of it."

"Take care of what?" she asks, confused. She hasn't even gotten to the Christmas shopping part of the conversation.

"Look, you and I both know you're not a people person. Even before the agoraphobia, you weren't exactly an outgoing kind of girl."

Lou frowns. She'd certainly been outgoing enough when she'd been at university. She'd had friends and even here in Ledoux, she'd gone to parties with her mother and enjoyed herself.

"I don't know—"

"You like being alone! Well, not all the time." He chuckles softly, intimately. He gives her a warm smile, loaded with memories.

Lou flushes, fidgeting uncomfortably beneath that look.

He says, in the same seductive tone, "I remember you telling me so many times that I was the only one you cared about. The only one you needed."

"Tha—"

"Anyway, I'm sorry, too," he says, and she closes her mouth with a snap, pushing down her annoyance. She tells herself he probably hadn't heard her start to speak, and besides, she did spring the news about Tessa on him without any warning.

He sits back in his chair and gives her a benevolent smile. "I'm sorry I got you into this mess in the first place. I didn't realize Ferrin would make such a push to get close to you and bring his girlfriend into it, too. I suppose I shouldn't be surprised, considering how desperate he is for money. I have to say, though, Tessa surprises me, but if she's in love with him, well, she'll do whatever he wants her to do."

She frowns. "What?"

Ike waves a hand, his smile becoming downright beneficent, making her grit her teeth. "Don't worry about it. I can't blame you for wanting to forget how everyone turned their backs on you and your mother, and give people a second chance. Besides, it's my own fault for leaving you alone and vulnerable, and in the care of a stranger. Well," he sighs, "what's done is done. I'll go over all your financials in the new year; make sure they haven't got into your accounts somehow." He nods and stands. "I'll go right now. You won't need to deal with them again."

She shoots to her feet.

"What the hell are you talking about?"

He pauses, eyes widening. "I just told you! I'm going to tell them we're on to them, and they're no longer welcome here."

"You most certainly will not!"

"Lou, we both know this is for the best..."

"No, I *don't* know! What I do know is that I don't want them to leave me alone, and I definitely don't want you to 'take care of it'! I think I'm old enough, and still sane enough, to know what I want!"

Ike laughs. "Oh, come on! Do you really think they

'befriended' you because they like you? At best, they feel sorry for you; at worst, they're going to rob you blind!"

She hisses in a sharp breath, and clutches her sweater.

"That is a shitty thing to say," she chokes out, "and it doesn't exactly make me want to listen to you! They've never asked for money or even anything about it! Why is it so hard to believe that maybe, just maybe, they like me? Why is that so impossible?"

Ike shifts uncomfortably, and he grimaces. "Come on, Lou, you know I didn't mean it like that," he mutters, and she feels a spurt of satisfaction that he realizes he might have gone too far.

"No?" she sniffs and lifts her chin. "I'm not sure what other 'meaning' there's supposed to be." She shakes her head as he opens his mouth. "No, just shut up and listen!"

He closes his mouth with a snap, a mutinous set to his jaw.

She steps closer and points a warning finger at him. "I'm telling you right now, Ike, I will not have you telling them to stay away from me. Have you got that? I *like* them! I like that they make me laugh and I like that they seem to enjoy spending time with me! You don't live here anymore, remember? And I'm only thirty! I am *not* going to spend the rest of my life locked up behind these walls, with my only contact with the outside world a guy who lives two thousand kilometres away and calls me once a week for fifteen minutes! These people, for whatever reason, want to be my friends. I'm going to grab this chance they're offering me with both hands, and if they end up hurting me, well...so be it. That's a price I'm willing to pay." She sniffs as she adjusts her sweater, her chin high. "Besides, it's not like it would be the first time."

Ike's eyes are big, sad pools of amber. "If I'd known moving to Vancouver was going to do this to us—"

"Oh, what? You'd have married me instead of Irish?" Lou barks out a harsh, cynical laugh.

"I'm trying to look out for you. I worry about you. I

care about you, you know that!"

This time she doesn't soften beneath the weight of his hurt-puppy eyes.

"Well, worry about it when I start asking you for large sums of money," she snaps. "For God's sake, you mean you wouldn't notice if I started spending more money than usual? What the hell am I paying you for?"

He glares but says nothing.

"Ferrin and Tessa want to be my friends," she says more quietly. "I won't have you doing anything to jeopardize that."

He silently considers her, then nods, and leaves without another word.

It isn't until the door slams behind him and she's slumped on the couch with her knees shaking and her rapid breath rasping in her throat, that she realizes she still hasn't figured out how to get her Christmas shopping done.

♠ ♥ ♣ ♦

Tessa leans on the bar that separates Ferrin's kitchen from his living room and grabs a handful of peanuts from the bowl in front of her. A smile spreads across her face as she watches him cook.

"Every time I see you in there, I wonder how you fit," she says.

He shoots her a mock-glare. "I'm not *that* big," he says.

"Yeah, keep telling yourself that, big boy," she says with a wink.

He gives her a stern look as he points at her with the wooden spoon he's using to stir the vegetables. "No flirting."

She sits up straight and widens her eyes. "Since when?"

"Since I have to keep my mind on my cooking. I don't

want to feed Juan, Delaney and their hellspawn burnt food. It's Christmas, after all!"

She laughs. "All right, I'll behave."

He grins his crooked grin, and she shakes her head, a suddenly sad look on her face.

"Why didn't we hook up, Ferrin?"

He blinks at her in surprise. "Did you want to?"

"Oh, God, no! No offense, but—ew."

He laughs. "None taken—and neither did I."

"But why? We're both reasonably attractive--"

"Speak for yourself! *I* am gorgeous!"

She throws a peanut at him, and he pouts as he rubs the spot where it bounced off his forehead.

"Fine," he growls, "you're gorgeous, too." He stirs the vegetables once more, then turns down the heat. He saunters to the bar and leans on it, eyes intent on hers. "What brought this on, anyway?"

Tessa shrugs. "I don't know. I was watching you be all domestic, and suddenly thought, 'there he is: tall, sorta dark, almost handsome, nice, and he frickin' cooks, too.' Face it, Ferrin, you're pretty much perfection on a stick."

He laughs. "Not according to my ex," he says, "but considering you thought I was a homeless drifter the first time you saw me, I guess I should be flattered."

She rests her chin on her hand. "You *were* a homeless drifter the first time I saw you—wearing nothing but a couple of horse blankets, remember?—and now look at you! 'Willing to get a job, buy real clothes, and work towards a better life'. See? Perfection. On a *stick*!" Her grin fades. "Seriously, Ferrin," she says, and there's no laughter in her voice now, "what on earth am I waiting for if I didn't even *think* about jumping your bones?"

He looks vaguely hurt. "Not even once?"

She shakes her head. "Sorry."

He sighs sorrowfully, and hangs his head, then looks up at her with a shrug. "I suspect you're waiting for somebody you do want to jump, that's all."

She thoughtfully munches a peanut, then says, "Okay. I can live with that." She sighs. "Have you been to Lou's place since Ike's been back?"

Ferrin shakes his head. "You?"

She shakes her head. "Her orders were pretty clear."

He takes a sip of his eggnog and raises an eyebrow as he takes in the pout on her face.

"What's going on in that rather frightening mind of yours?" he asks.

"I'm just thinking she's all alone. I mean, Ike's there to do odd jobs and to give her papers to sign and stuff, but he doesn't stay there. He doesn't play cards with her, or watch movies with her, or...anything, really. I'm a little worried she'll get used to being alone again by the time he finally buggers off back to Vancouver."

"Hm," Ferrin says, smirking, "that sounds familiar. Now you know how I felt. She was fine then, she'll be fine this time, too."

"He's here longer this time," Tessa says sourly, "and he knows about you. He'll work on her, just you watch."

Ferrin looks curiously at her. "You really dislike the guy, don't you?"

"Does it show?"

He lifts his hand with his thumb and forefinger held close together. "Just a bit."

She shakes her head and eats a peanut. "He reminds me of an ex of mine," she says, "the one I followed here to Ledoux, actually. Teddy. Smooth, charming, and a complete and utter asshole. That, and Ike hit on me while he knew I was with Teddy and expected me to just fall into bed with him." She takes a sip of her drink and shrugs. "Maybe I'm being too harsh on him. Ike, I mean. Projecting. You know."

"So, I take it you didn't want to jump his bones, either?"

Ferrin watches with interest as hot colour rises in her face.

"Oh, my God! You *did*!"

"Well, he's gorgeous," she mutters, "and I was still in my 'assholes are hot' stage."

"Yeah? When was that stage, exactly? Last year?"

Ferrin laughs as he dodges another peanut.

"Seriously, Ferrin, I just don't want all of Lou's progress these last few months to be for nothing, and the longer Ike's the only one she sees, the more likely that's going to happen!"

"So what are you suggesting?"

A devious gleam appears in her brown eyes. "A couple of things, actually. I think we should drop in on Lou tonight, and I think we should bring Juan, Delaney and their hellspawn with us."

His own eyes widen.

"Are you *insane*?" he breathes, horror dripping from every word. "She'll shoot us!"

Tessa cocks her head as she considers the idea. "I don't think she'd be able to find a gun all that quickly in that place; it's pretty packed in there. By the time she does, she'll have calmed down."

"You're assuming she doesn't have one close to hand!" He straightens, firmly shaking his head. "No. No, no, no! *Hell*, no. A thousand times no!"

Tessa grins, her round, pretty face lit with mischief. "Tell me what you really think, Ferrin."

He opens his mouth to do just that when the doorbell rings.

"Your delicate ears have been saved by the bell," he says severely as he strolls from the kitchen to open the door.

"It's too early for them," she says, spinning around to give the door an interested look. "Did you invite a date and didn't tell me? Or worse: you didn't tell Lou?"

His step falters for a fraction of a second before he rolls his eyes as he swings the door open. "Like the whole town wouldn't have known about it in five minutes," he says drily then stops short when he sees the man standing on his porch. "...Ike..."

Ike steps over the threshold and glances around the small house. He pauses for a moment as his gaze falls on Tessa, who raises her eggnog in salute.

"Hey, Ike."

"Good," he says coldly, "I'm glad I found both of you."

Ferrin raises an eyebrow as he closes the door, never taking his eyes off the other man. Ike thoughtfully assesses him, and Ferrin's eyebrow inches higher as he takes in his expression. A sudden hot shaft of fear slices through him.

"Is everything okay with Lou?" he asks, his voice sharp.

"No, everything is not okay with Lou," Ike snaps. "There's no other way to say this: you're fired. Don't go near her again, or I'll slap a restraining order on your ass so fast you won't know what hit you!" He slides his angry gaze over to Tessa. "Same goes for you, too."

Ferrin gapes, shaking his head. "Whoa, whoa, whoa— what the hell are you talking about? Why am I fired?"

"You know damn well!"

"No," Ferrin says firmly, "I don't. Now tell me what's happened!"

"She told me everything," Ike growls. "How you pressured her to let you into the house, how you're both constantly bothering her, eating her food, wasting her time, trying to force her to do things she doesn't want to do. I won't allow it!"

Ferrin gapes. "I—*what*? She told you that?"

"That, and more!" Ike snarls. He glares, his lip curling with contempt. "I know who you are," he sneers.

Ferrin wipes all expression from his face so he won't betray the fear slicing through his stomach. This is not the time to have his true identity revealed, although he does thank God that a lifetime rubbing shoulders with the Macon-Jones family has given him a good poker face when he needs it. Although, he thinks ruefully, *being* a Macon-Jones helps even more.

"Yeah?" Ferrin asks, his voice cool. "And who am I?"

"You're a fucking parasite! You've probably spent a lifetime cozying up to vulnerable women, then taking them for everything they've got. You must have thought you hit the motherlode when you saw Lou! At least this one is young!"

Ferrin goes weak with relief. He knows his friends in Ledoux won't be thrilled he's hidden his Macon-Jones connection from them, but being a rich bastard is still better than being a con man.

"You are out of her life," Ike snarls. "You won't call her. You won't go to her house. You won't even look in the general direction of her house! If I had my way, I'd have you run out of town on a rail tonight, but the cops won't do anything until they have evidence that an actual crime has been committed." He snorts with disgust. "I'm sure I'll find evidence soon enough when I start going through her financials with a fine-toothed comb."

Ferrin listens without moving, never taking his eyes off Ike. He's curious to see just how far this is going to go, although judging from Tessa's gasp, he knows Ike's bluster is doing its job on her. He hopes he looks appropriately intimidated even as he thinks Abram—not to mention any one of his other cousins—would crush this bully-boy before breakfast and forget about him before they even finished their eggs. He's putting in a good effort, Ferrin concedes, but he's nowhere near the level of a Macon-Jones. He has no...*finesse*.

Ike's eyes narrow as he continues speaking. "I'll be telling Juan to fire you, too, and I'll make sure you're blackballed everywhere in town. If you know what's good for you, you'll pack up whatever you've managed to accumulate these last few months and hit the road. If you leave tonight, I won't tell everyone in town what you've been doing and you can leave with some sort of reputation—such as it is—still intact." He shoots a contemptuous glance at Tessa. "You can go or stay, but either way, you don't ever go near Lou again, or I'll have you blackballed, too."

He turns and strides out the door.

Ferrin gives him extra points for his exit: the quiet click of the door closing behind him is far more ominous than any harsh slam could have been.

Ferrin turns his bemused stare to Tessa, who looks stunned, angry, hurt, and scared in equal measure.

"What the hell was *that* about?" she sputters, her eyes wide and bewildered.

"I don't know. But I know how we can find out."

"How?" she asks with a slight quiver in her lower lip.

His smile is slow and evil. "Let's find containers for all this food."

Lou starts as the doorbell peals, followed by heavy pounding on the door. She clutches her sweater and catches her breath. *Nobody* is supposed to be here tonight!

As she hurries to the door, all the potential disasters that might be waiting for her on the other side flash through her mind. Ike wouldn't have come back, and Ferrin and Tessa promised to stay away until Ike leaves again for Vancouver. That leaves the police, and that's never good news, but even she can't refuse to talk to them.

She puts her hand on the door's latch and quails. She takes two steps back then catches herself. She takes a deep breath, staunchly tells herself she can deal with whoever is on the other side of the door and whatever they have to say, and flings it open with panic licking at the corners of her self-control.

Her jaw is aching from gritting her teeth and she's so focused on preparing herself for disastrous news that it takes her a moment to realize she's staring at a familiar parka covering an equally familiar broad expanse of chest. She raises her eyes and stares at Ferrin's smirking face. She goes limp beneath a hot rush of relief and she grins before she catches herself and turns her grin into a fierce scowl.

"You scared me," she snaps as she steps aside to let him in, and her scowl only deepens as he's followed by Tessa, then a man and a woman she doesn't know, and—of all things—two nervous, wide-eyed children. She turns a dark, dangerous glare on Ferrin.

"You better have a good explanation for this," she growls.

"I do," he says smoothly, "but first, let me introduce Juan Martinez, his wife Delaney, and their children, Steebeth and Mateo."

Lou stares silently at them before she gives them a short nod as she tugs her sweater more tightly around herself and instinctively shrinks within it.

"Tessa," Ferrin says, and Lou's wariness grows when she hears the dangerous note in his voice and sees the sharp edge of his smile, "why don't you take the others to the kitchen? Once I've explained things to Lou, I'm sure she'll let us heat everything up and we can enjoy our supper."

"Supper?" Lou blinks, finally realizing that everyone is carrying a covered dish. She watches as the three adults and two children troop obediently in the direction of the kitchen. She blinks as Delaney rolls her eyes, and mutters, "Men!" as she passes Lou.

Once they're safely out of the room, Lou turns to Ferrin with fire in her eyes.

"Ike fired me tonight," Ferrin says cheerfully before she can speak. He stares at her with a patently false grin and equal fire in *his* eyes.

Her jaw drops. "*What?*"

"He said you told him we were taking advantage of you, forcing you to do things you don't want to do—like,

181

oh, talking with you in person. He told me to leave town tonight, and told Tessa to never come near you again. If we don't obey, he's going to go to the police to, I don't know, have us tarred and feathered and run out of town on a rail or something."

She closes her eyes with a groan and pinches the bridge of her nose. "...he just...he doesn't want me to get hurt," she mutters.

Ferrin takes a step closer. "*Are* we hurting you?" he demands. "Have I hurt you? Or Tessa?"

Lou gives him an exasperated glare. "Of course not! Do you honestly think I wouldn't tell you?"

Ferrin visibly relaxes at her words. "Well, to be fair to Ike, you did tell me to leave you alone."

She snorts. "And when I ordered you in no uncertain terms to stop coming to my door, you did. I invited you in, remember?"

He shifts, looking like a guilty little boy, and something softens inside her. She has an almost overwhelming desire to fling her arms around him and tell him everything will be all right.

"As far as I'm concerned, you're not fired," she says, abrupt as she firmly pushes the bizarre urge away. "That is, if you still want to work for me."

"Ike sounded pretty adamant that, yes, I was fired. And I had to leave town tonight."

She snorts. "What is this—the 1880s in the American west? Plus I think I can make my own decisions about who's working for me and who isn't." She glances at the kitchen door then back at him, her eyes wide with sudden alarm. "Is this a—a good-bye supper, then?"

Ferrin's grin returns, and this time it's coldly feral. "Hell, no. This is an ambush supper. It's time you widened your circle of friends again."

She scowls, her desire to comfort him gone as suddenly as it appeared. "That's not up to you!"

He ignores her. "And I'll be here tomorrow at my

usual time to play cards."

"*Tomorrow?* But—"

"Ike can kiss my ass," Ferrin says coldly. "I'll be here tomorrow and every day I can. Now, we have some hungry hellspawn, so we better get that food warmed up ASAP."

Lou grabs Ferrin's arm, tugging him back as he brushes past her towards the kitchen. His arm is surprisingly solid beneath her grip and they both freeze as they stare down at her hand then at each other. Lou realizes with a shock that this is the first time she's touched him since he fell off her porch and snatches her hand away as if he's burned her. He simply watches her, his eyes dark, his face stark with something she's too rattled to recognize and too terrified to even try to decipher.

She swallows, tugging at her sweater, and squeaks, "Hellspawn?"

He glances away and when he looks at her again, he seems lighter somehow, less dangerous.

"The kids," he says, his lips curving into his lop-sided smirk. "They're known for wreaking havoc wherever they go."

Her eyes widen, and he laughs.

"It's okay," he says, his voice a low husky rumble, "I think you can handle some havoc in your life."

She scoffs and says, "Oh? Because you haven't caused nearly enough?"

He raises an eyebrow and his smirk widens. "I have not yet even *begun* to cause you havoc!"

Her stomach swoops at the teasing gleam in his eyes and she takes a hasty step away, tugging at her sweater.

"Well...well, we better go see if my kitchen's still in one piece," she says, and is relieved her voice is only slightly breathless. She ducks her head and hurries away.

"I told you to leave Ferrin and Tessa alone."

Ike stumbles as he steps over the threshold but quickly rallies.

"I'm protecting you!"

"Well, stop it!"

"Lou, they're just taking advantage of you!"

"I think I can figure out if somebody's after me for my money, Ike!"

He barks a harsh laugh. "I seriously doubt that! Lou, listen to me—"

"No, *you* listen! I don't know why you're so suspicious and honestly, I don't care! I like Tessa! And I really like Ferrin, and I'm not going to let you run them off!"

Ike throws up his hands.

"Fine! Fine! It's your fucking life! And when it all falls apart—like it always does—you'll expect me to pick up all your pieces, like you always do!"

She hisses in a hurt breath.

He point a finger at her and says, "I'm warning you right now, Lou: if you insist on ignoring my advice, I'm not fixing things for you this time!"

She pulls her sweater close, a mutinous set to her chin. "Fine."

He lowers his hand, scowling. "What is it about these people? Or is it just the guy?"

She flushes, her fingers flexing restlessly against the wool of her sweater.

"Oh, my God! It is! For God's sake, Lou—what? Do you think he's falling in love with you or something equally ludicrous?"

"*Shut the fuck up, Ike!*"

He stops, staring, his mouth dropped open.

She pulls in a shaky breath, her fingers clutching her sweater, her knuckles white.

"I don't know why you're being so cruel," she says, keeping her voice calm with an effort. "I now have friends who aren't you, so you're not solely responsible for me anymore. That means I'm improving, and who knows? Maybe I'll even leave the house someday. As my friend, that should make you happy!"

He has the grace to look ashamed.

"I am happy for you," he mutters.

"Well, you sure don't act like it! Your concerns are duly noted, but I'm not letting you live my life for me anymore. That should make you happy! If you can't accept that, well...I don't need all those stupid investments anyway. Put everything back in my bank account, and you can go on your way."

Ike's eyes snaps to hers.

"Lou!"

"I *love* you, Ike! I've loved you all my life, and you know it. I'm grateful beyond measure for everything you've done for me for the last ten years but not even you can talk to me the way you just did. And not even you can force me to do something I don't want to do. You either accept my friendship with Ferrin and Tessa, or anyone else I choose, for that matter, or we can go our separate ways."

"*Lou...*"

Ike trails off, his eyes wide with disbelief, but for the first time in her life, Lou remains unmoved by the betrayed hurt in his amber eyes.

"I'm not changing my mind, Ike."

He stares at her for a long moment, until he finally, grudgingly says, "Fine...but I'm just trying to protect you. You know—"

"Ike."

He waves a hand. "Fine," he says again. "I'll stop interfering."

Her fingers relax, and she nods. "Good."

"But I reserve the right to say 'I told you so'."

"Of course you do," she says drily.

185

In the end, Lou digs through the boxes in one of the bedrooms and finds a pair of pearl stud earrings for Tessa, and a small water colour of the prairie landscape for Ferrin, and for the first time in years, Lou makes Christmas dinner for guests.

Tessa gasps and gives Lou a tearful hug when she sees the earrings and laughs when Lou warns her to make sure she disinfects the things since she doesn't know if costume jewelry turns toxic. Ferrin raises an eyebrow at the painting and slowly smiles as Lou mutters she's sure he has a blank wall or four at his new place. He, too, gives her a brief hug and she almost cries at how good it feels and hopes the others don't notice how those brief moments of physical contact affect her.

Ike doesn't say another word about her new friends but she's still relieved when he and Irish go back to Vancouver the day after Boxing Day. It feels like a weight lifts from her shoulders and her life eases back to her now-normal routine of visits from Tessa and Ferrin, only now also spiced up with visits from Delaney and others of the Martinez clan.

All in all, she decides as she readies herself for bed the day before New Year's Eve, it's been a pretty good year.

Ferrin leans back in his chair while Lou shuffles the cards. It's New Year's Eve. Tessa's at a party in Regina, Juan and Delaney are home with their kids, Willis is alone with a bottle of wine, and he's here, watching Lou push up the sleeves of her sweater before she deals.

"Okay," Ferrin says with a trace of amusement, "I think we've known each long enough now for me to ask this question without getting my head completely torn off..."

She glances at him with a questioning scowl.

"What is it with the sweater?" he asks.

She shrugs. "It was my dad's."

Ferrin raises an eyebrow and makes an obvious show of assessing what he can see of her and the sweater. She flushes.

"What?" she asks defensively, glowering in response to his smug, amused smile.

"I can't decide if your dad was seven feet tall and that sweater fit him to a tee, or if he just had an interesting dress sense."

Lou reluctantly chuckles. "My mom made it. It was the first one she ever made, and she misjudged the size." She grimaces. "Not to mention the colour. I understand my father praised it to the skies, and always wore it in the house when he was cold."

"Aw. That's sweet."

"But he absolutely refused to wear it when people could see it."

Ferrin laughs. "Good compromise."

Lou smiles. "My mom seemed to think so. She had almost finished a second sweater for him when the accident happened."

"I'm sorry," he says softly.

She sighs. "Me, too. I never knew him, you know; he died before I was born." She plucks at the wool and shrugs. "It's deplorable, but, you know...it reminds me of the way things used to be, and the way things might have been. It..." she hesitates, then ducks her head and mumbles, "it makes me feel safe."

Ferrin nods. "I can understand that," he says softly, "but you live in that sweater. Does that mean you live in the past?"

Lou shrugs. "Don't you?"

"Not really."

"No?" she asks with a skeptical lilt in her voice.

"How am I living in the past?"

"Have you dated anyone yet?"

Ferrin smirks and raises an eyebrow. "I didn't realize

that was a prerequisite to living in the present."

Lou shrugs. "It's a sign of living in the present, especially for a guy like you."

Both eyebrows shoot up to his hairline. "What kind of guy am I?" he asks, amused.

She flushes. "I don't know! One who dates!"

He laughs. "I'm flattered. I think."

She scowls as she leans back in her chair, the cards forgotten in her hand. "Whatever. The fact remains that it's New Year's Eve, and you're sitting here with me."

"There are worse places to be," he murmurs.

She blinks at him and he pauses for a moment to admire the beauty of her eyes. They gaze at each other in silence and a flush rises in her cheeks before she looks away and sits up straight.

"What were you doing last year at this time?" she blurts.

He blinks, then grimaces. "I was proposing marriage in front of friends and family."

"Oh. Right." She bites her lip. "Sorry. I forgot."

Ferrin shrugs and for a moment, he feels the weight of that rejection still heavy on his shoulders. "Well," he says, "you weren't there. What were *you* doing last year at this time?"

Lou frowns, her eyes studiously on the cards she's restlessly re-ordering in her hands. "This. Except alone. Hoping Ike would show up." Now it's her turn to grimace. "He was proposing, too."

Silence settles over them, wrapping them in somber intimacy.

"Tell me about him," Ferrin says.

Lou stares off into the distance, her forehead wrinkled in thought.

"Not much to tell," she says. "We grew up together, went to school together, were friends forever. He helped his dad look after us when Mom got sick, and took over management of our finances when his dad got fed up with us. Ike had finished his business degree by then. Anyway, he supported me through my mom's illness while all of her friends, including his dad, turned their backs on us. Then he helped me through the funeral, that never-ending ordeal of planning and then listening and standing, kneeling and pretending to pray, followed by an endless line of people giving hollow words of respect and grief—where had they *been* that last year? He took me home and I finally broke down. It had been a long five years, looking after her, watching her waste away, watching all of her so-called friends just...leave her alone to die." She pauses, then shakes her head. "*Finally*, after five years of hope and setbacks and despair, I was able to cry, and he took me in his arms, then he took me to bed. A part of me was ecstatic, because I've loved him—wanted him—for *my entire life*, but another part of me was screaming that his timing really fucking sucked." She makes a sound that might have been a chuckle, and rakes a hand through her hair. "Needless to say, that first time was a disaster, and the memory would be hysterically funny if it wasn't all tangled up with the pain of it all."

She pauses, a rueful twist to her lips, then says, "I stayed inside and slept for about a month. When I wasn't sleeping, I was grappling with my grief and trying to adjust to no longer having to care for my mother. Ike practically moved in, and I struggled to adjust to that, too. About six weeks after the funeral, I decided it was time to get out of the house, go grocery shopping or for a walk or something...and I couldn't get out the door." She shivers. "Those first panic attacks, when I had no idea what was happening...God, I thought I was dying! And I couldn't get out to see a doctor, and Ike couldn't convince anyone to make house calls, and—yeah. I learned that the only way to avoid the panic attacks was to stay inside.

"It probably wouldn't have been so bad, you know, these last few years, if Ike and I had stayed together, but when I didn't show any signs of improvement, he just...drifted away. It was so gradual, I almost didn't notice until one day, I looked up and realized he was gone. We never even officially 'broke up'; we just...stopped. You want to know what's sad? There was a part of me that was...relieved. Oh, I still loved him, probably always will, but it wasn't the right time. I always hoped we'd drift together again and this time, *this* time I'd get it right...but then he married Irish, and left me behind."

She stops speaking, staring at nothing, a sad twist to her lips. She shakes her head, gives him a wry smile, and says, "What about you? What's the story with you and your ex?"

He hesitates, trying to decide how much he can tell her without giving his secret away.

"We met at a party," he says slowly, which is true enough. It had been the Macon-Jones annual charity ball, where every member of the family and every corporate headquarters employee, from the CEO to the kid delivering the mail, is invited to attend. Of course, it helps that the kid delivering the mail is usually a Macon-Jones. Abram, for all his arrogance and dictatorial tendencies, firmly believes that any Macon-Jones interested in working for the company has to begin at the bottom and work their way up. Those cousins who couldn't accept that their heritage didn't entitle them to a free ride at the office quickly found other things to do with their time. To be fair to his cousins, there aren't many who make that decision.

Ferrin chose to stay away from the business because he has no real interest, and because he's never been able to shake the feeling he would be somehow betraying his older brother, who at twelve had already been passionate about the company, hanging on their father's and Abram's every word. If his brother had lived, Ferrin might have followed him into the company, just like he'd followed him everywhere else.

Until the one time he didn't follow...

He's suddenly back in that hot summer day, his brother forever twelve, his mother forever thirty-four, and both forever laughing and shining bright in his memories as they paddle away for the last time.

Ferrin's happy to attend the occasional board meeting, charm wealthy donors at Gillian's various charity events and the annual charity ball, attend the family's annual reunion, and give his vote to whichever cousin asks for it first, or wrings a drunken promise or two out of him, but as far as he's concerned, Macon-Jones Enterprises belongs to his brother, not him.

He pulls himself back to his current surroundings and Lou's concerned face, and opens his mouth to tell her all of it, to tell her everything...and stops short. He's not sure how she'll react and there's a very real possibility she'll never want to see him again. He shakes his head.

It's not the right time.

Besides, he's supposed to be telling her about Olivia, not his mother and brother.

The thought of Olivia causes a different kind of pain to twist through him.

"I met her at a party," he says again, "and she was the most beautiful woman I'd ever seen. I was particularly handsome and charming that night, and I was making a great first impression, too, until I spilled my drink on her." He grins suddenly. "Of course, it gave me an excuse to take her home, where all the clothes came off in a hurry."

Lou's jaw drops. "On the first night?"

"In the first hour." He shrugs, looking unbearably smug. "Let's face it: I'm irresistible."

"So is she, apparently."

He pauses, eyes widening, then laughs. "Point taken. Anyway, we were never apart after that. Well, I mean, she went to work, and all that, but we were just together immediately. And it was...easy. Fun. Exciting. We loved instantly, you know, and that was the first time I experienced that. It was...intoxicating."

"So why did she turn you down? Or why didn't you get married earlier?"

He cocks his head, frowning as he considers her question.

"You know," he says slowly, "after all my soul searching this last year, I don't think I've actually asked myself that. We talked about getting married, of course, a lot, in the beginning." He pauses, thinking how it hadn't seemed prudent to marry too quickly when she had only just started her meteoric rise in the company. The cousins, of course, knew the truth, but those who weren't related—and some within the press—would not have been kind.

He shrugs. "We just kept putting it off until the time was right."

"So were you really shocked when she said no? Be honest."

He frowns, considering the question. "Yes...and no. We hadn't talked marriage for at least a year or so by that point." He chuckles almost bitterly. "Looking back, I can see all the signs I didn't notice—or want to notice—at the time. We didn't make love like we used to, but that's just what happens after you've been with someone for a long time. But there were other hints. We no longer planned anything more than a few months out. She didn't share any future goals and dreams that weren't about work." He shakes his head. "Maybe, if I'd noticed, paid attention, I could have done something to change things, stop her from drifting away. I don't think she stopped loving me. I think she just allowed her ambition to overwhelm that love, just like I allowed myself to take her love for granted." He shrugs. "I don't know."

"Regrets?"

"Too many to list. All the things done and all those not done. That happy future I didn't notice slipping away..." he trails off and shakes his head.

"How do you move on from that?" she asks softly.

"Very slowly. And you don't really get over losses like

that, you know. You just learn to live with them and still be happy."

He falls silent as he once again thinks of his mother and brother until he shakes his head, chuckles, and says, "It's been a hell of a year."

"Sure has," she agrees with a rueful grimace.

"But not all of it was bad, right?"

A smile tugs at her lips as she says, "Maybe."

Ferrin gives her his best puppy look and her smile widens.

"It's had a moment," she concedes. "Maybe two."

"Hopefully we can manage three in the new year." He's struck with an idea and his eyes light up as he leans forward. "You know, I once read that what you do on New Year's Day is a sign of what you'll be doing throughout the coming year."

She raises an eyebrow. "Yeah?"

"Yeah. So, as a sign that the new year is going to be better than and different from the one we've almost finished, I think..."

Her eyes widen as the pause lingers, and for a moment, there's a wealth of possibilities in the silence.

"What?" she finally demands, and he grins. She rolls her eyes. "What?"

"Tonight. Just after midnight...I think you need to go outside."

Lou's mouth falls open and for a moment she desperately hopes she misheard him.

"*Outside?*" she squeaks.

Ferrin nods, eyes wide and eager. "Everything I've read about agoraphobia the last few months says that, most of the time at least, you can learn to control and sometimes even cure it by facing the things that trigger it...I mean, facing things in a controlled environment, of course. I've read it will even sometimes go away by itself. So, I say your New Year's Resolution should be to try to minimize your agoraphobia." He grins. "I'll help."

She shakes her head. "That's—I appreciate the thought, I really do. I don't know what you've been reading, but nothing will help, Ferrin. Back when it all started, Ike did a lot of research, talked to a lot of people—doctors, you know—and they all said nothing could be done." She frowns. "Why are you looking at me like that?"

He shakes his head. "No reason. Besides, that was then; this is now. It's been five years. Things change a lot in that time."

She shakes her head. "I asked Ike about it a couple months ago, and he said there was still no progress. No new theories or therapies or, well, anything."

Ferrin's eyes narrow. "Hm. Still, what does it hurt to try?"

She scowls. "Panic attacks are not fun."

"I'll be right beside you, and I'll get you back inside even if I have to carry you. Come on," he coaxes, his voice pitched to a low, seductive rumble, "it'll be an adventure."

She feels herself weakening beneath his persuasive charm before she shakes her head, her scowl deepening. "What makes you think I want an adventure?"

"Because it's with me!"

She rolls her eyes.

"Come on!" he says. "It's New Year's Eve! A time for outrageous resolutions you know you'll never keep, reckless daring, and at least one moment you look back on and say 'dear God, I hope no one had a camera'."

She bites back a smile and Ferrin grins.

He sobers and, suddenly very serious, he says, "Do you trust me?"

She hesitates and hears Ike's voice whisper that Ferrin and Tessa only want to use her. But it's faint and has no strength against the intense, cursedly seductive man in front of her. Besides, until Ferrin arrived on her doorstep, adventures of any kind had been severely lacking in her life and she can't help but be tempted.

Ferrin says, "I'll tell you what; how about this? Your New Year's Resolution is to go outside, after midnight, and stay outside for...let's say five minutes. Three? One! One minute! If you can handle that, if you can hold off the panic attack for a least one minute, then your second New Year's Resolution is to start taking baby steps to leave the house on a regular basis."

She opens her mouth, but he forestalls her.

"Oh, and I mean go outside into your yard, not on the porch! I'll be beside you the whole time. In fact, if it helps, I'll pretend I've fallen off the porch again, and you can check me out."

She frowns. "Don't you mean 'check on you'?"

He waggles his eyebrows with a suggestive smirk. She rolls her eyes and once again struggles to keep from smiling.

"Come on," he says, "what do you say?"

She sighs. "What's the temperature out there?"

After some searching, Lou finally digs out her boots from where she flung them after she was unable to leave the house to stop Ike's wedding.

It feels like a lifetime ago.

They pull on their parkas and head to the back door. Her steps slow as they get closer until she finally comes to a stop, staring wide-eyed at the plank of oak that is a twin to the one at the front of the house. The black panic begins to rise as her breathing speeds up. The door both looms and retreats in her vision, and in a far corner of her mind, she wonders what Ferrin would do if she dropped to the floor right now and curled up into a ball.

She jumps and yelps as Ferrin's hand wraps around hers in a warm, firm grip.

"You're okay," he says with an encouraging smile. "You're not alone and I'll take care of you. Trust me."

She blinks up at him and forces her mouth to curve into a faint, shaky smile.

"My hero," she mutters, but she laces her fingers with his and holds tight.

"I can always change into my Superman costume, if you'd like," he says, giving her hand a reassuring squeeze.

Sweat prickles her skin and black panic is licking at her corners as she says, "Maybe later."

Their gazes collide at that, and for a moment, they're suspended, an electric awareness humming between them. Her eyes widen and Ferrin leans closer, his chest lightly brushing against her shoulder, his own eyes serious and intent. Her lips part and suddenly she knows that if she leans towards him, just a little, she could fall into him and let him engulf her until she doesn't know where she ends and he begins.

It would be glorious—and utterly disastrous.

Lou knows she can't afford to lose herself in him like she once lost herself in Ike and her own home. She's so tired of being lost. Still, she's tempted and all she seems capable of doing is stare at him until the tension and that looming sense of trouble becomes too much for her, and Lou isn't sure if she's more afraid of going outside or of staying inside, in this moment, with Ferrin.

She pulls in a sharp breath as she abruptly turns, yanks the door open and rushes through, pulling him behind her.

The night is crisp, the sky clear, and Lou is shaking from the black panic lurking on her edges, waiting to rush in...but she isn't having an attack.

It's only after long moments stretch out as endlessly as

the prairie horizon that she begins to believe she's going to be all right this time, and tightens her grip on Ferrin's hand.

They stare up at the stars, twinkling in the cloudless sky above them. Their breath mists in the crisp air as they stand together, cocooned by silence and the cold and the dark. It's beautiful and ephemeral and so, so precious.

Lou swallows, then says, softly, "You ran away, didn't you? From Olivia, I mean."

Ferrin hesitates. "Yeah," he breathes.

"I ran away, too. I just ran in place."

He squeezes her hand as they stand beneath the stars.

Lou sighs and says, "We're a sad pair."

"Maybe. But maybe we don't have to be sad."

Their eyes meet, cloaked in starlight and shadow. Lou shivers and looks away, turning her gaze back to the sky she hasn't seen like this for far too long.

"Ready to go back in?" he asks.

She shakes her head.

He smiles and tightens his grip on her hand.

Lou honours her New Year's Resolution. She goes out every day with Ferrin and stands motionless in her back yard, soaking in the sky and the sounds and the smells and the cold of January. Those moments are glorious and beautiful and fill her with hope.

But there are also times when the panic overwhelms her and she stumbles back into the house, gasping and shaking and furious with Ferrin, with herself, with her weakness, and her fear.

In those moments, Ferrin gets her back inside as quickly as he can, soothes her, and simply encourages her to try again tomorrow. She both appreciates his support and hates it, and she's so fucking confused and happy and nervous sometimes when she's around him, she doesn't know which way to turn or even where to look.

Tessa's no help, not only because Lou doesn't understand what she's feeling enough to share it with her, but also because Lou hasn't had that many female friends in her life. Her heart-to-hearts had always been with her mother or Ike.

Well, she thinks as Ferrin finishes dealing and she picks up her cards, that's something to think about later. Right now, she has a card game to win.

She throws her cards into the crib, and returns her attention to Ferrin, big and broad and sitting across the table from her, frowning at his cards. She cuts the deck and he picks up the exposed card, then shoots her a lightning glance as he places it face-up on the deck.

Her eyes narrow. "What?" she demands.

He clears his throat and says, carefully casual, "I'm going to Toronto at the end of the month."

Lou freezes, scowling.

Ferrin frowns at his cards and sighs with disgust before he looks up at her and says, "This deal sucks. Are you playing or what?"

"Are you coming back?" she asks.

"As far as I know," he says mildly, and nods at the cards in her hand.

"Why?"

"I live here."

She rolls her eyes. "Why are you going to Toronto?"

"My family's there."

"You don't like your family."

"Not every day, no, but they're my family and I haven't seen them in almost a year."

"So? Is that the only reason?"

A slight frown creases his features. "Well, we have this annual...I guess you could call it a family reunion. My great-grandfather started the tradition and all of his descendants are expected to attend unless there are compelling reasons not to do so."

It's her turn to frown. "What kind of compelling reasons?"

He shrugs. "It involves bodily fluids flowing out of a variety of orifices. His will was quite specific. And unfortunately graphic."

Her eyes widen.

"My great-grandfather was a very colourful fella," he says with a smirk. "Grumpier than hell, more likely to growl than smile at you, and God help you if you pissed him off. Huh. Reminds me a little of you. Are you going to play?"

She ignores the mild insult. "In a minute. Your great-grandfather put this in his will? What do you get for going to this family reunion?"

"The chance to gossip about each other."

She snorts. "How long has the guy been gone?"

Ferrin frowns, calculating. "Ten, almost eleven years now."

She raises an eyebrow.

"He lived a long and fruitful life," Ferrin says lightly, then sobers. "He buried two of his four sons, though, including my grandfather, not to mention a grand-daughter-in-law, and a great-grandson." He glances at her with suddenly sad eyes. "My mother and brother. I remember Gramp sometimes being very sad, and he told me once that no one should bury their descendants, that it's the worst pain on earth to see those who should follow after you go before you."

He stares off into space, his face drawn with grief. "He held us together," he says softly. "My dad and me. Oh, the cousins tried, but really, it was Gramp. He stepped in and took care of me and my dad when we were incapable of caring for ourselves. He introduced Gillian to my dad about four years after the accident, and my dad came to life again. Well, to a certain definition of 'life', anyway. Gillian saved both of us, and we have Gramp to thank for it...although I think she probably curses him on a regular basis."

"Why would she curse him?"

"We're not exactly an easy family to get into and we're not exactly an easy family to stay in. We're almost certain we don't actually eat our own young, although just in case we do, several of my cousins have reproduced like rabbits, so we have plenty of them to go around."

"Charming," she mutters.

"You have no idea. Anyway, yes. We still follow Gramp's dictates." He shrugs ruefully. "All for our own reasons. Me? I do it partly because I'm the last of my grandfather's branch, but mainly because Gramp was good to me. It costs so little to honour his request, even if he's no longer here to see it."

"That's actually really sweet," Lou says softly.

Ferrin stares at her in silence and after a moment, a flush creeps up her cheeks as she holds his gaze. The silence stretches, deepens, until he gives a start and drops his eyes to the cards in his hand.

He clears his throat and says, "I'm sure my cousins have a different way of describing it," he says with forced lightness, then glances at her with his crooked smirk. "Now, are you going to play or are you going to forfeit the game?"

"Never!" Lou says, and slaps her first card down on the table.

Lou's bottom lip sticks out slightly as she frowns over the cards in her hands.

Tessa laughs.

"What's so funny?" Lou growls.

"You are! I'm sorry I'm not Ferrin but there's no need to pout!"

"I am not pouting!"

"You so are! Now, are you going to play or not?"

Lou makes a face, and throws her cards on to the table. "No. I just can't focus tonight."

Tessa laughs again, gathers up the cards and sets them aside.

"No kidding. You miss him."

Lou tugs her sweater around herself and sniffs. "I don't know what you mean."

"Yeah. Bad liar."

Lou frowns, looking anywhere but at Tessa as she pushes her chair away from the table and stands. "You want a drink?" she asks.

"Coffee and kahlua?"

"Okay."

They go to the kitchen where Tessa leans on the kitchen counter as Lou goes through the motions of making coffee.

"There's no crime in missing him, you know," Tessa says as Lou turns the coffee pot on.

"I don't miss him."

"No?"

"He's a drifter. I'm not even sure he's coming back."

"He said he's coming back."

"Sure, but that was before he left!"

Tessa shakes her head. "Okay, even I am having trouble with that one."

Lou sighs. "Look. He's back in Toronto, and he said he'd be seeing Olivia. His ex. Well, you know he's still in love with her. Why would he come back to Saskatchewan if he could stay in Toronto with her?"

"Well, for one thing, 'seeing' her doesn't mean he's 'with' her, and while they might end up having ex-sex— sex-ex? Whatever. Anyway, just because he's going to see her doesn't mean they're back together or that they're going to live happily ever after even if they are. For another thing, he left Toronto in the first place because he's in love with her and didn't want to see her all the time, so I think that's a pretty good sign he'll be leaving again.

Unless, of course, he's actually over her and he just doesn't know it yet. Of course, the bigger question isn't whether he'll leave Toronto but why he would come back here, to Ledoux, I mean. Small town Saskatchewan is a pretty far cry from big city Toronto." She pauses, considering her point. "I don't think Olivia's the real attraction anymore. It's more likely he'll decide to stay once he's reminded of everything he's missing by living here."

"Yeah," Lou mutters and thumps the bottle of kahlua onto the table.

"Now, my question to you is, why aren't you giving him a real incentive to come back?"

Lou mouth drops open. "What?"

Tessa leans forward with a wicked grin, her eyes gleaming. "Oh, come on! I've seen the way you look at each other!"

Lou blushes. "I don't know what you're talking about," she mutters.

"Oh, please! I'm not judging, by the way, I'm just surprised you haven't been knocking boots from the first day you laid eyes on him...no pun intended. I mean, he's what? Six-two? And I haven't seen shoulders that wide on a man since I moved to town! He's handsome, in an off-beat kinda way, and let's face it: that voice of his is pure porn!" She leans even closer and lowers her voice as if there was somebody else in the house to hear her. "Tell me the truth: you've given him the phone book and just told him to read it to you, haven't you?"

Lou's eyes widen with every word, and she stares, motionless. All she can think to say in response is, "Pure porn?"

Tessa carelessly waves a hand. "I saw that description on the Internet once and I had no clue what it meant. Then I heard Ferrin's voice and I get it now. I guess, just like with other kinds of porn, you know it when you hear it."

Lou stares in stunned disbelief then shakes her head.

"Have you ever given him the phone book and asked him to read it?"

"Hell, no! But then, honestly? He does nothing for me."

Lou raises a skeptical eyebrow.

Tessa shrugs. "I can't help it. He makes me feel very sisterly towards him, and I have no idea why. Maybe it's that pathetic look he gives me when he comes in for his morning coffee. I don't know. But that doesn't mean I don't know pure porn when I hear it!"

Lou's forehead furrows in confusion.

"That sounds way worse than I intended," Tessa groans. She shakes her head. "Anyway, if you're too shy to make the first move, get him talking and then, at just the right moment, let your hormones do the thinking." She beams.

Lou shakes her head. "What makes you think he even wants me to let my hormones do the thinking?"

Tessa laughs. "Oh, please! I don't think he even realizes it himself yet, but the way he looks at you? The way he looks when he talks about you?" She shakes her head. "It's only a matter of time, my friend."

Lou flushes hotly and busies herself with pouring the coffee. She gives hers a generous splash of kahlua, looks thoughtfully at Tessa then adds another splash for good measure.

Tessa shakes her head in mock-offense and grabs the bottle out of Lou's hand. "The poor guy better never play poker, because he'd lose his shirt." She perks up. "Ooh, there's another idea! Stop with the crib and start playing strip poker! Or play strip crib! You could probably both be naked in only two games if you do a piece of clothing per point!"

"Tessa!"

"Oh, please—stop with the scandalized innocent routine! You and Ike, remember? And there were a couple of guys in university, weren't there?"

"I can't believe I shared any of that with you," Lou groans.

"What can I say? I have that kind of face. Anyway, my point is, you're not a virgin!"

"It's been a while," Lou mutters, leading the way back to the living room, after grabbing the kahlua bottle to take with them.

"You and me both," Tessa sighs.

"I've been stuck inside my house for five years. What's your excuse?"

Tessa grimaces. "Bad choice after bad choice after bad choice. I finally decided I needed to take a break from men and just focus on being happy with me first." She takes a sip of her coffee and smiles in satisfaction. "Best decision I ever made. Although it's too bad I know all the guys in town so well now."

"Nobody you'd like to settle down with?"

Tessa shrugs. "I don't think I'm ready to settle down, exactly, but I'm almost ready to think about maybe finding somebody to explore the possibilities."

"That sounds remarkably vague, even for you."

Tessa laughs. "I'm not looking for anybody or anything, but I'm willing to reach out and grab the opportunity if it presents itself." She raises an eyebrow. "Can you say the same?"

Ferrin stands on the balcony and watches the milling crowd below him. The women are beautiful and colourful in their elegant gowns while the men are uniformly handsome in their black tuxedos. Scattered here and there, standing out in the crowd, are several far more flamboyant cousins who will, no doubt, be featured in the society pages the next day. He smiles as he leans on the railing. As much as he jokes about his family's cutthroat ways, he's missed them and parties like this.

He watches Gillian waft through the crowd, elegant and cool in amber silk as she floats from cousin to cousin. When she married Ferrin's father, she took on the role of hostess for most if not all of the Macon-Jones' public parties, including this annual charity ball that occurs the day after the Macon-Jones' annual and more private family reunion, and she takes her role very seriously. Ferrin can't help his fond smile as he watches his stepmother. Over the years, even the most arrogant of his cousins has learned to behave themselves during these gatherings, or at least during the charity ball, when they are all on public display.

His smile widens into a grin as he sees Gillian speak to Abram then turn abruptly away with a shake of her head and a lift of her shoulder that even from this distance radiates annoyance.

Well, most of them have learned to behave themselves.

He becomes aware somebody is standing behind him and glances over his shoulder. His gaze collides with Olivia's and for a moment, he freezes, memories of the first time they met flashing through his mind. Then he blinks the memories away and slowly straightens as she joins him at the railing.

They stand side by side, their attention ostensibly on the people below them, but he watches her from the corner of his eye, and notices she's watching him the same way. He tightens his grip on the railing, and holds his breath, waiting for her to speak.

"Hi," she says finally, softly, not quite looking at him.

"Hi," he says, equally soft.

"You're looking good, Ferrin."

Ferrin shivers at the way she says his name and turns to face her, his eyes wide as he drinks her in.

"So are you," he says, his voice husky and warm, filled with nostalgic longing.

She smiles almost bashfully as she meets his eyes.

"You've lost weight," she says.

He looks down at himself and laughs. "Optical illusion," he says ruefully, "although the tux does seem to fit a little better this year."

She smiles again, and her dimple flashes. "Where have you been?"

"Here and there," he shrugs, "but mostly Saskatchewan."

She wrinkles her nose. "I'd heard that, but didn't really believe it! Hard to imagine you out in the middle of nowhere. I mean, if you have to be out west, at least go to Alberta. Calgary and Edmonton are real cities!"

Ferrin chokes on a laugh. "Well, I'm sure people in Regina or Saskatoon would beg to differ."

Olivia grimaces. "Sorry. But not really." She turns to fully face him, her dark eyes—but, he notices, not as dark as Lou's—curious. "Seriously, Ferrin, what do you do all day? I mean, I find it hard to believe there are that many parties for you to go to, or a lot of high culture happening."

"Well, it's not like I went to the symphony or ballet every night here!" He shakes his head, his crooked grin warm. "You're such a snob! Aren't you from Sault Ste Marie? I mean, how big is that place?"

She laughs. "My point exactly!" She cocks her head as she considers him. "So, what do you do out there?"

He shrugs and turns to lean on the balcony's banister. He stares down at the people in the ballroom below. The guests to the public charity ball are beginning to arrive, and he watches his cousins as they mingle with the new arrivals and each other with a genteel civility that is all too often a thin veneer hiding their never-ending turf wars for power and influence within the company and the family. Three generations together in one room, and almost all of them wary of the family around them. Only Abram and Ferrin are removed from the bickering. Abram, because he already holds the power and he'll continue to hold it until it's pried from his dead, cold hands, and Ferrin, because he decided long ago that the family he had left meant far more to him than any power over the family or in the corporation ever could.

With sudden, heartbreaking clarity, he realizes Olivia was right: he's no use to her in navigating the rocky waters of the Macon-Jones' family when they're doing business, and he never will be.

He realizes Olivia is still watching him only now she's puzzled instead of only curious.

"Sorry," he says turning back to face her with an apologetic smile, "what was the question?"

"What do you do in Saskatchewan?"

"I help to build houses, mostly," he says, oddly reluctant to mention Lou. "I mean, I'm unskilled labour, so I clean up, tear down, haul shit away, run errands, that sort of thing."

He chuckles at her appalled expression and holds out his hands, palms up. "Look—I even have callouses!"

Olivia slowly shakes her head. "That's...so unlike you...or anyone else in the Macon-Jones family."

He shrugs. "It's been fun and different and exactly what I needed."

She looks vaguely guilty at that. "Are you...are you okay, Ferrin? Are you happy?"

It's like no time at all has passed when he sees her worried face and sad eyes. All of the same old, familiar protective instincts rush over him. He never could stand to see her be anything less than happy and he finds himself starting to reach out to touch her face, her shoulder, to pull her into a hug and tell her everything would be all right.

He stops himself and settles for giving her his most reassuring smile, and says, "I'm no long unhappy, Olivia." For some reason, the memory of Lou's face as she stood beneath the stars for the first time in years flashes in his memory. "There are even a lot of days when I'm very happy," he says. "Yes, I'm okay."

She looks relieved yet somehow unsatisfied. "I'm glad," she says, and that, he knows, is sincere.

"So am I."

"Do you have friends?"

He laughs. "I've been out there for almost a year, Olivia, of course I have friends!"

"But what on earth do you talk about?"

"We talk about work, and farming, and football. A lot of football." He laughs. "It's Saskatchewan; they bleed green, or so they tell me."

She looks adorably confused, and love and yearning almost overwhelms him, but it's all tinged with nostalgia and a melancholy acceptance that what they had is truly over. He's sorry they fell apart, and there will always be a part of him that wishes things were different, but on the other hand, he never would have ended up in that little town in the middle of nowhere, never would have met Juan and Delaney and their hellspawn, or Tessa, or Willis, or any of the others in his circle of friends. He never would have met Lou, with her heart-shaped face and messy hair, her perpetual scowl and amazing, almost-black eyes. He hides a grin as he pretends to listen while Olivia tells him about the last year at the office, and he has a sudden, sharp image of Lou, with her this-is-bullshit face, wrapped in that deplorable sweater, and wonders what she'd say about everything going on around them.

He feels a pang, and is surprised to realize it's akin to homesickness. He misses his life in Ledoux more than he thought he would.

He realizes Olivia has asked him something.

"Sorry, what?" he says.

"There was a time when you hung on my every word," she says with a sad smile, but her eyes narrow as she watches him. "I asked how long you're staying in Toronto."

"I leave on Monday."

"Oh."

She fidgets in awkward silence, then almost shyly says, "Would you like to go somewhere? Get a coffee? Talk?"

His eyes widen as he studies her expression before he slowly says, "I don't think that's a good idea. Do you?"

She looks at the floor, turns her shoulder to him, and shrugs. "I suppose not."

He feels a brief flash of guilt for putting that sad look on her face and is surprised it isn't as powerful as it was even just a few minutes ago. The realization startles and frightens him. He takes a half-step towards her, but he's interrupted by loud shouts from Carson, Dyson and Jack as they bound up the steps to the balcony area. He's never been so glad to see them, with their rapid banter and knowing, sympathetic eyes.

The Musketeers chat amiably with Olivia before they carry him off, because, they explain to her with the trademark Macon-Jones' charm on full display, the last of the guests has arrived, and it's time to mingle and persuade their fellow rich people to open their cheque-books.

He glances back to find Olivia staring wistfully after him.

His stomach lurches with a jolt of fear because he knows—knows to his core—he's walking away forever from something that had been so good, something as familiar as his own face, something that had been his life for five years, and his step falters. He has a sudden, intense urge to go back to her, to take her up on her offer, to see where this melancholy mood of hers will lead them. Even as he thinks it, he sees everything unfold, as clearly as a movie. They would go somewhere and talk, and one thing would lead to another, and he would end up in her bed, and they'd pick up where they left off. They might even get married this time, and the future, he's sure, would be...happy enough.

Only he isn't ready to give up Ledoux, and his life there as Ferrin Jones. He still loves Olivia, but he doesn't want to leave Lou and the others behind. Not yet, anyway. Not when Lou is just starting to show signs of interest...in the outside world, he means.

He stares at Olivia and she gives him a tentative smile, raising an eyebrow in hopeful question. The revelation that she's no longer his sole reason for being is exhilarating and terrifying, and he wavers for what feels like an eternity but is, in actuality, no time at all. When it comes right down to it, and his heart breaks at the thought, it really is a simple choice to make.

His smile is sad as he half-raises his hand in a gesture of farewell and turns to join his waiting, watchful cousins.

He doesn't look back again.

♠♥♣♦

Lou opens the door and tries to keep the relief off her face when she sees Ferrin standing on the porch, grinning, as big and broad and handsome as ever.

They consider each other in silence before she sniffs and steps aside to let him in.

"So," she says coolly, turning to watch him, "you're back."

He nods happily as he shrugs out of his parka and removes his boots.

She frowns. "What's going on?"

He straightens and stares, blue eyes wide and startled.

"What makes you think something's going on?" he asks.

She shrugs, pulling her sweater more snugly around herself. "I don't know. You have a weird look on your face."

"Really? What's weird about it?"

"I don't know—it's just...weird. Never mind." She brushes past him. "Do you want coffee? Tea?"

"I'm all tea'd out right now," he groans as he pads after her. "My stepmother's English—did I tell you? Anyway, I've got tea coming out my ears. How about some hot chocolate, made with real milk and lots of those little marshmallows?"

She raises an eyebrow. "What am I, a restaurant?"

He gives her his best puppy look that she's sure he's also trademarked. "Please?" he wheedles.

She scowls. "Irish Cream?"

"As if that's even a question," he says as he heads towards the living room and the card table.

She huffs loudly, but grins after she's turned her back to him. She happily hugs herself as she strolls to the kitchen.

"Did you miss me?" he asks when she finally rejoins him.

"Barely noticed you were gone," she says as she puts the cups on the table and sits down.

"Of course," he says, his eyes sparkling and filled with some indecipherable expression that makes her body tingle and her face flush. She quickly drops her gaze to the cards he's holding in his large, calloused hands. She has a sudden, visceral desire to feel those rough fingers rasp against her skin and she shivers at the thought. She hastily picks up her own cards and averts her eyes, hoping he hasn't noticed anything.

"Shut up and play," she growls.

Ferrin easily returns to the pleasant routine of his life in Ledoux as winter slips and slides towards spring. Before he knows it, it's March, and it seems the prairies are determined to have not only an early spring, but an unusually warm one as well. His first bicycle ride of the year is in mid-March, to the Martinez' spacious home on the east side of town.

He walks into chaos, but then again, the Martinez house is always in chaos, with at least half the town's kids running around at any one time. Well, hellspawn are, of course, the best friends to have, he thinks, amused, because it's never boring and you always have somebody to blame.

He makes his way into the kitchen, where, in spite of the general commotion going on around her, Delaney calmly greets him, directs a child or two—it's difficult to be sure how many—to the appropriate places for what they want, and expertly manages the cooking food, which fills the house with mouth-watering aromas.

He sniffs appreciatively as he put his offering of wine and cupcakes on the kitchen counter.

She thanks him with a smile, then says in her warm voice filled with the rhythm of the Caribbean, "Could you clear the dining room and set the table, please?" She rolls her eyes in mock exasperation. "Juan just got home and dumped everything in there as usual. Get him to help you."

Ferrin grins. "No problem," he says, and heads for the room in question, dodging running children and what appears to be a baby woolly mammoth along the way.

"That seems new," he says to Steebeth as she races by and is rewarded with her giggle.

He walks into the dining room and stops short at the sight of Juan, immaculate in a dark suit, his salt and pepper hair impeccably groomed, standing at the sideboard where he keeps the hard stuff. Juan half-turns, and Ferrin notes the tasteful tie, loosened and hanging slightly askew against his blindingly white shirt. Juan gives him a bleak smile as he pours himself a stiff drink.

"What's wrong?" Ferrin demands. He's never seen his friend and boss look so downhearted.

Juan shrugs. "Just got turned down by another bank for my dream project. Drink?"

Ferrin shakes his head. "Well, I guess that explains the

spiffy suit and hairdo. What dream project?"

"Trying to impress. I figured it couldn't hurt, anyway." Juan takes a healthy gulp from his glass and grits his teeth against the burn. He nods at the haphazard pile of papers on the table. "Take a look," he says.

Ferrin raises an eyebrow as he picks up the first piece of paper. It's a short letter, outlining a proposal to buy the abandoned hospital in the southeast corner of the town of Ledoux and renovate it into apartments.

Ferrin frowns, trying to visualize the location. "Are you talking about that big grove of trees?" he says. "I always thought it was just, well, a grove of trees. I didn't think there was anything there except maybe teenagers in parked cars."

"Well, around here, any grove of trees is something special, but that one is really special. Smack dab in the middle of it is the old hospital. Beautiful building. Just beautiful." The yearning is clear in his voice.

Ferrin raises an eyebrow. "Does Delaney know she has a rival?"

"I've known for years," she says from behind them and they turn to find her leaning against the door jamb with her arms crossed. "Considering I love her, too, I've learned to live with it."

Ferrin's eyes gleam wickedly. "Gives a whole new meaning to ménage à trois."

Two small, puzzled faces poke out from bed'hind Delaney.

"What does that mean?" Mateo asks.

Delaney and Juan both bite back laughter at Ferrin's horrified expression.

"It's...it's...it's...a pie," he stammers. "Like lemon meringue, only...chocolate."

"Oh," Steebeth says. "Sounds yummy. Could you make one, Mama?"

Delaney coughs then says, "I don't have a recipe, but maybe Ferrin has made one."

Now it's Ferrin's turn to cough, and Juan abruptly turns his back, his shoulders shaking.

"Can't say as I have," Ferrin finally manages and glares as both Juan and Delaney burst into laughter.

"What's so funny?" Steebeth asks suspiciously.

"Never mind, honey, it's a grown-up thing," her father says.

"About pie?" Mateo says, his nose scrunched up in confusion.

"We're just being silly," Delaney says briskly, and Ferrin sags with relief. "Come on, we have to clean off the table or we'll never get this army fed. Juan, go get out of those stuffy clothes."

Juan nods and tosses back his drink. He sets the glass down and heads for the door, removing his tie as he goes. "Ferrin, would you mind taking that stuff into the den?"

Ferrin nods, picking up the over-sized papers and the rolled up blueprints. He carries them into the den, then, curious, he opens one of the large coil-bound booklets, which he knows contains the architectural drawings and leans over them, humming beneath his breath.

"Hey!" Juan shouts behind him and Ferrin yelps and whirls, guilt written all over his face.

"Sorry, Juan, I should have asked—"

Juan laughs and waves away the apology. "Just wanted to get your attention because supper's ready and if we don't hurry, the hordes, including that food vacuum I was told was a dog, the liars, will have eaten everything. Besides, I already told you to take a look. If you're still awake after supper, I'll tell you all about it."

Ferrin's definitely still awake, although so full from the amount of food he's managed to put away he's groaning as he waddles after Juan into the den where he leans over the drawings, and listens to his friend explain his dream.

Juan takes him out to the site the next day, and smiles almost shyly when he catches sight of Ferrin's expression as they walk towards the massive building.

"I had no idea this place was even here," Ferrin breathes. The building is gothic in its architecture, built with heavy red brick and majestic even in its currently neglected condition.

"Built back when we were a much bigger town." Juan looks at the building, naked yearning in his eyes. "Look at those lines," he sighs. "She's beautiful, and now that we're growing again, she could be given new life."

They stand and stare, the silence that surrounds them broken only by the sound of birds and the occasional hum of a car in the distance. Juan heaves a deep sigh before he shakes his head and turns away.

"Well, you saw the plans," he says as Ferrin follows him back to the car. "It'll take millions to renovate the place into the apartments I have planned. I can't really blame the banks, you know. It'll never make money in my lifetime, and probably not even in my kids' lifetimes."

"Why not? Ledoux's pretty prime real estate right now, with the economy booming."

Juan grimaces, and opens the driver's door. "How long will the boom last? By the time the apartments are ready, we could be back to cheap oil and praying it'll rain or hoping grain prices won't fall so low that half the farms in the province have to declare bankruptcy." He shakes his head. "We're not Alberta; we haven't been booming long enough to think it's going to last forever."

"So you're just gonna give up?"

Juan glances back at the building, a determined glint in his eyes. "Hell, no. I said I understood the banks; doesn't mean I agree with them."

He grins, and Ferrin laughs, then says, "Have you thought about private investors?"

"They're all farmers and small business people around here. They couldn't raise enough, and most of them can't afford to take the risk or wait years for their investment to pay off—if it ever does."

"Have you at least bought the building?"

"The town won't sell it to me until I have a plan in place and funding to implement the plan. Believe me, I've tried! At least I'm half-way there." He sighs, his shoulders slumping. "She's just gonna be torn down," he says mournfully, "or be allowed to fall down. Such a waste."

"Hmm. Would you mind giving me a copy of your proposal?"

"Of course not," Juan says with a puzzled frown. "Why?"

"I know a guy."

♠ ♥ ♣ ♦

"You want me to do what?" Pierce says flatly.

"Look," Ferrin says, "his plan looks pretty solid to me. A gamble, of course, but what isn't? If you agree, I want you to pull a company together, maybe see if anybody else in the family wants to invest. I'll canvas people here, see what money they can scrape together."

"And if it doesn't seem like a good investment?"

"Then do it anyway, but I'll leave the cousins and the people here out of it. Juan and Delaney are good people; they deserve to live his dream."

"You're looking at funding their dreams to the tune of tens of millions of dollars!"

"We could all use a tax write-off."

"You've already bought that building with the coffee shop in it and that run-down little house for more than it's truly worth, and you don't want to know the strings I pulled so that vet could 'win' a new truck! You can't save everyone, Ferrin."

Ferrin pauses, his mouth twisting. "I know," he says, his voice rough, "but I can at least try and save the ones I can. He has a dream, Pierce. A passion. I doubt we'll ever make a profit, but then again, how do you measure what you gain from giving somebody a chance like that? It's not like I'm giving him my last million...unless there's something you're not telling me?"

Pierce snorts. "Not even you and your wastrel cousins can put a dent in your family's fortunes."

"Hey! We work hard for our money!"

Pierce's silence is loud with skepticism.

"Most of us."

The silence deepens.

"Okay, okay—most of them."

Pierce laughs.

"All right," he says, "I'll look at the proposal. I can't ethically advise you to invest if the deal isn't sound, you do understand that?"

"Of course. I wouldn't expect anything less. But I don't have to listen to you, either."

"Have you ever?"

"Now you're sounding like my dad. And Abram. With a touch of Gillian in there, too."

Pierce chuckles again and says good-bye.

Juan stares, his dark eyes wide, his face expressionless.

"You fucking with me?" he demands.

Ferrin shakes his head. "Look, Pierce thinks there's potential there and also thinks he can line up some investors. He's even willing to have people here buy-in, if they want."

"They can't afford it."

"He's looking at $500 a share. Even I could buy in at that price."

Ferrin doesn't even blink at the underlying deceit in his words. It's worth it, he thinks, to see the hope dawning on Juan and Delaney's faces.

"Don't get too excited," Ferrin warned. "Pierce drives

a hard bargain, and his contacts might say no."

Juan and Delaney exchange a glance before Juan smiles a tight rueful smile. "It's still better than the banks, who said no immediately."

♠♥♣♦

"You're not hooking them up with the mob, are you?" Lou asks, her eyes narrowed into suspicious slits.

He laughs. "The mob? Do we even have a mob in Canada?"

"Sure do. I saw a documentary on the History channel."

Ferrin grimaces. "Tessa told me I'd regret convincing you to get cable."

"Tessa is usually right...once you figure out what she's saying." Lou flashes him a quick grin, then sobers. "Seriously, Ferrin, where's this Pierce guy gonna get the money? And how do you know him, anyway? I mean, I doubt you travel in the same social circles."

"Thanks," he says drily. "'That guy'—and I really hope you meet him one day—is a business advisor. He has a lot of rich clients who are always looking for places to invest their money." They all just happen to have the same last name, he silently adds.

Lou gives him a doubtful nods. "And you know him...how?"

Ferrin pauses, and thinks this is his chance to come clean and tell her who he really is. But Juan and Delaney would likely refuse his help out of mistaken pride, Tessa would be royally pissed, Willis would yell at him, and Lou...

He looks at the woman in question, watching him with a suspicious frown.

Lou would feel betrayed and would likely kick him out and refuse to see him ever again.

His stomach twists at the thought.

He can't risk that. She's barely begun to trust plain old

Ferrin Jones, the homeless drifter trying to set down roots, and her odds of having a panic attack when she leaves the house are still fifty-fifty. His mind boggles at telling her he's actually Benjamin Ferrin Macon-Jones, and if he were to tell her, he'd have to explain that being friends with a Macon-Jones who's a Macon-Jones in public means dealing with the occasional paparazzi ambush and the odd run-in with the police, not to mention charity balls and a multitude of other social, business and media events where he sometimes needs to make an appearance as a representative of the Macon-Jones dynasty. She'd run as far and as fast as possible away from him.

Well.

She'd run into her bedroom and lock the door, and never allow him near her again.

"Ferrin?"

He starts and blinks. "Sorry," he says, shaking his head, and he isn't sure if he's apologizing for taking so long or because he's going to continue hiding the truth. "Pierce is an old friend of the family. I've known him almost all my life."

"Huh," she says. "A boy from the old neighbourhood who made good?"

Ferrin slowly smiles. "Something like that."

He shoves away the guilt. He'll tell her—he'll tell all of them—the truth. He will.

Just not today.

Even for a Macon-Jones, investment deals take time. Still, Juan and Delaney, and the new company Pierce pulls together, are able to buy the hospital and grounds from the town within six weeks. Juan grins like a kid on Christmas morning as they sign the papers and the town ceremonially hands over the deed. Delaney is just as giddy, and she watches her husband with a gleam in her eyes that bodes well for another hellspawn in the near future.

That night, as Ferrin waves to the friend dropping him off after the deed-buying party and staggers into his house, he can't help but feel smugly pleased with life.

♠♥♣♦

"What?" Gillian teases over the phone the next morning. "Do you intend to purchase the entire town?"

"A house and two business properties are not the whole town."

"Just majority landowner, then?"

He sputters with laughter, then winces as his hangover protests the noise. "Maybe."

"Well, I'm calling about the grand opening of the one thousandth Macon-Jones store."

"I remember. I know Carson, Dyson and Jack want an ever bigger bash but Abram's being a curmudgeon about it."

"Well, the curmudgeon has been bludgeoned into submission. There will be a week of festivities to mark the occasion."

"Good God—how did you get him to agree?"

"We put it to a vote at the Board of Directors. Yours was the tie-breaker. Carson, Dyson and Jack are very pleased you decided to side with them."

"Wonderful."

"We all know how the game is played."

"Well, warn the others that I'm off to the Dominican next month with the Musketeers, so my vote may be locked up for another three years."

"No more contracts on pizza boxes, please. It makes it even smellier in that boardroom than usual."

"Deal."

Lou scowls. "You're going where?"

"The Dominican Republic," Ferrin repeats cheerfully. They're both slouched comfortably on the couch watching television, a bowl of popcorn between them.

"You only just got back from Toronto!"

He laughs. "That's almost two months ago! Look, my cousins have a place. Booked." He grimaces and shakes his head. "Anyway, they've asked me to go, and it's been a while since the four of us have gone somewhere, and— hell. I'm not even sure why I'm trying to justify it to you."

"You do work for me," she snaps.

"Actually, I don't. Ike fired me, remember?"

"And I told him to un-fire you."

Ferrin shrugs. "He stopped paying me after Christmas."

She turns to frown at him. "But...but you've still been shovelling my walk and—and running my errands!"

"Yeah, because that's what friends do for each other."

Her eyes widen and her jaw slowly sags open.

He frowns. "What?" he asks, and reaches for more popcorn.

"I even pay Ike!"

He considers her thoughtfully, one eyebrow raised.

"Well," he says, his voice carefully neutral, "he also manages your investments, so I guess that's fair."

She glances away, pulling her sweater tight around herself. She stares at the TV, where a commercial is still playing out its song and dance routine.

"It's only for two weeks," Ferrin says. "Will you really miss me that much while I'm gone?"

Their eyes meet, and she finds she can't look away.

She feels a small frisson of electricity slide down her back. It's odd how he'd been such a stranger a year ago, something almost alien, and now he's as dearly familiar to her as her own face. Those crooked features are actually quite handsome, his eyes a compelling blue. She can now read so much into his lopsided smirk, and his raised eyebrows can make her laugh, or make her gnash her teeth in frustration. He's no longer alien, but a precious part of her life, one she doesn't want to lose and now is the worst possible moment to realize how much he means to her, when he's sitting right across from her with a raised eyebrow and puzzled puppy eyes, and she has a horrible desire to throw herself against his broad chest and kiss him breathless, then take him upstairs and lose herself in his arms—

That brings her up short and she catches her breath, instinctively withdrawing into her sweater, plucking nervously at its strands.

"Lou?" Ferrin asks, concerned. "Everything okay?"

"Yes," she says a bit more sharply than she intended. "Yeah." She forces herself to meet his eyes and smile. "We're missing the show."

He opens his mouth, but she turns up the volume and they go back to the adventures of the intrepid detective and her plucky sidekick. Ferrin keeps throwing puzzled glances her way, which she steadfastly ignores, even as she walks him to the door and says good-night without mentioning his pending vacation again.

A part of her curses and calls her a coward as she shuts the door behind him.

It's *complicated,* the other part of her thinks sourly as she stomps upstairs to bed.

The days feel oddly flat after Ferrin leaves on his holiday, but Lou can't deny there's also a sense of relief, like she's been granted a reprieve, of sorts. Short-lived, but still welcome, although she has no hope things are going to be less confusing by the time he returns.

Even with him gone, he's constantly in her thoughts. One minute, she's convinced she only thinks of him as a friend, and the next, she's daydreaming about his hands, and the moment after that, she hears Ike's voice telling her Ferrin's only interested in her money, and the moment after *that*, she's reminding herself Ferrin only thinks of her as a friend. Having Ferrin gone for two weeks will give her time to think in peace, or so she tells herself as she drifts rather disconsolately through the first couple of days without him.

She forgot about Tessa.

"So," that woman says, thoughtfully munching on a cinnamon roll, "why doesn't Ike know about you going outside?"

Lou freezes, then flushes. "What makes you think he doesn't know?" she asks, her eyes on her hands as she stirs her coffee.

"The fact that you kept telling me not to tell him when he was in town last month," Tessa says drily. "As if I have any reason to talk to Ike in the first place, especially after what he did at Christmas! Besides, he better not set foot in The Row, if he knows what's good for him! Be that as it may, though, sooner or later, those people who do talk to him are going to mention it. You're being seen, you know, and that makes people talk."

"God," Lou says bitterly, "I haven't even left the back yard yet! The way people gossip in this town, it's no wonder I've stayed inside for so long."

"Sure, because becoming a recluse in a small town is an excellent way to keep people from talking about you."

Lou hunches her shoulders, and shrugs. "Doesn't matter what they're saying," she mutters angrily, "so long as they're not saying it to me."

"Why are you so angry? Most of the people I've met in town are really, really nice."

"Sure, when you're healthy and don't need them."

Tessa's eyebrows shoots up. "Okay, you can't just leave me with that!"

Lou heaves an impatient sigh. "Once they knew my mother was dying, they stopped coming around. Ike was the only one who visited, the only one who asked if there was anything we needed, the only one who offered to help, then actually helped." She shakes her head. "I didn't mind so much for me, but my mom..." She blinks furiously against the sudden hot rush of tears. "My mom was so lonely that last year. I can't—I won't—forgive them for that."

Tessa rips off another piece of cinnamon bun and pops it into her mouth with a thoughtful air. She finishes chewing, swallows, and says, "Well, that does surprise me. A lot." She frowns. "Willis, too?"

Lou sneers. "He's the worst of the bunch! He supposedly loved her! Hah! That bastard."

Tessa shakes her head and pops another piece of cinnamon bun into her mouth. "I don't know what to say, Lou. I'm sorry that happened. So, is your goal to control your agoraphobia to the point where you can leave Ledoux? Move somewhere else and start a new life?"

Lou snorts. "Like where?"

"Vancouver, maybe."

She laughs. "I'm not going to Vancouver."

"Why not? You don't have any family anywhere and Ike's your best friend, right? So, why wouldn't you go to Vancouver? Which brings me back to my original question: why don't you want your best friend to know how well you're doing?"

Lou shrugs, and restlessly plucks at her sweater.

"Lou," Tessa sighs, "you know I'm not going to stop until you give me an honest answer."

Lou scowls, and shifts uncomfortably beneath Tessa's mock-glare.

"It's...complicated," she finally mutters.

"Why?"

Lou sighs and tosses down her cinnamon bun.

"Look," she snaps, "Ike was my only friend and my only link to the outside world for years. He's the only one who stood by me when I was looking after my mother, and then later, when I couldn't leave the house without collapsing into a puddle of panic-stricken goo at the door, he looked after me. I...I just don't want him to think..." She trails off helplessly.

Tessa's expression softens. "You don't want him to think you're getting better without him. Is that it?"

Lou shakes her head. "I don't want him to think he's the reason I never got better *with* him."

"Oh. Oh! I get it. But if he loves you—"

"Ha!"

"There are lots of different forms of love, Lou. Just because he doesn't love you in a romantic, let's-get-married-and-make-babies sense doesn't mean he doesn't still love you. He took care of you for all those years. That means something! And you have no idea how much it pains me to say anything nice about that man! But what I'm trying to say is, because he's your friend, he'll be happy for you. He might be sad that he wasn't the one who could help you, but, then again, if he hadn't left, you wouldn't have had the push to make a change, and so, he's still responsible for you getting better, whether he's physically here or not."

Tessa beams happily while Lou tries to untangle her words enough to follow her logic.

"I...guess that makes sense," she says slowly, "in a convoluted sort of way."

"Of course it makes sense!" Tessa leans forward, her eyes gleaming. "Look. Ike left because he wanted to make a life with Irish, right?"

Lou winces and nods.

"Well, in order to do that, he had to leave you behind. He couldn't have expected you to stay exactly as he left you, could he? Life doesn't work that way! So, really, you making the effort to get better, to get outside, to make new friends—well, you're just doing what he would want you to do, anyway, if he wasn't such a jerk."

Lou scowls.

VICTORIA BERNADINE

Tessa waves away her irritation.

"Okay, fine, maybe I'm totally projecting how I would react onto him, and he's really just as much of an asshole to you as he is to everyone else. The fact that he has a soft spot for you and seems to be in love with Irish are the only saving graces he has, in my opinion. All I'm really trying to say, Lou, is you better tell him how far you've come before he finds out from somebody else. It's something worth celebrating, and if he's as good a friend as you say, then he'll be nothing but happy for you." She raises an eyebrow. "Or are you still hoping he'll decide to come back to you if you come across as needy enough?"

Lou's eyes pop open. "What? No! I never—that's not—!"

"Well, from the outside, that's exactly what it looks like to me."

"No," Lou says firmly, "I don't want him to come back to me."

She freezes, her eyes widening as her mouth slowly sags open.

"Lou?" Tessa finally prompts when it appears she's never going to speak again. "What's going on? Are you okay?"

"I'm fine," Lou replies faintly. "I just...I just...I just *really* don't want him to come back to me."

"O-kay..."

Lou laughs. "No, you don't understand! I've loved Ike for so long—my entire life!—I just—I don't—I don't even know how to explain it!"

Tessa's eyes widen. "You're laughing. Like, really laughing. I've never seen you laugh like this before."

"I know! I feel so light, all of a sudden!" Lou laughs again, joyously, and she stands, stretching her hands above her head. "Oh, my God! I feel...*marvelous*!"

Now Tessa is laughing as well, albeit with a puzzled note to the sound. "I'm happy for you. Now, do you want to explain it to me?"

Lou walks to Ike's Chair—that armchair that only he ever sat in until Ferrin and Tessa came into her life—and flops into it, then laughs again, this time at Tessa's confused face.

"Don't you get it?" Lou says. *"I'm not in love with him anymore!* I'm sincerely and truly happy that he's happy, and in Vancouver, and with Irish, and that he doesn't love me, and he's just a friend, and—oh, my God—I'm free! I'm free now to do and be whatever I want!"

Tessa grins as Lou once again stretches her hands high above her head and laughs with joy.

"Oh, my God," Lou says, "I feel like...like dancing, or something!"

"Too bad you're not ready for it, otherwise I'd say let's go to the bar. Impress the town with our moves on the dance floor."

Lou leans forward, her dark eyes gleaming. "Will we scandalize anybody?"

Tessa's eyes widen. "Depends on whether you intend to dance on the tables or not."

Lou's grin turns wicked. "Dare to find out?"

In the end, she isn't quite that brave. They end up at The Row—it's only across the street from her back yard—where Delaney's holding down the fort for the few regulars who wander in for an evening coffee. Willis-that-bastard is also there with Juan, and Lou freezes when she catches sight of him.

Willis-that-bastard turns and sees her. His eyes widen, his grizzled face startled and wary as she hesitates just inside the door. She automatically clutches at her sweater as her eyes lock with the man who had been her mother's lover and closest friend, but who had left them alone in their struggle towards the end. His bright blue eyes turn hopeful and Lou thinks she might be brave enough to leave her house, brave enough to walk into a public place like The Row, even brave enough to consider going to a bar and dancing on a table or two...but she still isn't brave enough to actually confront Willis-that-bastard.

She slowly blinks, and turns away from him, and pretends she doesn't notice the look on his face when he shakes his head at Juan's questioning look.

Delaney and Tessa end up back at Lou's house, where they drink everything she has in the cupboards before a sleepily grumbling Juan arrives to take his staggering, albeit extremely affectionate, wife home while Lou and Tessa giggle helplessly as the couple meanders their way to the front gate before Tessa crashes on Lou's couch.

Lou goes to The Row several times over the next week and a half, where she carefully ignores Willis-that-bastard along with all the others she hasn't seen in five years. She goes, for the first time, on a solo walk around her block, even though she spends the last half of it in a life-or-death struggle with the panic trying to bring her to her knees. She even manages some grocery shopping with Tessa. All the while, she waits with growing impatience for Ferrin to get home. She can't wait to tell him everything she's accomplished while he's been gone.

When he returns, he's tanned and relaxed and more handsome than she remembered, bubbling over with stories of the things he and his cousins had done and the people they'd met. She hangs on his every word as he tells her stories of open air restaurants and neighbourhood bars, about long, smooth beaches and endless ocean, about his cousins who get him into so, so much trouble, but invariably get him out again. She studies him with something approaching fascination as he talks, paying attention to the laugh lines around his eyes, the shape of his nose, the exact way the dark scruff of his whiskers look against his tanned skin, the way his flashing, crooked grin lights up his eyes and face, how he laughs with his entire body.

"I think that Scottish guy kinda liked her," he's saying now, "until she got sick all over him during our fishing trip. Yeah, the seas were a bit rough, but who knew Jack was such a girl?"

Listening to his low, rumbling voice, watching his expressive face, Lou feels, for the first time in a long time, a real desire to see and experience these things for herself.

"Well, at least your cousin tried," Lou says wistfully. "I've never even seen the ocean."

Ferrin stops and blinks. "You've never seen the ocean?"

She shakes her head.

"Why not?" he asks, curious. "I mean, you didn't spend your entire life in this house!"

She shrugs. "Mom didn't like travelling so we didn't go far when I was a kid. When I was in university, I came home in the summers before I moved back. I've never even had a job, and after Mom died, well..." She ruefully indicates the room they're sitting in and by extension the rest of the house and the two heavy oak doors that have defined the boundaries of her world for years. "I've never really had the chance to go to the ocean."

Ferrin considers her thoughtfully, head tilted to one side, then says, "Would you like to go to the Dominican? Or, really, anywhere with an ocean beach?"

She blinks, then slowly nods. "I think I would, and for the first time in a long time, I think it may even be possible. Some day."

He raises an eyebrow in question.

She shifts nervously, then gruffly begins to tell him of her adventures while he was gone.

229

April drifts into May and Lou finds herself prepping for Ferrin's arrival every day. She tries different hairstyles, and she puts on skirts and shorts rather than jeans or sweats although her voluminous sweater still swallows up her figure. She finds herself blushing too much and becoming unfortunately tongue-tied far too often.

She hates it.

And she loves it.

As the days get warmer, Ferrin and Tessa, Delaney, Juan and their hellspawn, coax her a little farther away from her house for a little longer each day. She hasn't quite gathered the courage and determination to make it to Regina to shop, but she did make all the way through Main Street. The day she walked into The Row on her own was a cause for celebration and they all descended on her house that night with food and drinks. She spent the next day cursing them through her hangover.

Ferrin persuades her to go his house and she stands in his back yard, staring out at the broad, flat horizon, breathing in the scent of freshly-worked soil, listening to the low rumble of a tractor in the distance.

He anxiously watches her but she stands and smiles and soaks it all in, feeling like she's soil dried by a Saskatchewan drought, and it's finally beginning to rain.

May turns into June and Ferrin takes Lou out of town for picnics and drives, although she refuses to visit anyone and does her best to avoid anyplace—The Row is the one notable exception--she knows Willis-that-bastard might also appear. She glares and presses her lips into a thin, tight line whenever Ferrin asks her why she hates Willis-that-bastard so much.

But it's not her stubborn refusal to widen her circle of friends that's keeping Ferrin up at night—although it does concern him.

No, what's beginning to bother him is...*himself*.

He takes Lou for a picnic and finds himself admiring the way her hair tumbles over her shoulders when she lets it down, or how it shines in the sun, or the healthy glow of her tanning skin, or the shape of however much of her legs he can see when she wears shorts or a skirt beneath her ever-present sweater. He finds himself tracing with his eyes the curve of her lips or the lines of her chin and cheekbones, or the delicate arch of her eyebrows over those always-fascinating eyes.

It's distracting and dangerous and, he reminds himself every night as he heads home, utterly inappropriate.

"Have you thought yet about dating?" Tessa says one night with a bright-eyed grin and Ferrin immediately goes on full alert, wondering what's going on in her convoluted mind.

Lou wrinkles her nose. "Dating?"

"Yeah. You know: you go out with a person who's hopefully not too closely related, have a meal, maybe see a movie, then return home and have wild, screaming sex for three hours. Dating."

"Hey, now," Ferrin yelps, "I don't want to think of either of you like that!"

Tessa gives him an appraising look. "Of course you don't," she says drily and he flushes. She turns her attention back to Lou. "Well?"

Lou looks both disturbed and intrigued. "Three hours?"

"Come on! You and Ike must have had some great sex! At least once, right?"

"Well, not for three hours! I mean...what would you do for that long?"

"I'm right here!" Ferrin groans, burying his face in his hands.

Tessa starts to laugh. "Oh, come on, Ferrin! You've never talked about sex with women before?"

"With women, yes—not with the two of you!"

He knows he's made a horrible mistake the moment the words leave his mouth.

Tessa's still giving him grief by the time she leaves and once they're alone, Ferrin turns to Lou and says, "Are you going to keep giving me a hard time or are you going to kick my ass in crib?"

She sniffs as she adjusts her sweater. "Who says I can't do both?"

She does do both, and Ferrin's still grumbling while he puts on his shoes and prepares to leave.

"Oh, please," she says, rolling her eyes. "If you hadn't insulted us—"

"Accidentally! Come on, give me some credit! I'm much more creative than that!"

She raises an eyebrow and appraises him with a decidedly wicked smirk. "So, three hours seems about right, then?"

She sees the expression on his face and laughs up at him, her eyes shining, her sun-kissed skin glowing, and for a split second, he wants to swoop down and pick her up off her feet to kiss that smile and taste that laugh.

He must actually reach for her because she dances away, laughing even more.

"No tickling!" she says with a wag of her finger.

I don't want to tickle you, he thinks, and gapes at her, struggling to regain his composure.

"Tickling's what you get for teasing," he manages to force out and hopes she doesn't notice how lame he sounds.

Tickling, Lou thinks as she closes the door with relief on Ferrin's broad shoulders. She leans her burning forehead against the oak, closes her eyes, and groans.

She was flirting. Actually flirting—and if there's one thing she simply cannot risk doing with Ferrin, it's flirting and trying to make their relationship into something it's not.

Behind her closed lids she sees his crooked smirk and teasing eyes, his broad shoulders and long, long legs, and her knees tremble as sweat prickles her skin.

She wants him, she thinks. She wants to lay him down and crawl up his body; to burrow against him and lose herself in his strength and scent and taste.

She gently bangs her head against the sturdy oak door. There's nothing wrong with lusting after someone, and considering she hasn't really lusted after anyone but Ike in her entire life, the fact she's burning with sexual frustration right now is a good thing.

The bad thing is her desire to lose herself in him.

She straightens with a sigh and wanders back to the living room to take the last of their dishes to the kitchen.

She just spent five years lost in her own home. She can't afford to lose herself again.

Ferrin pedals his bicycle home like all the demons from hell are hot on his heels.

He wants her, he thinks. He wants to peel that ugly fucking sweater from her shoulders then peel off whatever else she might be wearing beneath it. He wants to tease her, explore her, make her laugh and sigh and squirm while he watches those incredible eyes darken even more with lust and pleasure.

On the surface, this lust is okay, he thinks as he coasts into his yard and puts his bike away. Considering he hasn't been with anyone but Olivia in years, lusting after another woman is good thing.

He bounds into the house and heads to the bathroom.

But not Lou, he thinks as he hurriedly strips down and starts the shower, making it as cold as his heated body can stand. He's the first man she's seen in five years who isn't Ike. He steps beneath the icy stream and grits his teeth against the pain of it. Even if she were interested and willing, it's not like she's had a whole lot of choice the last few years.

He could probably seduce her if he really tried but it's not only inappropriate, it's not fair. She's been locked away for years with only Ike for company; she deserves a chance to explore her options.

As June edges into July, Ferrin finds himself encouraging Tessa's teasing and forces himself to regularly suggest Lou expand her circle of friends, to meet new people, and open herself up to new possibilities.

And by 'new possibilities', he means 'men'.

"Juan has some pretty handsome youngsters on his crew," he says with a determined smirk as he picks up his cards.

Lou glares and cuts the deck.

"No," she says.

He turns over the top card and says, "Are you sure? I can bring you pictures so you can see for yourself."

She slaps down a card. "No."

He grins, this time genuinely amused.

"You sound a little uncertain," he says.

"Fuck off and play."

July drifts by, and Lou wonders if Ferrin has any idea how much tension is building inside her.

Whether wearing grey t-shirts and cargo shorts, or shirtless in cargo shorts, she's finding it more and more difficult not to forget herself and touch him the way she's been touching him in her dreams. He's big and broad and beefy, and she finds herself spending more and more time imagining herself wrapping her legs around his waist and frantically kissing him as he carries her to the bedroom. She wants to cling to him, burrow against him, lose herself in him—and it's that last thought that's always like a pail of ice water over her head.

She doesn't want to lose herself again. She can't.

It doesn't stop her from fantasizing, though, and one night, she steps towards him and almost kisses him good-night before she catches herself. Thankfully, he's too busy bantering with her to notice.

She thinks she could probably seduce him, if she really tried, because she occasionally catches a glimpse of his face when he thinks she isn't looking. She's almost certain there's something there, an ember of something burning beneath the surface that might burst into full flame if they're not careful.

Tessa—damn her—simply watches them both with knowing amusement but for once doesn't say anything.

Lou sometimes wonders if she should be concerned about that then decides she has enough to worry about without adding Tessa's thoughts to the mix.

August arrives and with it, a heat wave that settles over them all like a heavy down blanket in an over-heated room, and Lou is still enveloped in that stupid sweater even as sweat beads her forehead.

"Years sitting in this house in that sweater, and you never thought to get air conditioning?" Ferrin mutters, taking a long, grateful drink of ice cold beer from a bottle that's sweating almost as much as he is.

"Ike didn't know how to install it," Lou growls as she shuffles the cards, "and I wasn't about to allow anyone else in the house."

"Well, it'll cost you an arm and a leg if you were to try to get it put in this week."

Lou looks at him and raises an eyebrow. "If you want my house air conditioned so much, then you do it! I'm perfectly fine."

Ferrin smirks. "Right. That's why you have a droplet of sweat—" he reaches over, gently cups her chin and swipes his thumb against the corner of her brow, "—right there."

She freezes and stares at him, eyes wide and dark and getting darker, and he finds he can't look away or move his hand.

Then she ever-so-gently nuzzles against his hand and her lips part—

And he lurches across the table, and mashes his mouth against hers.

It's sweet bliss as she buries her fingers in his hair and returns his kiss with equal abandon...except for the card table digging into his stomach.

With a growl against her lips, he drags her to her feet and shoves the card table out of the way, cards and board and notebook and beer flying, and then she's *there*, in his arms, pressing against him like she's water and he's the desert and he's desperate to absorb her into his very core.

It's only when he picks her up and she wraps her legs round his waist, her hands tangled deep in his hair tugging him closer as she makes desperate mewling sounds against his mouth that sanity returns.

Reluctantly...but it does return.

As abruptly as he began the kiss, he ends it, putting her back on her feet and taking several hasty steps away.

She stares up at him, her lips red and swollen, her eyes dark and filled with a mixture of lust and bewilderment.

"I'm sorry," he says, panting, and knows he's said the

exactly wrong thing when hurt fills her face.

He reaches for her but she abruptly turns away.

He clenches his hands so tightly, his nails dig into his palms.

"It's not what you think," he says.

She sniffs and tosses her head but doesn't turn to look at him. "I'm sure it's exactly what I think," she grates out. "You should leave. Now."

He takes a step closer, reaching out his hand once more.

She hunches her shoulders and deftly avoids his touch.

"Can we talk about this tomorrow?" he asks.

She bows her head but says nothing.

Ferrin, heavy-eyed from lack of sleep, sets off on his bicycle for work the next morning still thinking about what happened the night before and wondering just how badly he's fucked everything up.

They'd been trapped in tense silence when he left the house and he's spent the night trying to figure out how to get Lou to talk to him about what happened—assuming she lets him back into the house. For a moment, he's lost in the fantasy of simply walking in and sweeping her into his arms and kissing her before he carries her upstairs to her bedroom and giving her the three hours of screaming sex Tessa had mentioned...if he could last that long, of course.

He shakes his head as he pedals.

Nothing has changed: she's had no chance to meet other men yet to determine if what's happening between the two of them is something she even truly wants. Most importantly: she still doesn't know his full name.

He pedals furiously, absorbed with worrying at the situation as he barrels around a blind corner—which is why it takes him several precious seconds to realize there's a load of lumber strewn crookedly across the road, a one-tonne truck parked on the shoulder, and two young men who look as shocked as he probably does as he hits the boards and flies off the bike.

In the split second before everything goes black, he wonders what it is about this town that makes him so *fucking* clumsy.

The doctor is handsome, calm, competent, and professionally impersonal. Lou hates him on sight, but that may have more to do with her terrified ride to Regina with Juan and the uncertainty of what they'd find once they finally got there.

"He's still unconscious," the doctor says now, his voice cool and brisk, "but the CT scan isn't showing any major damage. A concussion, but no fractures; he had a pretty good helmet on. He's also bruised and scraped up, especially along his left side, but again, no fractures. He should be just fine."

"Should be?" Lou asks sharply, her fingers digging deep into the wool of her sweater.

"He is still unconscious. Now, I'm not expecting any complications, but he does have a brain injury, so we need to be cautious. If you haven't already done so, you should contact his family."

"Why?" She's almost embarrassed by how strident she sounds but decides she'll apologize later.

Juan touches her shoulder but she instinctively shrugs him away.

"They should be told regardless," Juan says, his voice calm and much more soothing than the doctor's, "but the doctor means in case he needs to do surgery or something...right?"

The doctor watches Lou with a thoughtful expression. "Correct. Or do you have the authority to give permission for treatment?"

She gives a short shake of her head, folding into herself and shrinking into her sweater.

The doctor glances from her to Juan in unspoken question.

Juan says, "I have his emergency contact information on file at my office. I'll take care of it."

"Good." He glances back at Lou. "Well, it's just a precaution, so you shouldn't worry. You can go in now." He gives them an impersonal smile and a nod as he opens the door to Ferrin's room.

♠♥♣♦

Juan leaves her alone with an unconscious Ferrin while he calls Delaney then Ferrin's emergency contact. Juan returns to sit beside her for a couple hours before he tries to persuade her to take a break. When she refuses, he reluctantly excuses himself to check on his crew, stretch his legs, and find something to eat.

"Will you be all right on your own?" he asks.

She nods without taking her eyes off the man in the bed.

"Are you sure?" Juan persists. "I don't want you to be alone if you have a panic attack."

"Well, I'm in the best place for it," she says, distracted. "I'll bet they have some great tranquilizers round here."

He chuckles. "I won't be long," he says. "Hopefully no more than an hour."

She waves him away.

Fifteen minutes later, Lou's eyes widen as a man strides into the hospital room like he owns the place. He's tall, distinguished, and classically handsome with fine, delicately drawn features, black hair salted with grey, and dark blue eyes. He's dressed in a suit that even Lou can tell is well-tailored and probably cost more than all the clothes in her house combined, and possibly the furniture as well.

His face is grim as he flicks a glance at Lou, then turns his attention to Ferrin.

"How is he?" he barks with a distinct Celtic lilt to his voice.

"Who are you?"

He turns, his eyes coolly assessing as he takes in her messy hair, and the shapeless brown sweater. She feels herself shrinking back beneath the intense scrutiny then she lifts her chin and straightens her shoulders with a haughty glare of her own. Recognition flashes on his face and he gives her a smile that, even though it's fleeting, still manages to rock her with its charm.

"My apologies; worry has made me forget my manners. I'm Pierce Killian, Ferrin's emergency contact. Juan Martinez called me?"

Lou relaxes slightly. "Oh. Yes." She frowns. "I thought you lived in Toronto. How'd you get here so fast? It's only been an hour or so since he called."

"I do live in Toronto, but it's amazing how quickly you can get somewhere in a very fast, very private jet. However, I can't claim superhuman speed. I was already in the air on my way to Vancouver, so we arranged a detour." He smiles again, this time more slowly, and Lou wonders how many doors have opened and deals been made as a result of that smile alone. "You most definitely are Lou," he adds as he stretches out his hand.

Her eyes widen then narrow as they shake hands. They both turn to look at Ferrin and silently watch him until Pierce turns to her and raises an eyebrow in question.

"He's bruised and battered," she says, "but nothing's broken. He was briefly conscious about a half hour ago, but he just muttered something about purple monkeys and went back to sleep."

"Well, he always could sleep through anything."

She bites back a smile. "It's comforting to know this is normal," she murmurs.

"Trust me, my dear, there is nothing normal about

Ferrin."

This time she can't stop the laugh. "If we keep agreeing like this, we may end up friends."

Pierce turns and gives her an indecipherable look. "I have no doubt about it."

♠ ♥ ♣ ♦

Ferrin first becomes aware of the smell; that distinctive mix of odors that screams 'hospital' no matter where a person actually is when they catch a whiff of it.

He hates that smell; came to know it far too well when his father was dying and for a moment, floating between sleep and consciousness, he's confused. Is he still there in that hospital room? Is he still watching the shallow rise and fall of his father's chest, torn between desperately praying to see another breath and just as desperately pleading for his father's struggle to be over so he can finally be at peace? If he looks to his right, will he see Gillian restless on the couch, reluctantly convinced to nap, and Abram, sitting grey and drawn and stoic in the chair on the other side of the bed? Would one of the other cousins or Pierce walk in at any moment?

His face scrunches into a frown.

No, he thinks fuzzily, he isn't sitting in an armchair, and besides, that was a long time ago now.

His nostrils twitch and he cracks open his eyes. A face almost immediately looms over him and comes into focus.

"Good morning," Pierce says, his voice silky smooth.

"Hey," Ferrin mumbles through a dry as dust throat and mouth. His eyes slide closed and he drifts again towards sleep until he realizes he's just seen Pierce.

Here.

In Saskatchewan.

His eyes pop open in sudden panic and he tries to sit up only to fall back against the bed with an involuntary yelp as his body tells him there are a few things he needs to know.

He groans through gritted teeth, his eyes tightly closed.

"I realize I'm not quite as handsome as I used to be, but I really don't think I'm as awful as all that!"

Ferrin opens his eyes again, still grimacing with pain. "Yeah, it's really you," he croaks, then licks dry lips. He gestures for water and Pierce stands and holds the glass and straw as Ferrin takes cautious sips. When he's finished, he leans his head back against his pillows with a relieved sigh. "Nobody else could be so falsely humble."

Pierce grins, wreathing his face in crinkles which, to Ferrin's fuzzy annoyance, only serves to make him even more handsome.

"It's a gift," Pierce says with a graceful shrug.

"But you are here...wherever here may be?"

"You're in the hospital in Regina."

"Hospital?"

"Yes. You had an accident."

Memory returns. "Oh, God—on my bike." He closes his eyes and groans. "What a stupid thing to happen."

"Most accidents are stupid things that happen. The important thing, however, is that you're all right, and will be out of the hospital in a day or two."

Ferrin looks at him in sudden consternation. "Is Gillian here? Or any of the cousins?"

"Gillian's still in Europe and very relieved to learn you're mostly unharmed, and more or less yourself. She's leaving in the morning and will be here in a day or two, regardless of my assurances that your head is as hard as we always suspected." Pierce's lifts his hand as Ferrin opens his mouth. "This is Gillian we're talking about. You don't think she's more than capable of keeping your secrets?"

Ferrin subsides with a frown.

Pierce continues. "Abram's in Japan, negotiating that expansion agreement and has provided me with a thoughtfully crafted statement to give you if you chose to be seriously injured and he was forced to cut his trip short.

You should be relieved there's no need for me to share that now. Carson, Dyson and Jack are waiting for a word from me before galloping to your rescue while the other cousins are waiting with bated breath for news."

Ferrin breathes a sigh of relief. "Thank God. You haven't told anybody here who I am, have you?"

"You were admitted as Ferrin Jones, but I informed the hospital of your true identity so they could access your medical records, if needed. They've been persuaded to be discreet and will remain so once a substantial donation is made in your name. Your *real* name. I've also convinced them to move you to this private room and to tell your friends it's because you needed complete silence."

Ferrin grins a little, then winces. "Well, if I can get out of here without Juan or Lou figuring it out, I'll be lucky."

"You could just tell them," Pierce says mildly.

Ferrin shakes his head and winces again. "Things are...complicated," he says, "and now would not be a good time for them to find out the truth. Especially this way."

Pierce leans forward, his face serious, his eyes intent. "You've been gone from Toronto for what? Almost eighteen months? You can't keep running from your life forever."

Ferrin grimaces. "I know." He closes his eyes then opens them again, a pleading look on his face. "You won't tell them, though, right?"

Pierce sighs, and straightens, looking at him with reluctant affection. "I won't tell them," he says, "but I think you're going to be very sorry if they find out the truth another way. Sooner or later, Ferrin, something's going to slip. You know that."

Ferrin grimaces again and nods.

♠♥♣♦

"Oh my God, are you frickin' kidding me?" Tessa practically moans when they walk into The Row that evening. She gapes at Pierce's well-groomed hair and silk scarf that perfectly accents his beautifully tailored suit.

He raises one eyebrow, then turns his attention to the menu posted behind the counter. Tessa continues staring her mouth hanging open. He glances at her, then back at the menu, then back at her, and gives her a polite albeit uncomfortable smile.

She blinks, flushes, and rushes into speech. "I'm sorry, it's just that we don't often get people like you in this town, and definitely not in my coffee shop! And by 'people like you', I mean, you look pretty rich! What's that suit made of? And, seriously, dress pants? A jacket? A scarf that probably costs more than everything in this place put together, not to mention you're wearing a fucking scarf in August in the middle of a heat wave! Are you a lawyer? I can't remember the last time I saw anybody in a suit in The Row—oh, wait, I can! A month ago, when Scott Shelby's youngest boy got married, the whole wedding party was in here on the way to the pictures, and they all looked gorgeous! But suits like yours would be ruined pretty quick around here."

She stops, contemplates the rather glazed and terrified look in his eyes, and gives him a slow, wide, sunny grin.

"Did Ferrin warn you about me?" she asks brightly.

Pierce's eyes crinkle as he returns her grin. "He failed to do you justice," he says. "He's correct about one thing, however," he continues as he reaches out and lifts her hand from where it's resting on the counter, "you are utterly charming," he murmurs, and brushes his lips across her knuckles.

Lou turns her back and bites her lip hard as Tessa actually simpers.

Juan clears his throat, and says, "Tessa, if it isn't too much trouble..." he raises an eyebrow, and nods at the pots of coffee. "We need coffee and then we'll give you an update on Ferrin."

"Oh! Oh, right. Sorry, Juan." She straightens,

reverently touches the back of her hand, and smiles wistfully at Pierce. "Have you decided what you'd like?" she asks, and blushes.

His grin turns a little wicked but he only says, "A large, regular coffee, please. It was an early morning today."

She nods. "Gotcha. I can give you the regular stuff, or I can make you an extra-strong espresso, guaranteed to keep you awake and probably vibrating for the next five days."

"I'll take a cup of that," Willis-that-bastard says, the door chimes jangling as he pushes his way into The Row as Tessa finishes speaking.

Lou abruptly turns her shoulder to him and wanders away from the counter as Tessa looks around Pierce's broad shoulders, and mock-glares at the older man. "You get into more than enough trouble, Willis, without me adding fuel to the fire!"

"Have a heart, Tessa, it's been a long day, and it's shaping up to be an even longer night."

He gives her his best winning grin, but there's no mistaking the tired lines in his grizzled face.

"Then I guess it's the rocket fuel for you," she says briskly. "I'll bring it over in a minute." She gives Pierce one last, wistful look, then shakes her head, straightens her shoulders, and begins to fill their orders.

♠ ♥ ♣ ♦

"I don't see why I can't stay at my place," Ferrin grumbles as he limps into Lou's house flanked by Juan and Pierce. "Pierce can look after me."

Pierce laughs, loud and hearty.

Ferrin scowls. "Fine. Then I can stay alone."

"The doctor says you still need to get a lot of rest," Lou says, "and I know you, Ferrin. You'll be bored and wrecking the place within the first three hours. I'm going to get you some water so you can take your pain meds."

She hurries to the kitchen.

"She really does know you," Pierce says, a hint of admiration in his voice.

"Well, why can't I stay at Juan's place?"

"Partly because I can't deal with your whining, but it's mainly because my wife thinks you're cute," Juan says.

Pierce raises an eyebrow. "You don't trust your wife?"

"Oh, I trust her with my life, but she'd fawn over him even more than she does now. Pah! Turns my stomach!"

"It's never bothered me," Ferrin mutters, then winces and bites back a groan as Pierce and Juan ease him on to the couch. He leans his head back and closes his eyes, his face grey and pasty.

Juan glances at Pierce.

"You staying here, too?" he asks.

"God, I hope not," Ferrin mutters.

Pierce tsks, and says, "That's the thanks I get for rushing to your side in your hour of need?"

"Lou thinks you're cute and she's going to fawn over you even more than she does already." Ferrin opens his eyes and gives Juan a faint smile. "Okay, I get it."

Juan grins, while Pierce mock-scowls.

"I do not think Pierce is cute," Lou says, bustling into the living room with a glass of water. She hands it to Ferrin along with a painkiller.

"No?" Ferrin says, his lopsided smirk out in full force as he pops the pill in his mouth and takes a drink of water.

"I think he's *smokin'*," she says, and winks at Pierce and Juan while Ferrin coughs and sputters.

Lou walks into the living room the next day with a fresh tube of antiseptic ointment in her hands.

"Okay," she says, "time to change your dressings."

Ferrin looks up with a grimace, while Pierce abruptly closes his laptop and springs to his feet.

"I think we all need coffee!" he says, overly bright, and all but bolts for the door.

"Tell Tessa I said hi," Ferrin calls, and Pierce waves a hand as he leaves the room. They hear the front door close decisively behind him.

Lou turns rather helplessly towards Ferrin, who shrugs.

"He never could stand the sight of, well, anything, really. He'd almost pass out when I showed him my scraped knees as a kid." He grins. "Which just meant I always made a point of showing him, of course." His grin fades, and he looks almost shyly at her. "So, I guess this means you're stuck with helping me with this."

She shrugs. "Somehow, I'm not surprised."

Lou helps him remove his shirt, then she takes off the large white cotton bandages that cover the spectacular scrapes and bruises on his left side and back. She winces as she looks at them, the long, angry red marks just beginning to scab over. At least the sight of the scrapes keeps her attention off Ferrin's naked torso.

Or not, she admits ruefully, because even as she focuses on cleaning the scrapes and applying the antiseptic, she's intensely aware that he towers over her and is easily twice as broad as she is. Instead of feeling intimidated, though, she feels...*safe*. Protected. Like she could lean into him and he'd be more than strong enough to hold her up until she could stand on her own again.

"Are you supposed to use the entire tube of that stuff each time?"

Lou starts, and blinks up at Ferrin, who's watching her with that look in his eyes that always makes her nervous, but this time, it's in a good way.

"I—no. I don't think so," she says, and is surprised to hear the huskiness in her voice.

"Okay," he says.

They stand suspended, as if the entire world is holding its breath.

"I'm glad you're okay," she whispers.

"Thanks. I'm glad you're taking care of me."

She smiles and silence gently settles over them.

He turns to fully face her and reaches out to put a tentative hand on her hip. She draws in a sharp breath, her lips parting as he urges her closer.

She rises on her toes as he dips his head, and they bump noses with a mutual 'ouch'. She huffs a nervous little chuckle.

"I haven't done this very much," she says with a grimace.

"I'm not complaining," he murmurs and bends toward her again. Their lips touch, part, then touch again, exploring, testing, tasting, and it's awkward and sweet and strange and oddly familiar and somehow innocent, and Lou melts against him, sliding her hands around his back...right into the goopy salve that now covers his scrapes and he lifts his head with a pained hiss.

"Oh! Oh, shit! I'm sorry!" she blurts, releasing him as if his skin is burning hot.

She tries to step away, but he tightens his grip on her hips, holding her still. He winces at the sudden movement and hisses again, but he's laughing and his eyes are shining as he says, "I'll forgive you if you promise we can try that again. Maybe when I'm not covered with gunk and can barely move."

She frowns up at him, reality and memories setting in. "The last time we did this, you acted like I had turned radioactive."

He closes his eyes and grimaces. "I know. I'm sorry. It's just..." His fingers flex against her wool-covered hips. "Look. You've been in this house, alone except for Ike, for years. I just... you shouldn't end up with the first man you see who isn't Ike."

She blinks. "End up...? I don't want to *marry* you, Ferrin!"

She realizes what she's said and closes her eyes with an embarrassed groan.

"Are you saying your intentions are entirely dishonorable?" Ferrin says in scandalized tones.

She opens her eyes and scowls. "I'm saying you shouldn't get ahead of yourself!"

He chuckles then winces. "Still. I'm not particularly interested in being...I don't know...the first man you see and so you take me to bed because I'm the first man you've seen." He sighs. "I'm not explaining myself very well, am I?"

Her scowl slowly smooths away. "No, I understand," she says as she flattens her hands very carefully and precisely in the middle of his bare, broad chest. She savors the strong beat of his heart beneath her palms then says, "Look...I don't disagree with you. Besides...you..." She ducks her head then lifts her chin and gives him a steady look. "When I think about you...and me...and maybe...you know...well, I always end up thinking about how much larger you are than me and how much I like that, because it makes me feel safe and like I can burrow into you and you would shut out the rest of the world so it's just you and me. That scares me because I lost myself in my house and it feels like I'm just trying to replace one hiding place with another."

They stare at each other in silence, then Ferrin says, "I understand."

"So we shouldn't...you know..."

"No," he says, "we shouldn't."

"So we're agreed?"

"We're agreed."

They stand in silence, his hands warm where they're resting on her hips. She feels the rapid beat of his heart beneath her palms.

"Your hands are all gooey," he finally says, his voice a low, seductive rumble.

She ducks her head and looks up at him from beneath her lashes.

"I know."

He tugs her a little closer.

"They're a little smelly, too," he says, bending towards her.

"I know that, too," she murmurs and rises up to meet him. Their lips brush—

"Hey, kids, look who I found outside!"

They turn startled faces towards the living room door as Pierce breezes in, followed by an older woman with a slender figure, elegantly-styled grey hair, and an attractive face. Lou realizes she must be Ferrin's stepmother, Gillian.

Behind Gillian is a curvaceous and classically beautiful woman, with long dark hair, brown eyes, and a slightly worried expression.

Lou frowns, wondering who this woman might be as she slowly lowers her hands and Ferrin loosens his hold on her. She glances at Ferrin and freezes at his dumbfounded expression. He takes a step towards the newcomers.

"*Olivia?*"

Ferrin is limping and moving gingerly as he opens the door to his house and leads the way inside. Olivia follows him in and looks around with interest, then raises an eyebrow as she turns towards him.

"A few steps down from what you're used to," she says, her voice neutral but with a thread of amused condescension running through it.

"I'm trying to live within my means," he says and shrugs, then winces as the movement pulls at his scrapes.

Olivia laughs, tossing her jacket on the back of the couch that Ferrin now guiltily thinks looks shabbier than he realized.

"Come on, Ferrin," she says, "your 'means' can afford much better than this place and you know it!"

"I mean, I'm trying to live within the salary Juan pays

me." He gives her a warning look. "I know Pierce already told you, but I'm going to tell you again anyway: they don't know who I am here. I'd like to keep it that way." He grimaces. "Thank God Pierce was already at The Row when you walked in."

Olivia frowns. "Yes, Pierce gave us the whole story on our way to...Lou? That's her name, right?" Ferrin nods, his eyes narrowed as he assesses her. "Well," she says with a careless shrug, "I still can't help but ask: why on earth would you want to hide your identity?"

He gives a small shrug that doesn't aggravate his injuries.

"I'm one of them, Olivia. If they knew I was a Macon-Jones, *the* Macon-Joneses, then they'd treat me differently. I like this life. I'm enjoying myself."

"Yes, I noticed," she says drily.

Ferrin scowls. "That's not what I'm talking about," he snaps.

"Well, at least you're not saying it's not what it looked like," she says, deliberately casual as she drops her purse on top of her jacket.

"Why would I?" he says, surprised. "It's exactly what it looked like—although not really..." He shakes his head. "Anyway, I'm not sure why it would matter to you either way."

"Well, I did fly halfway across the country to see if you're all right."

"Because Abram asked you to?" he asks cynically.

She glares, then softens. "Carson, Dyson and Jack, actually, but I had already decided to hitch a ride with Gillian when she passed through Toronto."

He raises an eyebrow. "The Musketeers didn't trust Pierce's updates? That's odd."

"They just wanted another set of eyes on you...and Abram asked them to double-check. All the cousins know Pierce will do and say whatever you want him to. He loves you like a son, you know."

"I know," he sighs, "even if he does love me like a Macon-Jones father."

Olivia laughs. "Well, you either learn to love that way or you go insane."

Ferrin chuckles then sobers. "And that's another reason why I don't want anyone in town to know who I am. Lou and I...I don't know what, if anything, is really happening between us, but I definitely don't want to pile the whole Macon-Jones thing on her. Not yet."

She raises an eyebrow. "So you're going to spring it on her when, exactly? The honeymoon?"

He snorts. "She's already said she doesn't want to marry me!" He gives her a long, thoughtful look. "Why are you here, Olivia?"

She shrugs, running one delicate finger along the back of the couch as she wanders across the living room.

"I already told you."

"I know you. I know that face. There's something else going on. What is it?"

She bows her head then turns to face him, determination in the set of her jaw and the look in her eyes.

"I heard about your accident, and I couldn't pretend anymore. I couldn't deny what I've been fighting against since I saw you in February." She hesitates, then walks up to him, placing her hand flat against the middle of his chest. "I've missed you," she says softly. "I think we should try again."

Ferrin's eyes widen as his jaw drops. "Well...*shit*."

"My first home away from home," Ferrin says as Gillian strolls out of the rectory's kitchen and places a tray laden with teapot, cups, cream and honey onto the coffee table between the two sofas.

Gillian glances round. "Spartan, but functional," she

says.

"Quite a step down from what you're used to."

She gives him a slight smile. "We all make sacrifices for family, even when that family is the Macon-Joneses."

He grins at that. "It's good to see you," he says.

"Thank you, Ferrin," she says briskly, filling his mug with tea and handing it to him. "I must confess, I've been curious to see this quaint little town for myself. I now understand at least one of its attractions."

"It has many attractions," he says.

Gillian raises an eyebrow as she sits on the sofa opposite him and lifts her own mug to take a dainty sip. He gives her his best innocent look, and she sets the cup on the coffee table with a melodic clink which somehow sounds both authoritative and disapproving. It's a gift, he thinks, amused.

"For heaven's sake, Ferrin, it's been what? Eighteen months, more or less? It's time for you to stop this nonsense and come home once and for all."

He keeps his face carefully expressionless as he watches her.

A slight frown mars her attractive face.

"You can't simply intend to leave your life behind forever," she says.

That surprises a laugh out of him.

"What life?" he asks. "Everything I ever did revolved around Olivia."

"Oh, please! You have friends in Toronto. Family. Not to mention obligations, both social and business! Granted, you don't actually work at the company, but you are a member of the Board, and you could be more active in the operations if you so choose, either in headquarters or in one of the subsidiaries. If you must stay in Saskatchewan, there are always the new offices Abram's proposing to open out here."

He grins at the disgust in her voice, then says, "I thought my lack of interest in the company was my biggest selling point to the family?"

She ignores him and says, "And what about Olivia? She travelled all this way when she learned you were hurt. How can you repair that relationship if you keep yourself buried in these backwoods?"

"I don't know if you've noticed, but there are no woods—back or otherwise—in this part of Saskatchewan."

She impatiently waves her hand. "Stop trying to avoid the issue, Ferrin! You can't run away from your life forever!"

He takes a sip of tea then says, "I'm not running away from my life, Gillian." He leans back and looks steadily at her. "You said I could be more involved on the Board. You're also on the Board. Tell me, how much time does that really take?"

She frowns. "That's not the point."

"It most certainly is the point. I'm not going to deny that there's a lot to be said for the life of the idle rich, and yes, I'm sure Pierce would like me to come back so I can be more hands on with my personal investments. Even Abram wants me home, if for no other reason than to try and lock in my vote once my deal with Carson, Dyson and Jack is done. But, Gillian..." he hesitates, then leans forward, his eyes intent, almost pleading.

"I get up at an ungodly hour every morning," he says softly, "and I go to a job site where I freeze or boil my ass off as I haul out garbage and haul in building materials. Sometimes I'm sent for coffee and lunch, and sometimes I tear things down or hold things up, but no matter what I do, it's something tangible. Something real. It may not be on the same scale as Macon-Jones Enterprises, or a charity ball that raises millions, but it still matters, Gillian, and I get to see the faces of the people who directly benefit from the work I'm doing. In the evenings, I do Lou's yard work and run her errands and we play cards, and..." his expression softens as a fond half-smile curves his lips.

Gillian raises an eyebrow. "And?"

He flushes. "We talk."

Gillian's other eyebrow joins the first. "Ah, yes. You certainly seemed to be talking when we walked in yesterday."

His flush deepens. "We're friends."

"Hm," she says skeptically, and sips her tea.

He tells himself to shut up but finds himself saying, "Neither of us is interested in pursuing anything more than that."

"Really."

He never could withstand her scrutiny.

"Ah, bloody hell," he groans, and slumps down into the cushions of the couch, or as much as he can slump with his still-tender scrapes and bruises.

Gillian hides a smile behind another sip of tea. She lowers her cup and says, "Like that, is it?"

"I don't know what 'that' is! Good lord, I'm the first man she's seen in five years who isn't the man she's loved all her life! This could be nothing, or this could be the start of something amazing, or it could be a short-term thing, or it could turn into something incredibly...creepy." He pulls a disgusted face.

Gillian's smile widens. "Is it really that awful?" she asks, uncharacteristically gentle.

"I...yes. No. It's complicated," he groans, rubbing his face. "Besides the whole 'only the second person she's seen in years' thing, I was with Olivia for years. I wanted to marry her not even two years ago! Hell, she just told me last night she wants to try again! And I was kissing Lou yesterday but now Olivia's back and—I mean...how could I have moved on so quickly if I truly loved Olivia?"

"Olivia set you free. What did you think you were supposed to do? Pine for her for the rest of your life?" She frowns and becomes suddenly fascinated with her tea.

"Like my dad, you mean?" Ferrin says, his voice quiet.

Gillian heaves a sigh, places her cup on the coffee table,

and stands. She moves to where he's sitting and perches almost tentatively beside him.

"Now, you know I don't like to interfere," she says.

He slants her a skeptical glance.

"Much. But this woman—"

"Lou."

"Yes. Lou."

Gillian takes a deep breath, then hesitantly places her fingertips on his knee.

That startles him, and he stares, trying to think of the last time she's touched him. He feels vaguely guilty that he can't actually remember. He hadn't even hugged her good-bye the last time he left Toronto.

"Ferrin," she says, slowly and carefully, as if she's searching for each word, "when I married your father, I knew I would never be as important to him as your mother had been."

"Gillian—"

"No, no—let me finish. Your father was...*fond* of me. But he didn't love me. Not really. I thought I loved him enough for both of us. And most of the time, it *was* enough. But it's..." she closes her eyes, her lips pressed tightly together, then continues. "It's not easy being second-best to a woman who is forever young. Forever beautiful. Forever *perfect*."

"Gillian..."

"What I'm trying to say, Ferrin, is this: if you still love Olivia the way you always have, then leave this Lou alone. Settling for second best is sad, but *being* second best..." her voice cracks, "it's not *fair*."

Ferrin swallows past the painful lump in his throat.

"Dad loved you," he says huskily.

She smiles and grazes his cheek with her fingertips. "You're a good man, Ferrin. You have a kind heart. I've often resented your mother over the years, but I've always been grateful to her for you."

♠♥♣♦

Ferrin doesn't see Gillian again until the following afternoon, when he finds her, Pierce and Olivia in The Row.

He gives them a distracted smile and turns to Tessa. "Juan says he called in the order?"

Tessa nods and hands him a square box bottom filled with carafes, paper cups, creams and sugars. "Tell the boys not to break anything this time, okay?"

"I'll tell them," he says. "I think they just sent me on this errand because I can't do anything else."

"Well, of course," Tessa says with a grin. "That's usually why they send you on errands, isn't it?"

He rolls his eyes and turns, still moving gingerly, as the bells over the door jingle and Willis pushes his way inside.

"Tessa, you magnificent Caffeine Goddess," Willis says, "please tell me you have some rocket fuel ready for me?"

Tessa rolls her eyes. "You need to spend time in your own bed, Willis, instead of depending on my coffee to keep you going."

"Well, suddenly this town is sounding much more interesting," Gillian says.

Ferrin watches with amusement as Willis turns, a questioning scowl on his grizzled face that quickly morphs into an expression of intrigued interest.

"Well, with two beautiful women I've never seen before in town," Willis drawls, "I would have to agree."

"Are you suggesting I'm not interesting enough for you?" Tessa says with mock offense.

"Oh, more than interesting enough," Willis hastens to assure her, "especially when I see you with that nectar of the gods in your hands."

Gillian and Olivia burst out laughing.

"You're quick on your feet," Gillian says, "I'll give you that."

"And I haven't even been to sleep yet," Willis says.

"Oh, God, don't encourage him," Ferrin groans. "I have to get back. Even if Juan sent me here to get rid of me, they're probably still waiting for the coffee."

He leaves them, shaking his head, and hopes Gillian remember she's just a Jones.

That evening, Ferrin checks in with Lou, who helps him apply the antiseptic and change his bandages in stoic silence.

"Lou," he says, softly pleading, when she finishes and hands him back his shirt.

She shakes her head and turns away.

He leaves a voice mail for Gillian then goes to his house, where he walks in to the deliciously savory smell of food simmering in his kitchen.

Olivia pokes her head over the bar that separates the kitchen from the living room and gives him a smile.

"Pierce is having supper with Tessa," she says.

"Okay," Ferrin says as he strolls towards her. "Where's Gillian?"

"She rather charmed by Willis. She's out on a round with him."

Ferrin stops and sta….res, his mouth dropping open. "Out on a round? *Gillian?* She does know he's a vet, right?"

Olivia shrugs her shoulders with a shrug. "She knows. She even went out and bought jeans and a flannel shirt this afternoon, so she would be ready for anything."

He sits on a bar stool, his breath knocked out of him.

"Please tell me you took pictures!" he begs.

"Of course," Olivia says with an evil grin. "I've been around you Macon-Joneses long enough to know you never pass up the chance to gather blackmail material."

"It's sad that jeans and flannel can be considered blackmail material," he mutters and shakes his head. He leans on the counter and watches as Olivia moves about his tiny kitchen. She gives him a fleeting smile as she picks up a spoon and stirs what's cooking in the pot on the stove.

"Do you know what I'm making?" she asks, a teasing lilt in her voice.

"Of course," he says, with a rather melancholy smirk, "how could I forget? Your gumbo made from a 'secret family recipe'."

She laughs, and his expression softens as he feels a pang of regret and longing. She looks both alien and achingly familiar, standing there in his kitchen. For a moment, it's almost like he can see, overlaid on the present, all his memories of the past and all the possibilities of the future she offered him the other night.

"Your favorite," she says softly, and in a blink, there's only the present again. He sees her eyes are bright and shining, and she's looking at him the way she used to, back when they were happy and in love. She leans across the counter, and rests her hands on his crossed forearms.

Her voice when she speaks again is warm, husky and fond. "This brings back memories, Ferrin. Doesn't it? Good memories."

He raises an eyebrow. "Eating gumbo?" he teases, his voice deliberately light.

"With you." She tilts her head and her smile turns slightly wicked. "Gumbo always seemed to turn you on."

"Maybe it's all that spice," he murmurs, feeling like he's swaying, falling towards her, towards the memories and familiarity of the life they'd made together. The life he *thought* they'd made together. The life she said she no longer wanted and ended with barely a second thought.

That reminds him that she's a top executive in Macon-Jones Enterprises, and she's been part of the family's inner circle for a lot of years. Which means she has a certain amount of Machiavellian tendencies that has to be considered in almost every situation.

Including this one.

His smirk takes on a cynical twist.

"Do you think the gumbo's going to turn me on this time, too?" he asks.

Olivia frowns as she straightens, her hands sliding from his forearms.

"I wasn't suggesting anything," she says, and Ferrin can't help feeling a small stab of triumph at her slightly defensive tone. Perhaps he isn't quite as nice a guy as she seems to believe.

"No?" he says. "My mistake."

Olivia's frown deepens. "You're angry."

He laughs at that, incredulous. "Ya think? Yes, I'm angry. And confused. I mean, I understand why the cousins sent you. I even understand why you agreed to fly out here and check on me. If nothing else, we were together for a long time. But I don't understand all this." He gestures at her, the kitchen and the delicious-smelling food simmering on the stove.

Olivia has the grace to look uncomfortable.

"I told you: your accident reminded me of how much I love you," she murmurs, her gaze on her hands, still resting on the counter. "It also made me realize how much I missed you, and that maybe...maybe I'd made a mistake."

"So, you really meant what you said the other night? You want to try again?"

"Do you?" she asks with a hopeful look.

Lou's too stoic—and too silent—face since Olivia arrived flashes in his mind.

"I don't know," he says.

"Are you saying you don't love me anymore?" Olivia asks, her eyes wide and hurt and disbelieving.

He hesitates, so many words on the tip of his tongue:

angry, bitter, sarcastic, accusing—words he could never take back once spoken.

He swallows them down and says, "I don't know, Olivia."

Her face falls, and she nods, biting her lip.

"Well, we can at least enjoy the gumbo," she says with forced brightness and turns back to the stove.

Tessa chortles with laughter, but there's a tinge of hysteria to it.

Ferrin scowls at her, slouched over the table in her kitchen, his still-healing scrapes and bruises aching almost as much as his head.

"I'm sorry, Ferrin," Tessa finally says, "I know it's not really funny, but I'm not sure what else to do! I mean, this is something that happens in the movies, or romance novels, not in real life! Between Gillian and Willis making googly eyes at each other, and now Olivia wanting to try again, are you sure we aren't starring in some teen drama on TV?"

"I think we'd all be considerably younger if that were the case." He buries his face in his arms and winces as his injuries remind him of their existence. "You know they walked in just as Lou and I were kissing?"

"Oh, yeah. Pierce told me."

His head shoots up and his eyes narrow. "And why would Pierce tell you anything?" he asks, a dangerous note in his voice.

Tessa grins, and flutters her eyelashes. "Unlike you, he's not immune to my charms."

His jaw drops. "You're not—you don't mean—?"

She grimaces. "No, more's the pity, although I think he's weakening. Anyway, even if I never sleep with him that doesn't mean I don't appreciate him or that he doesn't appreciate me."

"He's old enough to be your father!"

"And I'm old enough to know my own mind! Besides, he's definitely not my father, and, really, Ferrin, if you were gay or a girl, you'd understand! He's...wow." She heaves a dreamy sigh.

"Okay, I...I think I need some serious mind bleach."

"Because of me or him?"

"Both!"

She rolls her eyes. "Anyway, why are we talking about me and Pierce? You should be grateful I'm not grilling you to within an inch of your sanity about your life in Toronto after seeing how well-off your friends and stepmother are! How did you go from all that to being homeless in a ditch?" She shakes her head and waves her words away. "We'll get to all that later. What are you going to do about Olivia?"

He sighs, and props his chin on his hand. "I have no idea," he mutters. "I mean, usually I do whatever she wants me to do, but in this case...I don't..." he hesitates.

"You don't know if you want to try again with her or see what happens with Lou, right?"

He nods as, for some reason, guilt floods him. "I'm not leading Lou on, you know," he says. "I really...I feel something for her. But Olivia...I know what I felt for her. What I could probably feel again, if I tried."

"Ah." Tessa wags a knowing finger at him. 'Probably feel again, if you tried'. You should think about those words very carefully before you do anything you might regret. Oh, and I hope you've told Lou you weren't leading her on! Have you seen her lately?"

"This morning, when she changed my bandages. I'm still staying at her place but she was already in bed when I got back last night from my supper with Olivia." He puts his hands over his face. "I suppose I should offer to stay at the rectory with Gillian, but those were pretty intense googly-eyes Willis was shooting her."

"You're worried you might cramp their style?"

Ferrin groans. "Thanks for that; I think I need another dose of mind bleach! But yes. Anyway, I still need to have my scrapes tended twice a day and Lou has been kind enough to continue doing that."

Tessa raises an eyebrow. "Even after Olivia arrived oh-so-dramatically?"

He nods. "Although she hasn't said a single word to me since. Lou, I mean. Olivia's been doing nothing but talk."

Tessa laughs again. "Can't say I blame either of them."

He groans, and once again buries his face in his hands.

"Where's Olivia now?" she asks.

"I don't know," he mutters, "and I honestly don't care."

♠♥♣♦

Lou opens her door and blinks at the sight of Olivia's smiling face.

"Huh," Lou says. She steps back to allow the other woman inside, thinking that not too long ago, she wouldn't have even opened the door. She rather misses those days, she decides with a flash of irritation as she turns to look at her visitor, who's now standing in the middle of the foyer, looking around.

Lou protectively adjusts her sweater, suddenly wishing it wasn't quite so shapeless or enveloping or ugly, feeling at a distinct disadvantage when compared to the other woman's sleek beauty. She watches Olivia with a wary scowl.

Olivia turns and smiles, a charming, bright smile that makes her already-beautiful face glow.

"Thank you for not slamming the door in my face," she says.

Lou shrugs, but tightens her hold on her sweater, her fingers flexing against the wool strands.

They stand in awkward silence. Lou is used to Ferrin

now, and Tessa, not to mention Juan, Delaney and their hellspawn. Even Pierce, after such a short time, has become an almost-familiar presence and she's sorry he'll be leaving so soon. But what, exactly, do you say to the ex-lover of the guy you were kissing a couple of days ago? Lou wonders if there's an etiquette book about that and bites back the urge to dissolve into hysterical giggles.

The silence stretches and grows and Lou shifts uncomfortably beneath Olivia's calm gaze.

"Can I, um, get you something to drink?" she finally offers with an air of helplessness.

Olivia smiles. "No, no, thank you." She glances around again, and says, "You're probably wondering why I'm here."

"I'm assuming it's because of Ferrin."

That surprises a laugh out of Olivia. "You're blunt, I'll say that for you!"

"Thanks. I think."

There's another moment of awkward silence, a thoughtful expression on Olivia's face as she watches Lou, then she shrugs, and Lou feels a stab of envy at her effortless grace.

Olivia says, "Yes, I'm here about Ferrin."

Lou sighs and bows to the inevitable, leading the way into the living room. She waves Olivia to a seat on one of the couches.

"I'm not sure what you want to know," Lou says.

"You and Ferrin seemed very...hm...*close* the other day."

"Yes."

Olivia raises an eyebrow, leans back on the couch and crosses her elegant legs. "Are you in love with him?"

"Is that any of your business?"

"Ferrin and I were together for five years."

"You're not together now."

"Did you know about me?"

Lou shrugs. "I knew he was getting over a bad

breakup."

"It wasn't a bad breakup."

Now it's Lou's turn to raise an eyebrow as she moves to perch on the edge of Ike's Chair.

"Really."

Olivia has the grace to look sheepish. "I mean, we didn't have any screaming fights, nobody got violent, and we certainly didn't viciously argue over our shared property."

"That's good to know. I suppose." Lou cocks her head to one side and considers her. "Are you still in love with him?"

Olivia chuckles. "We didn't break up because we didn't love each other. Love was never the problem."

Lou's stomach plummets to her toes and is replaced by a cold, yawning hole. She focuses on the faded design of the carpet, and distantly decides she needs to vacuum.

Olivia leans forward. "I don't want to be in competition with you," she says softly, sincerely, and even without looking, Lou can feel her intent gaze on her face.

Lou laughs and shakes her head, keeping her eyes focused on her dusty carpet. "Well, I'm not much competition, since I'm still getting used to leaving the house."

Olivia frowns. "What?"

Lou shoots her a quick glance. "Didn't Ferrin tell you? Or Pierce?"

"I—no. What are you talking about?"

Lou shrugs. "I'm the town recluse. Hermit. Nut job…whatever. Before Ferrin came along, I hadn't been out of the house in years."

Olivia's mouth sags open. "What? I had no idea! Why are you a recluse?"

"It's just…easier," she mumbles.

"Oh, come on! Seriously—how—why—what happened? How did you become a recluse?"

"Accidentally," Lou says drily, and grimaces at Olivia's

incredulous expression.

Olivia hesitates, then says, "Well, if you're a recluse, how did you meet Ferrin, anyway? And how did he end up here?"

Lou frowns. "Didn't he tell you?"

"I haven't had the courage to ask," Olivia laughs, and even her laugh is beautiful. For a moment, Lou is in very real danger of actually hating the woman in front of her.

"Ike hired him to look after me," Lou mutters.

"And who's Ike?"

"My best friend, who looked after me for years. But he got married and moved to Vancouver, and couldn't find anyone to take his place." Lou chuckles ruefully. "Lucky for me that Ferrin was homeless and desperate, I guess."

Olivia's mouth slowly sags open again. "Okay, wait, wait, wait!" She stares around the living room. "You know, I think I will take that drink now. There's—you—I have so many questions!"

♠♥♣♦

In retrospect, Ferrin probably should have been warned by the shoes haphazardly kicked off in front of the door.

That, and the gales of laughter coming from the living room.

He walks in and stops, taking in the sight of Olivia and Lou sprawled on the floor, backs against one of the couches. There are a couple of empty bottles of wine beside them, another bottle still half-full on the coffee table, and the glasses in their hands are tilting dangerously as they giggle over something in Lou's hand.

"Please tell me you're not talking about me," he says.

Two pairs of brown eyes blink owlishly at him.

"Oh, we stopped talking about you ages ago," Olivia says. "We've moved on to talking about Ike."

"Ike?" He belatedly realizes that what Lou is holding is

a small stack of pictures that she clumsily hides from view.

He scowls, and Lou grins and gives him her best innocent look, marred somewhat by the drunken glaze in her eyes. He shakes his head and mutters, "It's going to be a long night."

It *was* a long night, Ferrin thinks with rueful amusement as he helps Lou into bed, wincing as his scrapes pull while he lowers her onto the mattress. She's almost immediately asleep and he tosses a spare blanket over her before he leaves her still wrapped in her ever-present sweater and snoring peacefully. He returns to the living room where Olivia is already clearing away the debris from the impromptu party. Ferrin begins to help without a word although he feels the tension building in the set of his shoulders. He doesn't know what, if anything, Olivia let slip during her time with Lou and he's not sure how to ask.

Olivia watches him from the corners of her eyes with obvious amusement and Ferrin decides that this time, he isn't going to be the first to speak. Besides, he'll find out soon enough what Lou knows when she gets over her hangover. He relaxes a little at the thought, a fond smile tugging at his lips.

He realizes Olivia is standing still, watching him with an odd expression. He lifts an eyebrow in question as he leads the way to the kitchen and starts washing their dishes.

"I was going to tell her, you know," she says, grabbing a tea towel and drying a wine glass.

Ferrin's smile takes on a bitter twist. "Yeah?"

"Yeah. I was determined to stop your play-acting and get you home, where you belong."

He turns to look at her, eyes steady on her face.

"Why didn't you?"

She smiles ruefully. "Lots of reasons. She's rather charming, once she relaxes a little. She's also..." she hesitates, frowning. "Vulnerable isn't quite the right word." She shakes her head. "I couldn't bring myself to hurt her. Besides, I was watching your face tonight. You seem..." Her lips tremble as she says, "You never looked at me like that. I mean, you loved me, but you look at her...you never looked at me like that." She shakes her head and waves a hand. "It doesn't matter. Anyway, I didn't tell her for all those reasons, but mostly..." She pauses, staring off into space.

"Mostly?" he finally prompts.

"I don't want to be that person...that person who could deliberately cause pain to somebody else solely for their own personal gain. I was ready to tell her but when I looked in her eyes, I realized I wanted to tell Lou about you because I wanted you back and I didn't care how you or Lou might feel about it. It wasn't because I truly believed it was best for all of us if she knew the truth, only that it would be best for me. Now, how selfish is that?"

She glances at him, tears in her lovely eyes. "I've been incredibly selfish with you already. I hurt you so badly when I turned down your marriage proposal."

"Yes."

She gives a watery chuckle. "See? Lou's been good for you. You never would have told me that before."

He slowly shakes his head. "No."

She sighs. "You've moved on, haven't you? I mean, you've truly moved on."

He looks at her, his eyes sad. "Yes," he says as gently as he can. "Yes, I have."

"I'm happy you're happy, and I really mean that. I wish...I wish I hadn't been so stupid. I wish I hadn't let you slip...no, you didn't slip away, did you? I threw you away."

"I think we both let it slip away. There's seldom only one person to blame when a relationship ends."

"Still, I wish I'd tried harder...made my feelings known earlier...but we can't change the past." Her smile is almost painfully sad. "I hope you'll be happy with your new life, and that it works out with Lou. Once you tell her who you are, of course, because telling people the truth really is the best for everybody."

"I know it is, but thank you for not doing it for me. And I want you to be happy, too. I really mean that."

"I know."

She smiles, and he's blinded by both her beauty and his memories of their life together, but the moment is fleeting, and she is, he realizes with heartbreaking sadness, simply somebody from his past who he cares about and will always cherish.

She sighs, then begins drying another dish. "I'll help you finish here then I'm going to go back to your place."

"I'll drive you home."

"Thanks, but I'm okay. I let Lou do most of the drinking; she seemed to need it more than I did."

"You sure?"

She nods. "Lou invited all of us over for supper tomorrow, but I don't think she's going to be in any shape to eat, let alone cook. Do you mind if we stick around for a few more days?"

"Not at all," he says. "Pierce and Gillian don't seem to be in any rush to get back, either." He grins suddenly. "Gillian seems very charmed by Willis and Pierce seems just as taken with Tessa."

Olivia raises an eyebrow as they walk to the front door. "Well, Willis and Tessa are also on my list for some private chats," she says, and slips out of the house with an evil grin.

♠♥♣♦

Ferrin doesn't have a chance to talk to Pierce until the next day, when they drive out to inspect their investment property.

They wander round the site, and Ferrin patiently answers questions until Pierce finally nods with satisfaction.

"It's not a great investment," he says. "None of you will make a fortune from it—you know that already—but it should provide a relatively stable source of income to your great-grandchildren someday." He sighs. "I'll finish signing the papers before I leave."

"When do you think that will be?" Ferrin asks.

Pierce raises an eyebrow. "Trying to be rid of me? Don't you trust me enough to keep your secrets?"

Ferrin rolls his eyes. "Of course I do. You've kept quiet this long, haven't you? I was just thinking about the rest of the family. How are they managing without you?"

"Quite happily. Besides, surprisingly enough, there really is Internet access in this backwater, so it hasn't been much of a break from the family. More's the pity."

Ferrin laughs. "Stop reading your e-mails or answering your phone."

"Oh, if only it were so simple," Pierce says with a long-suffering sigh. "I'll stay until the deal is finalized with Juan. That may take another week or two, and I may have to be on the phone every day to Toronto in order to re-convince the more reluctant of your cousins to open their wallets."

Ferrin snorts. "Good luck with that. Still...that's longer than I expected you would want to stay. How are you going to manage here in this backwater, even if we do have Internet."

Pierce glances away. "It has its attractions," he murmurs.

"Like Tessa?"

"She reminds me of my younger days."

He's trying to be flippant, but Ferrin hears a wistful undertone that surprises him.

"She seems to like you."

Pierce chuckles. "I'm a rich old man who wears a suit every day. That's more than enough to fascinate a girl living in small town Saskatchewan."

"I don't think you're giving her enough credit. And I wouldn't call her 'girl' to her face, if I were you."

Pierce shrugs, deliberately nonchalant. "I'm old enough to be her father. Possibly her grandfather."

Ferrin snorts a laugh. "You're not that old, she's not that young, and you're really not giving her enough credit."

Pierce shakes his head but he won't meet Ferrin's eyes. "Her whole life is ahead of her. Most of mine is behind me." He stares into space with a sad frown then he blinks and gives Ferrin a determined smirk. "Doesn't matter. The flirtation is flattering, and it's always time well-spent when you're with a beautiful woman."

Ferrin frowns. "Well, so long as you're both on the same page."

"Well, we weren't the other night, but we've since had a good, long chat, and yes, we're both on the same page." He gives Ferrin a hard stare. "Can you say the same about Lou?"

Ferrin flushes, and now it's his turn to avoid looking at his companion.

"Soon," he mutters. "Once Olivia's gone and Lou understands I'm here to stay."

"Are you?"

"For the foreseeable future, anyway."

Pierce shakes his head. "You know I don't like to interfere—"

"Since when?"

"—in your love life, but in this case, I feel it's justified. You can't put it off much longer, Ferrin, and it's better if she finds out the truth directly from you, and preferably before the two of you do more than just kiss."

Ferrin nods, frowning into the distance. "I know."

271

The sun beats down on the backyard of Lou's house as Lou sips a margarita and watches Ferrin, Pierce and Juan argue over the barbecue the men had delivered that morning.

"What do you think they're arguing about?" she asks.

"How long to grill each side for the perfect steak," Gillian says.

"Whether the barbecue sauce should go on before, during or after," Delaney says.

"Telling Pierce what, exactly, a barbecue is," Tessa says, nodding at the older man who is dressed far too elegantly to be cooking on a grill.

Olivia laughs. "I know Ferrin," she says lightly. "He's trying to figure out how to turn the damn thing on."

There's a loud whoosh and all three men leap away from the sudden burst of flame.

The women laugh, and lift their glasses in salute as the men shoot them mock-glares before turning back to the barbecue.

"I should have taken bets," Olivia says, her smile smug.

Lou chuckles, then takes another sip of her margarita. She wriggles her toes, feeling the press of the sun on top of her feet and the texture of the grass beneath them. She'd forgotten how good it all feels, she thinks, tilting her face towards the sky and closing her eyes.

Delaney raises an eyebrow at Tessa and says, "Think we should go help those three before they burn the house down?"

"I think that is an excellent idea," Tessa says, and they stand and saunter towards the cheerfully arguing men.

Lou smiles, her eyes still closed as their voices mingle with the sound of birds, the wind, the insects, and the occasional passing car.

"When was the last time you were outside during the summer?" Olivia asks softly.

Lou blinks sleepily, glancing from Olivia to Gillian and back again. "A while," she says, and sips her margarita.

Gillian grimaces. "I'm sorry. We shouldn't pry."

Lou shrugs. "I'm not avoiding the question; I just...I honestly don't remember. I mean, I was house-bound for about five years, but I nursed my mom for almost five years before that. At the end, I wasn't exactly in the mood to sit outside and soak up the sun."

"I'm sorry."

"I'm not," Lou says with a sad smile. "Not about my mom, I mean. It's...tough, and I wish it hadn't happened, and there were days when I didn't think I could do it, but...yeah. I'm glad I was strong enough for her, at least."

Silence settles over and between them as they watch the others laughing and joking while Tessa and Delaney attempt to wrest cooking duties away from Ferrin. He holds the tongs over his head, well out of reach of either woman while Juan and Pierce cheerfully egg them on. Lou's attention is on Ferrin, who's still moving stiffly from his accident, wearing the same deplorable khaki shorts he's worn since last summer. While all three men are relatively the same height, he seems to loom twice as large, twice as broad, taking up twice as much space, and she feels that now-familiar soft yielding inside her as she watches his muscles move beneath the thin grey t-shirt he's wearing as he dodges away from the women.

Olivia and Gillian chuckle, and Lou glances rather uncertainly at them, flushing as she realizes she's been staring and ignoring the women beside her.

Gillian glances at Olivia then back to Lou. "I think I better go referee or else we'll never get fed."

Lou watches Gillian stroll towards the bickering knot of people then bashfully looks at Olivia, who's watching her with a twisted half-smile.

"He likes you, too," she says softly.

Lou's eyes widen and she flushes. "We're not...we decided...we...it's complicated."

"Doesn't mean he doesn't like you. Or that you don't like him."

"I...I know," she mutters.

Olivia looks away, blinking rapidly as she nods. "I'm glad."

Lou raises a questioning eyebrow. There's sadness in Olivia's eyes and around her mouth, but there's acceptance there as well.

"I'm sorry," Lou says suddenly.

Olivia smiles, and Lou catches her breath, truly awed by the other woman's beauty. She can't believe Ferrin would choose to stay here when this vision wanted a second chance.

"I'm sorry, too," Olivia says, "but I'm the one who told Ferrin it was over. I can't blame anyone but myself, can I?"

They share a remarkably understanding look before Lou says, "I still would. He probably deserves it for one reason or another."

They share a glance full of amused affection for the man in question before they turn their attention back to the group clustered around the barbecue, who appear to have finally come to some sort of agreement under Gillian's amused supervision. Tessa shepherds a protesting Pierce into the kitchen to presumably prepare the side dishes, although from the gleam in Tessa's eyes, it seems more likely that Pierce will soon be defending his virtue instead of tossing salad. Juan has a firm grasp on Delaney as they lean together to supervise Ferrin, who turns the steaks with an air of smug triumph.

Ferrin glances over his shoulder, and his eyes meet Lou's. He smirks his crooked, charming smirk, and she smiles rather shyly and lifts her margarita glass in a toast. His grin widens before he winks and turns his attention back to the barbecue.

"Do you think anything's going to be edible?" Lou asks thoughtfully.

"Not even close," Olivia says, and they clink their glasses together in perfect understanding.

♠ ♥ ♣ ♦

In the end, everything is remarkably tasty and Lou apologizes to all of them for ever doubting their combined ability to produce an edible meal.

"It was touch and go there a few times," Tessa says, shaking her head, tendrils of blonde hair escaping her ponytail to wisp around her face, making her look even more adorably cute than usual, if Pierce's ruefully smitten expression is anything to go by...at least until her words sink in.

He sits up straight. "We had it completely under control!"

"Which is why we had that second explosion, I suppose?"

Lou smiles as the good-natured bickering continues and glances at Ferrin beside her, his arm slung across the back of her chair. She marvels at the fact that she's here, in the middle of all these people, and outside.

Ferrin seems to read her mind, because he squeezes her shoulder as he leans closer and whispers, "You've come a long way, baby."

She gives him a shy smile, and allows herself to relax against him.

♠ ♥ ♣ ♦

Ferrin arrives at the rectory the next day to say good-bye to Gillian. She gives him a faint smile as she sets her small suitcase on the living room floor.

"Taking your new wardrobe back with you?" he asks with a teasing grin.

"Of course," she says breezily. "I never knew veterinary science was quite so...*fascinating*."

He grimaces. "You're my stepmother, Gillian!"

She laughs. "I'm not quite ready to be set out to pasture yet, my dear stepson."

He raises an eyebrow. "Not even with a vet beside you?"

"Willis is utterly charming," she says, her demure voice in direct contrast to her laughing eyes.

He shakes his head. "Never would have thunk it," he mutters.

Silence falls, then Gillian says, "You know you have to tell them who you are."

"I know."

"And you need to decide where your life is going to be. Carson, Dyson and Jack miss you, although I would dearly love to see the havoc they would wreak when they descend on this sleepy little town."

Ferrin shudders with mock-horror. "I don't know if this town could withstand the full force of the Musketeers."

"Especially once they're reunited with their D'Artagnan. They're looking forward to your visit next month."

He chuckles. "I'm not sure I'm going to be able to withstand the full force of the Musketeers!"

Gillian chuckles and they share a fond smile, then Ferrin shifts his weight from one foot to another and says, "Gillian?"

She raises an eyebrow.

He hesitates, then says in a sudden rush, "You know I've always loved you, right? I mean, I love you as much as I love my mom, only differently. You do know that, right?"

She rears back a little, then frowns at him. "Of course I know that."

"Good," he says, relieved. "I just...you're not second best to me."

Her mouth twists, then straightens, and she blinks rapidly, glancing away then back to him.

"This little town has made you sentimental," she finally says, but she can't quite hide the quiver in her voice.

"Perhaps it's not as dreary as I thought."

"Yeah, it has, and it's not," he says, and carefully wraps his arms around her. He hugs her warmly, breathing in the comforting, familiar scent of her perfume and her shampoo and *her*, and is suddenly, painfully conscious of the fragility of her bones. He's overwhelmed with a fierce desire to protect her, to wrap her so completely in his love for her that no-one can ever hurt her again, because she's right: his father had loved her, but never as much as he'd loved the wife he lost. After a moment's hesitation, she hugs him back, and there is strength in her arms, a resilience that makes him proud, even as he fights the urge to weep over her—something she would not appreciate, and would quite likely earn him boxed ears. That thought gives him the courage to gradually release her and step away.

"Call me when you get home?"

She rolls her eyes as she discreetly flicks away a tear. "Are you suggesting Abram's pilots aren't the best?" she says, striving to be as cool and sarcastic as ever, but falling somewhat short.

"They better be," he says with a chuckle as a knock on the door announces Pierce and Olivia's arrival. "I'll have their hides if anything happens to you on their watch."

It's a glorious August.

The days are long and slow and hot and Lou keeps carefully extending her time outside every day.

While she isn't exactly a fixture in Ledoux's social life, leaving the house continues to get easier as the days drift along. Her relationship with Ferrin remains, by mutual agreement, strictly platonic, although they occasionally have to pull themselves back at the last minute to prevent another kiss and potentially awkward aftermath. Lou admits, however, even if only to herself, that there's a sense of inevitability to it all, flavoured with an almost unbearably delicious anticipation.

Then it's the end of August and suddenly Ike's next visit is looming on the horizon, with Ferrin's next trip to Toronto scheduled to begin a couple of days after Ike's arrival. Even so, as she watches Ferrin getting ready to leave her house one night, Lou realizes she's happy: gloriously, glowingly, finally happy.

As for Ike, Lou can't wait to see him so she can see his face when she tells him about her progress. She knows he's going to be just as ecstatic as she is and she can't wait to share the good news.

Lou lets Ike into the house with an anxious smile and a warm hug then hurries to the kitchen to get the coffee. When she carries the tray into the living room, he's already settled in Ike's Chair, pulling a stack of papers out of his briefcase.

"You look great," she says cheerfully as she puts the tray on the coffee table.

He gives her a sharp look then frowns.

"What's going on?" he asks suspiciously.

She stares, eyes wide. "What do you mean 'what's going on'? Where? What?"

"You're..." his frown deepens, his eyes narrowing. "You're happy. What's happened?"

She laughs as she hands him a mug of coffee, then curls up on the couch, her own mug cradled in the palms of her hands.

"You make it sound like my happiness is a bad thing!" She grins suddenly, a little girl grin filled with the sheer joy of existence. She leans forward, eyes shining. "I've been going outside!"

Ike's face becomes an expressionless mask.

"Going outside," he repeats, his voice flat.

"Yes! I know, I can barely believe it myself! But I've been going regularly to The Row, and grocery shopping, and even Regina! Well, Regina was because of Ferrin's accident and it was an emergency, but you know, Tessa and Delaney and I were talking about going again to shop! God, I can't remember the last time I went shopping, let alone in Regina!"

Ike's expression doesn't change, although his shoulders tense as she speaks.

"Shopping. In Regina."

Lou nods. "I can barely remember what it's like to shop for clothes, or how to get money out of a bank! I'm not sure I even know where my bank card is, let alone my PIN number! Thank God you've left everything somewhere round here! I guess it's time to clean," she says, and laughs. "Anyway, we're going to go once you're back in Vancouver, and while Ferrin's in Toronto for a month for some family thing or other. We haven't quite figured out what to do with Juan but he can at least watch the kids. We're planning a girls' night out, too—maybe a lounge, and if I manage that okay, we're talking about going to a concert! A *concert*, Ike!" Her grin widens, and she almost bounces on the couch. "It's going to be so much fun!"

"Fun."

She frowns, wavers, then continues. "When Ferrin gets back home, and if I've managed to at least go shopping in Regina, he's promised to take me out to dine and dash." She laughs again, a light, airy sound. "He won't admit he meant 'dine and dance'. He says I'll just have to go out with him and find out for myself."

The ensuing silence is dark and dangerous, broken only by Ike's slow, deliberate breathing. She nervously grips her sweater and digs her fingers into the wool.

"More secrets," he finally says, his voice flat and ominous. "Why haven't you told me any of this over the phone? Or the last time I was in Ledoux? I thought we had a deal."

She shrugs as she forces herself to steadily meet his gaze. "Lots of reasons. I wanted it to be a surprise, plus I wasn't always sure I was going to be able to keep going outside. It hasn't been easy, you know. Ferrin and Tessa have helped me through more panic attacks than I care to admit, but they're still coming back for more."

"And your relationship with Ferrin?"

"There is no relationship with Ferrin! I mean, we're friends, of course—"

"Friends? Is that what you call it now?"

Lou clamps her lips together and glares at him through narrowed eyes.

He rolls his eyes. "Oh, come on! I know you, Lou! I know the way you look when you're in love!"

She flushes. "I'm not in love with him!"

He snorts. "You always were shit at lying, you know. Of course you're in love with him! It's written all over you! Have you slept with him?"

"It's none of your business if I have or not!"

"None of my—I've only been taking care of you for the last five years! And how many fucking years before that?"

"Well, you don't need to take care of me anymore!"

Lou almost staggers beneath the abrupt silence that follows her words.

She claps her hands over her face and says, "I didn't mean that the way it sounded."

Ike sighs. "I shouldn't have pushed so hard. I'm just disappointed at all the wasted—just tell me what's going on between you and Ferrin."

She slides her hands down her face and looks at him. "Nothing, Ike, I swear! We...we kissed a couple of times but we decided we're not ready for anything other than friendship."

"Yet."

She shrugs. "Maybe. Maybe never. Whatever's

happening with Ferrin is too..." she hesitates, trying to figure out how to explain. "There's so much other stuff going on in my head some days, it's a real struggle to keep going outside and not just retreat back into the safety of this house. Whatever I feel for Ferrin—or don't feel—it's too new for me to define. It scares me and it thrills me and I don't know if I feel like this because it's Ferrin or because I finally have the possibility of having a life again! A real life and not one that's just me drifting around these rooms until I die. Everything's just too...*too much* to really talk about yet, especially over the phone. I don't know what it is or how long it's going to last, but I'm happy, Ike, and excited about the future. Doesn't that count for something?"

"And like always, you'll expect me to pick up the pieces when everything comes crashing down around you."

"I don't expect you to do a fucking thing, Ike, except be my friend!"

They glare at each other, caught in a silent impasse, then he lowers his gaze to the cup on the coffee table in front of him. He picks it up, moving slowly, like his bones ache, and leans back in Ike's Chair. He takes a sip and returns the cup to the coffee table before returning his solemn gaze to her face.

"If you're happy, then I'm happy, Lou," he says.

She raises an eyebrow. "Why am I sensing a 'but' in there?"

"I don't want you to get your hopes up, that's all." He leans forward, amber eyes intent on her face. "I don't want to see you hurt."

She stares unblinkingly at him then puts her mug down on the coffee table with a decisive thud and gives him a perfunctory smile.

"Thank you, Ike. I know you're only looking out for me, like you've always done. I haven't forgotten what Willis-that-bastard and the others did to me and my mother, but I don't want to keep cowering in this house like a kicked puppy. I refuse to be a prisoner anymore in my own life! Why is that such a bad thing?"

"It's not!" He pauses, grimacing. "It's not, Lou. I'm glad you're leaving the house. I'm glad you have friends. I'm even glad you have a chance at having a—a—a whatever-the-hell you want to call him. I just...you don't know these people, not really, and I think I'm justified in worrying about you, even if it's from a distance." He gives her a fond look, then continues in a low, seductive voice, "We've been through a lot, you and I. We've been many things to each other. That means I'm going to be worried about you, whether you need it or not."

She tilts her head and considers him thoughtfully. "Thank you," she murmurs.

Ike pushes to his feet. "I think I'd better go."

She frowns. "I haven't had a chance to sign any of the papers you brought."

"Well, you dropped a lot of bombshells on me today. I need some time to...to process everything." He nods at the stack of papers on the coffee table. "I'll pick those up tomorrow."

♠♥♣♦

That evening, Lou tells Ferrin and Tessa what happened with Ike.

Tessa rolls her eyes. "I always knew he was an ass," she says.

Ferrin raises an eyebrow at the stack of papers on the coffee table. "He obviously hated the idea of your new life so much he left before you signed everything."

"You're not far off," Lou says with a grimace. "You'd think he'd be happy that I'm regaining my independence! Instead he acts as if I'm about to, I don't know, jump off a cliff because all my friends are jumping first!"

"Well, that's just stupid," Tessa says. "Where are you going to find a cliff in Saskatchewan? Although I suppose you can't really blame him. He's been looking out for you and your mom for years."

"I know. Anyway, he left before I'd even looked at those things—not that I ever really do, but still. He's going to pick everything up later."

Ferrin cocks his head as he studies the stack of papers. "Do you mind if I look at them?"

She tenses. "Why?"

"Because I'm curious."

Her eyes turn wary. "Why?" she asks again, more sharply.

He gives her a surprised look. "Olivia works for a major corporation," he says, "and Pierce is a business manager who regularly pulls together multi-million dollar deals. I'm just curious to see if I've learned anything at all from them."

She hesitates.

"I don't have to," he says hastily. "Like I said, I'm just curious, that's all."

She gives him one last, hard stare then shrugs.

"Knock yourself out."

"At least until we find something to watch," Tessa says, scowling at the TV as she works the remote. "God— eleven hundred channels; you'd think we could find something worth watching!"

Ferrin laughs. "Well, it'll be a race between you finding something to watch and me getting bored."

"And me getting more popcorn and drinks," Lou says.

She stands, picks up the almost-empty bowl of popcorn they've already devoured and heads to the kitchen. Tessa turns her attention back to the TV, and Ferrin picks up the top set of papers from the stack on the coffee table. It turns out to be Lou's financial statements, and he mentally raises an eyebrow at the total amount of her holdings. She isn't Macon-Jones rich, but she and at least two generations after her are definitely set for life.

He flips the page, and scans the list of investments and

current stock prices, and their comparison to the previous period's stock prices. His eyes stall on one particular item, and he frowns.

"What's wrong?" Lou asks sharply as she walks back into the living room.

He blinks and looks up. "Nothing," he says hastily, and suspicion is immediately back in her eyes. He flips the document closed and places it back on the coffee table. "I just realized I'm not as smart as I look. I can't make heads or tails out of that mess."

She relaxes and smiles. "Neither can I," she says. "It's why I leave everything to Ike."

"Do you have any idea what time it is?"

Even though Ferrin doesn't feel like laughing, Pierce's sleepily grumpy voice still makes him smile.

"Two a.m.," he says as brightly as he can while he runs a hand through his hair. He shifts on his couch, and thinks of Lou, hopefully sprawled across her king-sized bed while sleeping the sleep of the innocent.

He wishes with all his heart that he didn't have to make this call.

"So this is a deliberate interruption of my sleep," Pierce says, bringing Ferrin back to the task at hand. "Good to know. And remember."

"Ah, Pierce, I remember the days when you were always wide awake at this time of the night, although perhaps even more unhappy at being interrupted."

"You aren't old enough to remember those days."

"My father told me stories."

Pierce yawned. "Unlikely to be truthful, then, or most likely greatly edited."

"You hope."

There's a chuckle followed by the sound of rustling blankets, then Pierce, all sleepiness gone, says, "What's going on? You're cheerful, so there can't be any immediate threat to life, limb or relatives."

"Not exactly." Ferrin once again runs his hand through his hair. "Listen, does Abram still have that private investigator on retainer?"

"Of course. Why?"

"I need him to look into Ike Boisin, particularly his financial history and activities—does he have bank accounts in the Caymans, for example—and I need him to do the same for Lou. I also need answers as quickly as humanly possible...like, by the afternoon."

"What's going on?" Pierce is completely alert now.

"I think he's embezzling from her."

There's a long, thoughtful silence, then, "Why would you think that?"

"Lou let me look at some financial reports he left behind earlier today. It included a summary of her investment portfolio and the share prices as of Monday. There's at least one stock listed as being worth much less than it truly is."

"Which one?"

"Macon-Jones Enterprises."

Lou smiles as she opens the door, a smile that immediately turns to a glare as Ike pushes past her, already talking.

"Listen, Lou, I know you didn't want me to do any digging into Ferrin's background—"

Lou's eyes narrow dangerously as she spins to face him. "But you did anyway, didn't you?"

"Things have changed now! You're in love with him!"

Lou sighs tiredly and pinches the bridge of her nose as she leads him to the living room. "I've already told you: I don't know what I feel about him. Besides, why the fuck does that matter so much to you?"

"Oh, please! You're not that stupid! Now, just shut up and listen!"

Lou closes her mouth with a decided snap. She haughtily tugs her sweater into place, her fingers gripping it in an attempt to control her anger. His smug satisfaction at her compliance makes her grind her teeth.

Lou growls, "What makes you think I care what—"

"Ferrin isn't his real name. I mean, it is, but it isn't. It's *Benjamin* Ferrin *Macon*-Jones."

She frowns.

"Of *the* Macon-Joneses."

Her expression doesn't change.

"For God's sake, Lou! Like the stores! Like the family that's always in the tabloids!"

"I don't believe you," she says flatly. "He was living in his car when Willis-that-bastard pulled him out of the ditch!"

Ike pulls several folded sheets of paper out of his pocket and holds them out to her. She stares at them like she's never seen such things before.

"I've got proof," he says and his soft voice turns the very air into fragile crystal, as if the slightest sound or movement will shatter everything.

She hesitantly reaches out and delicately takes the pages. She unfolds them, and finds herself looking at three pictures, two from Toronto's local papers, and one from a national paper, all with Ferrin's face in them. One has him looking handsome in a tuxedo, a proud smile on his face and Olivia on his arm, at what is obviously a red carpet event of some kind. The next has him in jeans and a t-shirt, striding through a parking lot, cell phone and car keys in hand. The third is a formal portrait, and he's in the midst of a large group of people with a distinct family resemblance, and even she recognizes, front and centre, Abram Macon-Jones, the Chairman of the Board of Macon-Jones Enterprises.

The blood drains from her face and she sinks on to the

couch.

"I'm sorry, Lou," Ike says, "but you needed to know. You also need to know he's never held a real job. He's notorious for living off his family's money and for his party lifestyle. He's been arrested numerous times for drunk and disorderly conduct, usually in the company of the same three cousins. There's some suspicion that he's guilty of more serious crimes, since he lives a lavish lifestyle with no visible means of support. He's also a family joke because he's always taking on lost causes, some pet project or person to re-do or save until he gets bored and leaves them high and dry."

"Get out."

Ike blinks. "I haven't fin—"

"Don't say another word. Get out! I need to figure out how to deal with this."

Abram's private investigator is frighteningly efficient.

"Not that it was difficult," Pierce says drily. "Ike didn't do much to cover his tracks."

"Why would he?" Ferrin growls. "Lou trusts him implicitly. She never looks at anything he gives her, never questions anything. She doesn't even get her own bank statements! You don't need to hide much if nobody's looking."

"True."

"How bad is it?"

"Her bank accounts are almost empty. If Ike maintains his pattern, she'll be wiped out with the next transfer. There are no investments of any kind left. Once the cash is gone, she won't have long before the house is in foreclosure as well."

Ferrin groans. "He even took the house out from under her?"

"He mortgaged it through a Vancouver bank. She

signed the mortgage papers herself."

Ferrin pinches the bridge of his nose. "She never looks at anything he puts in front of her," he mutters and sighs. "Do I even want to know how this information was obtained?"

"You will wish to maintain plausible deniability."

"That's what I thought." He lapses into brooding silence.

"What do you want done?" Pierce asks.

"Well, first, we need to save the house, without her knowing we did it."

"Abram's already taken care of it."

"*Abram?*"

"He says anybody who's brave enough to return to the world after being a recluse for so long deserves a second chance, and of course, she's putting up with you. He did have to beat out Carson, Dyson and Jack in a race to the bank, though. Says it gave him quite the adrenaline rush even if the speeding tickets are going to be truly astronomical."

"How'd I end up with cousins like mine?" Ferrin says with a mournful sigh.

"Just lucky, I guess."

"Can't argue with that," he says and chuckles with genuine affection.

Pierce chuckles as well, then sobers. "The mortgage will be officially discharged tomorrow. Abram and the Musketeers convinced the bank manager here to be discreet, and they've come up with a convincing cover story for the branch managers in Vancouver and Ledoux. Forgotten stocks or some such nonsense. Really, Abram seemed to enjoy conspiring with the Musketeers a little too much, if you ask me."

"Maybe now he'll understand how they always manage to suck me in!"

"Yes, because it wasn't your idea to 'test drive' that police officer's speedboat, was it?"

"He offered! And the accelerator got stuck!"

Pierce tsks. "At least you know enough to stick to your cover stories. Well, there's something else you need to know before you go to Lou or the police."

"Oh?"

"Ike has been skimming for years, but his activities accelerated over the last year. He increased the speed in which he was selling her investments, and began siphoning the cash out of her accounts and into one in the Caymans. An account in the name of Ferrin Jones."

Ferrin's brain stops then stutters back into motion.

"I—I don't even want to ask how you got that information, do I?"

"Plausible—"

"Deniability, I know, I know. So, in other words, I appeared to be the perfect patsy for Ike."

"When did Lou tell him about you coming into the house?"

Ferrin frowns. "I'm not sure. Last September? Maybe October. Something like that."

"That tracks. Ike's activities began to escalate in October but the money really began to pour out of the accounts after the first of this year. He also took out the mortgage in January. He's kept enough cash on hand to keep making those payments, but barely. He certainly hasn't been the one transferring money between accounts to keep her from falling into foreclosure; that's been the bank manager in Ledoux."

"The sooner he could get me arrested, the sooner he could get the rest of the money," Ferrin mutters.

"Possibly. We suspect it's only because the bank manager in Ledoux knows Lou and her situation that the house payments have been made at all."

"The benefits of small-town living,"

"And one of its detriments. That same bank manager never bothered questioning anything Ike was doing, and Ike didn't bother to hide his tracks very well. I think he wanted enough of a false trail so he could leave the country before the police arrived with an arrest warrant."

"He didn't the police would even bother looking any further than me," Ferrin growls. "Think about it. I'm a homeless drifter, down on my luck, who weasels my way into the life of a lonely recluse then robs her blind. Happens every day. He likely expected me to take his threats seriously enough to leave town when he told me to and set things in motion so he could clean her out by the end of January. Then he'd break the bad news about me; she'd blame me and not him, and by the time she's thinking clearly enough to go to the police—if she could force herself to go at all—Ike and his wife would be safely out of the country. I'm sure my refusal to leave town with my tail between my legs caused him to change the timing of his plans."

"I hate to admit it, but it's not a bad plan. A homeless drifter has no resources, and who's going to believe him? Benjamin Ferrin Macon-Jones, on the other hand, is another matter entirely."

Ferrin chuckles grimly. "I'm glad Ike's never bothered to find out who I am."

"What are you going to do?"

"I'm supposed to be leaving for Toronto tomorrow. Can you see if you can rearrange that and make all the necessary apologies to Gillian? I have a feeling I'm going to miss my flight."

"I'll send one of the planes for you, shall I?"

"Please; I'll let you know when I'm ready to leave. While you're doing that, I'm going to have a chat with Ike."

"Don't you want to go to the police first? Those reports you saw could be reason enough to start an investigation. They'll be able to find most of the same information we did, and do it legally."

"If we're lucky, we won't need the police. Besides, it's well known around town that Ike and I are not the best of friends. If I go to the police, it would likely be seen as me trying to push the asshole out of Lou's life, once and for all."

"And, of course, without them knowing who you really are, everyone will also assume you're only trying to get control of the money. Not that there's much left."

"Exactly. I need to tell Lou who I am before I talk to Ike."

"One is tempted to say 'about time', but one shall refrain."

Ferrin snorts. "Don't strain yourself."

Ferrin knows something's wrong the moment he walks into Lou's house. She doesn't answer when he calls for her and he finds her huddled on the couch, her knees pulled up to her chin and tucked inside her sweater.

"Lou?"

He wonders if she's somehow found out about Ike's betrayal in the thirty minutes since his conversation with Pierce.

She surges to her feet as he approaches and slams a handful of crumpled paper against his chest.

"What—?" he stammers, grabbing them before they fall to the ground.

"I got some very interesting news today," she bites out.

He groans. So she has found out, somehow, likely because the local bank called her about discharging the mortgage. Whoever was so thoughtless will need to run for cover, he thinks grimly, because he and his cousins will eat them for breakfast.

But that problem will have to wait. Right now, Lou is glaring at him with tears filling her gorgeous eyes.

"I'm sorry," he says, "I wanted you to hear the news from me."

She snorts. "Really? When? Before or after you

buggered off back to the high life in Toronto?"

He blinks, wondering how this had become about him. He glances down at the papers in his hands and straightens them out. He looks at the pictures and swallows.

Oh.

He looks up at Lou, his eyes wide.

"Look, I can explain—"

"Ha!"

"Look—"

"No, *you* look! I've been trying to figure this shit out ever since Ike left and none of it makes any goddamn sense! All I can think is that I've been some sort of test case or—or—or charity case for you! What, was I your good deed for the decade?"

Ferrin's jaw drops. "What?"

"Aren't you the one who's 'famous' for your lost causes? The one who likes to rescue people, at least until you get bored? That's what Ike says! Is that what this—" she waves her hands, encompassing herself and her house, "—all about? Was I—oh, God—was I just something to do because you were bored?"

Ferrin closes his mouth with a snap.

"Why would you even think that?" he demands. "Why would you think I would do something like that?"

"I don't know you!" She wraps her sweater around herself, her glare hot enough to melt rock. "I have no idea what Benjamin Macon-Jones would do; I've never met him! Did we amuse you? Me, Tessa, Juan—everybody? What? 'Small-town Saskatchewan—how quaint'!"

"What? That's—where the fuck is this coming from? I go by Ferrin with my family and friends—I always have! And I've done absolutely nothing to make you think—"

"Nothing, except lie about who you really are! You don't think that's kinda important? Especially when you belong to one of the richest families in the country?"

"I..." He hesitates, then says, "Okay, yes, I should have told you who I was a long time ago. But I liked being just a Jones, and not a Macon-Jones. I liked working with my hands, and being liked for me, and not for my money or my connections. But that doesn't mean you're right about everything else! Why would you think I'd be that cruel and thoughtless?"

"I don't know who you are," she bites out.

"Lou—"

"Get out. Go back to Toronto and your rich family and all your rich friends! Oh, God! Pierce! And Gillian! And *Olivia*! They sat here, in my house, and *they knew*! They knew what you were doing!"

Ferrin takes a step towards her and stops abruptly as she darts away.

"Of course, they knew," he says with his most soothing tones. "You're just in shock."

"And whose fault is that?"

"Ike's! He's just stirring up trouble because—"

"Because he loves me! He warned me from the very beginning not to trust you! God, I should have known to listen to him! He cares, and unlike you, I know I can trust him!"

"Trust him? *He stole all your money!*"

She rears back and stares, her black eyes wide and disbelieving.

"Get out," she hisses. "You can't—Ike would never—*get out!*"

"Lou," he says softly, apologetically, and steps towards her. His shoulders slump as she hastily backs away. "I didn't mean to tell you like that. I was going to break it to you gently, all of it, about Ike and about me. But all right. I'll go. We'll talk about this tomorrow."

"There is no tomorrow, especially if you're just going to tell me more lies!"

"Then we'll talk when I get back from Toronto—and I'm not lying. Not about Ike."

"Why bother coming back?" she scoffs. "Do you enjoy laughing at us so much? At me? Hah! I don't care

293

if you never come back!"

His expression hardens. "I'm coming back, and we're going to work this out. I'm not giving up without a fight, and if you need time to learn that Benjamin Ferrin Macon-Jones is the same man as Ferrin Jones, then so be it."

He stomps to the door and opens it, then turns and glares at Lou, standing tall and defiant behind him, wrapped in that stupid brown sweater, her chin raised high, the colour bright in her cheeks.

"I'll be back next month," he growls, "maybe by then you'll be ready to listen to reason!"

"Not if you're going to make ridiculous accusations about Ike!"

"Ike made ridiculous accusations, too, and he was right. What makes you think I'm wrong?"

He slams the door behind him, just in time for the ornament she'd grabbed to shatter against it.

Ferrin isn't sure if he's grateful or not that Tessa isn't at The Row when he finally gets there an hour later. It's taken him that long to calm down and to make arrangements for one of the company jets to pick him up from Regina that night. On the one hand, Tessa's absence means he doesn't have to tell her just yet. On the other, it puts off the inevitable, at least with her.

He's not so lucky when it comes to everyone else.

Delaney's covering the store, and Juan and Willis are the only customers, comfortably sprawled at their usual table. Without Tessa, it makes telling them his real name a little faster, even if it isn't any easier to get them to believe him. In the end, he has to pull out the balled up pieces of paper Lou shoved at him.

"So," Juan finally says slowly, his face expressionless as he hands the papers to Willis, "you're a Macon-Jones. Of *the* Macon-Jones."

Ferrin nods with a hangdog expression as Delaney looks at the papers in her turn then hands them back to him with a raised eyebrow. He crumples them up again and shoves them back into his pocket while Delaney shakes her head and goes behind the counter. The sound of liquid pouring into cups is loud in the uncomfortable silence.

"And you've been living here," Willis says, his voice flat. "Doing manual labour. Really."

Ferrin grimaces. "Yes. Really. I understand your skepticism—"

"I highly doubt that!" Juan says. "You had nothing when Willis hauled your sorry ass into town! Nothing but the clothes on your back and a piece of shit car stuck in a ditch! What? Did you lose all your money in the casino, or did your family disown you?"

Ferrin spreads his hands in a helpless shrug.

"Neither," he says. "You all just assumed I had nothing, and then you got me a job and clothes and a place to live, and held out your hands in friendship. You gave me a place to call home at a time when I didn't even know I needed such a thing. I didn't want to tell you at first because I was enjoying myself, then after a while, I didn't know how to tell you."

"Just like this at any point in the last year!" Willis snaps. "Does Lou know?"

"She does now." He grimaces at their expressions. "She threw me out. Threw something at my head which thankfully broke on the door instead. I'm not sure she'll let me back in the house."

"Do you blame her?"

"Not even a little." He sighs. "I'm not giving up, though. She'll forgive me. Eventually."

Willis snorts. "I don't know if you've noticed, but Lou isn't exactly the forgiving kind."

"Well, we'll see about that when I get back."

"Back?" Juan sneers. "What about your vast Macon-

Jones business empire?"

"It's the twenty-first century, Juan. I can manage my investments quite well from here. Or, rather, Pierce can."

"Pierce?" Realization dawns. "Aw, shit—you're the investor Pierce found!"

"Well, technically, I'm the investor who convinced Pierce to pull the deal together. The others are a few of my cousins and Gillian."

"Oh, for fuck's sake! I don't need your charity!"

"I didn't need yours, either, but I learned to accept it in the spirit it was given! Besides, if you think my cousin Abram does anything out of the kindness of his heart then you are tragically mistaken."

Juan's scowl deepens even as his lips twitch towards what Ferrin hopes is a reluctant smile.

"How's Tessa taking the news?" Delaney asks as she holds out a cup of coffee to him. He glances at it, then at her.

"Did you put salt in this?" he asks.

"I tried, but Tessa's all out."

Ferrin gives her a tiny smile and takes the cup. "Well, that's a small blessing. No, I haven't told Tessa yet. In fact, I came here looking for her to do just that."

As he finishes speaking, the door bursts open and Tessa barges inside, the door chimes jangling. She comes to an abrupt halt at the sight of him and levels her index finger at him with a dramatic flourish.

"*You!*"

Ferrin gulps and eyes the distance to the door, wondering if feinting left before bolting right would work, or at least give him enough of a head start to save his skin.

Tessa stomps towards him, her brown eyes steely.

"I think she knows," Delaney murmurs, and eases away.

"Damn right I know! I was just at Lou's. She told me. At high volume."

"Is she crying into her beer?" Delaney asks with a

worried frown.

Tessa snorts. "Are you kidding—Lou? She's too busy ripping her furniture apart. *With her teeth!*"

"I'm sorry!" Ferrin blurts out.

She steps close, pointing a finger at his nose. "You should be! We've known each other for almost two years and not once—not once!—have you offered to get me an employee discount at your family's stores! Do you have any idea how much money I spend in that place?"

Ferrin's shoulders relax with relief.

"I can do that," he says eagerly. "Valid at any Macon-Jones store in the world."

Tessa huffs and crosses her arms. "Well, that's a start. A poor start, but a start. Of course, the fact you never told me you're rich also means I never had the chance to allow my greed to overcome my lack of attraction to you. I'm not going to forget that in a hurry, either!"

Tessa's stern look dissolves into a grin and he grins back, relief flooding through him.

"Aren't you pissed at him?" Juan demands.

Tessa cocks her head as she ponders the question. "No," she finally says. "Surprised. Shocked, actually. Bewildered." She shrugs. "Relieved."

"Relieved?" Juan asks.

"He could have been a serial killer or a bank robber. A spy, or a cat burglar, or a con artist, scamming us out of our life's savings. Instead, he's a member of one of the richest families in the country. I think we got pretty lucky, actually. I mean, if nothing else, he owes us all tropical vacations this winter."

The others exchange somewhat sheepish glances then turn to Ferrin.

"Yeah, I suppose," Juan mutters.

"And I'll bet anything that if any one of us had bothered to search his name online, we would have found out who he was right away. I mean, seriously, how many 'Ferrin Jones' could there possibly be?"

The others look thunderstruck, but no one more so than Ferrin.

"Never even thought of that," he mutters.

"Lucky for you, neither did any of us," Juan says and sighs.

Ferrin eases his bulky frame into a chair with an overwhelming sense of relief. He has no doubt they're going to make him pay for his deception, but at least now he knows they're going to forgive him in time. He sips his coffee, and coughs.

"You never asked about pepper," Delaney says demurely.

Lou scowls at Tessa and Delaney standing on her front porch, each carrying a case of beer and a bottle hidden in a brown paper bag.

"Really?" she demands.

Tessa breezes past her, beer bottles rattling cheerfully in their case.

"Really. Juan's looking after the hellspawn tomorrow, I've closed The Row, and you, my darling, need to vent and share, drink tequila, swear off men forever, crumble at the thought of his smile, have a messy, gross, snotty crying jag, and drink until you puke." She leans closer, and whispers, "The puking bit's optional."

Lou snorts. "What makes you think I need any of those things?"

Both Delaney and Tessa give her identical pitying looks.

"If we have to explain, you'll skip right to the crying part," Delaney says.

Lou snorts again and drifts after them as they put the beer in the fridge and reveal a couple bottles of tequila.

"For the drinking games," Tessa says.

"Of course," Lou says drily.

♠♥♣♦

The next morning, Lou pries her eyelids open and stumbles to the bathroom then the kitchen, where she slowly and cautiously drinks a gallon of water.

Well, it feels like a gallon of water, anyway. Her stomach gurgles, her head throbs, and she decides she's never drinking again. At least not tequila. Or beer. Or anything alcoholic, really, if it leaves her feeling like this the next day. She starts making coffee, hoping her head won't explode before she manages to drink that life-saving beverage, the thought of which is the only thing keeping her upright.

Delaney is the next to arrive, her eyes half-closed against the morning light.

"Why are we awake?" she rasps as she gingerly slumps into a chair at the table.

"My bladder was about to burst," Lou mumbles, leaning against the cupboard and willing the coffee pot to work faster, "and my head was exploding. You?"

Delaney rests her head on her arms and closes her eyes. "Same," she groans.

"Good morning, sunshines!" Tessa yodels as she bounces into the kitchen.

Delaney and Lou grunt in reply; Delaney doesn't even open her eyes.

"Coffee smells great!" Tessa continues. "Anybody hungry? I can whip over to The Row and get yesterday's leftovers."

"*No!*"

Tessa laughs. "In stereo, yet!"

"Aren't you sick at all?" Delaney moans.

Tessa slides into a chair across from her.

"Deathly," she says, "but I've learned that sometimes, you have to fake it 'til you make it."

Delaney opens one eye to glare at her then closes it again.

"Wake me when the pain leaves," she growls, "and by pain, I mean Tessa."

To Lou's surprise, the impromptu party actually does provide some measure of catharsis...or at least it does once the hangover fades. Her headache returns at the sight of Ike on her porch the next morning, smugly smiling and carrying more papers for her to sign.

As she listens to him say 'I told you so' without ever actually saying those particular words, Ferrin's accusations seem to echo in all the empty space he's left behind.

"Well," she says abruptly, putting down her pen and interrupting Ike in mid-gloat, "at least we know Ferrin wasn't after my money. He has way more than enough of his own."

Ike looks suddenly disconcerted, although, Lou tells herself staunchly, it only seems that way because of Ferrin's poisonous words.

"Well," Ike says, "who knows what he was planning or what he's done? It's the family that's rich, after all, not necessarily him, personally. I told you there are rumors that he may be getting his money illegally, right?"

She scowls. "Well, there's no way in hell he could have gained access to my accounts. Besides, wouldn't you have noticed if he had? You're supposed to pay attention to all that shit, aren't you? It's what I pay you for, after all."

Ike's eyes flicker away from hers then returns. "We-ell, I've been distracted the last few months. Irish, you know. I'll start going through everything with a fine-toothed comb when I get back to Vancouver."

Suspicion coils in her stomach.

She gives him a thin smile. "You know what? I'm tired. It's been a tough couple of days." She stands and adjusts her sweater. "Why don't you leave all *this*..." she carelessly waves her hand at the stack of papers with a grimace of distaste "...here, and you can pick it up tomorrow on your way of out of town."

His sudden frown causes her stomach to tighten even more, and for the first time in a long time, the black wave of panic licks at her edges.

"I don't know, Lou," Ike says, "I want to get an early start in the morning."

"Tonight, then." She heads towards the doorway then pauses and looks expectantly at him over her shoulder. He reluctantly stands and follows her.

"What are you going to do this afternoon?" he asks with a hint of worry.

She raises an eyebrow as she opens the door. "I have no idea," she says. "I might call Tessa or Delaney and go for a walk. Or I might just take a nap. What do you have planned for the rest of the day?"

"I was going to pack up and maybe leave right away, if I managed to get everything done." He gives her a persuasive smile and tilts his head in the direction of the living room and the papers sitting on the coffee table.

She forces a smile. "Well, I'm not going to get to those until later. If you're looking for something to do, you could go to Regina for me."

"Regina? That's an hour away!"

"I know," she says drily. "I just..." she heaves a sad sigh. "Look, I'm having a tough time getting my head wrapped around the Ferrin thing, and I really, really need our favorite ice cream." She shrugs and looks sheepish. "Never underestimate the power of comfort food. It's only sold at Macon-Jones—God." She bites her lip while Ike pats her shoulder. "You can only get it in Regina," she mutters, glaring at the floor.

Ike sighs. "Fine," he says, "I suppose it's the least I can do."

She flashes him a puzzled look.

"I'm the one who told you about Ferrin," he says with a shrug. "I feel a little guilty about that."

She grips her sweater and scowls. "Not your fault...but pick up a couple of litres. Maybe three."

Ike chuckles. "All right." He glances at his watch. "I'll leave right now. It won't take me long to pack and get on the road once we've finished everything here."

Her smile is thin and barely there. "Thanks," she says and closes the door behind him with relief.

It takes her three tries to get out the door, the possibilities of what she might discover driving her back to the couch in a black, shaking panic. In the end, though, she manages it.

Just as she manages to walk into the bank with her armful of papers, and ask to speak to a manager.

She follows the vaguely familiar, obviously dumbfounded, man into his office and thinks with a grim scowl that the truth damn well better set her free.

Lou steps into The Row and shakes her head when Tessa gives her a harried grin and holds up a coffee pot. Lou scans the crowd until her gaze lands on the person she wants.

Willis-that-bastard is sprawled in a chair at one of the tables, a newspaper held up in front of his face, oblivious to his surroundings.

She squares her shoulders and walks over.

"I thought paper newspapers were obsolete," she says, and is childishly proud at how normal she sounds.

Willis-that-bastard lowers the top of the newspaper and blinks owlishly at her over his reading glasses. The look on his face would have been comical under other circumstances.

She nods at the chair across from him.

"May I?"

"Of course," he says, sitting up straight and putting the paper aside. His hand trembles a little as he places his glasses on top of it.

She slides into the chair and slouches forward, her hands loosely clasped together and resting on the table in front of her. She looks at him in silence, noting the grey hair and new wrinkles he had acquired since the last time she allowed herself to see him.

Willis-that-bastard clears his throat. "Can I get you a coffee?" he asks, his voice gruff.

Lou shakes her head. "I have some questions for you."

He slowly nods, his eyes wary. "All right."

She drops her gaze to her hands, frowning.

He waits.

"When my mom was sick," she says, forcing each word from her mouth, "what did Ike tell you? Especially that last year."

Willis-that-bastard is silent for so long that she risks a lightning glance at him. Her heart clenches at the dark sorrow on his face.

"The truth," she whispers through numb lips. "Please."

He sighs, and says, "He told me you didn't want us around. That we upset your mother too much, because she didn't want her friends to see her like that. That all she—and you—wanted was to be left alone so she could die in peace." He pauses, staring into the past. "He turned me away from the house. Repeatedly. He finally begged me, with tears in his eyes, to honour Marigold's last wishes. If I loved her at all, I'd do what she wanted. I asked—begged—to see her one last time, to have the chance to say good-bye. He said he asked, but the answer was no. I gave up after that." He roughly clears his throat. "I've always regretted that. I should have told her one last time how much I loved her; how much I would always love her."

She stares at her hands, now gripping each other so tightly her knuckles are white. The sickening feeling she'd successfully ignored until this morning, that started when Ferrin dropped his bombshell, threatens to overwhelm her, and she swallows down the sudden desire to scream and rage and break something. Again.

Willis clears his throat again and says, "Why? What did he tell you?"

"He didn't know why people stopped visiting." Her voice is muffled, as if it's wrapped in cotton wool and coming from a vast distance. She feels her lips moving but her face is numb, as is her entire body, disconnected from her and everything around her. "He said he begged you and the others to visit, but you couldn't find the time." Her lips twist. "He told me, with tears in his eyes, how sorry he was that all my mother's friends turned their backs on us, deserted us in our time of need; that he was sorry he was the only one who really cared." The bitterness is vicious.

The sounds of the coffee shop and its customers fill the silence between them until Willis-that-bastard says, "I tried to see you after the funeral, you know. Several times."

She shakes her head, eyes still on her white-knuckled hands. "No. I didn't know."

"He never let me in. He insisted you wanted nothing to do with me or anyone else. It didn't seem to matter when I tried to see you, he was always there and I couldn't get past him. Then I heard others had tried to see you, too. Rang the doorbell, knocked, but you never opened the door. The last time I tried, he met me on the porch and told me you were going to slap a restraining order on me, citing harassment, if I didn't leave you the hell alone."

"And you believed him?"

"I had no way of knowing anything different."

She covers her face with her hands.

"I gave up then, too, probably far too easily," Willis-that-bastard says, "but I thought it was what you wanted. Who was I to judge how you wanted to live your life?"

She makes a muffled choking sound.

"You believed him, too," he says gently.

"I know."

She's an idiot.

Lou stares at her hands. She's mildly surprised to realize they aren't shaking at all. Perhaps she's simply drained from the revelations of the day, from her trip to the bank, from the conversation with Willis, from the last half-hour with Ike. His handsome face broadcast the truth the moment she confronted him, and now he's sprawled in his chair, which she's determined to take out and burn the moment this is all over. After ripping it apart with her bare hands. She'll throw the ice cream that's currently melting on her coffee table in with it, for good measure. She always hated that flavor, but it was Ike's favourite and she had always wanted to please him.

She's a *fucking* idiot.

Ike spent most of the last thirty minutes denying, defending, and rationalizing, and she simply watched him until he finally sighed and grudgingly admitted that both Willis and Ferrin were telling the truth. He's been pouting for the last five minutes, glaring at her like she's the one who's done something wrong. Finally, she lets out a soft breath and asks the only question that really matters to her.

"Why?"

Ike sneers.

"Look around you! This town has nothing—and I mean nothing! I've always wanted to get the hell out of here but to do that, and live the kind of life I wanted, I needed cash and lots of it. I sure as hell wasn't going to inherit it—my old man might be able to make money but he spends it twice as fast! And there you were, sitting on all that cash." He gives a dismissive wave of his hand. "Yeah, I felt kinda bad about your mom, but she never trusted me the way you did so I never could get anything past her. She questioned everything, even up to the week she died! But you...you trusted me so much, loved me so much, it never even occurred to you to question me."

He pauses, and she watches him, her face impassive.

He shrugs. "If it makes you feel any better, I intended to marry you, you know. I would have done my best to keep you happy while I siphoned off the money. I intended to leave you with a smile on your face, at least. Then I realized I didn't have to marry you, because you couldn't leave the house! I was already in control of everything and with you hiding in here, well...I could get it all another way. Slower, maybe, but I'd met Irish by then and I didn't mind hanging around for a while longer. Your agoraphobia was a gift, and you believed every word I told you about it! It was perfect, even if your dependence on me for *absolutely fucking everything* was so bloody annoying! At least there was a prize at the bottom of all that bullshit—two, actually: all that money and the woman of my dreams."

Her eyes flicker but her expression doesn't change.

"Come on, Lou, do you blame me? *You never used it!* You never even looked to see how much you had, that's how blind and spoiled you are!" Ike shakes his head in disbelief. "You had no idea—and it was just...sitting there. Like you."

He pauses and cocks his head to one side, an arrogant smirk on his face. "If it makes you feel any better, it wasn't personal. It was just business."

She looks at him, and thinks her heart is literally breaking. She shifts and pulls her sweater more securely around herself as she remembers the playmate from her childhood, her teenage crush, her lover, and realizes she has no idea what, if anything, about their relationship through the years has been real and what has simply been manipulation for his own purposes.

Just business.

"This is just business, too," she finally says and raises her voice. "You can come in now, Detective."

It's almost worth it for the look on Ike's face when the officers walk into the room.

The house darkens around Lou as she sits, silent and still, on the couch, wrapped in the sweater of a man she never met, made by a woman she desperately misses. The silence settles over her, like leaves, like dust.

Just two days before, her world had seemed so perfect. A budding relationship ripe with possibilities, great friends, and money enough to not have to worry about working, unless she wanted to, of course. Now the guy she thought might be something more than a friend turns out to be somebody else, her best friend turned out to be no friend at all, there's very little money left, and she's sitting in the dark with tears trickling down her cheeks.

What a difference forty-eight hours makes.

Well, she thinks, wiping moisture from her face only to have it immediately replaced, at least she still has the house.

She starts as the doorbell shatters the silence. She pushes to her feet, her bones aching in protest at ever moving again. She knows it will be Tessa and Delaney, come to sit with her in her darkness.

She swipes her hands across her face again as she swings open the door and finds not just Tessa and Delaney, but Juan, Willis, and several of her mother's friends, people she believed abandoned them but now knows had been there all along.

She stands and stares, tears trickling down her cheeks...then steps aside and lets them in.

♠♥♣♦

She doesn't really think about Ferrin over the next week. She's busy with the bank and the police and her fantasies about stomping Ike's smugly handsome face into the sidewalk. Her rage and humiliation as a result of the betrayal from the man she's known and loved all her life leaves no room to deal with how she feels about Ferrin's deception. She blesses the call display on her phone, though, and never answers when he calls each day at six, the time he would arrive at her house to do chores and eventually to play cards.

It isn't until halfway through the second week, still bewildered by the extent of Ike's treachery, that she hesitates when the phone rings. She longs to talk to Ferrin, to hear his voice, to talk to somebody other than Tessa or the others.

She resists.

At the the end of the second week, Tessa passes along a message: Ferrin won't call again but he'll see her when he gets back.

The message seems to punch a hole in her stomach even as she scowls and says, "As if he's coming back."

Tessa rolls her eyes but for once says nothing.

Lou's phone stays silent after that, and she's relieved...and saddened. She's closed the door, she thinks staunchly, and fights the urge to break things.

Over the next week, it's as if Ferrin never existed. No one talks about him, her phone doesn't ring, and it begins to dawn on her, now that all the shit she has to deal with because of Ike is starting to ease, that she...

She hates to admit it, but she misses him.

But she'll be damned if she'll let anybody else know that.

Tessa leans on the coffee counter and props her chin on her hand as she balefully watches Lou pace restlessly around The Row. Tessa finally straightens and smacks her hand on the counter.

"That's it! You're making me dizzy! Not to mention people are starting to wonder what the hell's in my coffee if you're pacing the floor like that! If you miss him so much—"

"I don't know who you're talking about," Lou snaps.

"Of course you don't," Tessa says sarcastically. "Look, why don't you just call him?"

Lou glares. "I refused his calls for weeks. What could I possibly say to him now?"

"Oh, I don't know! 'You were right; I was wrong; I miss you; come home'?"

"He is home!" All the anger drains out of her. "He is home," she says again, her voice soft and sad. "I somehow doubt he's going to care much about anything I have to say."

Tessa rolls her eyes. "I don't, but fine. Why don't you surprise him in Toronto? Actions speak louder than words, you know."

Lou scoffs. "And how would I get there?"

"Well..."

"Exactly. Besides, if he doesn't come back, then...well, then he doesn't come back, and I don't look like a lovesick idiot for chasing after him. I'm not hiding out in my house anymore, so I can't just ignore the gossip."

"Sure you can," Tessa says absently, "I do it all the time." She stares off into the distance, her arms crossed, her foot tapping as she ponders the question. She nods her head with decision and turns her attention to Lou, who's pacing again.

"Stop that," she says so firmly Lou stops in mid-stride. Tessa gives her a sunny smile. "You and me, Lou. We'll go to Toronto, see the sights, paint the town red. Finding Ferrin is just a bonus."

Lou stares. "And how would we get there?" she asks again, her eyes wide.

Tessa comes out from behind the counter with a broad grin and dancing brown eyes. "Road trip!" she says gleefully, bouncing with excitement.

"I'm agoraphobic!"

"When's the last time you had a panic attack? Caused by going outside, I mean, not because you found out your crush hid his identity and your best friend stole all your money?"

Lou scowls, opens her mouth then closes it again.

"Exactly!" Tessa crows. "No more using that old excuse, my girl! And just think: today a road trip to Toronto; tomorrow the world!" She pauses, her head tilted to one side. "Literally, in your case."

Lou doesn't know whether to laugh or cry or run screaming for cover.

Lou settles into the passenger seat and looks at Tessa with wide eyes, wondering if she looks as worried as she feels.

Tessa smiles then sobers and gives her a stern look.

"Are you going to be able to handle this?" she asks. "Seriously. If you do have a panic attack on the road, you're hooped, I hope you realize that. We're not going to have the luxury of being able to get back to your house."

"A little late to think of that now!"

"No, a little late is when we're half-way through Manitoba!"

Lou chuckles then sighs. "You're right. I haven't had a panic attack caused by leaving the house in months, and I've been out and about quite a lot, especially the last couple of weeks. If I can handle all of that Ike shit, then I can handle being alone with you in a car for three days as we drive across Canada."

Tessa gives her a slow, evil grin and puts the car in gear. "You think so?" she purrs and peels out of the driveway, gravel spurting behind them.

♠♥♣♦

"I have to say, you're doing really well," Tessa says as she slides into one of the beds in their motel room on the second night of their journey. "No panic attacks and you've actually talked to quite a few people."

Lou shoots her skeptical glance. "What? All five of them?"

"I'm almost positive there were six." Tessa snuggles down against her pillows with a relieved sigh. "This feels good," she says. "I'd forgotten how long it takes to drive to Toronto. I'll be glad when we get there tomorrow."

Lou frowns as she gets into her own bed.

"Lou?"

She glances at Tessa to find her watching her with a concerned frown. She blinks. "What?"

"Aren't you going to be glad to get there tomorrow, too?"

Lou's eyes slide away from hers. "Sure. Can I turn off the light?"

"Knock yourself out."

The room plunges into the semi-darkness that's common to all motels near busy highways. The only sound inside the room is the sound of their soft breathing, and for a moment, Lou is hopeful Tessa will drift off to sleep without further conversation.

No such luck.

"Why are you so scared?" Tessa almost whispers.

"I'm not," Lou says, her own voice just as soft.

"You've been scared ever since you found out Ferrin's full name."

Lou blinks up at the dark ceiling, and scowls.

"Lou? Is there something about Ferrin you haven't

311

told me?"

Lou half-groans, half-sighs, then says, "He lives his life in public. His family's in the newspapers, and on TV, and is followed by paparazzi. Their names are connected with numerous charities from coast to coast to coast. They negotiate multi-billion dollar deals and go to multi-million dollar fundraisers. They give speeches at international conferences, for God's sake! My former best friend and lover stole almost everything I own, we're staying in third-rate motels because it's all I can afford, and I didn't leave my house for five years! How can I...I can't fit into that world, Tessa!"

Tessa rolls onto her side and looks at her from across the space between their beds.

"Lou, I think you're worrying before you have anything to worry about. Ferrin's been living a pretty non-public life for the last year or so and he seems happy enough. There's no reason to think that's going to change any time soon. By the time it does, the two of you will have worked things out, one way or another."

"I can't compete with that life, Tessa," Lou says, her voice choked with tears, "and I can't join it, either."

"Lou," Tessa says softly, sadly.

Lou sniffles and swipes at her nose.

"If you feel this way, why are we going to Toronto?" Tessa asks.

Lou huffs and says, "Because I want to show him I'm willing to try."

Gillian snaps a couple of hours before the family's pre-party party is scheduled to begin and demands Ferrin tell her what happened in Saskatchewan to leave him moping all over the penthouse, and not even Carson, Dyson and Jack's antics can cheer him up. She's determined to enjoy a party she's worked hard to organize, she tells him, and she doesn't want it ruined by a sad-eyed stepson. It's almost a relief, and Ferrin feels like he's sixteen again, confiding in her about his first serious crush.

Gillian's face is as serene as it had been then as everything spills out of him.

"She's really pissed," he finishes softly.

"Do you blame her?" Gillian asks. "Honestly, Ferrin, what did you expect? Everything you did with her, you did under false pretenses."

"I did not! It's not like I created a whole new personality!"

"No?"

Both Gillian and Ferrin turn surprised faces towards Abram as he strolls into the room, handsome and carelessly elegant in an expensive custom-made black tuxedo.

Ferrin glares. "Is this really any of your business?" he snaps.

Abram raises an eyebrow, his lopsided, charming smirk firmly in place as he stares at Ferrin with a knowing glint in his eyes.

Ferrin's jaw hardens and his eyes narrow. "You're the head of the family business, Abram," he growls softly, "you're not the head of me!"

They stand in tense silence, blue eyes clashing with hazel ones, their identical shit-eating-grins nowhere in sight. Then Abram's lips twitch, and he says, his voice gruff, "And this is why I always wished you'd come into the family business." He tilts his head in acknowledgement. "Well played, son, well played...but my point still stands."

Ferrin blinks, taken aback. "Your point?"

"About creating a different personality."

"I didn't! I was just...me, maybe even more 'me' than I've ever been before."

"I think the point Abram is trying oh-so-badly to make is that you weren't all of you."

Ferrin scowls.

Gillian sighs. "Stop being deliberately obtuse, for heaven's sake! Yes, Ferrin Jones is you, and, in many ways, the best of you, but *this*—" she makes a sweeping gesture encompassing the large, elegant apartment, "and *that*—" the next graceful sweep of her hand takes in Ferrin's own tailor-made black tuxedo, bow tie and crisp white shirt, "are also part of you. Admit it, you like *this* and *that* just as much as you like building houses and trimming hedges and Lou."

Ferrin's glare softens as she speaks.

"I like Lou a whole lot more," he says.

"So why did you lie to her?" Abram demands.

"I didn't lie! I just...didn't tell her everything."

"Why?" Gillian asks, her voice gentle.

"She's a recluse," he says helplessly, "and agoraphobic, although she's doing much better now. How do you think she would have reacted if I'd told her about *this* and *that*?"

"That was her choice to make, not yours," Abram says, shaking his head as he moves behind the bar, where he pours himself a glass of the champagne that's chilling there.

Gillian watches him with a raised eyebrow.

"How surprisingly enlightened of you," she says.

He smirks and raises the champagne bottle in question. She nods and strolls to the bar.

"I'm sorry to tell you your husband raised an idiot child," Abram says, filling her champagne flute.

She shrugs carelessly. "I'm sorry to say your cousin did the same."

"Touché," Abram says and they toast each other, for once in perfect agreement.

Ferrin rolls his eyes. "How about some of that champagne for this idiot child?" he growls and joins them at the bar.

Abram obligingly fills another flute and hands it to him.

"So, what are you going to do?" Abram asks.

Ferrin sips his champagne and shrugs. "Do? I'll do what I should have done before I left. I'll throw myself at her feet and beg for forgiveness." He sighs, and his shoulders slump. "You're right, Gillian." He glances at Abram. "Both of you, as much as I'll deny you're ever right about anything, Abram. Lou deserved better from me. She deserves so much more than 'better'. When I get home, I'll stand on her porch until she sees me long enough for me to apologize, and then...yeah. It was—and is—her choice to make, and I never should have allowed my own fears to take that away from her."

Gillian considers him thoughtfully, then turns to Abram. "Perhaps I didn't raise such an idiot son after all."

"Perhaps not," Abram agrees and gives her a surprisingly warm and sincere smile as he lifts his glass in a toast.

Gillian turns back to Ferrin. "Home."

Ferrin coughs slightly on his champagne. "What?"

"You called Saskatchewan home. Is that truly how you feel about it? That...that little backwater town in the middle of nowhere?"

He shrugs helplessly. "Yes. I really do. Besides, Juan and I are going to renovate that old hospital, and it's going to be beautiful, you know."

"Is it going to make any money?" Abram asks. "Pierce was remarkably vague on that point even as he gleefully coaxed me into writing ever-larger cheques."

Ferrin grins. "It's not for making money, Abram."

"Then what's it good for?"

"A retirement home for all my cousins, especially you. No other place will put up with you."

Abram mock-glares as Gillian laughs her husky laugh. She saunters towards the hallway as she says, "Well, I have a few last minute things to see to before the rest of the cousins descend upon us. I'll leave you two to debate the merits of retirement living in Saskatchewan."

"I don't know about this," Lou moans.

Tessa puts her hands on her hips and glares.

"I didn't drive for three days just to have you turn tail and run once we got here, okay? At least not before you've actually seen him!"

Tessa moves to press the very-expensive-looking building's very-expensive-looking buzzer but Lou grabs her hand before she makes contact.

"What if he doesn't want to see me?" she hisses.

Tessa rolls her eyes. "Then we leave, and you know where you stand, and we'll have an awesome time in Toronto anyway, and you can stop moping all over my coffee shop, thank you very much."

She reaches again for the buzzer, but Lou stops her once again.

"Wait, wait, wait! What if he's not alone?"

"Then we leave, and you know—"

"Tessa!" Lou glances through the doors into the elegant foyer of the building, and her eyes widen when she notices the distinguished concierge at the front desk watching them with bright-eyed interest.

"This is a stupid idea," she groans. "Let's just go—"

Lou's interrupted by the sound of the buzzer and she spins to glare at Tessa's finger on the button before raising her glare to Tessa's smirking face. The smirk fades into wide-eyed uncertainty as the concierge, with great dignity, sails towards them and opens the door.

"For the Macon-Jones suite, I presume," he intones, and steps back to allow them into the building.

Tessa turns a bright smile on the concierge as she drags a reluctant Lou through the door. "Yes, how did you know?"

He gives them an enigmatic smile and says, "I'll call the elevator for you."

They ride to the top floor in nervous silence and tense

as the elevator glides to a gentle stop. The roar of voices that greets them as the doors open rocks them back on their heels and their jaws drop as they realize they're not looking out at some generic hallway but are instead in a spacious suite. They turn their shocked eyes to the quirkily handsome man waiting to greet them. He's dressed impeccably in a beautifully tailored tuxedo, ignoring the chaos behind him, and there's enough resemblance to Ferrin to immediately identify him as a member of the Macon-Jones family. He takes in their rather grubby jeans, t-shirts and sneakers, and his eyes linger on Lou's shapeless brown sweater before he smiles and invites them in with a welcoming sweep of his arm.

"Come and join the party," he says.

Lou and Tessa exchange terrified glances before they reluctantly step out of the elevator and gape, horrified, at the scene in front of them. The expansive living room is filled with milling bodies, discreet music, loud voices, and even louder laughter. There are beautiful dresses and black tuxedos and flashing jewels and Lou and Tessa draw together into a protective huddle.

"Maybe we should have found a hotel and at least showered first," Tessa mutters.

"I told you this was a bad *fucking* idea," Lou hisses.

"If you'd told me it was a bad *fucking* idea, I might have listened," Tessa hisses back.

The man who greeted them laughs, reminding them of his presence. "Don't be shy. We don't eviscerate people at the first meeting. Most of the time. No guarantees about the second meeting, though." He grins and winks. "I'll let the kitchen staff know there are two more for dinner."

Tessa opens her mouth, but he's already strolling away.

Lou doesn't notice. She's finally located Ferrin in the sea of black-clad men. He's standing with his back to the elevator, but she recognizes the set of his shoulders even if seeing them in a tuxedo is disorienting. As she watches, he half-turns to say something to Gillian, who's standing to his right. Lou belatedly notices Pierce is across from him, with Olivia to Pierce's left, looking stunningly beautiful as she listens to a grey-haired man standing on Ferrin's left.

Ferrin looks so handsome, she thinks as he laughs at something Gillian says, and frighteningly alien. She can't believe this cool, self-assured man standing so casually with a glass of champagne in his hand fell off her porch, been scraped and bruised from falling off his bicycle, shovelled her walk, kissed her like his life depended on it, laughed with her at horrendously bad movies, held her hand as she left the house for the first time, and coaxed her through more panic attacks than she cares to remember.

Gillian notices them on the threshold and does a discreet double-take before she lifts a corner of her mouth in a half-smile as she murmurs something to Ferrin. As one, everyone in their group looks towards the elevator, and Tessa and Lou move even closer together and stare back in wide-eyed trepidation.

Ferrin's jaw drops, his eyes widen, then his face lights up. He shoves the glass he's holding at the older man, who takes it with a startled frown, and lopes towards them with a huge grin.

He scoops Lou into his arms, lifting her off her feet to kiss her breathless, holding her so tightly she swears she hears her ribs creak. She briefly thinks she should tell him he's presuming too much, but then she's too busy kissing him back and wrapping herself around him to lodge a complaint.

She's completely forgotten there's anyone else in the room.

They finally come up for air and he sets her back on her feet with a broad grin and a gentle hand cupping her face.

"Oh my God, I've missed you!" he says, then blinks, and frowns. "Wait a minute! You're *here*! How did you get here?"

Tessa leans in. "Road trip," she says and leans away with a knowing smirk.

"Hi, Tessa," he says absently, never taking his eyes from Lou. "No, I mean...did you fly?"

"Drove," Tessa says, leaning back in when Lou can't seem to do anything more than stare up at him and grin. "That's what 'road trip' means, Ferrin."

"Drove?"

"It was fun," Tessa says brightly. "It's been a while since I've driven to Toronto, so we took it slow, saw some of the sights, flirted with all the boys we met along the way—"

Lou rolls her eyes. "Tessa!"

"Oh, you can speak!" Tessa mocks, "I'm impressed! I was beginning to think that elevator had stolen your voice!"

"Tessa," Pierce sighs as he strolls up to them, "I think they're playing our song." He puts an arm around her waist and begins to lead her away.

"We have a song?" Tessa asks. "Mind you, since you didn't rush over to lift me off my feet and kiss me senseless, I'm not sure I should dance with you even if we did have a song, and since there's no music playing right now, I'm beginning to think this is just a ploy to get me away from Ferrin and Lou and..."

Lou and Ferrin watch them go then she glances at the crowd in the living room, who all seem to be staring at them with great interest, and her smile fades.

"I don't know if I can do this," she whispers urgently.

Ferrin raises an eyebrow. "What? Meet my family? Well, I can't really blame you for that. Most of the time I wish I'd never met them, either."

"Not just the family," she hisses, smacking him in the chest. "You're obviously having a pretty high-class party here."

"That's only because the hard drinking hasn't started

yet. It degenerates pretty quickly after that."

"Ferrin!"

He laughs as he cups his hands around her face and looks deep into her eyes.

"You left your house. You let me into your life. You drove to Toronto with Tessa, and I don't think even I would have the courage to do that! You—"

"Had Ike arrested."

His jaw drops, eyes popping wide. "Oh," he finally says, then, "I'm sorry."

She grimaces and says, "I think I'm more sorry for Irish. She apparently had no idea what he was doing. She just thought he had a lot of clients."

He pulls her back into his arms and she presses her cheek against his chest with a sigh.

"I'm sorry," he says again.

"Me, too." She closes her eyes as they stand in a cocoon of silence, even as the roar of conversation starts up around them once again. She barely notices, listening instead to the steady and comforting beat of his heart against her cheek. She has a sudden thought and leans back to scowl up at him. "I'm not here because you're rich and I'm broke, you know."

"The thought never even crossed my mind," he assures her very solemnly as he presses her back against his chest, his hand gently cradling the back of her head as he holds her in place.

"Good," she mutters, "because I'm going to figure things out."

"I know you will. But that's tomorrow. Tonight we have a party to go to."

Lou shudders and burrows a little closer.

"Your life scares me," she whispers.

"It scares me, too, sometimes."

She chuckles and his arms tighten round her.

"I'm willing to show you how to get through it," he says cautiously, "if you want to give it a try."

She looks up at him, her eyes wide. She scowls in fierce thought then nods.

"I love you," he says fervently.

"I love you, too," she replies, just as fervently.

"And we're going to figure everything out."

She smiles. "Yes," she says firmly, "we are," and stretches up to kiss him again.

DREAM CAST, AND SOUNDTRACK

Anyone who's followed me for a while knows that I like to 'cast' my characters. With this novel, I learned that having a dream cast doesn't just help me get the 'feel' of my characters; it also helps me anchor their physical descriptions. Until I 'cast' her, Tessa had the same personality but changed eye and hair colour every time she appeared in the story. Now, I could have worked with the ever-changing hair colour, but the eyes were another thing entirely!

Dream Cast in Order of Appearance:

Benjamin Ferrin Macon-Jones – Nathan Fillion – because he's great.

Olivia – I just realized I don't have anybody cast for Olivia.

Lou Upjohn – Michelle Rodriguez – she was the best part of *Avatar*, and her looks are the perfect blend of sweet and bad ass that I needed to anchor Lou in my head.

Ike Boisin - Ryan Reynolds – not sure if he's as handsome as Lou thinks he is, but I can see why she fell for him.

Abram Macon-Jones – Harrison Ford – what can I say? He's Harrison Ford!

Gillian Macon-Jones – Helen Mirren – who wouldn't want Helen Mirren in their cast?

Pierce Killian – Pierce Brosnan – he would have fit

for Ike, too, in his younger days.

Willis-that-bastard – William Petersen – handsome enough to attract Gillian; ordinary enough to be the grizzled vet running around the countryside.

Tessa – Katherine Heigl – her 'look' captures Tessa's personality for me.

Juan Martinez – Esai Morales - he would have to skew a little younger than he currently is, because I always pictured Delaney to be within five years of Juan's age.

Delaney Martinez – Nicole Beharie - although maybe a little taller, a little older, a little plumper, and with a Trinidadian accent. Okay, maybe I should have cast somebody else, but Nicole Beharie is amazing and deserves to be in a meatier role than I gave her here!

Carson, Dyson and Jack – Jason Bateman, Joshua Jackson, and if anyone can suggest someone for Jack, I'd appreciate it! – they all have similar looks to Nathan Fillion and Harrison Ford.

Gramp Macon-Jones – Humphrey Bogart, because everything is better with a little Bogie.

Soundtrack:
I had a ton of songs in my YouTube playlist for this book. These are the ones that really anchored this story for me:

That's What's Up – Lennon and Maisie – Such a lovely song that really speaks to what this story is all about.

Getting Drunk on a Plane – Dierks Bentley – If anything illustrates Ferrin's binge at the beginning of the book, it's this song…along with…

The Weather is Here, Wish You Were Beautiful – Jimmy Buffett – if only for the title alone.

Drops of Jupiter – Train – Poor Lou.

One Horse Town – The Johner Brothers – hello, Ledoux. Added bonus: they're from Saskatchewan.

Additional songs:
Forty Days and Nights – The Rankin Family
Nobody from Nowhere – Jimmy Buffett
If the Phone Doesn't Ring, It's Me – Jimmy Buffett
The Weight (Take a Load Off Annie) – The Band
Nothing More – The Alternate Routes
Let My People Go Go – The Rainmakers
You and I – Ingrid Michaelson
Leaving on a Jet Plane – John Denver
Happily Ever After (Now and Then) – Jimmy Buffett

ABOUT THE AUTHOR

Victoria Bernadine (a pseudonym) is, as the saying goes, a "woman of a certain age". After twenty-something years of writer's block, she began writing again in 2008.

Victoria enjoys reading all genres and particularly loves writing romantic comedy and post-apocalyptic science fiction. What those two have in common is anybody's guess.

She lives in Edmonton with her two cats (The Grunt and The Runt). *Along Came Jones* is the second novel she felt was good enough to be released into the wild.

Find or support the author on the web at: https://www.patreon.com/victoriabernadine

Other Books by this Author:

A Life Less Ordinary

www.ingramcontent.com/pod-product-compliance
Lightning Source LLC
Chambersburg PA
CBHW032145190626
46814CB00005BA/1843